UNDER VENUS

PETER STRAUB

STEALTH PRESS

ISBN 1-58881-001-1 (formerly ISBN 0-425-07033-6)

FIRST STEALTH EDITION NOVEMBER, 2000

Stealth Press books are published by Stealth Media Corporation. Its trademark, consisting of the words "Stealth Press" and/or bomber logo is registered in the U.S. Patent & Trademark Office and in other countries. Marca Registrata.

For the friends of those days,
and the nights in Justin's house.
For Tom Donovan,
who was there.

CONTENTS

Light from the planet Venus, soon to set,
Be with us.

—*Evening-Star*, Louise Bogan

UNDER
VENUS

ONE

The Past in the Present

chapter 1

1969, December: a cold domineering wind, the sense of snow—invisible snow—hanging in the air. It is the true weather of an ending. At the finish of a decade of great hope and great foolishness, the Denmarks are flying home to America.

The skyline of Plechette City, like that of Chicago or Detroit, is abrupt and jagged, unplanned. At night when airplanes circle out over Lake Michigan, homing in to General Steenborg airport at the city's southern extremity, the passengers can look out of their windows and see the massed office buildings—these defined by light—and department stores built up about Grand Avenue, the principal shopping street downtown, and the dark huddled shapes of factories, breweries, other office buildings spreading out on either side. The War Memorial building, which functions as the city's art museum and is its most interesting structure, is too low to be distinguished at night from the taller buildings behind it, and the aspects of the city most distinct to the airplane's passengers are the huge revolving four-faced clock atop the Chambers Denmark factory, lately purchased by the Globe Corporation, and the blinking flame-shaped light mounted on the Gas Company building. The flame is blue in December, for the light is a weather indicator, and blue means *cold*.

The big clock is illuminated from within; the intricate Gothic numerals and hands stand out on the turning faces a pure dense black. It is in the city's guidebooks, and postcards with its picture may be purchased at the airport and art museum, for the Chambers Denmark clock is the largest revolving four-faced clock in the world: in the nineteenth century, a point of civic pride. The Gas Company flame is a more recent feature of the city's night landscape; the Gas building was constructed in the nineteen-sixties, and constructed according to the strictest principles of Mr. Mies van der Rohe. This is a few blocks to the north of Grand Avenue. The big illuminated clock shines out over the southern sections of Plechette City, the old Polish ghetto and manufacturing district, lately overtaken by Puerto Rican immigrants. The two great lights, yellow and blue in the week before Christmas, face one another across the expanse of the city.

From north to south, roughly parallel to the indented contour of the lake, runs the Plechette River, named like the city after Jean-Marie Plechette, the French Jesuit who was its founder on the site of an Indian settlement in 1684. Father Plechette Christianized the Indians, regulated the fur trading—southern Wisconsin was at this time largely forested, and bear, fox, deer and beaver were everywhere numerous—and gave French names to the local landmarks. Within the next two hundred and fifty years, all of these names had been changed, and the only trace of Father Plechette's industry, apart from the town and the river renamed for him, was the mural in city hall which depicted the Jesuit, idealized and sternly handsome, stepping rather garishly out of a canoe into a circle of fierce braves. By the time the mural was executed, the Plechette River had been already so polluted that the only fish to be caught from the abutments of the Grand Avenue bridge were carp, and the bears and deer and beaver had retreated to the far north of the state, and on into upper Michigan.

When Elliot Denmark's great-granduncle, Brooks Denmark, the founder with Charles Chambers of the Chambers Denmark Corporation and the first man in Plechette City to envision the four-faced clock, took a solitary trip down the Mississippi River as a young man, he passed town after town where the inhabitants chiefly spoke French. Even in the mid-nineteenth century, the great period of

French colonialism in America had left some perceptible residue. Think of the names of the towns: Racine, Prairie du Chien, Prairie du Sac, Fond du Lac. Brooks Denmark worked in little river towns, learned their language, and wrote back to his mother, sister and brother, *Dearest Mother, Eleanora, and Logan: My studies in the admirable language of the French progress apace, though I am uncertain of my ability to completely master the tongue. It is my most earnest desire to visit the homeland, the source of this language, where I feel with certainty that my studies would take on an even greater enthusiasm. My employer's family, the Mirceaus, speak of France as though it were the next state, and of Paris as though it were the home of all their finer sentiments. Perhaps we may all see it together someday in the future . . . Your loving son and brother, Brooks.* But this was to be Brooks Denmark's only *Wanderjahr*; he returned to Plechette City in the autumn, borrowed money from uncles and friends, and started his factory with Charles Chambers. In two years, he had forgotten all his French. When he was sixty, one of those boyish-looking, elated Americans in absurd shoes and Norfolk jackets who visited Paris in 1890, a little of his river French returned to him. He was shocked that no one understood it. But by then he was one of the leading citizens of a town which had tripled in size since his boyhood, he had ordered the construction of the huge clock which dominated one entire half of that city, he had helped found a private school and a hunt club, was a director of a hospital and a bank, and he knew that the value of his long-delayed trip to Paris lay as much in the allusions he would be able to drop into conversations as in the experience of actually being there. Yet he was stimulated by Paris, and at times almost intoxicated by it: like his great-grandnephew Elliot, not to be born for forty-seven years, he was responsive to what was beautiful, and was capable of a wildness, almost an abandon, in his apprehension of it. When Brooks Denmark first saw the banks of the Seine and the bridges and avenues fanning out from it, he thought immediately of transforming Plechette City. Paris was the only beautiful city he had ever seen. If he considered that he might make his hometown equal to his clock by making it more like Paris, he might be forgiven. Unlike many men of his class and time—new Midwestern manufacturing tycoons—Brooks Denmark would not have been dismayed to discover that one of his family would grow up to become an artist, a composer of music that most people would never hear and would not understand if they did, and a voluntary exile, with his wife, in Paris, and that this descendant would speak French like a Parisian born. (Perhaps, that is, a Parisian born in Marseilles: Elliot had often been told that his French was marked by a southern roll.) Brooks may have felt that he was getting some of his own back for the time a waiter spat on the floor when he suddenly remembered, as if by inspiration, six consecutive words of his river French. Brooks had no feelings about music, either one way or the other.

Music in Plechette City was largely an affair of brass bands, accordions and zithers. Especially in Brooks Denmark's time, it was imitative of German bands. It is not a coincidence that the first fortunes in Plechette City were made in the mid-nineteenth century. During this period, the city's first great time of growth, Germans seemed to come into town with every train from the East. Established families like the Denmarks admitted them with some condescension, but were, on the whole, grateful for the revenue and employment brought in by the breweries. By 1900, German was almost officially the second language in Plechette City, and unofficially, almost the first. It was regularly taught in the schools until the outbreak of the First World War; clerks in the new department stores along Grand Avenue were hired only if they were proficient in German. (Later, Polish was nearly as necessary.) By the year of Elliot Denmark's birth, the families most prominent in Plechette City were named Schallspiel, Van Blank, Denmark, Laubach, Nieder, Hockbein, Usenbrugge, Steenborg.

On the east side of the city, north along the long curve of the lake, these builders and entrepreneurs constructed their huge anomalous houses: some built on the model of the great family houses in Bonn and Munich, severe stone piles capped by turrets and cupolas, some, during the next three decades, oddly Spanish, almost Californian, imitations of Neutra. Others of these houses, shading into the new suburbs far north along Lake Point Drive, were multileveled brash constructions of imported stone, native woods, and a great deal of glass. Like Brooks Denmark, who could appear to them both charming and ruthless, both generous and a terrifying snob, the first suburbanites of Plechette City had a notion of the beautiful, and again like him, they cannot be blamed if it was aggressive and magazine-ish. It was the same impulse that led the fathers of the city to construct a park every two or three miles, so that, beginning at the strip of green between the Lake Expressway and the lake itself, you can walk all day in Plechette City and always rest your feet in the grass near a park bench.

On the last bank the plane made before circling down onto the landing strip, the Denmarks could see the lights of the western suburbs and old townships now annexed to the city, and beyond these illuminated windows, the dark mass of Nun's Wood, the fifteen acres of forest owned by a convent. These acres, thick with trees and enclosed by a high fence, were pricked at their center with light: the convent house, the "mansion" which had seemed so terrifying to Elliot when, eight years old, he had climbed the fence and stumbled, following the curving drive to the tall stone building, through the forest to the clearing, and seen the black figures gliding past the windows.

"I don't think I'm ready for this," he said to Vera, who was looking out of the windows to the now already vanished lights of her parents' suburb. "Maybe we should just stay on the plane and go back."

She smiled at him. "Our parents would be awfully disappointed if we did. And I'm sure you can bear it for three weeks." Then she said, brightening, "You'd also disappoint the thousands of admirers who think of your concert as the event of the season."

"Couldn't have been much of a season," he said. He folded a detective novel into his jacket pocket.

A minute later, lights and asphalt beyond the window, a quick dropping; then a hushed gravityless second: the wheels smoothly hit the ground.

"There's something moving on the runway," Vera said, grasping his arm. "Some animal. It's a dog, I think." She bent forward to see. "Can you see it? It's running around in circles up there."

"What kind of dog?"

"I can't tell, it's so far out there, way ahead of us. A raggedy little dog, like a terrier."

Her hand tightened on his arm. "Elliot, it's running right toward us!"

He put his head beside hers and peered out the window at the long gray expanse of floodlit track ahead and to the side. "I can't see anything," he said.

"Neither can I, now."

"Don't worry about it, dogs are smart. He'll just bark at the wheels."

One of the airplane's great tires thumped against something. *"No,"* Vera said. "We killed him!" The plane rolled on for several more yards, then halted. The lights overhead blinked.

A stewardess stretched above him, teasing her jacket up over her blouse, and plucked his coat from the luggage rack, then Vera's. "Is this yours?" she asked him. He nodded. She reached up again, and struggled the long score case, three yards of brown leather concealing Elliot's "secret" present to Vera, a bulky *Italian Renaissance Painting*, down onto his lap.

Vera propped herself on the armrest, her face tired in the beam of light from the panel above. "Didn't we just hit something?" she asked. "A dog? There was a dog ahead of us on the runway."

"Of *course* not," the stewardess crooned, professional. "Animals are kept off the runway." She turned away, saying, "You may de-plane through the front exit." Deplane: was that a real word?

Elliot Denmark, now thirty-two, had lived with his wife in Paris for four years. While Vera had been in graduate school, they had lived largely on grants from the Field Foundation, a documentary-film score he had written through a friend's recommendation (this work he had loved, and wished to do more of it), and occasional royalty checks from RCA, who had recorded his orchestral suite *Five Introductions*, Boulez conducting. After a euphoric two months while it seemed that the album was to be titled after his piece, it was released under the cowardly title *Mainstream Modern*, and Elliot thought that an ironic, painful, and apt category. Just when the second year of the grant had elapsed and when there was no offer to go to one of the lucrative summer arts festivals—in a year leaner than most, he a *Wunderkind* of twenty-seven, Elliot had spent a summer conducting an orchestra in Aspen, Colorado—Vera got her degree and began to teach at the American College in Paris.

Six years before, neither Vera nor Elliot had wanted to move back to Plechette City when he had finished with graduate work in the Columbia music department: but Elliot had been offered a good position at the college there when jobs in composition were difficult to find, the school had a good string quartet and a developing reputation for its music department; and in the end, they had lived in their old hometown only two years. When the foundation grant had come through, they were released from the school and the sometimes oppressive proximity of their parents. And Elliot was released, half reluctantly, half with relief, from Anita Kellerman, the widow of Frank Kellerman, who had been the chairman of the Plechette City University psychology department at the time of his death in an automobile accident. From their new flat in Paris, Elliot had written to Anita once, but she had not replied. Anita was a stern woman. From the first—within weeks of the beginning of their affair—Elliot had felt that he was an actor in some complicated game, a masque, where he had been set down without fully knowing the rules. Anita's husband had been twenty years older than she, an abstracted behaviorist in pink eyeglasses who had spent most of his time with his white rats and his rabbits in his laboratory. In the only picture Elliot had ever seen of the two of them together, Anita's fierce handsomeness, her blaze of heavy blond hair and black eyebrows (in a way which would not become fashionable for another twenty years, a shade too thick for standard beauty), her height, had made Frank Kellerman, a slight scholar's face and attenuated body in baggy Bermudas and a pullover, seem to recede off the photographic plate. Anita was scowling at the ground, walking a few feet before him, her whole attitude one of command.

Elliot had met Anita Kellerman at a party in the home of a cellist, Nathan Himmel. It was the first month of his return to Plechette

City, not long before the beginning of classes, a time of faculty meet-
ings and mimeographed letters from Jaeger, the dean of fine arts—he
threw them all away. "You won't stay here long, will you, Denmark?" Himmel had said. "This is no place for a real composer.
Stick around for a few years, get some work done, and then get out.
If you stay here, no one will ever hear of you. You'll be stuck in
academic politics, you'll make a few recordings on unknown labels,
you'll go dry. You could bitch up your life here but good. You could
turn into another old craphead like——." He named a famous,
though academic composer. Himmel's beefy face, its muscles slack,
had come close to his own. "You should see the letters Blamires at
Columbia wrote to Jaeger, recommending you. They'd knock your
eyes out. I *know* about your talent—it's a pretty talent, but you
haven't begun to develop it. I'm telling you. Don't let this place grab
on to you." The cellist seemed to inflate with sincerity.

"Why do you stay?" Elliot had asked him.

"I'm no composer, I'm a performer. The Melos Quartet is doing
very well. We can tour during vacations, all summer if we want. I like
teaching. It's a comfortable life. I'm making so much money I could
throw wads of it out the window. Hell, I'm a professor here! But
you're not even thirty yet, you shouldn't even want a comfortable life."

"Maybe I don't," Elliot said. "I don't think I care about that."

"Well," Himmel had said, "haven't you always had one?"

Everyone in the city knew about the Denmark family. Good Himmel, with his butcher's face, his advice and his touchiness about
inherited wealth—in Elliot's case, largely unfounded—he was still
there, teaching sweating young cellists throughout the winter, con-
certizing in the summers, earning his professor's salary. The previous
June, Elliot had spent two weeks in London, and he went to Wig-
more Hall to see the Melos Quartet play a concert of Schubert and
Beethoven quartets, a killing program. Himmel sat splayed over his
instrument, his meaty face tugged by concentration, sawing delicately, eyes closed, head wagging. Elliot had not the heart to go
backstage after the concert.

"Does it give you pleasure, writing music?" Anita asked him at
the party. "Doesn't it make it difficult to listen to other people's

music?" She looked like a Viking, a conqueror. A tall, solid body, deep in the thighs and pelvis: he had immediately wanted to put his hands on her, to see what she felt like.

"Pleasure?" he asked. "That's a funny question. It's all I've ever done. Sure, I guess it does. It saves me from having to do anything else."

"What kind of pleasure is it?" There was no trace of humor in these odd questions. He began to feel abraded. "Pleasure in the doing or the having done it, having finished something?"

"That doesn't last long," he said. Faced with this Viking of a woman—was this just arrogance? he wondered—he had to accept her seriousness. "That feeling slides off into depression, eventually. You don't know where the next one is going to come from. The best part of it is being in the middle of a long piece, waking up with it in the mornings, knowing it's going well. Seeing all those clean little marks on the paper. You push it around, hear it happening in your head."

"Don't use the second person when you mean the first," she said. "I'm no composer. I want to know what it feels like." When she smiled at him, her entire face changed. *My God*, he thought, *she's really beautiful*. It was like a bright blond sun coming out over a long tan field: her face seemed to kindle toward him. He felt as though he had been touched.

He bent to her face as if for a kiss. "To tell you the selfish truth, it feels like being made the king of Sweden."

"I hope you stay here awhile," she said. "We could use you."

Near the end of the party, Himmel played one of the Ciccolini recordings of the Scarlatti sonatas and Elliot made his way to the turntable, set into bookshelves. Himmel was standing by the machine, looking abstractedly at his party. "I know," he said, "it's not background music—but then, everybody hates background music. It's a lovely record anyhow, isn't it?"

Elliot nodded. Scarlatti reminded him of his piano lessons. Yet Himmel was right: it was a lovely record.

"By the way," the cellist continued, "I saw you talking to La

Kellerman. That woman can be a bit of a trial, if you're not used to her style of conversation. Did you know that she is a widow?"

Elliot had not known.

"Her husband and she lived two houses up from here. He was a dry old stick of a guy. I think she got that way of talking from him. 'Why do you do this? Why do you do that?' I guess he was pretty good in his field, but I used to go out and mow the lawn whenever he came over. Kellerman was the only man named Frank I've ever known who actually called himself Frankie. After he died, she wouldn't fade away, like most widows. The day after the funeral, she called up all their friends and said that she was going to keep on living the way she'd always lived. I never saw her shed a tear. You know what I mean? She's a tough woman. And she's got a tough job now, raising that kid and supporting herself besides. She's an assistant for the psych. department. The kid's a trial too, I guess— one of those problem babies. He never stops wailing. Well, I don't want to gossip. I like Anita, and she's a friend of my wife's. But something about her scares me. There's no bullshit about her."

"That shouldn't be scary," Elliot said.

"Well, it's not that. What I mean is, she looks at you like she's figuring out which part to bite off first."

"It might be a pleasure," Elliot said.

"Oh, she's good-looking," Himmel said. "She's the real Ice Queen. Look, just to change the subject," the cellist said, touching his sleeve, "are you one of *the* Denmarks? The family that owns the factory?"

It was a question Elliot had grown used to, though Himmel's phrasing was cruder than the usual mix of deference and curiosity. He grimaced into his glass. "Not really. Those Denmarks are my cousins. My father is in the industrial-real-estate business. And those Denmarks no longer own the factory. It was bought by the Globe Corporation, Ronnie Upp's company, five or six years ago. I've never even met Upp. No—I take that back. I met him once. We talked about our bicycles."

"Upp's the whiz kid around here," Himmel said. "I think La Kellerman knows him. I suppose if you've got enough money, nothing scares you. Me, I don't move in those circles."

* * *

The Glaubers were waiting for them in the lobby. Tessa held her arms out and permitted Vera to enter their circle. Taller than her daughter, hair skillfully kept to its ruddy shade of blond, severe strained dramatic face. "Vera! Vera! You're hours late!" Vera extricated herself from her mother's arms.

"We were held over in Chicago, Mother."

"Hello, Elliot." Herman Glauber, a stout man in a sports jacket of a crackling plaid, held out his hand. Elliot took it with gratitude. He had always liked his father-in-law. A big honest Germanic face, made owlish by his huge glasses.

"I told Tessa you'd be late, but would she believe me? I spent half of my week out here, seems like, waiting for some mucky-muck to come in and tell us what's wrong with our city, and they're never on schedule." His bald head shone with sweat. "The controllers in this country are going crazy, trying to juggle all the flights we got now. It's an impossible job, a man-killer. How was your flight?"

"Not too bad. Just long. I'm tired, though, Herman. I didn't sleep at all. How are you and Tessa?"

Tessa embraced him lightly. Long strong arms. He kissed her cheek. "Elliot," she said, "we fumble on. After the last elections, we collapsed for a week and a half. The Birchers almost caught up with Herman this time."

Herman, cradling Vera, looked up. "I'm in no trouble yet, though," he rumbled. "There's no danger of me having to go look for a job. I've been an alderman here since I quit delivering papers, I sometimes think. People have pity on an old man."

Disconcertingly, Herman Glauber shot an odd, nervous glance at his son-in-law. "Time for all that later," he said. "Let's get ourselves on the road. Honey, I'm so glad to have you *back*." He released his daughter, holding her shoulders for a moment. Then he dropped his hands and took the duty-free carton from Elliot's arms. "We'd better go down and get your bags," he said, "before somebody swipes them."

They rode down to the airport's main floor on the escalator. Tessa stood beside Elliot, gripping his free arm, Herman riding down before them on the same step with his daughter. "It's great to have you two guys back with us. I feel like I could stay up all night talking with you."

Elliot mimed staggering against the rail. "Not quite all night, Herman, unless you like talking to a sleeping man."

"Oh, you kids gotta get your rest. But I've been trying to set up a few things for you. Some publicity. Maybe I can help sell tickets to your concert, peddle a few records for you, maybe. Get your face around for the public to see it."

The baggage counter was directly to the left of the escalator on the ground floor. The suitcases were driven up on long flat carts and thrown out onto the pitched steel plane of the ramp, where they slid down to the waiting passengers. Elliot left Vera with her parents on the outer fringe of the crowd around the baggage slide and wedged through to the counter. A slight English girl who had been on the flight from Paris stood beside him, talking to a baggage handler.

"Please please be careful with my suitcase," she was saying. "I've got some glassware in it, and I'm terribly afraid it might be broken."

The handler, a fierce ebony black so dark his features seemed blurred, grunted. He muttered something the girl clearly could not understand.

"Excuse me," she said. "What did you say?"

"Ah know mah *job!*" he shouted at her. The girl jumped. The first cart pulled up and two uniformed men unloaded the bags, thumping them on the ramp and letting them slip to the bottom. Elliot felt an increasing pressure at his back. A fist, a hip dug into him.

Pale leather cases slid down the ramp. The girl pointed to them. "Those are mine, in fact. Could you get them for me?"

The man's face set deeper into rage. "It's *mah job!*" he bellowed. The girl flushed a pure pink. Elliot could tell that she still did not understand what the man was saying. The black man leaned out over the counter and wrenched the two cases up from the steel plane and in the same motion slammed them onto a cart. The girl seemed close to tears; her face loosened. "Please . . ." she began, but the handler had begun to bawl "CLEAH THE WAY," to violently shove the cart through the crowd.

chapter 2

"Food," Herman said. "We go nuts about food in this country. American food is the best in the world." Going westward, Jackson Drive was lined with small shopping centers, restaurants, Thom McAn shoes, cocktail bars—the Swordsman, Green Gables, Dillers, the Monte Carlo—hardware shops, furniture stores, big chain groceries with acres of parking lot, until Sixtieth Street, where the real west side began. There, Jackson Court, a ten-acre shopping center, sprawled, a nest of reddish brick buildings encompassed by shiny black asphalt; after it, a welter of McDonald's hamburger stands, miniature golf courses, pancake houses, Colonel Sanders chicken houses.

"A lot of this will be new to you," Herman said. "The franchise fad came in here in a big way about two-three years ago." They passed a series of prefabricated glass-fronted shacks blazoning famous names—impermanent-looking buildings. Their parking lots were neatly shoveled, the snow heaped into banks.

"*All* of this is new," Vera said. "There were some other shops here when we left, but I can't remember what they were."

"Who can? That's progress. Something comes down, something else goes up. That's what America means. If a ghost is standing in your way, you knock him down and get the job done. This whole stretch here is zoned for small businesses. Now, it might not look beautiful to you, but I think it's a good thing. You see, you get lots of guys in here, they're just looking for a break. These little franchise joints either make them some money or make them go bust. If they know anything about business, if they've got some training, some business education, they can make a better life for themselves. They've got the right to try. Of course, it's a little crowded here right now, I'd agree to that. But there you are, that's the zoning."

They passed a succession of flimsy neon-lighted buildings. The flaring signs marched down the long length of road. Elliot felt as though he had never seen this road before, as though he had been gone a decade.

Tessa twisted about on the front seat to face them. "Darlings, it's so lovely to have you back with us for the holidays. We've got a big Christmas Day party planned with your parents, Elliot, and I'm sure you've got tons of invitations to other parties while you're here. And Uncle Kai is very eager to see you."

"We'll call him tomorrow," Vera said.

Elliot looked out of the rear window, to his left, toward the south of the city. He could just see, revolving, the big gold top of the four-faced clock on its tower. It was miles away, on the other side of the industrial valley. It sent out great streams of light.

"You'd better call him," Herman said. "I've never seen him so pleased. He's finishing his book on Goethe, and I think he wants to talk to you about it. Hell, poor old Kai. He's such a recluse. I'll bet he never goes out of that gloomy apartment of his more than twice a week. Lately, the only times he talks to me he tells me how much he wants to die."

"Herman!" interjected his wife.

"Well, it's the truth. There's no sense in hiding it from the kids, they'll see it for themselves. He keeps going on about Germany. Germany! If I'd been through what he went through in Germany, I'd spit every time I heard the word."

Kai Glauber, Herman's older brother, now in his seventies, had been teaching at the university in Bonn during the twenties; and then, in mysterious circumstances, had been arrested and put in a camp. He apparently had false papers, and he had refused to leave the country. What had Tessa said? "Kai wouldn't believe in the war—he thought that if he ducked his head in some country town, it would blow away—typical. Kai runs away from things. If you want proof, just look at the way he lives!" Kai had been in the camp—"a small unglamorous machine, operating wholesale," as he would later say to Elliot—all during the war. When American soldiers came through in 1944, they had at first refused to believe that he was from the same country as they. He had forgotten all his English. During the five years in the camp, he had shrunk to seventy-five pounds, lost everything he owned, become another person. If Herman Glauber looked like an amiable spectacled bull, his brother Kai, by the time Elliot first met him, resembled an old sharp-featured fox. An enormous vein curled along one side of his forehead, knotting past the hard prominent lumps of bone. Long sleek white hair skimmed straight back across his skull. Since his return to America, he had never had a job, but lived on his brother's charity while working on the book about Goethe he had begun before the war.

A knotty, painful old man, Elliot had always thought. Kai was beyond judgment, in a sense, for he had been to the bottom of the world and had come back speaking another language.

The Glaubers' house was in the township of Richmond Corners, which name now applied principally to the little shopping center on the site of the old town municipal buildings.

"I'll bet it's nice to see your old neighborhood, isn't it, Vera?" asked Tessa.

"Sure it is," her father said. "It's always good to see your home. Isn't that right, Vera?"

"Of course, Daddy," Vera said.

"And you've got all your old friends from the college, you'll have a great time here. Elliot, I can't get over your father inviting us all over to his place for Christmas. Even Kai."

"Will he come?"

"You'll have to work that out with him. When I told him he was

invited, he just sort of nodded. But I'll tell you something, I think
it did him good just to be invited. Your father can be a thoughtful
man—I'll say that for him. He's got good manners."

"Herman," said Tessa.

"Tell us about Paris," Herman said. "What the hell is it like in
old Paree?" Elliot saw his clumsy hands, clad in brown perforated
driving gloves, clasp and unclasp on the wheel.

As Vera talked, they drove through the old township and on to
the Glaubers' three-story wooden house. On the old fields behind,
Elliot could faintly see, whitely limned with snow, the skeletal beams
of hard-constructed houses. One building, the only home finished,
was a dark undefined black before the night sky, dazzled with stars.
The car slushed onto the driveway to the garage Herman had added
to his house; the wheels spun on the ice before catching. Drifts on
either side of the driveway stood five feet high. In the pale winter
moonlight, they gleamed a bluish white.

Elliot had once done a serial composition based on houses like this,
To Walker Evans. It was one of the first pieces he had done after his
marriage. Their spareness, their linear quality, a Protestant dryness:
images in a book of Evans photographs Vera had given him.

It had been Tessa's idea to buy the house, he knew. Herman's
"study" was filled with maps of the city, his filing cabinets, a *Playboy*
wall calendar, his overflowing desk. The rest of the house was furnished with spindly antique furniture, colonial tables and rolltop
desks Tessa had found in farmhouses or at auctions. On every table
there were ancient nutcrackers, old beaten bowls for ashtrays. Pewter
mugs. A bed warmer like an elongated spoon leaned against the
fireplace. Each room on the ground floor had several hooked rugs.

In the first year of the Denmarks' marriage, Elliot a first-year
instructor fresh from Columbia, Tessa had shown him around the
house. "This old table was such a treasure I couldn't pass it up. Only
thirty dollars, and you know what's happened to prices! Oh, look
here, I got these from an old brewer who was just closing down his
brewery. I wish I could have bought *him*." She was pointing at a

jumble of rusted bottle caps in a brass bowl. "Selig's Family Beer, Est. 1801" was stamped on each flaking metal piece.

"We're putting you in Vera's old room," Herman said. "I hope you won't mind sharing it with some stuff Tessa moved up here from the living room. There's room enough to move around in, anyhow. I turned the heat way down, because I figured you wouldn't be used to central heating anymore." He opened a door and set the case on the floor, grunting.

Vera came in behind them. "Tell Mother not to fuss around in the kitchen, Daddy. I told her that we ate a big meal on the plane, but she went on in there anyhow. All I want to do is sleep. It's nice and warm in here. What's all this stuff?" She lay down on one of the twin beds. "*Umm*, delicious. Like sleeping in a warehouse."

Elliot laid both cases beside the beds and sprang open the locks.

"Well, it's ten o'clock," Herman said. "What time is it for you guys?"

"Four or five," said Elliot.

"Four," said Vera.

"You better get some rest. Elliot, first you should call your parents. Use the phone up here. The way we arranged things, you stay here a week and a half, then spend the last half of your vacation at their house. We'd love to monopolize you the whole time, but it didn't seem fair."

"I'll go downstairs and have a drink with you while I call," Elliot said. "I'm so tired I don't think I could get to sleep without one."

"Join me," Herman said. He had been pacing around the bedroom, dodging mirrors and chests like a huge plaid bee. "I can show you the publicity I arranged for you, the newspaper article."

Downstairs, Elliot dialed his parents while Herman made him a drink in the kitchen. The telephone was an old-fashioned wall model with a crank and separate mouthpiece and receiver which dangled from a cord. He heard the phone ring once, twice in his parents' home, and then his father's reedy voice came over the receiver.

"Hello, hello. Denmark residence."

"Hello, Father. It's Elliot. We just got in five . . ."

He heard his father calling "It's Elliot" off into space, and then heard the click as his mother picked up another phone.

"Hello, darling," she said. "It's so wonderful to hear your voice. Please talk lots. Did you have a good trip?"

"Oh, it was fine. But tiring."

"Well, it's fine to hear your voice again, Elliot," said his father. "How are you and Vera getting on at the antique fair?"

"Fine," he said.

Herman put a drink in his free hand, and he heard him slap a newspaper down on the table beside him.

"There's a silly article about you in the *Herald*. I assume your father-in-law was instrumental in having it written. We can only hope he didn't actually write it. Have you seen it?"

"No, not yet," he said. "It's here, though."

"Don't bother him about that, Chase. Elliot, can you and Vera come here for drinks and dinner tomorrow night? We are so anxious to see you. How is Vera?"

"I think she's asleep."

"Do tell her we're anxious to see her again, won't you?"

"Have you talked with Herman Glauber yet?" asked his father.

"Not really."

"He's said nothing about Nun's Wood?"

"Nun's Wood?" Elliot could hear Herman exhaling noisily, hearing the phrase. "No, nothing. Why?"

"Chase, I don't think you should go into that now," said his mother. "He'll be hearing about it until he's sick of it."

"Then he won't be the only one who is sick of it, Margaret," his father said. "Elliot, keep an open mind, and we'll see you tomorrow night. About six."

"Okay," Elliot said. "We'll be over. It'll be good to see you again. Good-bye for now."

"Good-bye, darling," said his mother.

"Good night, kid," said his father.

Turning from the phone, he saw Herman Glauber's broad plaid back going into the kitchen. He swallowed a mouthful of his drink and lifted the newspaper from the table. It was folded back to page three of the second section, the arts page, where a headline read BAD-BOY COMPOSER RETURNS TO GIVE CONCERT. The date was a week in the past. He skimmed the article. "Elliot Denmark, at thirty-two one of the country's foremost young composers and a native son . . . iconoclastic modernist . . . His music is tough going, except for the *au courant* . . . a series of puzzles . . . shockability . . . A spell at Juilliard led to . . . many performances at festivals . . . *Mainstream Modern.* Mr. Denmark is the son of Mr. and Mrs. Chase Denmark of Plechette City and Chicago, and the great-grandnephew of Brooks Denmark. On January 3, Denmark will conduct a program of his own works in the Usenbrugge Concert Hall of Plechette City University."

He took the newspaper into the kitchen. Herman was holding an ice tray under the hot-water tap, splashing the water on his sleeves. Herman glanced at Elliot through steamed opaque lenses, then turned his face back to the ice tray. He jiggled it. Ice cubes clattered out into the sink and began to diminish in the stream of hot water. "Damn," said Herman. "Do you want more ice in that drink? Or don't they use ice where you come from?" He fished in the sink for the slippery cubes. "You read the *Herald* article?"

"Yes, it's fine," Elliot said. "It might bring some people to the concert."

"That's what *I* thought. That 'bad-boy' stuff, I wasn't responsible for that. It was a cute idea of the city editor's. And I couldn't tell you why they ran it a week ago—a lot of people think you've been here that long. I gave them a little hell for that over the phone."

Elliot yawned hugely. "I'm sorry," he said. "I think I ought to get some sleep. Don't be worried about that article, Herman. It was good of you to think of it."

"One more thing. With a little help, I got a slot for you on Ted Edwards' TV show in Chicago. The taping is sometime next week, and we can just run down there for the afternoon and come right back. Is that okay with you? I know Edwards might not be to your taste, but it's a little more publicity, a TV audience. And since it's only a local show, not syndicated, there's nothing to be nervous about. How about it? You could probably cancel, if you want to."

"No, that's fine, Herman." Elliot yawned again, then sipped at his

drink. "It was good of you to arrange it. It might be fun to do."
Privately, he had some reservations. He could remember the Edwards show. Ted Edwards was an intense snakelike man, handsome
in a gangsterish fashion, known for harrying his guests, disguising
his rudeness with a smooth delivery. Celebrities he fawned over. Still,
in his exhaustion, Elliot thought that he could deal with Ted Edwards.

"Did your father see the article?" Herman fidgeted with the objects on the kitchen table: he slid a battered brass salt cellar back
across the scarred wooden surface. "What am I saying, of course he
did. Kai called me on the afternoon it appeared. He told me I was
an idiot. What could I say? That I didn't write it?"

Looking at Herman Glauber's earnest puggish face, Elliot thought
of his own father, his dandyish clothing, his dandy's white mustache,
his slightness, his dryness. What was there in him to threaten Herman Glauber? Just that he was a Denmark, this man who had not
done a single practical thing in fifteen years. The name continued to
impress. His father had once been grand master at a Chicago debutante's ball. Was anybody convinced by this nonsense anymore?
Even Chase Denmark had become "relevant," had involved himself
in committees on social thought, ecology; he sent checks to convicted
black rapists and murderers. All of this had happened over the past
two or three years.

"Herman, you're being too sensitive about something," he said.

His father-in-law tilted back his glass and drained it. Taking it
from his mouth with a snap of his hand, he bumped the base of the
glass gently on the roughened surface of the table.

"He mentioned the Nun's Wood business to you, did he?"

Elliot nodded. "But he didn't go into it."

"It's a little problem we're having out here. There's a question of
sale and development. Ronnie Upp is involved. Ronnie and I have
worked out a scheme that will leave as much of the woods intact as
possible. We could get it rezoned in a minute, except that some
people came into our first open meeting and made such a ruckus
that Max Festlinger, the head of the planning commission, put off
the whole thing for a public hearing." Herman looked grimly down

at his own hands for a moment. "Look, it's four in the morning for you. You'll hear about this tomorrow, I'll tell you all the details. The main thing is that your father and I are on opposite sides of the fence in this thing. Look, let's hang it up for tonight."

He stood up abruptly and gathered some letters off the counter. "You might just want to look at these. It's the mail you got delivered here." He pitched the envelopes onto the table in front of Elliot.

"Do you promise to talk about this tomorrow?" Elliot began to ask. "I don't think I understand the position . . ." and then he saw an envelope in the stack which was addressed solely to Elliot Denmark, in a stark black hand he knew. He tore it open. There was a single sheet within. In the middle of the page was typed *Call me sometime when you come in. It would be so good to see you. A.*

"What's that?" Herman said, standing behind him. "A? Must be a woman. Am I right?"

"An old friend. Anita Kellerman. We knew her at the university."

"Oh, I know her," Herman said. "That is, I met her. She came out here one evening with Ronnie Upp. A tall blond doll, good looker?"

Elliot fought with his surprise a moment before replying. "That's right, I heard she was a friend of Upp's."

"Maybe she wants to talk to you about this business. Come on, it's time to hit the sack. We'll see you guys in the morning."

They went up the stairs together in the dark.

In the morning Elliot's nose bled a thick syrup. He felt dizzy, disoriented. The room was surprisingly noiseless. The window at the opposite end of the room looked out to a clear featureless white. Everything was different. Blood flowed sluggishly toward the back of his throat, tasting of unsweetened chocolate and brass. His mind shuffled through a list of places. Then he saw the spindly chair on which he had hung his shirt and the stained desk behind it, a carved American eagle at its top between two in-curling wooden waves, and he remembered. He looked at his watch: ten o'clock.

"I feel terrible," he heard Vera say. "I'm so *dry*."

While Vera showered and dressed, Tessa told him the entire story.

They sat in the dining room, and he ate the eggs and toast she had made for him. The dining-room window opened onto the back garden, and while Tessa talked he let his eyes rest on the soft pale length of snow, swollen over hedges and massed at the edge of the driveway. Snow capped the head of the stone cherub at the end of the garden. His white stone arms were dusted, like the branches of trees, with inches of snow.

"You know how Herman has fought to bring development into this ward," she said to him. "And I do mean fought. People think aldermen do nothing but smoke cigars all day and make promises at elections, but I can tell you how hard that man works. He couldn't even stay at home this morning, as much as he wanted to. He had to go down to his office. The big hearing is right after New Year's, and he couldn't rest, knowing how much work he has to do. And the phone calls! Every time a dog bites somebody, every time somebody sees a rat, not that we've got rats out here, they jump to their telephone and screech at Herman."

"So," he said, breaking into her digression, "this Nun's Wood business has something to do with development? I gathered that it was that from the little he'd tell me last night."

"Why, of course," she said. Her ravaged face was white with a morning tiredness. "Do you want some more coffee?" She poured a thin black stream into his cup. "That's what I was telling you. The convent is closing down. The superior heard from Ronnie Upp soon after she made it known that they were going to sell, and I guess he made her a very reasonable offer for it. He must be Catholic, don't you think? They like to do business together. Anyhow, since Herman is on the planning commission, Upp called him to see what could be done about rezoning the convent grounds."

"What did he want to put up?" Elliot asked. "A subdivision?"

"No, it's much better than that," she cried. "If he were going to do that, it wouldn't have to be rezoned. The way he explained it to Herman was that he was going to build an industrial park. The emphasis is on the *park*. The old convent house could be used for one of the office buildings, and he's planning to put up two others at widely spaced intervals on the property." Elliot could tell that she was repeating someone else's words, whether Ronnie Upp's or her husband's. "It would be done as tastefully as could be. They would leave sixty percent of the existing trees standing, and the buildings would be set into the natural contours of the land features. There'd be IBM, a big life-insurance company. Ronnie's offices, lots of other big names, companies people respect."

"What's the problem with the plan?"

"The problem? What's the *problem*? The problem started with the families who live across Wiltshire Drive from the convent grounds. All these people, these six or seven families, they think their property values are going to go down. They think they have a God-given right to protect their little property values, like nobody else counted. Buster, it makes you take a long look at so-called democracy. They sent around a petition and got lots of names of people who didn't understand the plan at all! You live in a special world, you know. You don't come in contact with unreasonable people. These people, they packed the public meeting and forced the commission to delay the final vote for a public hearing. Then the newspapers started in. There have been articles all winter long about Nun's Wood. Well, the superior says she wants to sell before February, and if the commission is blocked from rezoning, she'll just sell to the highest bidder and some developer will get it—some Catholic developer. Then there won't be any park at all! There'd be another row of houses, a lot of imitation mansard roofs and carriage lamps, like Tudor Acres back here in the old hayfield. Not that Tudor Acres is the worst of them. Ronnie's behind it, and some taste has gone into it, judging from the model home. But anything that would go up in Nun's Wood would be worse than the industrial park. That's the part they don't understand."

"'They' including my father, presumably," he said.

She ignored his invitation to tell him what he already knew: Tessa's tact was often misplaced. "They want the city to buy the land and keep it the way it is. Or they want Ronnie Upp, who's been an angel through this whole mess, who's been all over the papers, to just plunk down his money and donate it to the city as a park. Now, nobody's saying he can't afford it. But is that a reasonable thing to expect?"

"I suppose it isn't," Elliot said. He was thinking: he is doing it to thwart Ronnie Upp. He still cannot forgive him for owning the Chambers Denmark factory. Elliot could imagine his father hiding his rancor behind the curtain of a humanitarian motive.

Ronnie Upp had been sent to boarding school in Connecticut when he was just a child. Then, a boy, he had returned one summer on his vacation, and the awful thing had happened. Harrison Upp, the father, lived near the Denmarks in the Lake Point area on the east side. In that year, 1951 or 1952, there had been a series of burglaries in Lake Point homes. They were all supposed to be the work of one burglar. Elliot's parents had put new locks on the doors and installed alarms on the windows, which were connected to a panel in the Lake Point police station. Harrison Upp, more swashbuckling than Chase Denmark, had a pistol. Sometimes he carried it in a shoulder holster. Elliot could recall his shock of delight and fascination when Harrison Upp had negligently let his jacket slide past the roughened black butt of the revolver; he had been standing in the door of the Denmark house, leaning on the jamb, his face florid in the June dog-heat. On a July night of that year, Ronnie Upp had heard a noise from the outside. It sounded like a man softly, quickly crossing their lawn. He had raced to his father's room, snatched the pistol from a drawer, and fired through the bedroom window. When the police came, they discovered that he had shot and killed his own father. Quite suddenly, it seemed as if everyone were saying, "Of course, Grace is an alcoholic, she's not responsible," and when Grace Upp died by her own hand in a nursing home at the end of summer, no one had seemed particularly surprised. Ronnie had gone away to Connecticut, then to England, and had not returned until he was a grown man. He owned property in downtown Plechette City, houses and land in many other cities; and he was almost legendary for his wealth. Upp was a member of the country club, but was never seen there; the same was true of the Town Club, the Plechette City Club, the Athletic Club and the Hunt Club. Anita, four years ago, had told Elliot that he was "sad." "I thought you must have known

Ronnie," she said. "Of course, he is a rather sad person. He is innocent."

Elliot could at least admit that Upp had strange psychic baggage for a tycoon.

Tessa took his breakfast plates into the kitchen. Elliot continued to look out at the snow-drowned garden. At the far end, before a hummock that was a buried hedge, the stone cherub lifted his fat white arms. Anita Kellerman's note was in his jacket pocket, where he had put it, folded in quarters, the night before. He tried to make out the features on the cherub's face: they looked blank and open. Soft parted lips. He heard the gurgle of the dishwasher beginning its cycle. There seemed to be a faint promise in the cherub's face, an expectancy for which the blank features were the expression. It looked, its arms lifted and weighted with snow, as though it would shortly ascend into the cloud-heavy sky. He decided to call Anita.

Elliot leaned forward over the table and peered into the kitchen. Tessa's back, her fluffy ruddy hair and long slim trunk, was turned to him. She was fussing with something at the oven. He swiveled to the phone and stood up to dial. Then he realized that he no longer knew her telephone number. He replaced the receiver on the hook, picked the directory, clad in a blue denim binding which bore the name of an antique dealer, from the top of the phone box and flipped through to the K's. Kellerman, A. The Leecham Street address. It pleased him that she had not moved. He dialed.

The phone rang once before he heard her voice. In the instant of its trill, his heart seemed to swim beneath his ribs.

"Ronnie," she said. "I want—"

He hung up.

When he looked away from the phone, Vera was coming through the door from the kitchen, dressed in blue jeans and a blue turtleneck sweater.

"You look like Jack Kerouac's girlfriend," he said, his hand still on the wooden box of the telephone.

"Were you calling someone?"

"Here." He fished the note from his pocket. "This came in a letter addressed here. Herman gave it to me last night with the rest of the mail, mostly Christmas cards, judging from their shape. I didn't open them." She unfolded the note and bent her head over it. "It sounds unhappy to me, so I just tried to reach Anita, but her line was busy. Your father thought it might have something to do with the Nun's Wood business."

"With what?" Vera's face showed both puzzlement and suspicion.

"Oh, Christ, you haven't heard about it yet. Just wait till I call Anita and I'll explain it to you."

"Ve-ra," her mother called from the kitchen.

"Oh, another thing," he said. "We are supposed to go to my parents' house tonight at six for drinks and dinner."

"Of course," she said, and went through the door to the kitchen. The door closed, and through it drifted Tessa's voice. "What's the point of staying here if you're going to go running across the town on those icy roads . . ."

He dialed the number again.

"Hello?" her clear voice said.

"Anita, this is Elliot."

"Welcome back, Elliot Denmark!" Her voice was entirely friendly. "Was that you who just called?"

"No," he lied. Then, remembering that Vera might be listening, he said, "I did try to call you just now, but the line was busy."

"I was waiting for a call from Ronnie Upp," she said. "That's not important. I suppose you're calling because of the note I wrote you."

"I would have called anyhow," he said. "I'd like to see you sometime soon, if you're not too busy."

"What does that mean?" He could hear her smile. "Never mind. Elliot, dear, I was confused and tired when I wrote that note to you. I read that awful thing in the *Herald*. How is Vera?"

"Vera is fine," he said.

"You're not angry with me? I had a rough spell, but I'm over it now. Please call me later, when I'm not so rushed, will you, darling?"

"How is Mark?"

"Getting on. Getting older. He's seven now. Duck, I have to run now. It was lovely of you to call. We'll get together later in the week. All right? Good-bye, sweet."

The phone clicked and the dial tone began to buzz.

He hung up. The voices of Vera and her mother, Tessa's pitched higher, came from the kitchen. One of them had swung the door, and he could see Vera's blue back, standing straight and alone near the oven: she was shorter than her mother, but her legs were long in those jeans. Her hair fell darkly down from her shoulders. Elliot looked out at the cherub, still on the verge of ascent, weighted by the powdery snow, its lips open as if to utter some statement about all this surrounding matter. He went toward the women in the kitchen.

chapter 3

When Elliot began his affair with Anita Kellerman, he knew that the sense of infallibility she gave him was illusory, but he could not dampen the surge of confidence she had aroused in him. He knew too that the motives for this flaring out of emotion were entirely primitive: Anita Kellerman was a big-bodied powerfully attractive woman—she seemed to blaze with purpose and design— and she loved him; he possessed her, at least as much of her as was not given to her son. If the world could be divided into survivors and victims, Anita seemed chiefly a survivor. What she touched in him was the level of feeling that had been all his life given to music. Anita's relationship to his work seemed profound. Since adolescence, he had instinctively valued those composers in whom the disorderly eruptive life of the emotions was made unrhetorical and implicit in form. The strength of the work he did in graduate school made him a small name, at least among other graduate students. Blamires, his supervisor, had been enthusiastic about these works, and Blamires knew everybody, Virgil Thompson, Cage, Sessions, Foss, Schuller, Tippett, everybody. As Himmel had implied, it was Blamires who had gotten him his job. After Elliot began his involvement with Anita Kellerman, he wrote a song cycle based on poems by Theodore Roethke, and allowed himself to be wilder, looser, more ragged.

Yet even the new music was highly conscious: it was as though he could transport the spirit of Anita's masque directly into it. Performed at the Donaueschingen Festival in 1968, *Words for the Wind* was his first real success. *Five Introductions* was written later that same summer.

Elliot had left the note in his pocket for weeks after Himmel's party. His classes had begun, he and Vera were buying things for their apartment, they ate dinner with one set of parents every weekend; Elliot felt as though, after the long grind of graduate school and nighttime writing, he had at last moved out into an actual life in the world. He enjoyed the business of teaching, and for some months it occupied him fully. He spent his evenings working out his lectures and planning exercises for his students, who were all seniors and juniors—music majors. He knew within the first month that most of them would never compose a bar of music once they left his course. They were too lazy. Many of his students would take jobs teaching music in Wisconsin high schools. Some, like Himmel's best pupils, would find jobs in orchestras; others would drift on into graduate schools. None of them reminded him of what he had been like at their age: compulsive about writing music, always ducking off to a practice room to toy with a piano.

He taught Monday, Tuesday and Friday afternoons, and Wednesday mornings. Wednesdays, he fell lazily into the habit of eating in the student-union cafeteria with Roy Baltz and Susan Stringer, both students. Baltz was a big farmboy, not long out of a crewcut, emphatic in his judgments. He loved Bruckner and Wagner, but seemed to despise the work of all other composers, including Elliot Denmark. He let it be known that he was working on an oratorio for rock band and orchestra. "Pardon me, Mr. Denmark, but all this stuff being done now is *so* minor." He looked to lank-haired Susan Stringer for confirmation. She nodded solemnly. "Where's the inventive music of today? It's not coming out of the academy. It's not old-fashioned so-called 'modern' works by guys who never thought beyond Webern." (Elliot knew that this was, for Baltz, a polite reference to his own work.)

After a month of listening to Baltz, he remembered Anita Kellerman on a clean aching mid-November day. He left the room after one of the Wednesday sessions and went upstairs to his office to use the telephone. When he arrived at her house, fifteen minutes later, she met him saying, "The arrival of Elliot Denmark." He had looked at her, puzzled. She seemed almost angry with him. He was uncertain of his intentions.

A record was playing inside her house, and he could hear it from where he was standing, outside the front door. Some slippery, piercing thing: jazz. He had a quick mental flash of Harrison Upp, his seersucker jacket pulled carelessly back over the cross-hatched butt of a gun.

She led him into the kitchen. It was a sunny yellow room into which the music drifted from the hall. Anita gave him a drink. "I'm glad you came," she said. "I was waiting for you."

Watching her move across the sunny kitchen, opening a can of soup, putting a pan on the stove, Elliot was moved by the clarity of her gestures. She did everything surely, finally: her face taut, cheekbones almost Slavic.

"You know," he said, "I'm not quite sure what I'm doing here with you."

"Does it make you nervous, being here?" She turned her head over her shoulder as she stirred the soup. Her face looked anxious.

"No," he said. He felt as though he were soothing her, though he knew this was not the case. "I'm not serious. What did you mean, you were waiting for me?" He felt a small flutter in his stomach. He had the sense that something definite was expected of him, an action he was not sure he wished to complete: sitting there in the bright kitchen with the jazz music floating through the door, and watching this tall solid blond woman pour soup into bowls, he felt as if there were a role here, a definition he was supposed to embody. Her gestures were delicate, precise.

She set the steaming bowl before him. Was she one of those women who collected musicians or academics? She did not look the type, but you could never tell anything by looks. He felt both foolish and irritated.

"I just wanted to talk to you," she said, sitting across from him.

"Yes, I'm lonely. People are different when a woman becomes a widow."

In a short tan skirt and white blouse she looked feline and healthy. He was conscious of long sleek legs. Her being widowed gave her another dimension, took her somehow beyond his reach. He could not be responsible for so much past.

During lunch, he felt himself opening up to her, talking about his teaching, his music, his ideas. She delighted him with her intelligence—that too seemed graceful. "Have you ever been entirely close to anything?" she asked him. "Close enough so you have a total understanding of it as another life, something you can understand without wanting to own it or possess it or change it?"

"I don't know," he said. "Maybe the closest I get to what you are talking about is with music."

"Other people's music," she said.

"That's right. I've spent all my life listening to it and trying to understand it, analyzing it, but I could never feel that I owned it or possessed it."

"You've never had this with a living being?"

"Have you?"

"Perhaps with Mark," she said. "I can remember seeing him in the hospital, seeing his red wrinkly skin and his tiny hands and feet. I felt as though I were looking right through, to see his veins and his heart. He's alive, I thought, he's another life connected to mine that will outgrow mine. That's the closest I've ever felt to anything. Frank was already dead when he was born." Her voice was level, uncomplicated; directed to some internal point. Yet he was sure that she meant him to take this speech as a kind of metaphor.

As he had to, he asked, "May I see him?"

She led him upstairs. The backs of her knees were smooth and girlish above the tender bulging of her calves. Watching her legs ascend the stairs, Elliot felt the beginning of a sexual tension, a current between them. He wanted to touch her. At the top of the stairs, she moved softly to a closed door and peeked in. Then she soundlessly entered and motioned to him. Her hand was slightly knotted about the joints and knuckles, the long strong fingers nearly the size of his own. "He's still asleep," she said. He moved beside her to the small bed. Mark lay on his back, thinner than most babies. He stirred, flung up an arm. Elliot, unthinking, put his arm around Anita's unfamiliar shoulder. She moved closer to his body.

She said nothing, but looked at him gravely, a long direct gaze that touched him squarely. They left the room together. In the tiny hall she put her hand in his.

Then she smiled at him, making his legs weak. "A lot of men find me forbidding. I'm too uncompromising. I always know what I want."

He put his arms around her. She felt solid in his arms, a denser presence than Vera. Anita's broad face hovered before his own, looking up at him. She seemed illuminated, as if by a private joke. Her eyes really were green, and lighted with humor.

She led him into her bedroom, the door next to the baby's. "Oh, my God," Elliot said. "I've got to teach a class in half an hour."

"Then don't take long," she said. "There'll be another time." He could not think of another woman in the world who could have said that at such a moment.

In moments of detachment and self-loathing, he saw his whole life from a great height: his big unathletic body, his heavy intellectual face, racing between two houses and the school, all this shrunk into dollhouse scale, his figure going in and out of beds, panting, groaning, embracing with two women, one taut and blond, one soft, dark. In front of his classes, he gesticulated, mouthing words in a fury, sometimes seeing saliva spray in the light, words about *purity, neatness, form. Bareness.* All the while cherishing his tangle of emotions, seeing his panting, ridiculous self as flawless.

Vera and Anita met for the second time at an end-of-term party at the home of Jaeger, the dean of the fine-arts school. Anita had come with Himmel, whose wife was in bed with flu. Jaeger was a tall thin greyhound of a man with the manners of a Japanese diplomat. "He gives good parties," Himmel had told Elliot, "but his only other talent is being good-looking."

"I've been hearing great things about your song cycle, *Wind Words*, is it?" Jaeger said. *"Winter Words?"*

"Words for the Wind," said Elliot. "Benjamin Britten wrote *Winter Words*."

"Yes, that's it," Jaeger said. "I hope you'll excuse my memory. Nathan has told me that it's a fine solid piece of work. I hope it's a great success at that wonderful festival. Where is that again?"

"Donaueschingen," Elliot said. "But it's not this year, it's next year."

"Yes. Quite a significant place, I gather. You'll be staying with us here at the school for a number of years, won't you, Elliot? We need a man like you to make our fine-arts school the place I know it can be. You and the Melos Quartet make us a powerful draw." He withdrew, smirking gently, to the side of a famous abstractionist who had been hired for the summer session. "Ah. Mr. Raciewicz," Elliot heard him purr, "it was so good of you to leave New York to join us here in the provinces." The painter was a small dumpy man, sweating through his denim shirt. He customarily worked on twenty-foot canvases, and Elliot heard him begin to complain about the size of his studio.

Elliot moved across the room to Himmel's side. The cellist waved his glass at him. "Ah, your first year in serfdom draws to its close. Did you know that you'll get Baltz next year, in your graduate class?"

"He told me," Elliot said. "He says he wants to change the whole program. He's going to petition the dean to do away with the requirements."

"Jaeger will just throw it back on us. With an infinitely courteous note. Fortunately, the good Baltz is practically friendless, as far as I can see. If he could get a majority of the first-year graduate students on his side, Jaeger might feel that he had to think about it. Then we'd be in trouble."

"I hate this administrative jiggery-pokery," Elliot said.

"Didn't I tell you?" Himmel's face began to look as cheerful as it could. "Don't get involved in this business, Denmark, or they'll end up making you an assistant dean. Then you can watch your life going down the drain."

"Don't you have any worries about it happening to you?"

"Me? I'm a helpless fiddler." Himmel seemed to radiate joy. "One of the court servants." He looked around. "Where's my date?" Himmel pretended to hold binoculars to his eyes. "Oh, date! Date!"

"I think she's in the other room," Elliot said. He had consciously avoided Anita throughout the party.

"Then let us adjourn," Himmel said. "The good Kellerman will have something illuminating to say about the Oversoul. Perhaps she is the Oversoul." He took Elliot's arm. "Come on. She doesn't really bite. I tried."

Anita was in the other room, sitting on Jaeger's floral couch with Vera. Still gripping Elliot's arm, Himmel led him before the two women. "Ladies, your court," he said. "Your friends from the animal world. I represent the Canadian goose and Denmark here is the sole surviving platypus. Only a kiss will restore us to human form. Make me human with a kiss." He bent down, offering his slab of forehead. Anita kissed his head lightly. "Alas," Himmel said. "I'm still a goose. Now the squire's turn."

He pulled Elliot's arm, urging him toward Anita. Elliot glanced at Vera, who was smiling at him. He bent. Anita's cool lips grazed his forehead.

"Transformed!" hooted Himmel. *"Un miracle!"* He collapsed on the couch beside Anita. "My dear, grant me a moment of bliss before you once more deliver me to my wife. A stray pet, a stray tickle among friends."

"I think Squire Denmark and I will grant you a stray cup of coffee," she said. "Will you help me?" she said, looking at Elliot.

"If you need help."

"I don't think it's Anita who needs the help," said Vera. She looked with amusement at Elliot. "Some coffee might be a good idea."

I shouldn't go in that kitchen with her, Elliot was thinking. We have to be more careful than that.

"Well, come on then," she said. He followed her toward the kitchen.

She closed the door behind them.

"Now I've got you," she said. "I told you I was greedy."

"This isn't very smart."

"I don't care. When I kissed your forehead I thought I'd faint. I wanted to put my hand inside your shirt." She smiled at him: the orange sun, that warmth. "Once I had my horoscope read, and the old lady who did it said that I was lascivious."

"She wasn't far wrong."

"No. She was dead right. I'm a lascivious bitch, and I'd love to make love to you on Jaeger's kitchen table."

She moved forward and put her hands on his shoulders. Elliot touched her lips with his: but she was still cool, playful. "You'd better lock the door," she said.

He took his arms from around her and went to the door. The lock was a simple lever below the doorknob. He clicked it to the left, then tugged at the door. It held. He went back to Anita, who stood smiling at him with a cat's face, and put one hand to her breast, the other lightly to the small of her back. Her mouth flickered beneath his.

"Now let's make the coffee," she said.

She took the pot off the stove and carried it to the sink. It was half full of old grounds and cold coffee, which she swilled down the drain. Elliot discovered some Maxwell House in a cupboard, the cups on a shelf close by.

"What did you and Vera talk about?"

"I wanted her to talk about you. My masochism, maybe. I wanted to see how she thinks about you." She heaped three, four, five spoonfuls of the coffee into the percolator, clamped the lid down, and put it on one of the burners. Twisted a dial. "But I couldn't get far. I kept wanting to find out about *her*, too. You've never told me anything about her."

"What did you find out?" He felt uneasy, slightly invaded.

"She loves you. She's a lovely girl. She knows you're a good composer, and she wants you to quit teaching. I think she's the kind of girl who always is first in her English class, but with more warmth than that type usually has—do you know what I mean? I guess I liked her. I just like you more."

"Vera doesn't like most women," he said. "She thinks they're vapid. I suppose you are the kind of woman she'd like, if she didn't feel overwhelmed by you."

The doorknob rattled. The door thumped slightly, pushed from the outside.

"Come in," Anita called.

"Is it locked?"

Hearing Vera's voice, Elliot smoothed his hair and went toward the door.

"I think it is," Vera said. "Why . . ."

Elliot opened the door. Vera's hand was still on the knob, her face pale, vulnerable.

"I don't know how it got locked," he said. "I think the coffee is almost ready."

"Nathan wandered away, and I got bored, so I thought I'd come in to see if I could help."

He saw her scrutinizing his face. Elliot felt himself beginning to flush. From the main room, he could hear Raciewicz, the abstractionist, bellowing about the teaching of art. "*Nobody* teaches painters," he was shouting. "Painters damn well teach their own greedy selves. Only pansies and hacks think you get anywhere by teaching art. You fucking well give the little sons of bitches pencils, and that's teaching art."

Jaeger's thin bland face appeared in the doorway. He smiled fractionally, a movement of his lower lip. "Our famous acquisition appears to be a little out of sorts. Have you really made some fresh coffee? I've never had such helpful guests before."

"I think it should almost be ready," Vera said. She moved to the stove. "I'll get it for him. Then I think we have to go home." She looked at Elliot. "Unless you want to stay and go home with Himmel."

"No, of course not," he said.

When they left, a woman was refilling Raciewicz's cup. A large brown amoebalike stain was spreading on the carpet where the painter had dropped his first cup.

They drove home in silence. Vera stared straight ahead through the windshield. As they put the car in the garage beneath their apartment building, Vera said, "Well, I've met your ideal woman, haven't I?"

"It'll work out," he blurted.

They lay together on the bed, the moonlight brightening the window through the white curtains.

"I don't know what to do about it," she said. "You must be in love with her, or you would never have done it."

"I am. It was just something that happened. But I love you too."

"How long?"

"Just a couple of months." Six? Seven? Nearly nine. His chest thudded under the weight of those nine months.

"It must be very good for you. She's beautiful, isn't she? Does she love you?"

"I think she does, yes. But I think she loves her son more than she could ever love anyone else."

"Elliot, how am I supposed to act, what am I supposed to do? I knew something was happening, but I couldn't bear to think about it before. When I talked to her, I just knew. I *knew*. And then it was so transparent—that kitchen business. How am I supposed to handle this, Elliot? It can't keep on."

"It won't keep on. You're right, it can't now. But . . . I do love her. I suppose I should feel sorry about that, but I don't. It makes me feel stronger. It's just love. She's good for me."

"It would help if you didn't assault me with my inadequacies."

He said nothing. What do we do? he wondered.

"You used to meet her during the day?"

He nodded.

"Did you make love every time you saw her?"

There was a long silence. Elliot watched the moon, hung like a button in the sky beyond their window.

"It makes me feel so degraded. I don't have any dignity anymore. I'm so uncertain. I feel weak."

"What I have to ask is that you let things go their own way for a time. I don't want to lose you, you know that. And I haven't left you. That would be impossible for me."

"I'm your *wife*," she said. "Your *wife*. I hate her."

He put one arm about her shoulder. Her body felt rigid, as if he had struck her.

Since the telephone's invention, adulterous lovers have required it. The next day Anita called Vera and spoke to her briefly on the telephone. Elliot had already phoned Anita while Vera was out of the apartment. "Yes," Elliot could hear Vera say, "yes. Perhaps we should. I don't know what I have to say to you though . . . I thought that. In Plechette Park, down at the lakefront . . . Five minutes." She hung up.

"That was your girlfriend. She could tell that I saw what was happening. She's very intelligent."

"You're going to meet her?"

"She wanted to. Along the lake. What am I supposed to say to her? That I want my husband back?"

"I don't know what you're supposed to say." He opened his mouth to speak, then realized that he had spoken the truth; he could not imagine what Vera might say to Anita. "You're brave," he said.

"I'm not brave. I'm shaking."

"You don't have to go." Yet inwardly, secretly, he felt as though this meeting would testify to some deep symmetry in things, a comprehensibility.

He stood by his desk as she left. He saw himself ascending, a feather borne up by his emotions. The two women, Vera Glauber and Anita Kellerman, walked beneath him by the edge of a huge body of blue water. The women talked, talked, came to some unimaginable agreement. They held his world together. He was saved. Music poured from his head.

chapter 4

Elliot moved his hands across the lid of the piano, miming the actions of playing. He was doing one of the Scarlatti sonatas, the E Flat Major, doing it reflectively, hearing the music ripple across his mind. Vera moved indistinctly to his right, looking at his father's books. His fingers thumped on the polished dark wood. *Cantabile*. He had never been anything but a competent pianist. Maybe if he had practiced more, as Ladnier, his piano teacher, had insisted. He saw withered old Ladnier moving him aside on the bench, touching the keys. "So," he said. "Play it so." "So," Elliot said, the word a totem. He ruffled his fingers: I'd have got it that time, Ladnier. He abandoned the Scarlatti, coming up against a blank space in his memory; he could hear the ghost of the music arching, effortless, in his memory. A small, perfect room. Now his hands were doing something curious: a pun. He was making big swing leaps with his left hand, Teddy Wilson piano, embroidery with his right. His father's music. Elliot folded the lid back and continued this on the keys. He sensed more than saw Vera turning toward him in surprise. "Tea for Two." He began, as a joke, deleting bars.

"The boys in dance bands used to do that when I was a young blade," said his father, coming through the door with a tray of drinks. His shirt gleamed a soft mauve. "They got bored. Most of the band leaders couldn't tell the difference, and the Lord knows that nobody they were playing to could. You're still a little stiff in the bass, by the way. Still no competition for Teddy Wilson. Take a drink and let me have a go at it."

Elliot stood up and moved to one of the couches, taking a glass from the tray. Vera sat beside him. Elliot caught a vibration from her, an uneasiness; Tessa had retold the Nun's Wood story that afternoon. In my parents' house, he thought, she should not feel herself on enemy territory. Elliot felt a tiny flicker of anger, then realized that it came from his own discomfort.

Elliot's father sat at the piano bench. "Now," he said, "I think we could use a little 'Sheik of Araby.'" His left hand moved effortlessly up and down, gently striking the chords. "This is the most elegant kind of jazz piano there is." To Elliot, it sounded as trivial as it always had. Thank God Anita had not played this stuff. She was at least a bit more modern. What was all that about on the phone? She had sounded distant, offhand. *Ronnie.* He took Vera's small hand in his. His father's dandyish face, sprouting white mustache above his colorless lips, winked at him over the top of the piano. "Do you see what I mean, Elliot? Utter elegance. Of course I can't do what Wilson does."

His mother came in from the hall door. "Dears, I hope you'll excuse my absence. I just had to change clothes, and then I thought I'd supervise Robert in the kitchen. Chase, don't be antisocial. Come and join us."

Elliot's father ended by playing a series of runs, and smartly closed the lid of the piano. "Well, I hate to pass the blame or to my only son, but when I came into this room, he was doing things to 'Tea for Two' that would have made Teddy Wilson turn green!"

"I'm sure Teddy will forgive him," said Margaret. "Now join us and talk to the children." She patted the cushions beside her.

"We're having some of your old admirers in after dinner," she said. "Some of our friends are dying to see you again. Pierce Laubach practically begged me to have him over, and Hilda Usenbrugge, who is an old dear, of course, wanted very much to see you, so your father and I invited them both for later this evening."

"Sure," Elliot said. "It'll be a pleasure."

Dr. Pierce Laubach was a thin baldheaded man, acid as fresh grapefruit juice, recently retired. He had been a gynecologist practicing among the circle of his friends. One of the old ladies whose illnesses had made him rich had almost certainly been Hilda Usenbrugge, the unmarried aunt to a large brewing family that had been in Plechette City for a century and a half. Elliot could remember her only as a scatty, rather shy old woman, her face the wreck of what must once have been a striking girlish prettiness. She had never shown any particular interest in him, and he could not imagine why she wanted to see him now. Nor Dr. Laubach either, though he was closer to the family. In shiny black dancing pumps and a wicked-looking tuxedo, Dr. Laubach had haunted his parents' parties while Elliot was growing up.

Elliot's father tucked up the knees of his trousers with a remembered movement of his wrists and sat where his wife had indicated. "You're all settled in over at the Glaubers'? We've rearranged your old room for you here, you know, so it will be ready for you when you make your great move." He smiled at them, his fine old eyes, the color of an August sky, wrinkling at their corners. "Vera," he said, "you've heard about the little disagreement between your father and myself. That's an unfortunate thing—it's unfortunate, I mean, that Herman should be on the wrong side of the fence—but don't waste time feeling nervous about it. We'll give him a bit of a thrashing, or at least I hope we shall, but you must know the respect I have for your father."

"Thank you," Vera said. "I think the best thing for Elliot and me is just to stay out of that question. I don't really understand it, anyhow."

"You don't understand it, my dear? It's quite simple. A gang of developers is going to despoil ten acres of the finest woodland in the entire county for the sake of a few irrelevant office buildings. Total disregard for the land, total disregard for the average citizen. And, I should add, for the sake of slipping a few extra dollars into Ronnie Upp's pocket."

"Chase," Margaret Denmark said. Her powdery pretty face inclined toward her husband. "There will be time for all that later."

She turned to Elliot and Vera. "For weeks Chase has been involved in this Nun's Wood affair. It's all I've heard, morning to night. Lord preserve us from our husband's enthusiasms, don't you agree, Vera?"

Vera wryly agreed.

"Not that Elliot has ever been terribly interested in anything but his music. Chase and I never thought that our son would go in that direction, but we could see from the time he was the tiniest little boy that it was his whole life."

"Of course, Vera," his father said, "even people in the arts owe something to the world of ordinary human beings. Responsibility. I can't tell you how forcefully I feel this. Now if someone of Elliot's stature were to declare himself on this issue we have here, I think it would do good for the entire city. I've been toying with the concept of getting the really *responsible* people, the responsible well-to-do people, together with those they can help the most. The blacks, the Puerto Ricans from the valley, the Indians. In this instance, the Wiltshire Drive people who could use an area of parkland. Rona Bender and her cohorts. I think we could raise enough money, if the people of this section of Plechette City could be stirred, to settle the Nun's Wood question for good and all."

His father's voice had taken on a stridency Elliot had rarely heard in it. Things really have changed, he thought. For a moment he pictured his parents' living room populated by angry blacks and Puerto Ricans in black berets, Indians in feathers and warpaint, haranguing sleek Pierce Laubach and dotty old Hilda Usenbrugge while his father played "The Sheik of Araby" as background music.

After dinner the six of them sat in the upper living room, where his father had drawn the drapes and made a fire in the big brick fireplace "to welcome home the prodigals." The room seemed much too warm to Elliot.

Dr. Laubach was even more saurian than Elliot remembered him, though, four years previous, he would never have worn striped trou-

sers (and, Elliot noticed, trousers discreetly flared). Hilda Usenbrugge
remained unchanged. She was still the type of the maiden aunt, shy,
feathery, still carrying the unsettling wreckage of her prettiness. Elliot remembered, now that the reason for their inclusion in the evening had become apparent, that she had always had a penchant for
lost causes. She had, years ago, formed a group to protect the Plechette River; before that, when he had been in prep school, there
had been something to do with bird sanctuaries in marshes.

"Oh!" Her spotted ringless hands described a vague shape in the
air. "Elliot, I can't tell you what your father has done for us."

"Just so," Pierce Laubach purred. "Without Chase's help we may
never have got off the ground. All of us on the committee are very
grate-ful for his help."

"Why, it's true!" Hilda Usenbrugge appeared to be startled by her
own enthusiasm. "There were the concerned Wiltshire Drive people
and the Landmark Preservation Society. They came to us first thing,
you know"—and he did know, for she had repeated this several
times—"and we were all just casting about before Chase gave us his
help. He was a real strongman for us."

"The news-papers," Dr. Laubach drawled. "The lovely newspapers. The lovely pub-licity. With Chase's help, we've given them a
good clean fight. Vera, my dear, you see the necessity for this kind
of thing in our society, don't you?"

"Yes," Vera answered. She looked acutely unhappy. "But I think
Elliot and I should remain uninvolved."

"It's your privilege, of course," said Dr. Laubach. "And nobody
would misunderstand your reasons for doing so. But we are merely
asking for your husband's signature on the newspaper statement to
be pub-lished the day before the hearing. It's a small matter, a *small*
matter."

"But not so small as all that," his father said.

"Just one name among many." His eyes glittered at Elliot.

"And two days before the concert! Just think! It's a real chance
to express yourself, to help us in what we're doing . . ." Hilda Usenbrugge's voice trailed off confusedly. "We must stop this young
Upp."

"Or just give him a crown and the keys to the city and let him rule us," his father said. Elliot could see a delicate flush begin to ascend his father's face. "We could just turn everything over to him now and forget our responsibilities as citizens. But I for one am not prepared to do that."

"I'm just a musician," Elliot said. "I don't even live here." Uncomfortably, he remembered Himmel. "I haven't made up my mind on this whole thing yet. I haven't been here long enough. And I can hardly do what you ask without causing personal problems I'd rather avoid."

"There are responsibilities," his father said. His mustache sprouted whitely out of his delicately reddened face: a little flag, a call to arms.

"Con-sequences," said Pierce Laubach. He wiped his hands together, making a dry scraping noise. "Every action entails its consequences. I think you might consider what we ask for a few days before giving us your answer. I will mail you a copy of our statement. In the interim, you might stroll about in Tudor Acres and gain some insight into the alternative to the position the three of us hold. That is another of Upp's little extravaganzas of taste. Vera, my dear, have your parents expressed any opinion of that assemblage of excrescences?"

"No, they have not," Vera said. Elliot held his silence.

"As a composer's wife, you must have an i-dea of taste. I advise you as well to see what our friend is capable of putting up."

"As a composer's wife, I have an idea of keeping us in groceries," Vera snapped. Elliot, taking her hand, could feel her trembling.

Dr. Laubach blinked expressionlessly as a lizard.

His father might be more refined, Elliot thought, but Herman Glauber was certainly more civilized, if civility implied a regard for another person's provinces of feeling. In his father's house, detachment had always been a Golden Mean, despite his mother's attempts to elaborate out of household ritual a kind of warmth. Elliot had never outgrown his childhood feeling that in the Denmark house he was a guest who had to ensure his tenure by politeness. At dinners all during his growing up, he was wordlessly expected to contribute one-third of the conversation: any digression into chatter about school was gently corrected. "*Not* very interesting," was his father's comment. That was in the settled days, when Chase Denmark was a vice-president of the Chambers Denmark Company, before the financial troubles he could catch, like a lake breeze against his skin, in his father's noncommittal letters, before Ronnie Upp had returned from his exile in England to purchase the factory—and before Chase Denmark had found himself out of a job at the age of fifty-one. After the great change in his life, he had studied for a realtor's examination and taken a job with a tennis friend; as far as Elliot knew, he had not sold a site in his nearly ten years with the firm. He possessed an office with an aerial view of Plechette City, he inspected properties in his English suits, he took customers to his clubs—Elliot thought that his father's advantage to the firm might lie chiefly in the accident of his knowing nearly everybody of importance in the cities on the western shore of Lake Michigan.

During his two years of teaching at Plechette City University, when he had feared his marriage might at any moment dissolve into ether, to a harsh gas, Elliot had considered that a man might go to a normal father for advice or understanding. But with Chase it was a clear impossibility; Elliot needed neither irony nor a lecture. This had been a rough passage. It had been months before Vera told him the details of her talk on the shores of the lake with Anita Kellerman. During this period, Elliot had felt himself being drawn thinner and thinner, to a thread: it would not have surprised him if he had awakened, one of those mornings from June to September, to find himself unraveled on the floor. Anita spent the summer in Sweden, after saying on the telephone, their last conversation before she left, "You know my position, Elliot. I don't make compromises, and I'm certainly not going to compromise myself. You know that I love you. I'll see you when I get back." There was a therapist in Sweden who was famous for his work with disturbed children, and Anita wanted Mark to spend the summer with him. Mark was nervous, taut as piano wire. Elliot had once watched him digging in the yard behind Anita's house, and the boy had screamed for minutes after catching sight of his face in the window. When Anita had calmed him and discovered the reason for his panic, she explained it to Elliot: "Seeing you, he didn't think it was his house anymore." A worse moment was the boy's entering his mother's bedroom and, screaming, flinging himself upon Elliot; the screams had pursued Elliot for days afterward.

During the time of greatest immediate strain, the first period of adjustment to Elliot's unfaithfulness, neither Elliot nor Vera had many excuses to take them out of the house. He was teaching only four hours a week in summer school, and she was not teaching at all. Sometimes Vera's students came to visit them at midday, and these were the only occasions when they were drawn upward out of their personal miseries into at least the show of normality. Elliot dreamed of Anita nightly during the first weeks of her absence. He felt tremendous dislocations. Groggy at three-thirty in the morning, his mind still turning slowly from an embrace, he would touch his wife and think *she's here: what luck this is* and draw Vera to him, feeling in her lighter body the lineaments of the woman he had dreamed. Such moments were very nearly their only lovemaking. In his dreams Anita was saying "You go into that room, to the blue chair, and I'll be right with you." In the mornings, Vera said, "You kept saying her name last night. You must have been dreaming about her."

"I don't remember," he said. "I might have. I can't be responsible for my dreams, can I?"

By her pouchy eyes and loose facial skin, he knew that she was sleeping little. "It all comes back on me, then. You want too much."

There was no one beyond themselves who might offer insight or comfort. Elliot's closest friend at the school was Himmel, who would have been of no help at all, himself half-infatuated with Anita Kellerman. Vera's friends, with the exception of one girl named Joanie Haupt, were all over the country, most of them back in New York, some in London, California, or Italy, and if single—like Joanie Haupt—themselves relied on Vera's capacity for sense to aid them in their love affairs; if married, they had begun their families and sent letters which were single sheets of paper folded about photographs of their babies. At his worst moments, Elliot wished that he had a confidant, even if the other person were to do nothing but listen sympathetically: at those times, he thought of what his father might have been.

After three months he knew the worst was over. Vera began to regain her lost weight, and she became more explicable, less a tense blue sky in which electricity was latent at every point. The week before Anita was to return from Sweden, Vera finally told him what the two of them had said in their talk on the lakefront.

"I was so nervous," Vera said, "that I had to put my hands in my pockets so she couldn't see them. But at the same time, I felt very purposeful. I knew what I had to tell her."

"Was she nervous?"

"I don't think she's ever nervous, do you? She was already there when I got down to the lake, and she was eating a hot dog from the little stand. She even offered to buy me one. When I said that I couldn't eat, she finished it off and wiped her fingers with the napkin, and the two of us started down the beach. We just said what we both had to say, I guess."

"What did she say?" His real question, unspoken, was *what did she say about me?*

"She said I had to share you. She wanted me to understand that she knew how I felt, but that she wasn't going to stop seeing you. She loved you, she said. She even said that she loved *me*. That almost made me sick. There was lots of stuff about what she felt like when her husband died. I could see why you would love her. She seemed so vital, and those big green eyes almost touched me, they were so intense. If I were a man, I would have fallen in love with her."

"I'm glad you had that talk," he said. "I'm even happier that you can talk about it now."

"It's not easy. But let me finish. When we had nearly got as far as the overhead bridge, after what seemed like miles of walking, I finally said that she couldn't see you anymore. Not in that way. Or I'd go crazy. I told her that I'd never leave you unless you did something absolutely brutal to me. And she agreed."

"She agreed?"

"So that part of it's over. I want you to promise. Otherwise I wouldn't be able to stand it next year. I wouldn't be able to stand you. Us."

He promised.

It was, he thought, a promise impossible to keep. But when Anita returned, he was only partially surprised to discover that she had resolved to honor her word to Vera: it was a reversal so complex that he could not see to its bottom. "I'm not even going to do the abandoned-woman stint—asking you to make a decision. Don't think this is easy for me. I've gotten awfully used to relying on you, you know." Thus they had spent the following year seeing one another only at odd times. Anita had coolly retreated, it seemed, into the life she had lived before his coming, as if she had sewn up a seam that had only shortly parted for him. But he was constantly reassured of her love for him, by her looks, gestures, and tones of voice. It was enough of what he needed—just enough. His love for her, blocked in this way from any conventional resolution, remained undiminished.

"What I envy most about your way of life, Elliot," Dr. Laubach was saying, "is your apparent ability to live wherever you choose. Your proximity to wonders that to us appear hopelessly distant. You make me feel terribly pro-vincial." His skin wrinkled about his eyes in a smile, and Elliot thought for a moment that Pierce Laubach would not forgive any man who made him feel provincial.

His mother must have sensed some of this, for she broke in saying, "But, Pierce, you've traveled so much more than any of the rest of us. Surely nobody could make you feel that way."

"These days, of course," he purred, "I am primarily an armchair traveler. I find that my insight into the places I've been has deepened immeasurably. Think of the Florentines! The Japanese! One has too much to read, I've found. But you *will* think about signing our statement, won't you, Elliot?"

Well, he thought, if it means no more than that, perhaps I will. He decided to go out the next day to walk around the unfinished Tudor Acres. The name was an unfortunate omen. Surrey by Lake Michigan. Signing the document would please his father, newly interested in such things; in any case his natural inclination might be to sign, especially since he knew the cause was almost surely lost from the beginning. The last planning-commission hearing would almost certainly result in a victory for Herman Glauber and Ronnie Upp. Signing would do no damage. But why involve himself at all? He had seen Herman and Tessa's seriousness about the Nun's Wood question: they would inevitably see his signing statement as a betrayal. Perhaps Herman could be made to see the meaninglessness of his signature. He was free to make up his mind on the question, he decided.

"You will think about it, Elliot?" repeated his father. Looking at the slim figure in his Savile Row suit, he thought: He is after all my father. And it is a small thing.

"Elliot is already thinking about it," said Dr. Laubach.

"I don't know how I could have forgotten this," Hilda Usenbrugge said in her rushing, breathless voice. "I think I'm getting too old. Age is a terrible burden. I've had it on my mind all day, Chase."

Elliot saw his father shift his attention with the slightest signs of difficulty from himself to the old lady. Nobody else, except his mother, could have noticed Chase's irritation. He twitched the flaps out of his jacket pockets—a gesture as habitual as the upward jerk to the knees of his trousers before sitting—and regarded her. Hilda Usenbrugge was not at all his father's type. "Excuse me, Hilda?"

The old woman colored. "I should think it is important, for a Denmark. And for anybody, really, who is interested in the Plechette City heritage. Why, that tower . . . I don't know why these things come all in bunches. He may have planned it. To confuse us, don't you think? The Preservation Society is so busy now with the wood, and then when I heard about it today, I thought we might need to delegate a subcommittee . . . Oh, I haven't explained it yet, have I?" Her color deepened.

"No," said his father. "What is the problem, Hilda?"

"Young Upp, of course. He's making plans to remodel the clock tower, to modernize it. He's going to tear the whole thing down and put up a new one."

"By God, we'll stop him!" said his father. Elliot for a moment saw the four older people in the room gaping at one another, their eyes wide. His mother closed her mouth.

"He can't do it," she said. "We all know that. It's a trick."

"It's blackmail," said his father. "Pure and simple."

"Or else he's perfectly serious, as he does own the building," said Pierce Laubach. "We might pause to consider that possibility."

"I don't believe that for a moment," his father said. "Hilda is right. Upp is trying to deflect us."

"We'll ignore it," his mother said.

"I think I'd better decide what to ignore," said Chase. "How did you find out about this, Hilda?"

The old woman looked increasingly cheerful. "It's terrible, isn't it? Money without conscience, money without principle. Always dangerous. One of our secretaries at the Preservation Society, Maggie Huebsch, told me about it. Her sister is a secretary at the Globe Corporation. Upp's company, the one that—"

"I know what the Globe Corporation is, dear," Chase interjected.

"Oh, of course. Excuse me. As I was saying, Maggie's sister is a secretary for one of the men there, and she told Maggie that she had seen plans for the new clock tower. And the architect's drawings, the renderings I believe they are called, of the new structure. Maggie's sister was most surprised that the new tower will not revolve. It was quite an attractive design, she thought."

And very likely it would be, Elliot thought. At least, it could with little difficulty be more attractive than the clock tower his great-granduncle Brooks had designed, that square-headed Victorian monument that turned and turned, sending out its conspicuous light. When he was a boy, people were still speaking of it as a "triumph of engineering."

"That clock is a triumph of engineering," Chase said. "Anything put in its place would be sheer modern gimcrackery next to it. I wouldn't put it past him to plan some sort of outright obscenity, like that damned imitation flame on top of the Gas building."

"It's a crime," said Margaret. Elliot thought that she was overstating out of an insufficiency of interest in the question of the tower.

He began to understand how the changes in his father must have confused her.

"Criminal," agreed Chase. "Of course, old Brooks's tower has begun to look a bit old-fashioned by now." He had recovered his habitual manner: perhaps Margaret was not at all confused. Chase gazed distantly at his son. "Elliot, you seem to bring us excitement." Then his gaze flicked to Vera. "Dear Vera, perhaps you should not discuss our conversation this evening with your father. On Christmas Day I may have the opportunity to . . . sound him out on the matter of the clock tower. We will inevitably have some private words together, if I know your father."

Vera made no reply. Elliot saw that his father thought he had made a joke, and that Vera was upset by the reference to Herman's directness. She merely nodded; and then his father looked, if only for a second, offended. It came to him that the public commission meeting would be nearly on the night of his concert. The room seemed unbearably hot.

The telephone began to ring when the guests were leaving. Helping Hilda Usenbrugge into her heavy camphor-smelling fur, Elliot heard the telephone racketing in the back hall. After a moment Robert appeared by the hall door. Elliot caught his glance and knew that the call was for him.

He rushed back into the hall as soon as Hilda Usenbrugge and Dr. Laubach had been seen into the doctor's Lincoln, and the car had backed massively down into the street and begun to inch toward Lake Point Drive. Dr. Laubach was a notoriously slow driver.

In the moment he picked up the receiver, he knew who it was. "Hello, Anita," he said.

"Elliot. Elliot, come over here. I have to see you. I called you at the Glaubers', and Herman told me that you were at your parents' house. That's not far away. Please come over as soon as you can."

"What's happened, Anita?"

"Just come."

"Should I bring Vera?"

"No. Oh, do what you want. No, don't bring her."

He hung up silently, for a second seeing her wholly.

"Vera," he said, while his parents, rubbing their arms, went into the lower living room, "that was Anita on the phone. She's upset about something, and she absolutely ordered me to drive over to her place to see her. I can't imagine what's happened, but she sounded very upset."

"Then you'd better go, hadn't you?" Vera took his arm. "I didn't mean it that way. You have to go. Should I come along?" She looked at him intently, then said, "No, I guess I shouldn't. Try to calm her down, Elliot. But please, don't be gone too long."

"I'll be back as soon as I can," he said, impatient to leave. He kissed her. "It might not take too long."

He hurriedly explained to his puzzled parents that he had to rush out to see a friend, then left the house, calling goodbye. He threw on his coat on the way to the Glaubers' car, which was parked against a snowdrift at the side of the street. After the heat of the living room, the cold night air felt fresh and alive on his face. The car jerked forward, skidded a few feet on the packed snow, then moved smoothly the few blocks up to the stop sign at Lake Point Drive.

He turned west on Windmere, then south again on Leecham. Anita's three-story frame house was the only home on the block that was undecorated with Christmas lights. Himmel's, just down the block, was outlined in red and green blinking bulbs.

Elliot stopped the car and climbed out into the white street. As he crossed to her porch and ascended, he heard from the unlighted house the swift dark downpouring of the jazz music.

chapter 5

Y ou don't look married," Anita said, "but then you never did."
Her taut Nordic face, above the strong column of her neck and the
narrow green jersey the color of her eyes, was wan, white; she looked
very tired. Anita had lost weight over the past four years. As she led
him from the hall into her living room, he saw that her body was
slighter in outline, more fashionably thin, than it had been when he
was her lover. She had cut her hair to a severe mannish bob, still
shiningly blond, which emphasized the smooth planes of her face.
The music, that constant background against which she moved, was
unchanged; it grew louder as they approached the living room, the
rapid fluent chatter of a saxophone. It was so familiar to him, this
being led into the room he knew, this counterpoint of the lyric jazz.
His chest fluttered with recognition. *My woman*. She made him a
drink, and he could see her hands shaking.

She sat facing him. She was almost colorless. For a moment that
was like a panic, a moment of utter loss, he wondered if he still
loved her, the real bodily woman who had continued living in Plechette City and had not answered his letter. Then he saw with a
shock that her face was slightly bruised beneath the cheekbone, a
faint trace of a discoloration. "What happened to your face?" he
asked.

"An accident. It's not important. Thank you for coming."

"I thought you were putting me off for good, this morning on the phone."

"I was," she said. "At least I was trying to. But I can't ever act on the basis of principle. I always end up acting on the basis of need." She smiled at him: a brief flash of her old assertiveness, her warrior's humor. "I used to say that I had gotten used to relying on you, and it seems I still do. I just wish there were a way to do away with the unfairness."

"I think *I'm* unfair to *you*," he said. "We've already worked all this out, a long time ago. My relation to you depends on our not being married." How much of this is only a role, a part I have learned to play and from which I am too lazy to escape? Perhaps my relation to Anita depends on not seeing her, he thought. But knowing the mechanism, is the emotion made invalid? He thought of how many times, in his first years in Paris, he had held her in thought, made love to her in memory. The emotion persisted, no matter how wrong its causes.

"The only time you were unfair was in that letter," she said. "It made me furious."

"Why?" He felt baffled by her again.

"It was dishonest. And I kept hearing this undertone in it that said, 'We can't ever meet, we'll never meet again, and that's why I'm whipping up all this emotion.' Well, I didn't feel that way. So I said, well, I'll be damned if I'll answer that kind of letter."

"Well, I didn't know what to say, after the main thing had been said. 'I love you and I miss you terribly.' That leaves a lot of blank page." He was deeply pleased by her response to his letter—it seemed to pin him again to a reality. "Then the more I wrote, the more hopeless the situation appeared to be. I could see you just drifting away out of my life. *That's* my unfairness. I want the old thing to keep steady between us, but I also want you to have a good stable life, to get married again, and to know that my affection is always there. At the same time, I have to say, I'd be torn apart with jealousy if you did get married again." It came out of him in a rush: he had not expected to commit himself so thoroughly. This must be the truth, he thought, it just says itself. He smiled at her. "But that would be only temporary."

"I'm never getting married again," she said. "Don't waste your time worrying about that. I feel like a nun."

This statement, superficially a relief, compounded his sense of guilt. "I see."

They sat in silence, regarding each other.

The music stopped, and Anita got up to turn the record over. An alto saxophone, disarranging "Indiana."

"Tell me what's wrong," he said.

"Mark is getting worse," she said. "He's too nervous to play with other children. He's being tutored at home now, and he has sessions with a psychiatrist—it's a kind of class—every week. I'm afraid that I may have to put him in full-time professional care."

"In a home?" Elliot was profoundly shocked, knowing Anita's devotion to her son.

"It's a possibility. Mark needs more care than I can give him. He's getting a lot of professional care now, but it doesn't seem to be enough. Emotionally, he'll always be difficult."

"Are you positive about that?"

"I don't want to be," she said. "Let's not talk about Mark."

"I want to talk about what's bothering you. If I can't help you with whatever it is, then everything that was ever between us is meaningless."

"Everything is meaningless," Anita said. "But I know what you mean. I'm grateful for it." She touched the faint bruise on her cheek.

"Herman said that you had been out to his house with Ronnie Upp."

"I've been seeing Ronnie," she said. "He's an old friend of mine. You never met him, did you?" When he shook his head, discounting an encounter with Upp when they were both children, she continued. "I'm having a party next week, on the twenty-third, and I'd like you and Vera to come. Ronnie will be here. Some other people. Nathan and Helen Himmel, if Helen can bring herself to come." She leaned her head against the back of her chair and closed her eyes. "I haven't been getting any sleep."

"Will you tell me what's wrong?"

"I don't know what's wrong," she said. "Maybe it's just middle-aged loneliness. I'm being impossible to you, dragging you over here from your parents' house. I wondered if you'd come." She opened her eyes. "Your father is being a fool about this Nun's Wood business. He and his friends are just delaying the inevitable. They can't beat Ronnie Upp. He has too much money and too much influence."

"I know," he said. "But I can see their point too. They asked me to sign a newspaper statement."

"That won't make any difference. You don't know about people like Ronnie. They do anything they want to."

Then from upstairs came a sudden series of screams—he jumped, spilling some of his drink. He heard footsteps, an automatic-sounding, thudding noise on the ceiling. Someone was running. The rapid clatter of footsteps sounded wrong, disturbing in the subdued house. Elliot felt a brief irrational moment of fear.

"Mark," Anita said. "He walks in his sleep." She stood just as the door opened and a small thin boy in pajamas windmilled into the room. His face was distorted with terror. "Out!" he shouted. "Get him out!" His body shook as he stood motionless for a second, and then he catapulted forward again and dove behind a chair. Elliot was certain the boy's unfocused eyes had not registered his presence. Anita bent over the boy and stroked him gently, quietly making his stand. She spoke to him softly. Mark's eyes blinked rapidly.

"He got downstairs before I could get to him," said another woman's voice. Elliot wheeled, still startled by the boy's high-pitched screams, and saw a woman in the doorframe. She was dressed in a shabby blue nightgown missing half the buttons. Her bare torso gleamed whitely in the interstices.

"Andy . . ." began Anita.

"That's all right," the woman said. "It doesn't matter." When she walked into the light, Elliot saw on her face a beautiful tracery of red scars. She glanced at him as she led the boy back out into the hall, her ridged face careless, free of shame.

*   *   *

After the girl left with Mark, Anita seemed to recover herself and become more the woman he had known. "Andy French was a student of Frank's," she said, "but she left school after her accident. She was in a terrible automobile crash, and she went back to live with her parents in New York for two years. I think she was very bitter then. She wouldn't have been more than twenty-one. She came back two years ago, and finished work on her master's. She's a therapist, and she plans to work with disturbed children. She's very good with Mark."

"Does she live here?" Elliot asked. He was haunted by his sight of the girl, her red-traced face and white gleaming trunk.

"I knew she didn't have any money, so I asked her to live here and help me take care of Mark. As I said, she's wonderful with him. And when I have to work late or do research at the library, she can see that nothing happens to him."

"Your Andy looked very competent."

"Oh, she's competent," Anita said. "We probably know one another too well. There was some trouble about a boy, a medical student in New York. Apparently he ran away from her after she came out of the hospital. She was uncertain about him, she says, about his reaction to her. To her scars. But it was a terrible shock when it came. It decided her to go without plastic surgery."

"Have you tried to change her mind? She looks strong enough to know her own mind, I'll admit. And . . . it seems odd, but she's still beautiful, in spite of it."

"I know," said Anita. "I know she is." There was an extra unplaceable resonance in her voice.

"I love you," he said, touching her hand. He raised his other hand to her cheek. In the same impulse, they stood. Anita's arms clasped him tightly. Her head buried against his jacket. "I love you too, Elliot. These stupid words we have to use. You're good for me." He could feel her face moving with the words. "It's late. You'd better go back to your nice wife. I won't ask you what you think of America, or how you like being home."

"Nobody's asked me that yet," he said, feeling both grateful for her words and rebuffed by them. He kissed her. A flash of the familiar playfulness in her mouth.

"I almost forgot how nice and big you are," she said. "But now it's time for you to go." She walked him to the front door.

"How long have you been here, anyway?" she asked. "Isn't it about a week?"

"This is my first full day," he said.

"Oh. Oh! I thought . . ." Her breath drifted in the dark air.

"What?"

"You're crazy, Elliot."

"Probably." This had been crazy.

Big damp drifts of snow fell onto the street. The cold air bit at his face. "Merry Christmas, Elliot Denmark," she said. "Call me tomorrow." She closed the door. He was alone on the cold porch.

Elliot walked down the porch steps to Herman's car. He looked at his watch. "My God," he whispered. When he looked back at the house, he saw, in an upper window, the white face of the girl, Andy, gazing expressionlessly down at him. Even on the street, he could hear a skirling ghost of the music.

chapter 6

In the jumbled green light of dreams, he was dreaming that he was standing on a long lawn, a summer drink in his hand. Two people were in front of him, listening to his conversation. At first the people were Herman and Tessa Glauber, but as he talked, they imperceptibly metamorphosed into Dr. Pierce Laubach and Vera. Andy French, her face unscarred, was talking to his father some yards away: he knew they were discussing him, for their faces kept swiveling toward him. His father looked amused and detached, Andy angered. Her words, imperfectly audible, came to him as "... make it stronger, stronger." Dr. Laubach was caressing Vera's hand. Faint and distorted, as if it were played across a body of water, *Harold In Italy* shattered and threatened; he had always disliked it. "Vera, why are they playing this awful stuff?" he said. Vera's mouth moved soundlessly. Feeling an irresistible urging in his bowels, Elliot felt himself toppling backward, spilling his drink. Immediately as he fell, he began giving birth to a series of puppies. They streamed out of him, smeared with his shit. Andy walked to his prostrate body and began to rub each little dog with a towel. They were small and black, with floppy ears like spaniels. "Push," she said, "push." Everybody's face was turned, greenly, whitely, toward him.

He woke with blood pouring from his nose. He put his hand

where, in the Paris bedroom, the box of tissues would be, and felt
the smooth leathery edge of a jewelry case. He fumbled, and it fell
to the floor. Elliot sat up sharply, holding his hand to his streaming
nose. Vera's bed was made. He was alone in the room. He threw
back the messed sheet—during the night he had tossed off the blan-
ket—and stood by the bed. His legs wobbled; and for a moment his
eyes swam; he thought he might faint. The box of tissues was pushed
far back against the wall on the bedside table. He wadded a handful
of limp paper to his face. The thickened blood tasted on his lips.
Elliot glanced at his watch: it was ten-forty-five. He tilted his head
and walked slowly to the bathroom, using the wad of tissues to dab
at his face.

By the time he came downstairs, showered, shaved and dressed, the
nosebleed had stopped. Vera and Tessa were talking quietly in the
kitchen. When he opened the door from the dining room, the women
turned, smiling, to him. Vera's eyes were underlined with gray. They
had suffered a short conversation about Anita Kellerman when Elliot
had returned to his parents' house.

"We've just been looking at the tracks on the lawn," said Tessa.
"What kind of animal do you think made them?" She poured coffee
into his upheld cup.

He looked out the back windows of the kitchen. On the thick
flawless carpet of snow, a trail of indistinct tracks dotted a thin line
to the back of the garden. He stood up and looked closer. He carried
his cup to the window. "A dog?"

"It may be a dog. But it looks like a fox's tracks to me. Everybody
says there is a family of foxes in Nun's Wood. One of the neighbors
saw one last week, running across his back garden."

"I thought all the foxes had left this part of the state years ago."

"You'd be surprised," she said. "Of course, they'd be better off leaving. Apart from the fields, Nun's Wood is the only really safe place for
them down here, and that won't last long, as we know. A deer was
killed on the I-94 to Chicago last winter. When I was a little girl we
lived on a farm and I could hear the wolves howling up on the ridges,
and that was only a day's drive away from Plechette City. The deer

used to come down to browse in the fields, and I guess the wolves followed them. Sometimes winter drives them south. Once I saw a wolf from our kitchen window. He came stalking out of the edge of the woods into our land, and he gave me a real thrill of terror. He was such a shock! I can't tell you. It was like seeing a red Indian with a tomahawk. He was a big gray gloomy creature, skinny, and he just trotted along the edge of the fields. I never told my father, because I was afraid he'd shoot him. And do you know what? Someone claimed they saw a wolf in Meadow Heights last week, not five miles from here. There was a picture of it in the paper—the woman's husband took it. You could only see this big foggy blur."

Elliot turned back to look at the tracks. They led to the stone cherub, now more thickly dusted with snow. He seemed to be wearing a conical white hat; beneath the knees, his legs vanished into the powder. The expression on the plump knowing face was still of expectancy, promise. But there was a difference in it. The little smile seemed faintly sinister, as if the cherub were plotting some anomalous wickedness. The tracks led twice around the babylike figure and then went into an obscure place beneath some boughs.

"I'll go out and take a look," Elliot said. "Maybe I'll be able to see him."

"Oh, he'll be long gone," Tessa said. "You'll catch your death, Elliot dear." Prompted by an irrational, wheedling logic, she added, "And both of you look so tired and worn out today, from staying up so late last night."

"If you want a real worry, there's always my concert."

"It's your health I'm worried about, not your concert," she said, but he was already putting on his topcoat and going out the back door. He closed it gently.

In front of him to the left, the garage door gaped open, revealing Herman's Pontiac parked at an angle within. Lawn mowers and rakes hung from hooks behind it. Vera must have driven her father into town and returned with the car. He remembered that they were to see Uncle Kai that afternoon; presumably Vera wished to do some Christmas shopping that morning. To his right the snow-filled back garden bulked whitely in his vision. The air was surprisingly warm, compared to last night's bitterness; it was a clean abrupt chilliness which he immediately heard as a sound, a pure piercing held note on a French horn. He had forgotten about such days, and the sense of animal good health with which they filled him. He inhaled deeply.

Elliot walked across the asphalt turnaround, plowed that morning while he was still asleep, and plunged into the garden. His shoes sank to their tops in the snow. Tessa, visible in the back window, was mouthing the word "Boots." He waved, signaling that there was no need to worry, and pushed through the snow to the tracks. Lobed, fingered, with tiny claw marks. He walked beside them all the way to the statue. The brisk unsentimental air felt to him like his natural element, a blessing. The tracks reeled about the statue and then seemed to drift in series, as though the animal had many times trotted back and forth.

As he bent down to look more closely, he found himself only inches from the stone face of the cherub. The blank wide face, the half-smile, seemed devoid of any meaning at all, stupid with happiness. He brushed the snow cap from the cherub's head. There was a quick rustling noise from beneath the snowy hedge. Elliot propped himself on one hand and bent lower. Still he could only see the flurried tracks disappearing.

Tessa will have a fit, he thought, and lay down flat in the snow. He had forgotten to button the topcoat, and he felt the white powder fasten coldly to his neck. His hands and ears were tingling with their exposure to the chill air. Then he saw the fox, first as an undefined brownish-reddish mass in a little hollow beneath the hedge, and then, as his eyes adjusted, clearly. It was lying down, its legs out to the side, regarding him intently. Elliot seemed to see each hair of its hide, each quill-like, puffed hair of its thick tail. Its eyes were focused on his face, and the fox breathed in short, quick pants, the long mouth open and seeming to smile. It was a perfect, quick, alien little creature. "Hello, fox," Elliot whispered. The fox leapt to its feet and darted beneath the hedge before he had finished speaking. On the light covering of snow where it had lain was a pattern of glistening drops. It was a moment before he recognized that they were blood.

*   *   *

"Blood?" Tessa said. "Was it injured?"

"I couldn't really tell. The fox didn't look injured, and I was just about four feet away from it. It stared at me for a second and I stared back, and then it bolted away. I've never been that close to a fox before." He still felt his elation, liquid held within him as in a spoon, and he feared to lose it. "I can't really explain why it should be, but the sight of it affected me very deeply. It looked so bright and alive. In another second I would have tried to pet it."

"Oh *no*," Tessa gasped. "You might be dead of rabies right this minute."

"But it didn't look sick. That's why the blood was such a surprise to me."

"It must have been hurt," said Vera.

Tessa required a second of thought to take this in, and then her response was final. "I don't think we need discuss it anymore," she said. "It was just a poor beast. Vera dear, weren't you going to the shopping center this morning? I think I'd better start the laundry. What are your plans, Elliot?"

His elation was wholly gone—trying to talk about it had been a mistake—and Tessa's attempt to neatly package him into an approved plan for the morning depressed his mood even further. She often made him feel rebellious: he had forgotten this. "I was thinking of taking a look at Tudor Acres," he said. "I'm curious to see what it looks like."

"Please, Elliot," Vera began, but seeing her mother's sudden attentiveness, she hesitated. "Don't forget about our appointment with Uncle Kai this afternoon. Try not to get lost."

"Why, that's absurd," Tessa said. "Elliot can't possibly get lost. It's right in back of the house!"

"Yes, of course," said Vera. She gave him a direct, warning look. "Elliot's a darling, but he really does have no sense of direction. He can get lost walking to the corner."

Tessa set down her coffee cup with a smile, clearly not believing Vera's comments, though they were not untruthful, and said, "I'm sure you'll like Tudor Acres. We hated to see Fleischer's old field go, but I do think the houses Ronnie is putting up there are fine.

Oh! I made a joke! Well, you'll see what I mean. They're going to be lovely old-fashioned houses. They will attract the right sort of people. I did love the old field, but . . . things go, I guess." She looked brightly at the two of them. "I'd better start the laundry if I expect to get to the auction in time."

She went upstairs to inspect the beds, then after a moment they heard her coming back down the stairs, crossing the hall, and continuing to the basement. The washing machine began to chug beneath them.

"Elliot," Vera said, "you aren't going to sign that ridiculous statement, are you?"

"I haven't decided yet. And we don't know it's ridiculous, since neither of us has seen it."

"Don't you think it would be better for us to stay out of it altogether?"

"Maybe," he said. "But it really does seem like a small matter to me. In six months, Upp will be bulldozing the woods, your father will have won, and nobody will remember whether I signed the silly thing or not."

She was right. But they both knew that he wanted to sign the statement.

Elliot called good-bye to Tessa down the basement stairs and went out the front door of the big frame house and along the walk to Willow Road. He had dressed himself warmly for the walk, pulling on a turtleneck sweater after he had come in from the outside that morning. He had also changed his damp shoes for Wellingtons, and in place of his topcoat had taken one of Herman's stouter many-pocketed khaki jackets, lined with fur, which was inches too short in the sleeves and bound him tightly across the shoulders while flopping and sagging in the front like an upright sleeping bag.

When Elliot had nearly reached the side street leading into the Tudor Acres lots, a blue Falcon passed him and turned into the Glaubers' driveway. It was the car of a Richmond Corners friend of Tessa's, with whom she was going that afternoon to an auction. This was at an old farmhouse that had belonged to a man named Romer who had died

intestate and heirless the previous month. Herman had mentioned to
Elliot that the city would put in a bid for the land. Tessa had invited
them along to the auction, and she had seemed slightly hurt by their
evident unwillingness to go; Elliot felt that only Vera's mentioning the
afternoon visit to Kai had assuaged her feelings. Elliot had never understood Tessa's attitude toward her husband's brother. It mixed a
protective, maternal solicitude and a kind of impatience. It was Tessa
who talked most of getting Kai out of his apartment and prodding
him into finally finishing his book on Goethe. She had told Elliot and
Vera that he could easily get a university position again, if the book
were published, and she seemed to feel that Kai needed this reenga-
gement with the outer world. This vision seemed to overlook most of
the salient points about Kai, his bitterness, his solitariness and fragility.
Kai had retreated into his dark flat, into his mind, and, one supposed,
into his memories; the attempt to bring him out seemed to Elliot a vi-
olation. The book would presumably be finished soon, and then, according to what Herman had said, Kai wished only to die. He lived
beyond ambition and sex and the possibility of comfort; he was abrupt
with his brother and Tessa—Kai had refused, in words of one syllable,
to come to dinner at the Glaubers' "for a meal with the children"—
and so was perhaps beyond even love. This reduction of customary human ends and solaces chilled Elliot. He thought he could see why the
old man had so long delayed the completion of his book. And yet even
that, over the past four years, had taken on an unreality. Elliot had
heard brief allusions of Kai's work ever since he had met Vera, and he
now recognized, walking in the brisk light December day, that he had
gradually ceased to believe in it. He wanted more than ever to see Kai.

Elliot passed the giant TUDOR ACRES sign and found himself at
an intersection of three raw, planed-out roadbeds. Unfilled ditches
for sewer pipes lay on either side of the new roads, and the stiff
heaps of dirt beyond the ditches were heightened by their covering
of snow. Tudor Acres was circumscribed by the two outer roads,
Laura Drive and Annabel Drive, which formed a dual crescent about
the four acres of the property. The middle road, Carriage Avenue,
led into a crossed network of similar raw streets in smaller crescents.
On all of these were visible the gaunt frameworks of half-constructed

houses. Elliot turned up Laura Drive. He could see the raised area
of the prospective green, now only a jumbled mound of dirt and
concrete blocks under snow, through the timbers of the houses.

He was moving toward the only fully constructed house in the
subdivision, the model home behind the Glauber house. A long barn-
like roof of some imitation "English" tile, half-timbering on the
white stucco, wooden ornamentation on the windows, and a carriage
lamp on a black iron stand at the end of the driveway.

His own country gave him culture shock.

He walked up the flagstones to the front door of the model home.
Experimentally, he tried the doorknob and heard a *click* as the heavy
door swung in. He was standing at the entrance to a hallway. A mel-
low red light suffused the interior, and it was a moment before he saw
that it entered the hall from the room to the left, where he had noticed
stained glass inserted at the top of the picture window. He stepped
quietly onto the carpet. The house was entirely mute. Elliot softly
closed the door and moved down the hall in the mild red light to the
front room to his right. He saw with a shock that the house was fully
furnished. Of course: he should have expected that. In the living room
were a spiky black chair, three other chairs, these padded, about a
small white table, a bowl of freesias, a sofa with a nubbly tweed covering, Utrillo prints on the wall. On a low stand near the entrance lay
a *New Yorker* with a Eustace Tilly cover. Broken patterns of light, cast
by the sun on the leaded windows, swam on the far wall above the fireplace. The room was like a suite in a pretentious freeway motel, and it
made him appreciate Tessa's idiosyncratic furnishings. He prowled
the room until the strangeness dissipated.

But when Elliot walked out again to the hall and glanced into the
kitchen and dining room, the dreamlike feeling he'd had on entering
the house returned. In these rooms the light could be seen to be not
merely red, but laid with green and blue and yellow, in spangles and
splashes against the wall and floor. It was impossible to see anything
out of the tiny leaded panes, except for swarmy blotches of mass and
color. Elliot felt as though he were transported to another dimension,
suddenly made very small, as though he were drifting about in a
dollhouse. He began to perspire inside Herman's coat.

On the carpeted stairs his feet made no noise. The stairs went up into a kind of tube, the narrow brown walls seeming to shrink together ahead of him. At the top was another door, past it a corridor stuccoed like the outside and flecked with paint in a manner that Tessa described as "taffeta." The plaster was drawn up into little points like whipped egg whites. Brown doors with odd gold doorknobs. He opened one of the doors at random. Except for a chair and bed set near the open window, the room was bare and very cold. A breeze from the window stirred up some feathers.

In the instant that he closed the door, Elliot heard a savage beating of wings—a big dark shape took off from the head of the bed. Elliot's heart stopped. His death seemed to be flying toward him, a hawk or owl, coming too quickly to be seen. When Elliot backed against the door, too frightened to think of turning his back to open it, the bird flew past his head, missing him by what seemed to be only inches. The bird seemed to blaze in the dim cold room. It made an appalling unearthly racket. Elliot felt paralyzed by Herman's binding, sagging coat. Then he saw that, grasped by the heavy claws, a rat hung limply down. Carrying its food, the bird beat once more about the walls of the room, and then suddenly dipped and escaped through the window. Elliot ran across to slam it shut, and for a moment he saw the heavy brown bird mounting over the rooftops of Richmond Corners, making for Nun's Wood. When he turned back to the room, he saw that the floor was littered with bird and animal droppings, to some of which were gummed thick coarse feathers. His entire body seemed to be trembling.

"One lives or one doesn't," Kai was saying, "one works or one does not. What happens to the individual is an irrelevance. I am satisfied with my life, and I resist anybody's attempt to alter it. Another man would be shamed by the necessity of living on his brother's charity. I am not. I like to think that it gives us both pleasure."

The white-haired old man looked more feline than ever, his face almost transparently white, his shoulders and arms under the red wool shirt thinner than Elliot remembered them. The whole effect of the man was of neatness and quickness, of mentality. It was as though he had been born at the age of seventy, enjoying the spectacle of all those other people who had entered life with passions and illusions.

Passions: Elliot had once asked Herman if his brother had ever had a mistress or girlfriend. "I never saw one," Herman told him, "but he was a good deal older than me. Kai was always a loner, though. Why don't you ask him?" But the tiny apartment, the drapes closed against the sunlight, could never have admitted a woman. It was spotless, as orderly as a ship's cabin. Even the desk where Kai was sitting was un-cluttered. Kai's dictionaries, his editions of Goethe, Heine, Kafka, Paul Celan and Theodore Storm, were lined on two shelves above the desk. Beside the old blocky typewriter was a square pile of yellow pa-per. A squat gray filing cabinet stood beside the desk, its drawers marked MSS and CORRESPONDENCE—GOETHE. On the bottom drawer the label read PERSONAL. Kai's little box of a record player was stowed in a corner, his records stacked beside it.

"That's not true," Vera said. "And I know that you're trying to change the subject. I really think you should get out more. Daddy said you never even come over to their house."

"If I tried to change the subject, Vera, it may have been because the topic of my welfare had gone as far as it could." He smiled at her. "Yet I am grateful for your interest."

"You always make me feel like a child," she said. "I'll stop. I was only concerned about your happiness. I don't know how you could be satisfied with staying indoors all the time."

"I can assure you that I am happier in my room than I would be in this terrible weather." He patted her hand. "Do you want some tea? I think it must be ready by now." Kai stood up and went across the room to the kitchen, a stove and refrigerator concealed behind a curtain. "Sugar? Do you take something in your tea?"

"Milk and sugar."

"Elliot?"

"Nothing."

"I apologize for having no coffee. I have few guests." He reap-peared with a tray in his hands.

"I hope you will come for Christmas at my parents'," Elliot said.

"I have not gotten so misanthropic that I enjoy spending Christmas by myself. I would like to come, yes."

"Thank goodness. I hate to think of you just sitting in here."

"Then do not think about it, Vera. Most of my sitting is done at my desk. Now that I am reaching the end, it takes up more time than ever before."

"It," of course, was the book on Goethe. "Are you really almost finished?" Elliot looked again at the neat desk. There was no sign of a manuscript.

"Very nearly. Have you read much Goethe?"

"Not much," Elliot confessed. "For a German course, I read *Faust* in college."

"At least you read it in German. Goethe was a genius at manipulating his own language. He was certainly the greatest genius of his century, and his century had a disproportionate number of them. The range of his interests! He became increasingly involved, as you probably know, in scientific problems as he grew older. Mineralogy, botany, zoology. Always the exact, and the love of the work. He was interested in light, and worked with prisms, trying to disprove Newton's optics. Do you see what excites me in this? He outgrew poetry even as he became a greater and greater poet, and turned himself to the world. All of this side of Goethe's life moves me. Yet I know much of his poetry by heart.

Durch allen Schall und Klang
Der Transoxanen
Erkühnt sich unser Sang
Auf deine Bahnen!
Uns ist für gar nichts bang,
In dir lebendig;
Dein Leben daure lang,
Dein Reich beständig!

If you were going to set poetry to music, Elliot, you could have chosen better than Roethke."

He ran his thin hands over his face, rubbing the tall white forehead where the vein curled into his hairline. "But I'm talking too much. And this interest of mine, this hobby—because it could never be more than that—is something I've lived with so long that it seems like another person, something entirely outside me."

"Shouldn't it be just the other way around?"

Elliot still heard Kai's harsh voice reciting the lyric. He had understood very little of the German, but the voice, chanting the poem, had nearly brought him to tears. He realized that Kai had not answered Vera's question. "That's what I would have thought too," he said.

"I can't believe that," Kai said. "Does a pianist become the music? And after reading these books for half my life, I've become almost bored with them. I'm certainly bored with my own work on Goethe. Poetry is for young men. Nobody reads Goethe now, but for a few scholars. Perhaps it is different in Germany. If I could afford the fare, I'd go to Germany to die."

Where he very nearly did die, Elliot thought. Even Tessa had never been able to learn from Kai what had happened to him in the camp.

"Germany is a sentimental country," Kai said. "But perhaps not more sentimental than America. Here the disease takes a different form. Elliot's father is sentimental about his family, Tessa is sentimental about wordless artifacts from the past, the young are sentimental about themselves. Huxley would be a sage if he were alive now, he'd have a television program."

They finished the strong sweet tea.

"Now I am tired, and you must go. I see so few people that talking tires me. And I have been egotistical, talking about my work, that fool's invention. Thank you for coming, my dear ones. Elliot, someday when you are not busy being written up in the newspapers you must return so that we can discuss music." He stood. "Before I saw that piece in the *Herald* I had no idea you were such a difficult composer."

"I know you didn't!" cried Elliot.

chapter 7

"A nita was going out for the day," Andy said, "and that's all I
know. She doesn't tell me everything she does. In fact, I sometimes
think she hides things from me, conceals things. It's not easy for two
women to live together. It would be impossible if we were living in
one another's pocket. So I just don't know where she is."

"But she told me to call her the other day. I had the feeling that
something was wrong that she couldn't tell me about after I got
there the night before last. The note she wrote me, her urgency on
the phone, those things for me add up to some pressure she's under.
I was just hoping that you could tell me about what is happening in
her life, what she's been doing these past four years."

"And I just explained why I couldn't. If you need a reason."

Elliot was driving aimlessly west on Jackson Drive with Andy
French; it was, from the first, an awkward meeting. When he had
telephoned that morning Andy had said that Anita was out, presumably for the day. When he had pressed her, she had invited him over
to the Kellerman house, saying, "Well, if you really want to talk, I
suppose you can come over. Mark is at his weekly appointment this
afternoon, and I'm all alone with nothing to do." He had been hoping that Andy could help him to understand Anita's contradictory
behavior. Vera had gone out for lunch with her high school friend

Joanie Haupt, so he was free to use the Glaubers' car. He'd had no clear idea of what he wanted to talk about with Andy French: the notion that he wanted to pump her for information about her friend and employer was repugnant; yet he admitted to himself that he was uneasy about Anita's situation. He was driven to know the truth about her.

Elliot knew that he was succumbing once again to Anita's complex appeal for him, that he was again being drawn into her masque. But perhaps his strongest reason for accepting Andy's grudging invitation was his curiosity about the girl herself, apart from her relationship with Anita and whatever she might know about Ronnie Upp.

"I'm a little jealous of your relationship with Anita," he said. "I'm puzzled by her, and when we lived here—well, I was puzzled by her then, too. She's the kind of woman . . ." That was an Anita Kellerman way of beginning a sentence. "She's very strong. When I knew her before, before we left for Paris, she seemed to be able to ride out any difficulty she had. And I think I was closer to her than anyone else was. I don't know what she told you about our relationship."

Andy was smiling to herself, looking straight ahead out of the windshield. Why do girls wear those big sunglasses on overcast days? he thought, and then said to himself: she wants to hide her face. "Very little. But I've seen enough to think that you're being a fool about her—I think you are the kind of man who, without intending to, disrupts things. You have a wife, don't you? I think you are acting in a foolish way."

"I haven't acted at all," he said.

"You came over to our house in the middle of the night, didn't you?"

He turned again to look at her. The girl seemed very distant, despite her frankness; the pattern of red scars was almost a veil.

"Well, I *am* fond of her, and I think you are too. We both want the best for her. I don't feel as though I have any hold on Anita at all. All I'm interested in doing is helping her in whatever difficulties she's having. And to do that, I need your help."

"Well, I've been trying to give you my help."

"Will you just answer some questions I have?"

She nodded. "Any reasonable questions."

"I suppose the first thing is, what is going to happen with Mark? Will he have to be institutionalized?"

She answered him squarely, without hesitation. "There's at least some doubt about it. I've been seeing Mark daily for two years and working with him, but his condition has deteriorated so much recently that he simply cannot play with other children. It's pathetic and terrifying, and it is a strain for Anita, not to mention what it does to the other children. Mark attacked little Saul Himmel last year—he went for him with a hammer. One way to deal with it would be to put him into full-time professional care. Anita is just delaying her decision until I go, I think. Whenever that will be, in a year or two."

"Will he ever be normal?"

"He will need a controlled environment for several years. Anita knows this by now."

"By God."

"But that doesn't mean that he can't be happy. 'Normal' is not a very helpful concept. Mark will be able to have a satisfying life as long as he can live in such way that ordinary pressures and threats are reduced. Living in an ordinary home might be of enormous help. He's an intelligent boy, you know. He won't need professional care forever. I'm sure that he will be able to go it alone in a number of years, if the care is thorough enough. Does that answer your question about Mark? After two years, I'm involved with the boy too, you know."

"What about Ronnie Upp? What is his role in Anita's life?"

She gazed out of the window for a long moment before replying. "It's nothing for you to worry about," she said. "He is a very old, very good friend of Anita's. They help one another in many ways. I think he dotes on her. She talks to him about his problems." She ran her hand along the padded edge of the dashboard. Elliot saw the fineness of her hand, her slim beauty. He turned to see her face again. "I guess she helps him. I guess he wants help. Ronnie is not the kind of man who ordinarily has much use for women."

He felt an enormous rush of gratitude. Andy seemed to be holding something back, some deeper resentment than she showed him, but his relief momentarily overrode his desire to go deeper.

"You've heard about the Nun's Wood business?"

"Ronnie's been talking about it for months."

"What's going to happen? Do you know?"

"He'll get his way. I don't think that Ronnie can be defeated very easily, once he has decided he wants something. He has too much money and influence, and he's too devious. At least in principle, I'm for the people who want to save the park. Ronnie is getting the land cheap, and he's going to charge an enormous rent for the buildings. If he bought it at the agreed price, he could save a fortune in taxes by leaving it untouched. At least, that's what I've been hearing. It's been quite an issue here, you know."

"I guess we are on the same side," he said. "My father and some of his friends want me to sign a newspaper statement about Nun's Wood."

"Is Chase Denmark your father?" She gave him a quick scrutinizing look through the enormous sunglasses. "I wouldn't have guessed it. He's been on the news programs now and then, along with that incredible old woman with the funny name. Hilda something."

"Hilda Usenbrugge. And yes, Chase Denmark is my father. I never expected him to turn out to be such a concerned citizen."

"He doesn't look like the placard-and-leaflet type, does he?" They smiled at one another. The self-conscious figure of Chase Denmark helped to remove the awkwardness and tension Elliot had felt during the long drive. Only now, in fact, did he realize how long the drive had been, taking them almost to the Meadowbrook turnoff on Jackson Drive, past the white unbroken fields on either side.

"We can be friends, can't we?" he asked.

"If you want. Being friendly is no strain. I *would* like to go to your concert. I heard the piece you wrote for that Boulez record, and I thought it was lovely—I still think it's lovely. Anita bought the record the day it came out. Were you upset by the piece in the *Herald*? Anita was furious when she read it."

He was touched by this, her unspoken and unadmitted connection to him during the years when she did not write, and touched also by Andy's kindness in telling him. "No, I wasn't particularly," he said. "I'd be much more upset if you didn't come to the concert. I'll send you tickets."

"I'd come anyhow. I really am interested in it. I don't know much about music, except that I like what everybody else likes. Stravinsky, Beethoven—you know. Living with Anita, I've learned to like jazz. I took some music courses at Hunter, but I'm utterly ignorant about theory or anything like that. Even about modern composers."

"Thank God," he said. "Otherwise we might have to talk about it." He passed the Meadowbrook turnoff. "I seem to be abducting you. It wasn't my plan to get this far out of the city. Should I turn around?"

"No, go on a couple of miles further. Since we're out here, there's something I want to show you."

The only car on the road, they continued down the straight length of road. A mile to the right, a huddle of houses he recognized as Richmond Corners appeared, then winked past them.

Andy rapped on the windshield. "There is a little drive just ahead, into this field. Turn in there and park."

The field was fenced by white rails, and looking ahead, Elliot saw the gap in the fence where the drive must be. The gate, when they approached it, had been left open, and Elliot turned off the main road onto the field. For about ten yards, the little drive was paved with stones, but it then degenerated into two rutted tracks—in summer there would be a grassy mound between them—that trailed off into the middle of the field, toward a line of trees at the far end. These were firs, and stood out a dark mossy green across the field of snow. Between the end of the drive and the trees were innumerable ridges and dells, lightly covered with the snow, cropping out at intervals into rises matted with last year's long grass, brown and hummocky. The white fence bordered three sides, and went into the firs at the opposite end. Looking at the hilly expanse of land, Elliot thought it must be at least twenty acres. He got out of the car. Andy, on her side, did the same. They looked at one another across the top of the Pontiac. The girl's beautiful scarred foxy face, between the upturned collars of her coat, was radiant with good humor—where did that come from? he wondered.

"It's warmer than I thought it would be," she said. "And the snow is sparse out here. Would you mind taking a walk up the path? I want you to see the whole thing. Come on, city slicker," she said. "You won't get your feet wet."

They set off together, walking in one of the narrow tracks, she a few feet ahead of him. The path went up a small rise, then down into a bowl and back up again. "All this land," she said, "belonged to a farmer who used it to graze his cattle. It takes in the trees at the back, too, and they run for at least four or five acres more. The new owner has not touched it, because he says he wants to keep it just the way it is, to preserve it. As you can see, it's practically useless for farming anyhow. But in the summer, it is beautiful out here. All the little rises are covered with Queen Anne's lace and wild daisies. We've been out here for picnics lots of times."

"So the owner . . ." he began. It was inevitable.

"Is Ronnie Upp. He bought it just a year after he came back from England. I wasn't here then, but Anita told me that he drove out here three or four times a week, just to get away from the city and enjoy the feeling of having preserved some thing from the developers. Having done *that*, he felt he was free to join them, I guess. Free to make another fortune by doing the very thing he objected to in the other developers."

Elliot wandered up the path, thinking. "It doesn't make sense. You are saying that if he could do this kind of thing once, there is no reason why he could not do it twice. I don't think that is being quite fair to Upp." He looked back at her, a slim brown-haired girl in a long carcoat. The beautiful violent face was looking at him intently.

"He didn't buy this as an entirely philanthropic gesture," she said.

"And I'm also thinking that you don't like him very much."

"I don't like him at all," she said. "I hope you are going to sign that statement for the papers. He once struck Anita in the face, and gave her a bruise she's still got. I think he's trying to get her to fire me—he thinks I'm too pessimistic about Mark, but the real reason is probably that I saw him slap her. He can be so charming, as you will probably see at Anita's party, but . . ."

"Well, for his own good then," Elliot said, smiling. The news about Upp striking Anita had gone through him with surprising ease: as if he had known it from the first. "My wife's family will probably never forgive me."

"Don't they forgive your missteps rather easily?" She glanced up at him. "Excuse me. I'm being bitchy, and I don't really feel that way at all. Maybe I'm jealous of the way you feel about Anita. I've only had one serious relationship with a man, and that ended with this." She lightly touched her face.

It moved him so much, this gesture of her fine hand to the beautiful marked face, that he blurted, "Don't worry about that, ever. You're lovely. In fact I think you are beautiful. I thought so the first time I saw you." Looking down at her, remembering, he said, "Listen. You weren't embarrassed then, so please don't be now."

"Oh, I know. I'm not embarrassed. Though I usually don't walk about practically half nude in front of strange men. I guess one of us had to mention it. Like my face. You have to talk about it once, and then it is out in the clear, and you can forget about it."

"Then talk about it." He brushed the snow off a flat slablike boulder, wide enough for the two of them, and sat. She really is just a girl, he was thinking. Andy sat beside him. Before them, the bowl leveled off in a long bumped whitish line to the trees.

"You can't think I'm angling for your pity, or that I want it at all. I detest pity."

"I'd never waste my pity on you."

"I've never liked weakness of any kind." She took the sunglasses from her face and put them in one of her coat pockets. "That's one reason Anita and I get on. We learn how to be tough from one another. We both like things to be clear." She darted a quick stabbing look into his eyes. "I was in an auto accident, of course, and I suppose I'm lucky to be alive. I'm sure I am lucky to be alive. I'll skip the details. But when I came to after the operation, I knew what had happened—my face felt as though it were on fire and I thought I must have been burned—and I would have been happier right then if I *had* died. I felt the same way when I first looked into a mirror. The horrid thing was that I knew my whole life had changed, and I couldn't know in what way. For at least a week, I was sure I was going to spend the rest of my life in a room. I can remember thinking: I'll never be vain again. When my lover defected I really hit bottom. He was so horribly polite, and I could tell that he was revolted and shocked by my face. He had a point, it was much worse then. He was a coldblooded doctor type, Mike Zeigler by name, and his reaction shattered me. But I didn't have a breakdown. My mother thought I was going to, and I think she was a little bit put out that she wouldn't have all those delicious months of taking care of me and talking about me with her friends. When I saw what sort of future I was likely to get, I determined to take my new face out into the world and let what would happen, happen. And I'll be damned if I'll have plastic surgery. This face has cleaned up my life unbelievably, and I'm not going to pretty it up."

"I don't think you should," Elliot said. "You're marvelous. In Africa you'd be a queen. Why don't you let me take you back to the city and buy you a cup of coffee?"

As they walked back to the car, Elliot glanced over his shoulder and saw a man come out of the firs and stand, a slight lean figure in a brown jacket, his arms akimbo. The figure was perhaps two hundred yards away and dwarfed by the distance. He carried a shotgun under his arm. The man seemed to be looking at them. He said nothing, but remained stock-still before the line of trees, watching. It must have been Upp. Tiny, so far away, the figure yet expressed amusement—it was in the body's carriage, the set of the small head, the loose handling of the shotgun.

In the car Elliot paused a second before backing out onto the highway, and bent forward, looking for the slight figure in the brown jacket, but it had disappeared, probably gone below one of the ridges between the gate and the line of trees. In the distance, he could hear a dog barking. Then he heard the faroff blast of a shotgun.

Andy slipped her hand into his.

TWO

Venus and Mars

chapter 8

DECLARE YOURSELF: SAVE NUN'S WOOD
Plechette City has a proud heritage of parks and green areas:
it has long been a city which values natural beauty and tran-
quillity, given to us on trust from the past, and which has
sought to achieve a balance between conservation and industry.
Our lovely parklands and woods are one of our most distinctive
and unique features as a city. We are aware of the rape of
woodlands and wildlife by careless development in other areas
of the country. Other cities have been heartlessly damaged by
industrial blight due to lack of planning and the indifference
of their citizens. We believe that the people of Plechette City
will not countenance this tragedy at home—we believe that
Plechette City must and shall fight the erosion of its heritage.
THE DECISIVE COMMISSION MEETING ON THE NUN'S WOOD
ISSUE IS AT CITY HALL AT 8: P.M., JANUARY SECOND. Attend
this meeting if you have an interest in the future of your city—
and DECLARE YOURSELF.

It was an uneasy statement, Elliot thought, written by committee.
"Rape" and "heartlessly damaged" must have been contributed by
his father, the acolyte to activism; "countenance" was pure Pierce

Laubach: Elliot could hear the old man ticking off the syllables in his precise, affected voice. His ear, too, told him that "proud heritage" and "erosion of its history" came from Hilda Usenbrugge—they were quavery, old woman's phrases. He was sure that Hilda had written the final version of the statement from drafts and suggestions submitted by the two men. Elliot wished, for a gleeful wicked moment, that he could see the statement his father had submitted to Hilda.

The note accompanying the statement read:

Dear Elliot:

The enclosed, as promised, is our poor effort to awaken our fellows. Doubtless we are unlikely Paul Reveres, but the statement is at least a clear espousal of our cause. If you should decide to sign it, mail it either to me or to your father. The other names, besides your own, will be those of doctors, lawyers, university people, prominent men in the city who support our position. Many thanks for your thought on this issue. I am certain you will do the right thing.

Yours,

Dr. Pierce Laubach

Dr. Laubach's letter had come that morning, and after reading it, he had folded it into his pocket, promising himself that he would later show Vera the statement. He had by now decided to put his signature to the paper: Elliot had felt Upp's presence on the snowy field as a blast of freezing Olympian air. He could not help thinking that the man had intended to frighten him, to warn him off, mockingly. And Andy's opinion of Upp was a further incentive. The girl interested him greatly: she burned with a fine clear fire of intelligence. They had gone for coffee at Longman's Hotel on Grand Avenue, where he and Vera had often gone during their two years in Plechette City, and coffee had lengthened out into lunch. He had been unsure of himself, taking her there; unsure for her sake, not knowing how Andy would take being subjected to stares in the self-conscious atmosphere of the Edwardian Room. It was on the top floor of Longman's Hotel, a dark circular chamber lined with windows where patrons could look out over all of Plechette City, the dim blue length of lake spreading out past the Art Center to the east. The men who regularly used the Edwardian Room were not his sort, nor, he was sure, Andy's. They were businessmen from midtown, lawyers, secretaries: beginning at five, the round oaken bar in the middle of the room filled up, with men in blazers and double-breasted suits, neat short haircuts and bright neckties. But at two o'clock, there was only a scattering of these, dining at tables littered, in these precomputer days, with graphs and lists of cost analyses. Andy had walked through their glances, a queen in her brown car-coat and loose brown hair, as if she did not notice. Across the room through the south windows, Elliot could see the four revolving, perhaps doomed faces of the Chambers Denmark clock. Their conversation, spun out over the coffee and then lunch, had been primarily about her. She was working in the charged, emotional territory between brain damage and child psychology, territory disputed by generations of therapists, and was planning to get a job in a clinic in a year or two.

What was Frank Kellerman like?

Like? A rabbit. A very dear, very intelligent rabbit. He was a weak, charming sort of man, and he was a surprisingly good scientist. He would have been much happier as a zoologist than a psychologist. Frank loved the lab. Also, I should add, he was a good teacher.

Is Anita?

In a brutal way. She hates it, you know. But she works very hard and she's quite clever, so it doesn't show up too glaringly. Ronnie is good for her because he takes her out of academe now and then.

Tell me more about yourself.

What's to tell? I was born in Queens. I guess I had a sheltered life, unlike what you hear about New York kids. I never fell in love until Zeigler, and you know what happened to that. Oh, gloom and doom, get me on another topic. That's your clock over there, isn't it?

Ronnie Upp's clock. Tell me—do you mind my asking about this?— What happened the time he hit Anita?

I thought we were going to talk about something cheery. No, I don't mind—but I don't really know what happened. I was out that day, and came in at the end of it. Ronnie was in a rage over something, I don't know what. She said something that made him furious, and just when I walked in, he slapped her. I could hear it all the way to where I was, by the door. When he saw me, he ran around the room, picking up his things, and left. Anita wouldn't explain. She was very calm. Her face, across the table from him, was slightly flushed from eating, and the raised tracery of scars less visible. *I think Anita has needed me this past year.*

That morning and the next he woke comfortably. The crowded room, a repository for Tessa's "finds" since Vera had left home (the "finds" were either moving downstairs, rediscovered, or up into the limbo of the attic), and for that reason bizarre with little wooden objects, nutcrackers and pepper mills and frail chairs, the walls hung with plaques and old advertisements, was cool and airy on these mornings, perfect for sleeping. He woke with a clear head, his dreams mere fragments and fragrancies and broken memories of broad fields through which he had been walking with a woman. He was relaxed, as he had not been since his return. After three days back in America he felt his distance from it as strong as ever, and was grateful for it, but the strangeness of the country had drained: it felt again like the place in which he had been born.

"Everybody envies us," Vera said to him. "You should have heard Joanie Haupt going on yesterday."

"What for?" Vera had mentioned little about her lunch with her friend.

"Joanie kept talking about how she would like to live in Paris— I'm afraid she might come to visit us next summer. She spent three days there once, on a tour. She kept talking about the Musée Grévin. There's another reason, of course." Here Vera looked at him wryly, half-deprecatingly. "She is having an affair with Lawrence Wooster. From Walkins School, remember him? Apparently he is married, and he's treating her badly. She wants to get away from him."

Elliot could remember Lawrence Wooster: he had been a cheerful outgoing dishonest boy at Walkins, a prefect, captain of the football team. A banker now. They had never particularly been friends. Elliot could remember a time two years after graduation from Walkins when Wooster had come to Columbia for a weekend from Brown—they met at a mixer in the dining room beneath John Jay Hall. Wooster was carrying a bottle of bourbon, and maintained a breathless awfulness throughout the evening. He had rushed about the room, still athletic in his stride, biting girls' behinds. Leaving for the bathroom, he had said, "Gotta bleed the lizard."

"I told her we could put her up," Vera went on, "if we were in town. There was no way I *couldn't* say it, and I wouldn't mind, anyhow. She's more interesting than she used to be. Even though she is being very dumb about Lawrence Wooster, she seems more intelligent than she used to be."

"Good for Joanie," Elliot replied. He remembered Joanie Haupt as a loud-voiced bouncy girl, devoted to Gestalt therapists, a reader of genteel detective novels, a faddist of health foods and popular music. "I don't suppose it's Wooster's influence."

Vera sat down opposite him at the table. "What are you going to do about that statement? I've been expecting it to come any minute. You are going to sign it, I suppose."

He took it from his pocket with the note and held it out to her.

When she read it, her face puckered with distaste—that was for Dr. Laubach, he knew—and she said, "I'm happy he is so confident about what the right thing is. Paul Revere." Her eyes slid toward him, and they both cackled with laughter.

Two days passed, a peaceful time in which Elliot and Vera stayed in the Glauber home, spending hours reading or watching television. Nathan Himmel called him, inviting them for dinner, but Elliot invented another engagement, wanting only to be by himself, separate from others for a time. In the end, he told Himmel that he would talk to him at Anita's party, then only six days away. The television interview with Ted Edwards was to take place a few days before that, and this and the upcoming rehearsals gave him an added excuse.

"We have some good kids in the university symphony now," said

Himmel, "and I heard them rehearse for your concert once before vacation, so they should do a decent job for you when the time comes. They're all eager to meet the great man himself. You only get three rehearsals with them, will that be all right?"

"Will it be enough?"

"Sure," Himmel said. "Most of them will ignore your conducting anyhow. But the tenor, a guy named Rod Ettenheim, is the best thing we've had for years, so you won't have to worry about the singing. He's a difficult sort of guy, but the bastard really has talent. Don't worry about any of it, in fact. The laymen will love it no matter how it sounds, and your old colleagues will be quietly malicious, just as they always were."

"Do you see much of Anita?"

"La Kellerman? Not so much these days. Mark scared the piss out of our Saul last spring, and Helen's turned a little cool toward her. I see her around school now and then, though. Have you seen her live-in psychologist? The au pair Cerberus?"

"The girl—Andy? I've talked to her," Elliot said. "An interesting girl."

The next day Elliot parked behind a Jaguar, a low green car like a large old cat, which was drawn up before the iron gates around Nun's Wood. Across Wiltshire Drive he could see a face peering around the half-closed drapes in the picture window of a white two-story house, a building that looked oddly detached from its neighbors—but all of these houses looked like that to him, used to row houses and streets which seemed to have been made all at once and by the same hand.

A woman came out of the white house just as he was approaching the gates to see if they were unlocked. She picked her way toward him across the street.

"Do you work for Mr. Glauber?" the woman called. Her voice was assertive, grating. Elliot saw that she was wearing only red house slippers on her feet. The woman was about his age, a short dark-haired aggressive figure pulling a heavy coat over her shoulders.

"No, I don't," Elliot said, turning to her. "I'm his son-in-law, Elliot Denmark."

"I saw you were driving his car." The woman scanned his face as if searching for a weakness. "That's Herman Glauber's car there."

"Yes, it is."

"You come out to inspect the wood before the bulldozers get at it?"

"Something like that."

She shot a bleak little look at him, then glanced downward, her face hardening. She moved her feet in the red house slippers.

"Didn't even have time to put my boots on. I might give myself double pneumonia out here." She moved her hand in a jabbing motion toward the gates. "I want to talk to you about that, if you'll listen. We're going to make trouble for your father-in-law, mister, and for you too if you're on his side."

"I'll listen to whatever you have to say," he said. "I don't have any real opinion."

"Well, you'd better get one, in one hurry too, if you don't mind my saying so. Herman Glauber is supposed to be our alderman out here, and he's selling us down the river. It's a double cross, and you . . . you can just go back and tell him so." She hesitated on the last phrase and looked down again at her feet. These must have been very cold. Elliot saw that there were fluffy red balls on the toe of each slipper. "He's our representative, but it looks to us like he's feathering his own nest, him and that Ronnie Upp."

Elliot sighed impatiently. "I don't believe that, Mrs. . . . ."

"Mrs. Bender. Rona Bender."

"Mrs. Bender, and I don't think you believe it either. I'm sure Herman has made the decision he thinks is the best one to make."

"Selling off the only wooded area close to Wiltshire Drive? Everyone around here knew that convent was going to sell, and we all want a safe area for our children to play in."

He looked at the white-covered trees beyond the fence.

"In summer." Mrs. Bender glared at him. "And has your precious father-in-law thought about the value of our houses? I said it was a

double cross, and I'll say it right to his face. At the public hearing."
She stamped the ground with her feet, making a soft squashing noise.

"I don't think you're going to get anywhere by being angry, Mrs.
Bender," Elliot said.

"Being angry is the only way to get anything done in this country.
Do you think that people pay any attention to you if you speak in a
soft voice? You have to make yourself known, mister, you have to
buy yourself a drum and bang on it. Look at the blacks." She touched
his chest with a steely index finger. "Yeah, look! Bunch of welfare
bums and work-dodgers, they make enough noise and the rest of us
support them. You'd be angry too if you lived here. I'll bet you don't
even live in this ward."

"No, I don't," he said.

She blinked, then tugged the coat more firmly about her shoulder.
"I don't care where you live." Then she looked at him slyly. "You
say your name is Denmark?"

He nodded.

"Are you related to Chase Denmark?"

"He's my father."

"And you just came out to get a look at Nun's Wood?"

"That's what I wanted to do."

"Well, you needn't think we can't draw conclusions," she said
triumphantly.

The lock on the gate hung uselessly from one of the iron rods: at
his push, the gate opened. The path up to the convent house had
not been driven on since the last snow. Only two pairs of footprints
marred the surface, dotting an irregular pattern on the path. Elliot
set off, following the wandering, irregular pattern of footprints.

chapter 9

W ell, that was Rona Bender, all right," Andy said. "She's one
of those frustrated housewives who go batty from minding the babies
all day long. She was on television last spring, when all this started,
and the newsman couldn't shut her up. That awful voice! And she
has an ass like a horse's. You should have seen her in blue jeans,
trotting around with a picket sign in front of your old factory."

"Was that on television too?" Elliot asked. They were in Anita's
living room later that afternoon, the pale winter light showing a film
of dust and fingerprints on the windows. Anita's housekeeping had
slipped in these past few years. Books were heaped on the little table
beside the couch, and a pile of papers, scrawled in a messy childish
handwriting that must have been Mark's, was untidily heaped on
the floor. Record sleeves lay atop a row of books near the turntable.
Elliot felt depressed by this disorder; he wished suddenly that he
were elsewhere. He wanted to open the window and let in the cool
winter air.

"Oh sure," said Andy. "All of the Wiltshire Drive people were
out there carrying signs. Anita, thank God, had sense enough to stay
away. She was furious that they would picket Ronnie—and she had
a point, you should have seen some of the signs. Mostly women, of
course. Rona Bender was definitely the leader. One of the newsmen

from WBAC was covering it, and she ran up to him—galloped up to him—and practically commandeered the microphone. She wouldn't let go of it."

Elliot had driven over to the house after he had left Nun's Wood, wishing to speak with Anita. She was at the library, Andy had told him, and Mark was out. He knew that.

"I'm happy I don't live here anymore," Elliot said. "My comrades in arms would just about do me in. Thankfully, in a year or two nobody will remember the Nun's Wood business, except for the fanatics. My father will have begun to dominate the local chapter of SDS, and everything will be back to normal."

"It's probably a good thing you don't live here," she agreed. "You're lucky, you know, in being able to live wherever you want. Artists have the best kind of life."

Elliot stood up and wandered to the bookshelves. He looked at the record sleeves scattered across the books: his own was not among them.

"Aren't you happy here?" he said.

"Very happy, as long as Anita is happy with me. I've got everything I want." Andy's voice, now that he could not see the beautiful tribal face, sounded somewhat defiant. He could imagine himself answering such a question in that way, as if he were slamming a door.

"But not quite everything," he said. He ran his hands along the spines of Anita's books. "You must want more than this, living in someone else's house, being a graduate student."

She made no answer for a time. Then: "When I need to have my satisfactions questioned, I'll bring you in for a consultation."

"Who does the housekeeping?" he asked. His fingertips were gray with dust where they had brushed the books.

"We split it," she said. "Week by week."

"Wouldn't you really prefer to have your own place?"

"No," she said. "To be blunt."

He had driven over to see Anita about what he had witnessed in Nun's Wood, and this enforced conversation with Andy unnerved him, set him obscurely on edge. The girl had met him with evident unselfconscious warmth, but their conversation, lagging, had inexplicably become irritable. He thought he might be keeping her from her work, but when he mentioned this she said, "Don't be silly. If I wanted to work, I'd just excuse myself and go upstairs." Yet they were uncomfortable. He thought he might be making a fool of himself. He wanted to tell her what he had seen.

When he had pushed open the gate and followed the tracks down the snowy path toward the convent house, he had no idea that he was, in fact, doing just that: his intention was to look at the woods and try to decide to what extent Ronnie Upp's projected office buildings would destroy it; at base, to satisfy his curiosity about the woods themselves. In childhood, this had been forbidden ground, mysterious territory. That afternoon he had still the sense of trespassing.

After Elliot had gone fifteen yards up the drive, the trees on either side thickly branched and heavy with snow, he had found himself turning on the drive's gentle S deep into the woods, and the sense of an outer world beyond the gates had vanished. He soon felt lost. The convent grounds were perfectly quiet. Big leafless trees, the old oaks of Plechette City, interspersed with gleaming birches, spread, darker than the ground, before him. Elliot walked slowly up the curves of the long drive and felt himself disconnected from the civic problems caused by the wood. Even Anita and her obscure problem fell away from him. He did not wish to be seen, to be talked to: he was grateful for his momentary aloneness. Elliot had, in those first five minutes within Nun's Wood, a sense of secrecy, of isolation— the quiet wood itself, in which no motion could be detected, seemed to answer it. His heart kicked in his chest.

Then at the base of a tree not far from the drive he saw a quick stirring, a motion like that of a leaf, and directed by his feeling of inconsequence and isolation, he walked toward it, leaving the drive. The snow had hardened, here where it was not driven into white-gray slush, and it crisped beneath his shoes. Ahead of him—he had by now lost his sense of direction, and could not tell if he were going back toward the road or off into the acres of untouched wood to the west—he saw, for only an instant, the upflung insolent brush of a fox. The animal darted into an area of pure white, and was gone. His feet going *pock pock* on the snow, Elliot reached the tree where he had first glimpsed it. At the oak's base, rough sectional bark and roots tangling half in and half out of the layer of snow, he saw a dark hole. He knelt to peer in. A stale, bitter odor floated to him. The smell was oddly pleasing.

Standing again, Elliot looked back at the path, fixing it in his mind. This made him feel foolish, for he knew he was no more than minutes from the convent gates, but the woods had so disoriented him that he wished to take no chances of getting lost and walking either straight toward the mansion or condemning himself to a long tramp in the wood, his bearings lost. Keeping the drive directly behind him, he moved deeper into the bare trees, using a thick white birch trunk before him as a landmark.

Within minutes, he was truly lost. The birch had become one of a stand of birches, and once he was within their ring, he could not tell which had been his landmark. His footprints were nearly invisible, except for the crushed, beaten layer of snow where he had walked back and forth within the ring of white trunks, admiring them. He could, of course, always find his tracks, so he was not absolutely lost: though the snow was light and hard, it cracked beneath his feet. By "lost," he meant that his sense of direction had apparently been reversed, for his instincts told him that he had come into the ring from his left, but the faint impress of tracks straggled off farther into the wood on his right.

After he had backtracked, following the dim markings of boots, he saw that he had been mistaken. The tracks led to a narrow paved footpath which he had never seen before. This meant, he recognized, that instead of going back toward the drive, he had continued moving west: his original notion of direction had been correct. But now where was he? North of the drive, certainly—but he had no clear idea of how far north. Three hundred yards, perhaps more, he thought. The path itself had been shoveled since that last snowfall, which must mean that it was frequently used. This in turn might mean that it led directly to the convent house, or that it bisected the drive. In either case, people from the convent might appear on it at any time. It came to him with a shock that the footprints he had been following were not his own.

A black figure appeared before him on the footpath, as if it had been waiting behind one of the oaks. It moved forward slowly, its head bent, aware of him but not looking at him. For a moment, Elliot felt an absurd desire to run into the wood, to hide—but the leafless trees offered no refuge, unless he were to crouch like a thief behind one of the trunks. His heart pounding, he stood on the little square of pavement, waiting for the nun to address him. He could always say that he had been unaware that the land belonged to a convent, that he was from out of town . . . He stared off into the wood. Bright yellow daubs of paint on some oaks before him riveted his eye.

The nun looked up at him, and smiling, swept past. No words had passed between them. Elliot turned to watch her gliding down the little path, he exhaling a white ribbon of steam, until she turned, still following the path, deeper into the woods. Even then he could see her black outline moving between the trees.

The trees crudely marked with yellow, huge gaunt oaks, were scattered closely up a small hillside. The gaudy paint, trilled down between the coarse rills of bark, seemed to him to make the oaks more desolate and wintry. Of course, he thought: they are to be cut. One of the two new office buildings would be built on this hillside; presumably, the other would be set on the other side of the drive. The little pathway would be widened to a road. The nun must have thought that he was one of Upp's men, out inspecting the new property.

Elliot imagined that the nun must have been coming from the convent house; the path probably went back in the direction of the drive to come out somewhere at a smaller gate on Wiltshire Drive. He pushed his hands deep into the pockets of his topcoat, clenching them for warmth. He began to walk slowly down the footpath. Up in the boughs of an oak he saw the black mass of a squirrel's nest. Sparrows, scrappy city birds, tore out of a hollow, cheeping excitedly, high overblown flute notes, Bach's trumpets at the top of their range.

He went some thirty feet, near to where the path turned, and stopped. At his feet, trailing off the path into the snow to his right, was a smeared line of blood. Aloud, Elliot said, "The fox." The word instantly translated into warm gouts of steam. Where the path turned stood a large stone statue of Christ pinned to the cross, his face tilted sideways in pain or unconsciousness. There was a stone bench set before it. Looking farther down the footpath, where it curved to make a gradual arc back up toward its origin—so it wound backward to the house—Elliot saw, intermittently blocked and revealed by the bare trunks, a series of statuary and friezes.

The fox had run this way. But the bleeding was not the spotting he had seen in the Glaubers' garden; it was wound bleeding, great splashes pumped from the body. The patch he saw before him trailed onto the snow, then another lay farther on, back in the way the statues went, in the area of wood between the loop of the footpath. He left the clean squares of pavement and stepped onto the crackling of snow. The red gouted splashes, regular as the beats of a drum, made another path, a blazed trail, straight for a brush heap. Elliot moved slowly toward it. The tangled pile came clear in his eyes, as if drawn there, wrongly, overclear. He came close enough to pull at it, and thrust aside a snowy branch, hard as a steel pipe and brittle-seeming in his hands. He thought it would shatter like glass when he tossed it aside, but the branch thudded firmly into the crusted snow. Using both hands, he pushed smaller branches aside, leaves dead-brown and molded. The blood was a thin mapping on the ground, threading into the pile. Then, at the bottom, just now ceasing to breathe, the animal lay, its mouth baring the two rows of teeth. It was not the same fox he had seen before, this one bigger, more muscular in the doggy hind legs and shoulders. A male. A thin childish-looking arrow's shaft jutted acutely from its side. Voices, a man's and then a boy's, came to him from the right, where the loop of the footpath wandered past the statues to the convent house. Elliot crouched beside the still body of the fox, and saw a slim dark-haired man in a brown suede jacket approaching, his face working in anger; beside him was a small slight boy Elliot recognized as Mark Kellerman. Dangling from the boy's hand was a bow. The

man talking softly, angrily, the boy sobbing, they moved quickly past
him, going in the direction he had come.

"Ronnie gave Mark the bow last year on his birthday," Andy said.
"Anita didn't want him to have it, and it seemed irresponsible to me
too, giving a weapon to a boy with Mark's emotional problems. Even
if it was a toy, it was still a weapon. Those arrows are not rubber—
you saw the proof of that. Anyhow, she hid it, but Mark kept finding
it. She probably should have broken it or burned it, but I suppose
she knew Ronnie would ask her about it."

"Why didn't she just explain to Upp that she didn't want Mark
to have the bow?"

Andy faced him very calmly. "I suppose she didn't want to hurt
his feelings. Ronnie has never wanted to acknowledge Mark's problems. He adores the boy."

"It was a shock for me to see them together," said Elliot. "I knew
that the man was Upp, although I hadn't seen him before. Well,
that's not quite the truth. That day you showed me Upp's farmland,
I saw a man coming out of those woods at the far end of the field.
He was too far alway for me to see his face, but I could see his
jacket, a brown thing that looked like suede. I knew it had to be
Upp."

Elliot sat on the floor beside her chair. It was now late afternoon,
and the room had darkened. He could see her face by tilting back
his head and propping himself on his elbows. The scars seemed to
have darkened with the failing light; no longer red, they showed as
brown across her temple and cheek.

A moment later Andy stood and moved to the window, where she
was seen doubly by him, her slim back, the patterned shirt above
her trousers, and a blurred light figure reflected in the window. Elliot
rose from the floor and sat where he had been earlier, in the padded
chair near the bookshelves. The car outside had already stopped, and
they could hear the footsteps rushing along the walk to the porch.
The outside door opened, then the second door.

"How cozy you look," Anita said. "I'm so happy to see you here,

Elliot. I didn't get a thing done at the library. I think the students must be stealing all the books from the stacks. Though why they pick such obscure titles to run off with is beyond me. Maybe the resale value is higher!" She removed her coat and slung it over a chair, dislodging a stack of papers. "Oh, damn. There go the term papers. Get me a drink, will you, Andy dear? I'm simply exhausted. Is Mark back yet? Make a drink for Elliot too."

Andy went quickly to the kitchen.

"I just saw Mark this afternoon," said Elliot. "The circumstances were rather unusual. That's why I'm here, really."

"Oh? That's a pity. I thought you came here to see me. Or Andy. Were you properly entertained while I was out?" Anita was going across the room, ruffling her bobbed hair, to the turntable. She pulled a record from the shelf, took it from its sleeve, and set it on the turntable. The jazz boomed from the speakers. This was a wall between them; the music irritated him, as did the hard chatty brightness of her manner.

"Could you turn that down just a bit, Anita?" he asked. He held out his hand, twisting it in the air as if turning a dial. Anita's expression, as she went back to the components, was surprised: a tinge of mockery? She lowered the volume slightly.

"As I was saying, Anita, I really came because of Mark. Andy has been telling me that he and Ronnie Upp are close—something to that effect, anyhow. That Ronnie is trying to help Mark."

"That's not quite accurate," she said. "Ronnie likes Mark, and consequently he does help him. I knew they were going to spend the afternoon together, if that's what your news is." From the kitchen came the sound of ice falling into glasses. "They often do. I think Mark ought to spend some time with a man, don't you agree? There are too many women around him."

"Elliot's going to be on television," Andy called out. "Has he told you yet?" She appeared in the doorway, a tray in her hands. "I should have asked before. Is Scotch all right for everybody?"

"Elliot is a great Scotch drinker," said Anita. In fact, Elliot disliked whiskey. But he took the glass. Upp liked Scotch, he supposed.

"What are you going to do on television?"

"Not much," he said, exasperated by this deflection of his purpose. "It's just the Ted Edwards show. Herman Glauber roped me into it. I don't very much want to do it."

"Oh, that's just cowardice," said Anita. "Ted Edwards is a cream puff. He and Ronnie are friends."

He did not want to postpone his revelation any longer—it seemed to him that the events of the afternoon stood almost as an epitome. Once spoken, they must cause permanent change. He saw again the body of the dead fox, pierced by an arrow. Elliot repeated his story.

"How dreadful," Anita said. "It must have been awful for you. I'm sure it was an accident. That he hit it, I mean. Markie's only seven, after all. Ronnie must have thought it would be impossible for him to actually hit anything with the arrow. It was an unhappy accident for all concerned, including the fox. I am pleased someone was there to tell him off, aren't you?"

"Sure. But . . . I thought you'd show more concern."

"I'm showing as much as I feel," she said. "I am sorry that he found the bow again, and I wish Ronnie didn't encourage him to use it. Maybe now he will see why I don't want him to have the awful thing." She sipped at her drink, then looked at Andy. "Why was our dear Elliot in the wood in the first place?"

Andy turned her face to him. "Elliot and I agree about Nun's Wood." She smiled, and he was reminded again of her youth.

"That's unfortunate. You went out there to see what would be done with the property?"

"I suppose so," he said. "Pierce Laubach and my father sent me a statement they want me to sign, and I thought I'd better see what all the fuss was about before I made up my mind."

"Fair-minded Elliot," said Anita. "I suppose that's the reason we all love you."

"But you think I'm foolish to worry about it at all."

"It's your privilege to be as foolish or naive as you wish. Or concerned, if you object to those two words. But I can assure you that Ronnie will get that property."

"I won't argue with that," he said. "But there is still a meeting. It is still an issue." The two women seemed to be closing about him.

It was impossible to talk to Anita alone; with Andy present, they had to shuttle back and forth on secondary issues—nearly everything but his love for Anita now seemed secondary. He wished that Andy would leave the room. This conversation, the music, their drinks, even the early darkness that had entered the room from the street, blurring outlines and suppressing details, seemed to imply that all was as it had been years ago, when he had lingered here on so many winter afternoons. In those days, however, there had been no Andy French to sit beside Anita, crossing her trousered legs, regarding him calmly. He felt like an intruder.

"I don't think I will like Upp very much," he said.

Anita glanced at Andy, then smiled at him, opening her face, all her warmth going toward him. "Now you *are* being foolish. You've never met him. I think, though," she added, "that a lot of people don't like Ronnie. He doesn't give the impression of needing many friends." Again, and despite the smile—her old smile, full of tenderness for him—there seemed to be a complicity between the two women.

"Mark will be back any minute," said Andy.

"That's fine," Elliot said. "I'm just going."

The momentary stillness broke: Andy took their glasses back into the kitchen, and Anita stood, turning on a lamp. Light fell in a pool about her couch. "We are friends," she said, leading him to the door. She hugged him once; her arms tight about his waist, then left him alone on the cold porch.

chapter **10**

Roy Baltz joined Vera and Himmel in the empty auditorium seats during the rehearsal while Elliot was leading the symphony through the third section of *Words for the Wind*. After four hours of rehearsal, Elliot knew that the orchestra was nearly as bad as he had feared. It was no help, he knew, that he was at best an inexperienced conductor. Yet he knew, more than anyone else, how the music should go: and he had a good ear. The problem, apart from some misplaying in the sections that could possibly be remedied, was that the individual sections themselves had trouble hearing what the rest of the orchestra was doing. The Usenbrugge concert hall, a giant theater in one of the new university buildings, bounced the sound from the walls, distorting what could be heard from the stage.

"Cellos," he said, "you are going to have to get your cues from the tenor in this part, if you don't look up at me. I'll indicate the beat you come in on, but remember to retard a moment before your entry." They looked up at him, a black with a bushy Afro, two thin girls with glasses, then looked back down at their music. "Mark it in the music, if you can't remember. And look at only my left hand in this passage. I'll give you a signal on the beat before you come in."

He waited a moment for the rest of the musicians to look up at him. "If we had enough time, we'd go through it all the way from the beginning now, just so you could hear how it should fall into place. But you know the schedule as well as I do. So let's not waste any time fluffing." Again, they began. The tenor, picking up beautifully, glided into the time change at the cello's entry. They did their best.

"Second cello," Elliot said. "Keep your eyes open." The girl squirmed under his gaze.

They went through the passage again. Elliot could hear Himmel, behind him, talking to Vera.

"I want a little more noise from the percussion section," he said. "Percussive noise, if you can manage it. Tympanist, don't be afraid to really hit it. From number twelve, and those eight bars. Try it along with the cellos."

In two attempts, they had it. Elliot could feel their uneasiness, their weakness, and then saw the black student flash a V sign toward Himmel after they had finally drawn together. "No games," he said. "Himmel isn't grading you."

A laugh.

The tenor, Ettenheim, was as good as Himmel had promised: a controlled, thick voice—it seemed to come from the back of the throat—but the boy was extraordinarily attentive to phrasing, the real gift. His voice constricted in the top of the range, but he kept it afloat, a dense bell of sound, moving like a bird through the rhythmic changes. With Ettenheim, at least, he could be confident: the boy could manage anything. Just for the pleasure of hearing him sing, Elliot conducted the piece through to its end, beginning with the third section, the tenor gliding up the glissandi, using the proper harshness in the short phrases. The strings began to lose their place, the cellos again rushing their entrance, and faltered, trying to follow his hand signals, but Ettenheim did the last difficult section perfectly, ringing out the somber closing lines and harshly biting off the last word, so that the listeners mentally leaned forward, thinking there should be more.

"Interesting," Elliot said when they had finished. "If you let the tenor down in the performance, you should all be shot. I think we can pull it together. See you once more before Christmas. And for God's sake take your music home with you, so you can practice."

A few handclaps from the orchestra as he stepped off his stand. Elliot felt full of energy, larger than his true size. He looked for Ettenheim. The boy was picking up his coat, a battered toggle-buttoned parka, from the floor.

"I thought we weren't going to go all the way through it," the boy said. He was short, with black eyes that went up and down Elliot's person, seeming to dismiss him.

"You didn't mind, did you?"

"Mind? I suppose not."

The boy looked bristly, assertive. Elliot sought for something to say that would overcome the distance between them. He wanted to be as generous as the boy deserved.

"I'm glad you are here, Ettenheim," he said. "You'll make this a good concert."

"I suppose I'll do that," the boy said. He was buttoning his coat, and did not look up.

Afterward, in the empty auditorium, the four of them stood awkwardly, putting on their heavy coats. The janitor leaned against the wall, far up at the back where the doors were, his hand resting near the light switches. Baltz talked volubly, enthusiastically; he had not heard the orchestra's confusion. Perhaps he had heard it, and thought it was intentional. Baltz liked things aleatory. Elliot hesitated to go, looking at Vera, wishing to be rid of Baltz.

"Thank you," he said to his old student. "But we've got a lot of work to do before we punish people's ears with the concert."

Baltz turned to Vera, smiling: he looked as though she had just cashed a dubious check for him.

"Look," Himmel said. "It's still early. What have we got to look forward to but another long winter night? Let's go for a drink."

Vera looked briefly at Elliot; she too was wondering, he knew, how to shed Baltz. They went out by the side door near the stage, to a concrete slab on a graveled yard. The parking lot was close by, and they began to drift toward it past the lighted library. The sky was already dark.

"We'll follow you," Elliot said to Himmel. "Lead on." Baltz hovered by the door of the Denmarks' car, still talking about the rehearsal. In the end, they simply started the car and drove off, leaving Baltz in the freezing parking lot.

chapter 11

He had been cold yesterday with Baltz, willing himself to be distant and only half-friendly, and was unsure of his reason for it. He knew now that the concert would never be the perfect, disruptive event he had hoped for—it might, indeed, only lie passively before the audience, a poor wounded set of intentions—but that was only part of it. Nor could he excuse himself by blaming his rudeness on Rod Ettenheim and on the verdict he had read in the tenor's manner. That had been only an unpleasant shock. Ettenheim must have thought that Elliot had been unsure of his capacities and had been testing him by the decision to let the piece roll through to its con- clusion. You should have trusted me, the boy had meant; if you were a musician you would have seen that I could leap through any fiery hoops you can put before me. And it was true: he had seen it.

Baltz's very manner had put him off. That had been a profounder annoyance than Ettenheim's assertion of his own ego, his own worth. Baltz's ignorant approval of what he had heard had offended Elliot; it was an implied assent, remembered well in Baltz, of everything done, every human activity, however sloppy, as long as it was new. Walking about in the long arcades and hot little chambers of the art center with Kai, Vera lingering in another room behind them, Elliot was grateful for Kai's own distance, his consciousness of standards

and ironies. Erect, almost glamorous in his old gray gabardine suit
and duffel coat, Kai had been unmoved by the current show, strolling
among the dwarfed, rubbery sculptures in the shapes of hands,
breasts, fetal figures, smiling faintly at it all. He had liked only one
section of the new exhibition, a random-looking assemblage of metal
pipes and tubes, some heaped and scattered on the floor and others
fixed to the wall. It looked as though the builders, in the midst of
some complex project, had left for their lunch. "This I find myself
liking," he said to Elliot. "I hope you think that odd."

"I think it's stupefying," said Elliot.

"But it makes no demands, no assertions," said Kai. "All these
other things"—he gestured around at the hands and breasts—"all of
them, they are so importunate."

"It astonishes me that you're interested in that kind of art," Elliot
said. "In antiart."

"I'll confess that I have little faith in the lyric impulse, Elliot. So
many of those flowers turn out in the end to be plastic. There was
a guard in my camp"—he looked down at Vera, who had stiffened.
He put his free hand over hers. "The guard could quote Goethe as
well as I. I think he was the last person I've met who had a positive
enthusiasm for Goethe. And could you guess? It has become a com-
monplace to mention such men."

"Someday," said Vera, with more heart than tact, "someday, Uncle
Kai, would you talk with us about what happened there? I'm sure
it would . . . I want to say, help you, but I don't mean that you need
help."

"My dear Vera," said the old man, now walking with them into
the main galleries. "Perhaps. But not to you. To Elliot." He smiled
at Elliot, his face white and ravaged, handsome, the sleek hair pulled
back above the vein knotted at his temple. "Yet, in the end, I don't
think either of you should be interested."

But even as he said this, even as he so clearly meant it, Elliot
thought he could hear in Kai's voice, for the first time, that he
wanted to break through all the silence he had built about himself
for twenty-five years.

Then they divided and went through the rooms separately. For a time Elliot lost sight of Kai and Vera, and stared unseeing at the paintings, brooding on Baltz and Kai. Then he turned a corner, passed a dozing blue-uniformed guard, and saw them again.

Vera and Kai were standing before a Zurbarán monk. She loved it, he remembered. Kai too seemed to like the painting; he stood as if for once not impatient to move on, staring into the tiny flame cupped in the monk's hands, the entire shrouded body plucked out for the painting's long moment from the surrounding dark.

chapter 12

I'm glad you've managed to spend some time with Kai," said Herman Glauber. "I worry about the old bastard. He was always older than I was—when I was a kid, Kai already seemed like a grown-up to me. He was in another world entirely. And Kai hated the old man, my father. We don't use the word 'enemy' much anymore, but that's what they were, enemies." His glasses glittered toward them. He put his fists up to his chin and jabbed the left into the air before him, quick punches.

"It wasn't really that bad, was it, Daddy?" asked Vera. She rocked slowly back and forth in her chair, her eyes on the fire.

"Well, it never really came to blows, as far as I remember. But it was that bad, it really was. Kai wasn't usually a demonstrative guy, but I can remember him storming around the house, slamming doors and kicking things. He wasn't even in the U.S. when our father died—he cleared out quick, once he made the decision. He lived here in town for a couple of years, then *boom*. Away he went."

"Don't forget his teaching," Tessa said. She had a dry, attentive look, flipping the pages of a catalog.

"I did forget. When he was somewhere in his twenties, he taught at a little school up in the western part of the state, near the Mississippi. Not far from Tessa's parents' farm. He always did just what he wanted to do. I'll say that for him. And now, when I think of him in that miserable little room down on Ward Street, working all alone, never seeing anyone, I wonder what good it was, all that independence. Those fights. He reminds me of the old man, in his last days before he passed away."

"How did your father die?" asked Elliot.

"Cancer," answered Tessa. "He was a wonderful man, a man who could do things. He knew how to be charming with women. It seemed like such a waste of a man when he fell ill. He was a big healthy fellow when I met him, and strong as a bull. He worked with his hands all his life. Like my father."

"Well, he did," said Herman. "But Tessa only knew him when he was getting old. Not that he ever really did get old. My father was only in his late fifties when he died. And then he was a changed person, a big wreck of a man. I'll never forget how he looked, lying there in the hospital. His face got so terribly thin. He was in constant pain, awful pain, and nobody could do anything for him. The nurses were terrified of him. An awful thing happened one of the last times I saw him there—he was no more than a shriveled old bag of sticks, and he wanted to die. I came in the way I always did, but he looked at me in a funny way. He looked uncomfortable to have me there, and I knew that he'd always welcomed my visits. Then he said, 'You came back, did you?' and I knew he thought I was Kai. I was terror-stricken. 'Are you happy now?' he asked me. I was thirty-four, and I damn near wet my pants. My father didn't live long after that, and he didn't want to live, either. Oh, it was bitter."

"It was a long time ago," said Tessa. "Kai is another man now. He's crawled inside and locked the door."

Vera smiled a little flickering smile.

"We never had any trouble with Vera," said Tessa. "She was the world's best girl. We could always depend on Vera. Herman's father felt the same way about him."

"Hell, I was the peacemaker," Herman said. There was a comfortable irony in his voice, and in the set of his hands folded before his large bullish face. He clasped them together, then ran the joined hands over his scalp. "I had to be. All the time I was a kid, I was in constant terror that everything was going to fly apart. I didn't know what was going on. At night, up in our room, I could hear my parents arguing about Kai, my mother's voice pleading, and then my father's big bass growl. You couldn't really hear their words, but I knew what they were talking about. Kai just sat at his desk ignoring it. Then later, when we knew he was in trouble in Germany—nobody knew about the camps then, and we tried desperately to get word to him—I used to think about those days. I realized what he must have been going through, hearing those arguments— but he never moved a muscle! God, emotions are awful things."

"Emotions are beautiful things," said Tessa, "as long as they don't go amok." She looked to Vera and Elliot as if for approval. "It's like sex in movies. Who can get pleasure from looking at naked people? That's what I call something running amok."

"It wasn't emotion killed my dad," said Herman calmly. "It was lung cancer. My mother died of a heart attack two years after."

"They were both beautiful people," said Tessa.

"I suppose so," said Herman. "Let me show you something." He left his chair and went out of the room. They heard him going up the stairs and crossing the wooden floors to his bedroom; the creak of a drawer.

"Did Kai look healthy?" asked Tessa. She had put the catalog down on an old wooden school bench near the window, and leaned forward, facing Elliot, the ruddy hair coiled tensely behind her ears.

"He looked fine, Tessa."

Vera nodded, rocking in her chair. To Elliot, she looked sleepy, and impatient with her mother.

Herman came back into the room with a manila envelope in his hand. He pulled from it three photographs, brown sheets in spotted holders. "These are pictures of my parents, and one of their wedding." He thrust them toward Elliot. "Vera's seen them already. The big one with the mustache is my dad."

After Herman had gone upstairs to bed, taking the old photographs with him, Tessa sat in the kitchen talking with Vera and Elliot. She was preparing the morning coffee and warming some milk to take with her sleeping pill. "You don't know what it's been like around here, these past months. Herman has been slaving, working his fingers to the bone trying to get the Nun's Wood business through the planning commission. He can sleep like a log. But you know he's a worker." She nodded her pale dramatic face at him, narrowing her long eyes.

"That's why he was going on so about Kai," she said. "About Kai and his father. He thought it would take his mind off his work. Do you know how long it's been since that man has talked about his family? Well, I can tell you. It's been since we were married. In all that time I have not heard him mention his family once. Oh, he loved them. You can bet on that, if you know Herman. But you heard what he said tonight—he lived in constant terror that everything would go to pieces. That was your Uncle Kai's work. Herman thinks that Kai was bleeding when he listened to his parents fighting about him, but he's wrong and I know it. Herman was the only one who was bleeding. Kai was just trying to get to the end of the chapter in his book. Your uncle has always been a selfish man, and Herman has always been too good-hearted to recognize it." She turned down the heat beneath the milk. "You can see how all this is affecting *me*. I'll never get any sleep tonight."

"I don't understand you," said Vera. "You've always taken the side of Uncle Kai. When he lived with us, you took such good care of him. You're always trying to get him into things again, to get him out of his flat. It was you who first suggested that Elliot and I call him up, the day we got back."

"Of course I did," said Tessa. "Don't you think that I respect that man? That I respect his experience, his mind? If it hadn't been for that foolish trip to Germany and all those years wasted on his book, Kai Glauber could have done anything. He could have been a college professor, one of the old-fashioned scholars, I mean, not one of these radicals." (The radicalism of professors was a concern of these times.) "He could have been a doctor, a partner in a law firm, anything he wanted to be. If Kai had gone into politics, he would never have stopped at the local level, I can tell you. He'd be a senator. And look what he is instead. An old man in one room, living off our charity, surrounded by Puerto Ricans down on Ward Street. That smelly fourth ward. I learned a long time ago that your uncle had brains but no judgment. He never got back into the mainstream again after he got back from Germany, and that's another thing that is eating at your father's heart. Kai has been wrapping himself up in that book, it's like a cocoon for him."

Elliot felt that she was expressing, in veiled fashion, her resentment against him as well as her disappointment in Kai—Tessa was never far from thinking that Vera was supporting him in an arcane and profitless hobby.

"I think you're overlooking what happened to him during the war," Vera said. "You can't expect a man to go through that and come out unchanged."

"Are you telling me that Kai couldn't get a *job?*" Tessa's voice was fierce. "Hansel and Gretel. When I look at you two kids, I think of fairy tales."

Tessa poured the warm milk into a cup and drank half. She took a red tablet from the table and swallowed it with the remainder of the milk.

"We know all about Kai," Vera was saying. "I can't imagine him teaching, I can't imagine him as anything but what he is. And you've been lovely to him."

"You don't know everything about him," said Tessa. "For example, you don't know that I met him a long time before I knew your father. He was teaching in the town near our farm, Highland Junction. This is something I've never told your father, Vera, because I knew how it would hurt him. You know what I mean—your father is a terribly sensitive man. I would have sworn that Kai and I were going to be married."

"You mean that you were in *love* with him?" It was nearly a gasp. She stared in astonishment at her mother.

"I didn't have any idea what love meant, I was just an eighteen-year-old girl. I *thought* I was in love. I didn't meet your father until two years later, when I moved down to Plechette City. He was a friend of my cousin Jacey's, and I met him at their house. Jacey said his name was Herman Glauber, and I said, are you related to Kai Glauber? I said I'd seen his brother in Highland Junction, where he was a school-teacher, but I didn't want to say any more. I knew what kind of man your father was just by looking at him. We saw each other for two years before we were engaged, and then it was too late to tell him. Sometimes it seemed important, and other times I knew it wouldn't make any difference at all. But Kai was in Europe when we were married, and he never said anything about it in his letters to Herman— though there were few of *those*, you can be sure. There were reasons for his silence about me, and I knew he wouldn't tell Herman that we had met. And then he came back after the war, and he was already an old man. I wasn't sure if he even remembered."

"Well, what happened?" Vera asked.

"Nothing happened," said Tessa. "Nothing at all happened. I used to meet Kai near the school in the evenings, and he'd talk to me for hours. He knew everything, he'd read everything, he knew about history—oh, it was thrilling to listen to him! I was just out of high school, and I was so eager to find out about the world, to learn things. I was like you then, with all your dreams. I must have seen him nearly every day. I told him everything about myself, all my hopes. When I think about it now, it seems sad. He was only ten years older than I, and what had he done? But he knew so much! We'd go up into the woods near town with sandwiches and we'd spend hours just talking. He was very handsome then, not like the boys I knew at school, the boys from the farms. They were clumsy people without an idea in their heads. Kai was another world from that. He was reading all the people that were famous then— Fitzgerald, Sinclair Lewis, Joseph Hergesheimer."

Tessa had again astonished her daughter. Elliot guessed that Vera had never before heard those names in her mother's mouth.

"But then everything changed. Kai began to avoid me. He had a friend who started coming up to see him, a man his age with a big yellow car, the kind of car we used to call a roadster then. On the weekends I used to see the car parked outside the boardinghouse where Kai lived. Sometimes Kai and his friend would go off for days together, Chicago, St. Louis, and in the summers to New York, on the train from Plechette City. His friend's name was Harrison Upp."

*   *   *

Tessa had first seen Harrison's Upp's car on a Friday afternoon, traditionally a time when she and Kai went for a walk. She had, in the past year, been growing closer and closer to Kai Glauber, and now it was the beginning of the summer of 1925, a close, breathless summer in western Wisconsin, and Tessa thought that she knew the pattern of her future. It seemed inevitable that she and Kai would marry: they had spoken vaguely of moving south, to one of the big cities there, Plechette City or Chicago, and getting teaching jobs. Kai was restless in Highland Junction. Tessa knew that he wanted to move to a higher-paying school district, one close to good libraries, and then begin graduate studies. Tessa was dreamily thinking of herself as a professor's wife, living in a colonial home in Princeton or Cambridge, herself a part of the world she knew only from novels and Kai's talk. In her imagination, it was a world of good china services and fast clever conversation, of effortless achievement; women with white dresses and intellectual husbands, long dinner parties that would seem to pass in a moment. She already saw herself, her hair cut short and somehow clinging close to her head like a brilliant helmet—Tessa was vain about her hair—walking across a college green to her new home. She had no doubts of Kai's ability to achieve all this for her: it would be a natural consequence of his conversation.

The yellow roadster seemed an omen, a portent of this life. She had never before seen an automobile like it. The heavens had moved, and brought her closer to the gorgeous careless future: touching the shiny metal of its door, she felt confirmed in her hopes. She knew that its owner must be a friend of Kai's, that he already had some connection with the universe they would later inhabit together. No one else in town could know the man who owned the car. Standing in the dusty street before Kai's boardinghouse, she thought that she had never loved him so much. ("Later," Tessa said, "I was horrified that what I thought was love had so much greed in it. But maybe it always does.") Playful, she honked the big horn at the driver's side of the car, squeezing the black rubber bulb.

Kai appeared in the doorway of the boardinghouse, followed after

a second by a florid balding man who was dressed in the most beautiful clothes she had ever seen a man wear. Tessa was startled, and
looked up at the house in her embarrassment. The other lodgers
were standing at the windows, peering down at her. They were
mostly clerks in the shops or traveling men, people who seemed to
her to have purposeless, eventless lives, like her parents. The new-
comer—Kai's friend—made them all appear shabby, grimy from
their years of doling out parcels and change, or of endlessly circling
about the western counties in rattly old cars and buggies. She could
have stepped into that car and never seen them again.

She did get into the car, helped by Kai's friend, and they drove
to another town, to a restaurant. By this time she had been introduced to Harrison Upp; he was the most sophisticated man she had
ever met. All during dinner, he talked about the places he had seen,
cities in Europe Tessa knew she would never see unless Kai took
her to them. He was nervously quick, sarcastic, talkative, leaning
slightly across the table toward Kai or gesturing with one hand in a
way that made Tessa think of the young men in novels she had read.
He knew Paris, Austria, Switzerland, Germany, and latent in his
descriptions and anecdotes was the implication that Kai would know
them too. It was all a prodding kind of flattery which must have
been attractive to the young man Kai was then, about to begin his
thirties in a small midwestern town for which he had no love. Tessa,
watching these two, felt an odd mixture of emotions: envy, excitement, an unlocalized kind of fear. She knew that everyone else in
the restaurant was watching them. Back at home that night, she sat
in front of her mirror trying to see in it the face of the woman she
was to become, who would be able to enter a restaurant that way
and concentrate it about herself.

But, as she told them, there had been an omen "all right," and she
had not read it correctly. Kai's attitude toward her began to change.
He became more openly dissatisfied with the town, with his job. When
she talked with him a few days after Harrison Upp's car had swept out
toward the trunk road, raising a great feathery plume of white dust,
Kai said many bitter things to her—he savagely lampooned the
school's principal, Royce Watkins, and the bank president, Walter

Bumpers. He frightened her with his wit. She knew that he was in a rage to leave the town. The next week he and Harrison Upp went to Chicago, and Kai came back with new books and two new neckties. Tessa knew that Upp had bought the ties for him.

One day after Kai had returned from Chicago, Tessa walked into town and up the road to the boardinghouse. She could see Kai at his window, watching her approach the house. When she was about to walk across the porch, he motioned her to stay where she was, and in a moment, joined her outside. They walked out of town toward the fields. Kai was uneasy and uncommunicative. He thwarted her questions with brief replies until she asked if he would stay teaching in the town another year. It had been their plan, she thought, to move separately to Plechette City the following autumn, though they had never spoken of it directly. Kai said no, he could not stay on in Highland Junction; nor would he move to Plechette City. Everything was slipping past him, he felt. He had to go somewhere where he could work on another degree, somewhere in Europe. Harrison Upp knew about these things: he had taken courses at the Sorbonne; he had friends in German universities. The two of them sat in the broad grassy field, plucking stems of grass from the matted ground. Listening to him talk, Tessa felt herself condemned to a lifetime of this, the confined little town, the fields that rolled on west to the river, all of it deadeningly familiar.

For the rest of that summer she saw Kai infrequently. It was clear that he avoided her. Too proud to chase him when the other boarders told her that he had gone over to the school to "read," she hovered across the street, watching from the windows of the general store. The yellow car appeared on the weekends and Tessa could catch glimpses of the two men in Kai's window, or out in the fields around the town, slowly walking, Harrison Upp wearing a bright straw hat. Their trips began soon after, sometimes lasting weeks. In August one of the men at the boardinghouse caught up to her on the street and gave her a note from Kai. He had moved out, and left with Upp for Europe. For three days she had been watching an empty room. Tessa went back to her parents' farm and began to make plans to move to Plechette City. Her mother reminded her of Jacey, her sis-

ter's boy, who had married a Plechette City girl and lived there with
his family. He could help her find a place to live. On the winter day
she finally left, her parents watched her pack with inarticulate astonished amazement: even her mother, she knew, had not expected that
she really had the will to leave. It had taken her six months.

Not until she had met Herman Glauber the year following and
known him for several weeks did she learn that Kai had never returned from Europe: he was then living in Harrison Upp's apartment
in Paris, and attending classes at the Sorbonne. He stayed there two
years, then broke with Upp and went alone to Bonn. He had little
money, but in his infrequent letters to his family said that he was
very happy. He had friends, he found a teaching job, he had begun
to do research for his book on Goethe.

Elliot and Vera lay in their beds in the dark cluttered upstairs room.
From the bedroom across the hall they could hear the deep fluttery
snoring of Herman Glauber, echoed by a gentler snoring from Tessa.
"In the morning," Vera said, "she'll tell us that she didn't get any
sleep at all. She is at least that predictable." After a moment: "What
are you thinking about?"

"That story."

"So am I. It's funny to think that I don't even know my own
mother. I never thought about how it was for her on the farm with
her parents. She always used to make it sound so idyllic—you know
Mother. She made it sound as if I should be jealous. But she must
have hated it, Elliot. The other strange thing is that Uncle Kai could
have been my father."

"Not if I understand the story," he said.

"Your parents knew Harrison Upp, didn't they?"

"Sure. He was a neighbor of theirs. Of ours."

"What was he like?"

"A red-faced kind of man, very bluff, a jovial type. He drank a
lot, I remember. Both he and his wife were supposed to be alcoholics.
He liked the way my father played the piano. I don't know what
else. He had a little rim of white hair. His family was very rich, and
he was very rich, and he took his whole family to Africa once when

I was a kid. We got postcards from them. They were on safari. He was a flamboyant man."

"Do you think Uncle Kai knew about the shooting?"

"It was in all the papers. I'm sure he must have seen it. I can't imagine what he thought about it."

"Oh, Elliot," she whispered, "I can't wait to get home. To have all of this over with." She turned to face him across the space between their beds. "Will you come in with me?" she said softly.

Elliot had been thinking, during this conversation, of the afternoon two days ago at Anita's house. He had, he realized, obscurely enjoyed the close world he had felt about him. He wondered what the two women had talked about when he was gone. He had tried to call Anita the morning of the rehearsal, the day after he had gone to her house to discuss Mark, and Andy had been parrying, protective.

How is she? Can I see you sometime tomorrow?

Dear Elliot. Aren't you awfully busy now? Don't worry about us. Anita and I were going to go shopping tomorrow—we are both last-minute types. In the background, he had heard his record playing.

Do you like that? The record?

I think it's beautiful. It reminds me of you. You should do things like that all day long.

He slipped from his bed and crossed to Vera's. In the darkness, her oval face looked tired, pale, pretty.

"Tell me about Anita," she said.

If Elliot had forgotten about Ronnie Upp's plans for the Chambers Denmark clock, his father had not. Tessa met them at the door as they returned to the Glauber house, saying that Elliot's father was on the telephone. "He called just this minute," Tessa said, "and I told him that you two were out for a walk, but then I looked out the front window and saw you coming up the driveway."

Vera, at a look from Elliot, took her mother into the living room.

"What the devil did you say to Rona Bender?" His father's voice was reedy, crackling. "She's one of our best women out there. I got a call from her the other day saying that she saw you snooping— that was the word she used—around Nun's Wood at the same time that Upp scoundrel was there. She as good as accused me of selling out the people on Wiltshire Drive and making a clandestine deal with Upp."

"That's because I was in Herman Glauber's car. You could have explained the situation to her."

"I did, believe me." Elliot could hear his father make a sigh that might have signified amusement. "I told her that you were a musician. And she told me that she didn't know how I could let a thing like that happen. I think she imagines you are one of those witless guitarists. Perhaps you should get a haircut."

"It's too cold for a haircut," Elliot answered, smiling.

"And Rona Bender can be a bit much at times. She was receptive to reason, however. I think she was rather ruffled by the tone you took with her. Rona is accustomed to rather less *hauteur*, I should imagine."

"Well, I don't think I said anything to disturb her. She just wanted to complain about her property values."

"A great complainer," said his father, his voice amused. "An inspired complainer. We're counting on Rona for some fireworks at the commission meeting. All that is by-the-by, really. I got a call from Pierce this morning, Elliot."

"Yes?" he asked, knowing what was coming.

"He had not received your signature on our statement. You are planning to declare yourself on our side, aren't you?"

"I am, yes." He waited for an indication of relief or approval, but none came. "But before I do, I've got to talk with Herman."

"Tread lightly, boy, tread lightly."

"We have to drive into Chicago for a TV taping the day after tomorrow, and I think I'll bring it up then. I'm sure you'll be able to calm Dr. Laubach in the meantime."

"Pierce is unimaginable any way other than placid," Chase said. "Unlike the good Rona, who is his opposite number, as it were. People on the west side of town seem to be more impulsive than ourselves." It was this sort of judgment, so typical of his father, that rankled within Elliot. "Don't even bother to contradict me," Chase continued. "I know one can't generalize. Especially in these days.

And perhaps there are special categories for creatures like Ronnie Upp." Chase paused significantly, as if wanting to hear the next beat.

"I don't think I followed that," said Elliot.

"I'm talking about the clock. I hope you have not forgotten."

"I think I had," Elliot said. He had a moment's flash of boredom with everything to do with Plechette City. "Is there anything new about that? Any new information?"

"Confirmation, if not information. Perhaps you have also forgotten about our spy in the embassy, Hilda's good coworker."

"I remember now," said Elliot.

"I should hope that you do. At any rate, the Huebsch girl has told Hilda that an agreement has been made with a firm to demolish my great-grandfather's structure, work to begin this spring, after the weather changes. That gives us time to plan our attack, even file suit, if necessary. Oh, we will stop him, I assure you."

"I'm happy you are so confident."

"Confidence is a necessity. Especially for us." Chase still sounded amused. "I've been to a lawyer on this matter, and he could give me little assurance that we could save the clock tower. It must be officially designated a historic monument. When I pressed him, he of course agreed that it was a historic monument. Hence the need for a citizen's group. We must present our case before the Monuments Commission, and then stir up public sentiment. Most of the members of the Monuments Commission are themselves monuments. Hilda tells me that the commission has not held a meeting for the past fifteen years. One can assume that they would love to be consulted again."

"Shrewd of you, Father." Elliot smiled. "Are they all still alive?"

"In body," said Chase. "You won't forget to inform Herman Glauber tactfully of your decision on our little matter, will you?"

"No, I won't," said Elliot. "Oh, there's one more thing I wanted to ask. What was Harrison Upp like—can you remember?"

"I'd rather forget," said his father. "He was a bit of a scamp, however. Why are you interested in the father?"

"You might call it psychology," said Elliot.

chapter 13

In 1963, Jefferson Glee, then a first-term Plechette City alderman and a creamily brown-skinned gold-spectacled raccoonlike man who owned a string of laundromats in the valley to the south of Grand Avenue, introduced at a Common Council meeting a bill to alter the name of Grand Avenue to John F. Kennedy Avenue. In 1945 an earlier alderman from the same ward, Roman Zawocki, had proposed renaming it Roosevelt Avenue; and in 1937 Route America had been proposed by Wilton Zamon, who later became the mayor and held office until VE Day, when he died of a heart attack at his desk, having just been informed that his son Roy had been arrested during a raid on a Booker Place nightclub described in the *Herald*'s account (which included a photograph of General Mark Clark pinning a Silver Star on Roy Zamon) as a "hell." Both of these bills, like Mr. Glee's, were defeated.

Grand Avenue had been for a hundred years the principal shopping area of Plechette City, a conservative mile of its largest and best shops. Second Street, intersecting it near the river, had been its chiefest rival from the early twentieth century to the nineteen-fifties; the big department stores had branches on Second Street, and many small businessmen had chosen to rent or build shops there. In the sixties, Second Street was gradually—and in the view of these men, fatally—overtaken by the blacks who had been displaced from the valley by Puerto Ricans. What the new shopping centers had begun, the black population finished; and after the riots of 1968 in which millions of dollars of property was destroyed and seven men killed, Second Street was lined with failing pawnshops, storefront churches, taverns, and the boarded-up facades of the department stores. Grand Avenue was the last, threatened center of urban life in Plechette City, and the city council did not wish to toy with it. Elliot had been therefore surprised to see in the *Herald* that a week after the mayor's Model City plan had been rejected, plans were being drawn up to close Grand Avenue off to traffic and make it a shopping mall: in the newspaper drawing, an arcade lined with trees and benches. A shopping center with nowhere to park. At the bottom of the page had been a curious paragraph (WOLF IN GARDEN) about a man named Leroy Zim, who had seen a wolf loping across his backyard. Zoo officials were summoned, but had been unable to find the animal. Mr. Zim described it as "no dog I ever heard of, not after I looked at it twice."

Another article in the same issue (OUR DYING DOWNTOWN) reported that the volume of pre-Christmas business had declined by eight percent from the year before. Elliot, in the midst of a thrusting mob within the Gimbels Grand, could only be grateful. He loved these big old-fashioned stores when he was a boy—he had loved, in fact, all the prosperous crowded length of the avenue—and had come shopping that afternoon with Vera to recover his old sensation of absorption into a varied and rushing mass bent on work and pleasure.

The store still had some of its old aura for him: those glass counters of expensive scarves and belts, the dark wood of the elevators and the paneling of the men's department. The elaborate women, brokenly seen through the crowd, behind the cosmetic counters. Tall boots on wooden wall ledges in an alcove. Going up on the narrow escalator to the second floor (Notions, Perfumes, Toys, Books, Women's Clothing II—Young Modes), Elliot looked over the crowded, rambling expanse of the floor below. A steady swell of people pushed through the revolving doors below the GRAND AVE-

NUE sign and the enormous gilded iron clock set into the wall above it: three-twenty.

Women's Clothing II—Young Modes, an arcade of booths and counters exhaling rock music, butted against the elevator like a more exotic continent. Vera led him into a row of long dresses with Spanish collars and great puffed sleeves through to a second enclosure. This was lined with satiny calf-length clothes, green and pastel blues and yellows, soft tan shades. Thick brown belts studded with bullets draped from hooks in the walls. The thin pained voice of the singers filled the air about them: ". . . and the eagle flies with the dove," rushed by drums. Elliot wondered for a moment if it might be Roy Baltz. He had not even asked Baltz if he had made a record.

"I think my mother would be happy if you got something and charged it to her," Elliot said. "That's what she wanted you to do. And if it looks expensive to you, no matter what it costs, think of Paris and get it. She'll be pleased." The offer of the charge card, Elliot thought, was Margaret's way of apologizing for Vera's embarrassment at the Denmark house.

"Don't worry about me," he said to Vera. "I'll just browse around. Take your time and find something you like."

Vera turned to the dresses, her face skeptical and concentrated. Elliot moved toward the little room's entrance and nearly bounced into a salesgirl.

"May I help you?" A harassed-looking girl, blue smudges painted below her large eyes.

"Just browsing—and so is my wife," he added, to protect Vera. He smiled at the girl's tired face. She looked no more than high-school age beneath the clown's paint. He earned a brilliant smile in return.

"Ask me if you need any help," she said, and went into the next enclosure: sweaters, Elliot saw, following. More belts with bullets. A new voice began on the tape, boyish and thick: "I'd like to be . . . Under the sea," a cowboy's unlikely lament. ". . . in the shade," comically mournful.

"Can't you shut that crap off? What is this anyhow?" The stumpy woman before the counter was staring aggressively at the girl he'd just spoken to, looming her heavy face up at the girl from beneath a wild mass of black hair. "I asked you, what is this? I been waiting fifteen minutes, listening to that crap." She leaned on a fluffy pile of sweaters, her arms in the shapeless blue coat jutting out at the elbows.

"I'm sorry," said the girl. "It's just the tape they play here."

"*Sorry.*" The woman glared at the girl. "I been waiting fifteen minutes, and you're sorry. That's a big deal, huh? All I get out of you is fifteen minutes of stupid music and a big sorry. Is that what you call service here?"

"I'm sorry you were waiting," said the girl. "I'll help you if I can."

"All you can say is sorry, is that right?" The woman pushed herself back from the counter with a fat jerk of her short arms and picked the top sweater from the pile. It was a small turtleneck, cut skinny in the chest: in the woman's hands, it looked no more substantial than a handkerchief. "I want to try this on," she said. "If you're over being so *sorry*, maybe you could show me the changing room."

The girl's tired face, now set into bored hostile lines which seemed to leak the blue eye makeup over large flat areas of her face, focused toward the skinny sweater, then back to the heavy little woman in the blue coat. "I don't think it looks like your size," she said.

"I'm trying to see if it's my size," she retorted. "It's the biggest you got, up in this section."

". . . in the shade," went the cowboy voice, filling the silence while the salesgirl put her hand to her eyebrows and Elliot hung indecisively by the entrance.

"Isn't that why you got changing rooms?" the woman insisted. "You don't expect people to just buy this stuff right off, do you?"

"But it's too small for you," said the girl. "Everything in this department would be."

"I don't have to take that from you," hissed the woman. "Someone who made me wait."

"This is Young Modes. The right department for you is downstairs." The girl leaned forward across the counter to take the sweater, balled in the woman's hand. Elliot knew that the gesture was a mistake.

"You're just one of those kids, aren't you? One of those filthy schoolkids. What makes you think that you can order me downstairs? Order me, *period*? You and your kids. Snotnose college brats. I'll bet you go to college, don't you?"

"Yes, I do," the girl said. "At night."

"I know what you do at night," crowed the woman. The girl looked toward Elliot, appealing for help. "Night, is it?" It came out like a dirty word. The woman walked backward two steps, still clutching the sweater. "Night's all you're good for, painted up like a whore." She followed the girl's glance toward Elliot, lighting on him with inflamed eyes. "What are you gaping at, mister? You stay out of this. This isn't your fight. And you stop staring at me."

"There isn't any *fight*," the girl said. "Just give me back the sweater."

The woman gave Elliot a wild, triumphant glare and, tilting her head very slightly, carefully spat on the sweater she held bunched in her hand.

"Oh, no," groaned the salesgirl, standing frozen behind the counter.

"Stare at that, mister," the woman said. She dropped the sweater to the floor. "Now I'll try another one on. A real nice one." She thrashed sideways and clutched another sweater from the stack beside her. "This one."

Vera appeared in the doorway beside him, gaping at the woman. "Get the manager, or a clerk, or someone," Elliot said. "Something's wrong with her."

"It ain't wrong with me," the woman shouted at him. "With this store. This little tramp who goes to college." Vera broke from him and disappeared down the line of arcades.

"Listen," Elliot began.

"You listen," she said. "You got no right to tell me what to do, you hippie." Her voice raised to an assertive command, a fishwife's edict. "You can get out, you got no business here. You don't belong up here anyhow, up here in the lady's department. A creep, that's what you are, a creep, a creep, a creep. Go on, get the cops, I know what you are." She closed her mouth like a bulldog, the mad black

hair waggling about her head. "*You.* Don't make me laugh." The
music, now a boy's wail over a strummed guitar, filled in again when
her voice subsided—*I see rain*, sang the boy.

"He thinks he's seen rain," the woman said, more quietly, and
moved forward toward the counter. Before Elliot could reach her—
and just as Vera appeared with a tall broad man in a blue suit, a
salesman's pacifying smile on his face—the woman had reached the
counter and kicked her foot through the glass. Blood welled out
through her stocking, down the thick gray leg. The woman fell
heavily, rolled, scraping her leg against the broken edges of the glass.
Her blood smeared against the disarranged, twisting sweaters within
the counter.

"Where is my son?" she said. "Creeps and bastards. I'm hurt."

The salesman rushed forward. "Lie still," he ordered. "Phyllis, get
me some bandages and tape from the office, and call the police."

"And an ambulance," said Elliot.

"No, just the police, Phyllis." The man turned around from where
he was squatting on the floor beside the woman. "And will all you
people please leave? Everything's in control. Just an incident; just an
accident," he amended. "Nothing to see. Please leave the room."

Elliot took Vera's hand—she was gripping a GIMBELS GRAND
shopping bag—and led her out into the row of arcades. Looking up
from her shocked face, he saw Andy French and Anita Kellerman,
close in talk and seemingly not noticing the knot of people pushing
him and Vera from the enclosure. They paused at a counter stacked
with gloves, lifted a pair striped like racing shoes, smiled at one
another, and continued down the row of counters into the next arcade. Out of the enclosure, the music was quieter, a barely audible
thrumming interleaving with the woman's groans. He led Vera toward the escalator, neither of them speaking.

"Vera isn't used to seeing things like that," Herman said, steering
the Pontiac onto the interstate freeway toward Chicago. "She's always been a tender sort of person, maybe too tender for the sort of
world we're stuck with. I guess she inherits that from me. Tessa has
always been the tough one in our family. I'll tell you, Elliot, marrying

that woman was the best decision I ever made in my life. She's kept me going through all the rough spots. The first time I ever met her, one afternoon at her cousin's house, I could tell that she was the girl I was going to marry. The old man fought it right down the line, down to the bone—he thought I was too young, there was Europe to worry about, and he chewed me out for weeks. Until he met Tessa. She won him right over. The old man, my father, knew a bargain when he saw one. He always liked a woman who could speak her piece. Of course, Kai was the important one, in *his* mind. It would have been the happiest day of his life if he could have gone to Kai's wedding, feeling that there was peace between them."

Herman stopped talking, obviously deep in thought about Kai, and the car sped down the freeway, now dense with cars and trucks going south toward Chicago in the cold morning sunlight. There was a lacing of frost on the edges of the windshield, and snow piled whitely, enormously in the space between the two branches of the freeway and in the long prairielike fields to their sides.

The Pontiac drew up to a toll booth, and Herman tossed the coins into the basket. He rolled up his window again, blowing out steam for a moment.

Herman said. "You remember that guy who went to the Chicago World's Fair a long time ago, or wherever it was, and came back saying, 'I have seen the future and it works'?"

Elliot nodded.

"The only difference between him and us is that we know he was wrong. The past works, not the future. We thought that we were going to go on and on, more and more freeways, more and more cars, more and more money—you name it. Airpanes, solar power. Monorails. Then we wake up and the city is full of crazies, nut cases, lunatics. You can't get out of your house at night. Everybody's scared of something—muggers, rapists. All the papers get to look like *The Police Gazette*. I sometimes wish I'd been born fifty years earlier, so I could have been around in the 1880's. The Gilded Age. The country was about power, making money, expansion—all positives. Then, everybody had some kind of ideal. Things might have been less easier materially, but the country was hopeful—hopeful in a crude way,

but people had values. For wars, what did you have? Teddy Roosevelt charging up San Juan Hill, instead of this Asian mess nobody
understands. Other times, of course, I can tell myself, listen. This is
the most exciting time in the most exciting country in the world.
You got a frontrow seat on history. Problem is, I don't know if I
believe it. But I don't think I could ever leave this country. I don't
mean to offend you—you know that?" He twisted his big head to
look at Elliot.

"Of course I do," Elliot answered. "I just thought there were
things to be learned by living somewhere else. What did you think
when Kai went abroad? Did that bother you?"

Herman grunted with amusement. "Kai always did just what he
wanted to do."

"Good for him," said Elliot.

"I can respect that. What the hell, everybody's got his own life to
live." He tilted his bullish head to regard Elliot. "There's just one
thing I want. That's for Vera to be as happy as any person can be
these days. Does she ever talk about coming home?"

"Now and then," he said. "We both do, Herman. But we've got
jobs and advantages in Paris that we'd have to look for a long time
here. In fact, Vera is probably more at home in Paris than I am—
she speaks perfect French and has a good job at the American College. And we love our house." That wooden extravagance in which
the pipes froze and there were too many rooms, always the threat
of dry rot and damp—it was theirs only by luck. A colleague of
Vera's at the college, Emmet Vevres-Moore, lived in the apartment
next door with his seven children and efficient Ohio wife; when
Poltovnin, the old Russian, had died, Vevres-Moore had shown them
around the old man's crazy palace. They wanted it immediately: the
wandering old apartment was so unlike them. Old Poltovnin had
filled it with elaborate tea services, silver samovars, great wooden
desks stacked with émigré magazines. Editions of Akhmatova and
Pushkin alongside bound copies of *Nature*. Dickens and Trollope
too, on those stout dark shelves. Elliot had first read *Emma* because
Poltovnin's house had held it, and had spent a week carrying the
book to his studio, to rehearsals, to restaurants, reading it all over

again on the day he finished it. Most of these things they had kept, along with a framed copy of the front page of *Combat*, a Resistance paper, with a grainy photograph of Nazi officers stiffly watching a group of Russians herd into a railroad car.

"I worked in one of those flops once," said Herman, pointing his finger toward a Howard Johnson's Motel and Restaurant that was just now slipping over their heads, built across the freeway on an overpass. Herman's hand followed its progress until his finger was pointed at the car's roof. "It wasn't a Howard Johnson's, of course, and it wasn't built spreading its ass over a freeway, but it was the same kind of thing. Longman's Motor Court, out on the old highway fifty-seven. It was owned by the same people, the same family, that put up Longman's Hotel down on Grand Avenue. Old Bing Longman and his kids—the kids, at least the son, still run Longman's. It was one of those motels that was built during the war. Ten-fifteen little block buildings, all white or pink stucco, set up around a parking lot with a central office where the manager stayed. You just had a cot, a stove, and a crapper. Bing Longman was out for the fast buck, and he didn't even put a heater in the manager's cabin. Elliot, managing that motel was a full-time job. You got your rent free, and now and then Longman would pop for a case of beer and a few steaks, just to keep me happy, but I stayed out there from 1939 to 1943. When no one showed up in the cabins in the middle of the week except for some hotpants kid from Racine, I would hightail it into town to see Tessa, but that was just strictly on the quiet. Longman gave me a hundred bucks every Christmas on top of salary, and I thought I was riding the world like a bicycle going downhill. Later, Tessa made me quit and get a job at the Penney's store in town, selling T-shirts and jockstraps. I'll tell you what I was like then. I was jumping around like a kid. Just about your age. I only grew up after I'd been married to Tessa for a couple of years."

Elliot tried to picture a young Herman Glauber—Herman at thirty. He seemed like a man who had always been gentle, slightly ponderous, in one place with a single life.

"I grew up somehow, at least," said Herman, "some because of Tessa and some because of that motel. It was far enough out of town so a lot of the politicians from Plechette City would go out there for a shack-up on the weekends. The best mayor the city ever had, Wilt Zamon, used to come out with a little doll who worked in the Gimbels store on Second Street. And his son, Roy Zamon, would park his car in the woods behind the cabins so his father wouldn't see it." He smiled at Elliot. "I never saw any Denmarks there, if you're worried. But I did see a lot of the kids from the east side—Jimmy Steenborg's boy, the one who died in Guam, Chip Schallspiel, one of the Nieder boys, Ralph, who later got a Silver Star in Germany and came home with one leg and shot himself in his girlfriend's bedroom. All those kids in high school and at Walkins who were just killing time until they got into the war. And there I was, ten years older, running ice to their cabins and cleaning out their shit afterward. With the rich ones especially, you had to get out of bed at five to make sure they didn't get out without paying. Sometimes you'd have to burn the sheets. You never knew what you'd find when you went in to clean up. Twice I found dead cats—one hanging from a lightbulb, one stuck down the toilet. I had to get it out with a knife. I must have called taxis for a hundred girls—black eyes, nosebleeds, faces all bruised up, their clothes torn apart all over the room. They were picked up at dances, usually by servicemen who were so screwed up by boot camp that they had to beat up on something that couldn't hit back. The poor little dopes thought they were going to bed with heroes. In 1940, a guy took a shot at me with a Smith and Wesson .38, and in 1943, another hotwire tried it with a service .45 that put a hole in the plaster you could hide a dog in. Both times I was trying to bust up a fight—you knew something was funny if they turned up Glenn Miller on the radio so loud I could hear it in the cabin. When I hear 'American Patrol' now, I think I'm going to have to shove some bleeding little girl into the showers so she can remember her name and address. Old Bing didn't give a damn what happened as long as we got the money out of their pockets and kept the place out of the papers.

"There's nothing you can name," said Herman, "that I didn't see or have to clean up afterward. My war. I'd read the newspapers in that rotten little cabin and see the pictures of the generals—Patton with his boots and pistols, that dictator, that fraud MacArthur, counting how many days until he'd be President—Willie and Joe washing their socks in their helmets—and in the morning I'd have to wash some GI's shit off the wall where he wrote 'Fuck You' with it. 'Kilroy Was Here.' If I could have met Kilroy, I would've strangled him. Who the hell else but Kilroy would hang a cat in a motel room? Or beat up dumb little girls from the farms who felt sorry for you? They thought if they could open themselves up wide enough, they could win the war."

Herman squeezed the Pontiac out from behind a truck and pushed his foot heavily on the accelerator. They cut across two lanes, the innocent white fields reflecting the sun seeming to career toward them, and swung into the farthest lane. Ahead were the turnoffs for the outer suburbs, doll villages on the left horizon, set down on the fields like tumbled blocks.

"I'll tell you how I lost my job at the motel. I quit, but it wasn't just because Tessa wanted me to work in town. I quit because I was going to be fired. They had my ass on a griddle.

"I told you about Wilt Zamon," he said, "a man I admired. He was an honest mayor and a good man, a man a lot like my father. He was liked and respected in every part of the city, except maybe the east side. Wilt got all his training in the unions, and that was a rough way to grow up, during the thirties. You had all the unions fighting with themselves, and the manufacturers fighting them. Some very hard boys came out of that situation. Anyhow, Zamon was a mayor when he used to come to the motel. Roy Zamon, his son, was about twenty-five, twenty-six then—the handsomest man I ever saw. He had a big curly head of hair, and shoulders on him like an ox. Roy had a closetful of medals. In those days, early in the war, you saw his name in the paper every other week. And he used to write a column back to the *Herald* about what the war was like, what the GI's were doing. Willie-and-Joe stuff, but people loved it. In April 1942, he came home with his left foot blown off but he got fitted out with an artificial foot and he was all over the *Herald* again. Mostly the social columns, but he also was busy making speeches all over town, VFW, the Legion halls, the Polish-American League. If he'd run for office in town, he would have won hands down. I used to read about him like anyone else. I guess I envied him. He couldn't do anything wrong. I always thought he was a little stupid—his speeches were just the usual wave-the-flag stuff—but he had enough glamour to put on a Broadway show all by himself, and if you stuck wires into him he'd light up the theater too. Well, the first time he came out to the motel he checked in with a soldier—I figured they were going to have a big party, so I told him to keep the noise down. Mr. Zamon, I said. He gave me a look that would grill a hamburger and pointed to the register. 'Mr. Clark,' he said. 'Mr. Bill Clark.' And that was the name he signed under. 'You call me anything else and I'll knock your teeth out for you.' Then he pulled his car around to the back of the cabins where no one could see it and he and the soldier went inside. They stayed in there two days, just going out for some food and a couple of bottles. When he checked out he gave me ten dollars over the tab and asked me my name. When I told him, he grabbed me by the necktie and said, 'Glauber boy, keep your mouth shut, or you'll be sorry.' Real gangster stuff. Then that big war-hero smile that was in the papers.

"You have to understand Wilt Zamon to understand what happened next," Herman said. "He loved his kid so much he couldn't stop talking about him. Zamon used to put his son into his campaign pictures, he made speeches about 'our fighting men,' all that kind of thing. Any scandal would have ruined him. And it did, eventually. Roy probably came out to the motel nine or ten times, each time with a different soldier, when he wasn't smart enough to go fifty miles down old fifty-seven to the next joint—he thought he could get away with anything anyhow. Where he went when he didn't come out there, I don't know, but I know he used to cruise the bars on the weekends, and he couldn't have gone without any too often. I guess he didn't understand rumors, that you can't kill them once they're started. No matter how many girls he got himself photographed with, he couldn't stop people's tongues. There wasn't much talk, you understand, but by 1943 there was enough to get back to Wilt. Wilt called Bing Longman and asked him about it. Old Bing denied everything. I can hear him do it, he was so smooth. Then Bing got out to me and asked me about it. I said I'd never seen Roy Zamon, whether with a girl, with a man, or with a sheep—that I hadn't seen him at all. Well, that was my mistake. I lied to protect that bastard, and in the end it bounced back on me. Wilt hired a detective to follow his son, and they got pictures of him driving in there. Must have been quite a scene in the mayor's house *that* day. Wilt must have been too ashamed to tell Roy that he'd had him followed, because Roy came back with blood in his eye, threatening to kill me. He thought I'd blown the whistle to his father. I talked with him for an hour and got out of it with no more than the black eye he gave me when he busted through the door. I had a gun under the counter, but I didn't want to bring it out: he would have grabbed it away in a second, gimpy or not gimpy. The next thing I knew both Roy and his father called Longman, ordering him to fire me. Wilt said to give me a thousand dollars to keep my mouth shut; you can imagine what Roy said. So I quit instead. I wouldn't take the money. And about a year later Roy was caught by the cops in something a lot funnier than an illegal card game, although that was all the papers said, and Wilt Zamon dropped dead at his desk, still holding the telephone. Roy got off with a fine, and left town after his father's funeral—he had guts enough to go to that, I'll say that for him, but he just vanished somewhere. He just went into thin air. California, they said.

"And here's the real ending to the story," said Herman. "When I was thinking of running for alderman for the Richmond Corners area, Bing Longman got in touch with me and offered to pay my campaign fees. If it hadn't been for that, I probably couldn't have afforded to run, not without mortgaging my soul. It's a screwy world."

"It's a good story, anyhow," said Elliot.

The interstate freeway had melted into a series of expressways dividing Chicago, and Herman crossed two lanes in the heavy traffic, horns erupting around them, to get onto the wide belt expressway going south along the lakefront, backed by miles of hotels and offices. The city looked deeply rubbed in grime, a heavy gray layer on the facades; to their left, the lake was an upthrown gray rib, a frozen curve.

"It's a better story now than it was then." Herman looked toward Elliot, his meaty face good-natured. "All that business out at the motel taught me one thing—you can't interfere with what people are. You can't change them. There's too much insanity in the way people live, too much unreason in the world. If you have some kind of design, you have to chip away at it, settling for expedients. Increments. But with your own family, I guess you always want something more than that. Listen, Elliot: the last thing I want to do is interfere between you and Vera."

"Yes?" said Elliot, surprised. "What is it?."

"She's been looking tense to me, the past few days. Tense and unhappy. Vera shouldn't be that way. Is it being home that does it to her?"

"No, Herman, not at all," Elliot said. "Of course not. It's probably this Nun's Wood confusion—my father working against you. They've asked me to become involved, and that's what is making Vera tense."

"Who is they? Chase? His sidekicks, Hilda Usenbrugge and that Bender fireball from Wiltshire Drive?"

"I suppose so, yes. And Pierce Laubach. They sent me a statement they want me to sign. I've been meaning to talk with you about it since it came, but I've never had the time. I wasn't sure how to bring it up."

Herman wiped his hand over his face, grinning. "Hell, go ahead and sign it. You can probably guess what I think of Chase's position, but what the hell? He's your father. I don't care if you sign the statement. I'll fix it up with Tessa. Everybody does what he has to do."

He looked over at Elliot again. "The battle is really over, anyhow, as far as I can see. We just have to get through the public hearing. Some speeches, a little ruckus, and it will be all over. In the past few weeks, I've got nearly a majority of the council with me. They'll go for the rezoning just to get me off their backs. The clincher will be the black vote, Jeff Glee and his two acolytes. Nobody knows which way they might jump. If they give Nay votes, we're blocked from rezoning. If they go Aye or Abstain, we're in. So we got two chances out of three." He smiled to himself. "Elliot, get that business off your mind. You got Ted Edwards to worry about now. We're almost at the studio."

chapter 14

Driving back from Chicago on the freeway, Herman sat silent beside him. His remarks on the Ted Edwards show had surprised them both, and clearly wounded and perplexed Herman. Edwards had begun by asking, "Mr. Denmark, does serious music have any relevance to us today? Aren't most modern composers simply working in a vacuum?" Facing the red eye of the camera, Elliot had unexpectedly relaxed: the question was so predictable, so various in its possibilities, that he had immediately shed his nervousness, the sense that he, sitting before the artificial background of a sitting room—a plaster wall painted to look like brick, a painted fire in a painted fireplace—was contingent, an accidental presence which could only simulate opinions and arguments. He had felt this unreality when Edwards had come into the dressing room where a girl was smoothing makeup into his face. Edwards stood behind them, smiling into the mirror at Elliot. "I'm Ted Edwards. Welcome to the catacombs. Denmark, your bit is fifteen-twenty minutes. Just a friendly chat about music, Plechette City, anything interesting. You get me?" His face was a shock: tauter and older than it appeared on the screen, smoothly suntanned, a corrupt face, just on the verge of disintegration. *Ronnie Upp*, Elliot had thought. His eyes, nostrils and mouth were all the same dark shape, as if they had been slit in his mask with a razor. "I think I get you, yes," Elliot said, unwittingly repeating Edwards' words. "All right, then, let's make it a knockers-up show. If you tighten up, I'll get you out of it, okay?" At Elliot's nod, he vanished from the mirror, and the girl's fingers resumed coolly rubbing the makeup into his face. Elliot saw that she had a small blue star tattooed on the back of her left wrist. Her breasts grazed the back of his head.

"It's just a competition thing," the girl said. "Don't worry about it. It only lasts fifteen minutes anyway."

"Did it hurt when you got your tattoo?" he asked, fascinated by its appearance and disappearance in the mirror.

"I didn't feel a thing," she said. "I was flying the whole time. I was real relaxed."

Elliot looked up at the girl's face in the mirror: wide, permanently startled eyes, a broad businesslike chin. He remembered the girls Herman had told him about, bedded and beaten by soldiers in motel rooms.

"Could you get me a job in music?" she said.

Seated near Ted Edwards on the couch between the cameras and the pasteboard wall, Elliot could see Edwards' face adjust itself to the unseen presence of his viewers; the razor slits in his face opened and formed questions, the man's brown mask signaling for the camera to roll toward him. Then he had talked—endlessly, it seemed. Edwards' face had changed during Elliot's long answers. *I'm serious*, it had signaled, *observe me listening*. Talking, Elliot could still feel on his face the girl's smoothing fingers: he was relaxed.

But what had he said? It had come out in such a rush, all that talk.

The first half of the interview had been easy.

"I don't know how you guys do it," said Herman. "I guess I'm just stupid. The average guy, he can't make head or tail of what you were saying about music. It has no meaning to him, what you were saying. The average guy hears a tune, he tries to hum it, and that's it."

"You could understand it if it were your job," said Elliot.

"Well, maybe. Spirals?"

"Oh, Herman, I was just talking. Gassing." This was a hidden reference to what he had said about Nun's Wood, and Herman took it up.

"Well, plenty of gassing is what I'm going to have to do with Tessa."

This time they passed the Howard Johnson's Motel without comment. Elliot switched on the radio as they sped through the flatland, and for a time they listened in silence to country music, songs about heartbreak and divorce and drunkenness. The flat white country layered out on both sides of the freeway.

"You should try writing this kind of stuff someday," Herman advised. "Then I'll expect a Rolls-Royce for a birthday present."

Both were grateful that Elliot was moving the next day from the Glauber home.

"I'll have to sort of warm Tessa up for the showing," Herman said.

For the twentieth time, Elliot stared at the blue wall: it was of a flat shining blue that looked metallic, like a tinted skin of aluminum. "Your father and I wanted to brighten your old room up a bit," Margaret had said. "We didn't take anything out except for some of that old furniture you had in the Walkins School, but we had the room repainted, and then had these bookshelves installed. Chase loves that blue. Don't you?"

"It's very contemporary," he said.

"*Tant pis,*" Vera muttered behind him.

"What was that, Vera dear?"

"Suits me," she answered.

Now Elliot lay back in his bed staring at the blank shining skin of the wall while Vera silently took her clothes from her suitcase and hung them in the closet. *His* bed was familiar, despite the new mattress he could feel beneath him, but the companion bed across the room was not. His stereo components, lovingly assembled while he was in high school, were now concealed behind a sliding panel, as were his old records. Elliot had been agreeably surprised that his old stereo system still worked. *Petroushka* was now uncoiling into the room: he had always loved the beginning, two trumpets playing in different triads.

The new blue wall, the new bed, the new wallpaper, the tubular and the ovoid lamps, the glass table: clearly, his room was now a guestroom. It struck him as a feeble pun that he should now be its guest. The bed's guest, the wall's guest. His parents had taken his books from the carved and battered old bookshelf and arranged them by size on long sleek shelves mounted to the wall. Thus spread and scattered and interspersed by vases, pots of ivy, a bust of Freud (*Freud?*), his childhood and prep-school books had lost their look of familiarity and seemed vulnerable, open to judgment. Old textbooks, science fiction, Sinclair Lewis and John Steinbeck, biographies of Mozart and Beethoven, *Generation of Vipers, Le Grand Meaulnes, Conversations with Stravinsky*. They had the look of books in a library, of the unopened volumes in an advertisement for shelves.

Yet the room was his. It reminded him, by the disposition of its volumes, by its dimensions, of his childhood. The boy he had been hovered within his consciousness; a thinner self inhabited his body. Old Ladnier bending his strict white face to say *Clumsy, but you are capable of better. At least that.* He began to think of school. In those years he had been intense, happy, moderately popular. He had at times been cruel or offhand to other boys, but such behavior was almost encouraged by the school—the caste system at Walkins was heartless. In senior school, the prefects were always the tallest, blondest, most Anglo-Saxon of the boys, the earnest athletes, dullards. Lawrence Wooster was one of these: the masters had loved him, especially those who were ardent football fans. Wooster had been able to throw long accurate passes. Later, he had played for a year at Brown. Elliot could remember Wooster gently opening the top of his desk during French class, peeking at the crib sheets he had hidden within. Elliot had spent over five years with most of his friends from Walkins, and with a handful, all twelve years of his schooling there—within three years, he was seeing only two. The two old classmates who remained still his friends were William Pittman, now a twice-divorced novelist living in Alicante with three cats and a sixteen-year-old German girl, and Minor Van Blank, a brilliant student who had earned a Ph.D. in economics at Harvard in three years and was now making a fortune in consultation fees. He was on the board of a New York bank, and could outplay Elliot at the piano. When Elliot was in New York, they played four-handed duets. Pittman hated music, and talked with Elliot mostly about his wives; Van Blank could talk about anything. Apart from women, they were his closest friends. He quickly banished the image of Anita: too complex a problem for the moment—and Vera, closing the closet doors, was tense and hostile.

Too complex. No, that would not do. Yet he could not think about Anita now. Vera was sitting by the little mahogany desk, another new acquisition whose guest he was, glumly looking toward the window. In a moment, he thought, she will ask what am I thinking. Elliot knew that the quarrel was not serious: Vera was angry primarily for her mother's sake, and that was not motive enough for a drastic bitterness. But the lower part of her face was set like a statue's.

He closed his eyes, and was swept over by the sensation of being back in his old room: another deflection. The unaltered volume around him seemed to shrink to the size of his body. His fingers grazed the wallpaper. He began to remember a story his father told about Mr. Von Heilitz, an old man who had been their neighbor during the forties. Then he remembered another thing about the man. Chase had once killed Von Heilitz's dogs, two wheezing and odorous spaniels, who had been sleeping in the Denmark driveway when his father had backed out of the garage in the morning. Mr. Von Heilitz had raced to the end of his hedge and fallen on his knees at the bottom of the driveway. His white jacket had soaked a little in the blood. Elliot, running from the house, saw with horrified fascination the crumpled animals, the blood draining down to Mr. Von Heilitz's white-trousered knees. Chase had detested the two dogs, as Von Heilitz knew. When he opened his eyes, he was looking at the blue wall.

"What are you thinking about?" Vera asked.

"About my father," he said. "During the war, he ran over two horrible old dogs that belonged to a neighbor of ours. He killed

them. It was an accident, but the neighbor, an old man named Lamont Von Heilitz, wouldn't believe it, even though he knew the
dogs had been asleep in our driveway. He thought it had something
to do with his being German."

"That sounds like your family." A grim smile, and a scorching
glance. Meaning: anyone connected with you could deliberately run
over a dog.

"And before that I was thinking about Walkins—about school."

"A real little orgy of nostalgia, wasn't it?"

"I suppose it was." He was determined not to be provoked by
Vera, who had the right to some bitterness. "There was a cat named
Moorish, the school mascot, that used to pace around the halls and
the school grounds like one of the masters. It was a huge black
creature. The smaller kids were traditionally afraid of him. I just
remembered now that one day in geometry class I saw Moorish going
very slowly across the front lawn toward a sea gull—he kept to the
edge of the bushes, and then sort of circled in toward him. At the
last possible second, he leapt at the bird; flew at him, really, and
pinned him down with one paw. The sea gull fought and tried to
escape, but Moorish had him captured. In twenty seconds he had
him ripped from top to bottom. The bird exploded feathers like a
burst pillow. And in ten minutes the sea gull was absolutely gone—
nothing left of him—just eaten up. All you could see was a perfect
ring of white feathers on the lawn. I was the only person who saw
it. For weeks afterward, I had dreams about it: a black thing devouring a white thing. Ugh."

She bent her head to the desk.

"I also just remembered a funny story about old Von Heilitz and
my father. Do you want to hear it?" Any conversation was good.
Drain off the tension in chatter.

"Elliot, did you *have* to talk about that Nun's Wood business on
the program? In front of my father?"

"He knew what my opinion was. I told you that. We talked about
it on the way down."

"That wasn't enough," she said, and he knew what she meant. It
was not enough for Tessa. Tessa had not been prepared. Herman

had tried to cushion Elliot's apostasy, but Tessa had not let herself be assuaged. "You aren't with us?" she said, her face strained and her voice high and incredulous. "You're not on Herman's side in this? Why didn't you tell us?" Then, at last, he had pulled the crumpled statement from his pocket and smoothed it out on the table. "And you actually talked about it on television?" She is overdoing it, he thought, but a look at her shocked face had dispelled the idea that she was acting. "It wasn't for very long," Herman rumbled. "Just a couple of minutes at the end." "Five minutes," he said. *"Five minutes!"*—as though the number of minutes he had spoken of Nun's Wood would be reckoned at the last judgment. "Calm down, Tessa, we talked about it in the car." "Nobody talked to *me* about it," she cried . . . on it had gone, Herman pacing around the kitchen, Tessa standing sternly by the table where he was seated, Vera nervously watching. "He was going to tell you about it, Mother," she broke in, "but Elliot didn't know for a long time if he was going to sign. He was under a lot of pressure." "Pressure," retorted Tessa. "What you two know about pressure wouldn't boil an egg." The evening had spent itself somehow. At dinner, Vera and her father carrying a limping conversation, Tessa had said, "You never understood what Herman's job has been. How could you? You gave up the only job you ever had." He had blazed out at her. Then raged at himself, and at his childishness in allowing himself to be provoked. "Well, I suppose I can't wait to see what Elliot actually said," Tessa crooned, "if he feels so wrought up by it." She smiled a wounded smile.

"She was defending my father," Vera said. "I know she was upset, but that was only because she thought she had to protect my father's feelings."

Elliot could feel the tension draining away into the ordinariness of talk.

"But I do think it was inexcusable of you to bring up Nun's Wood on a television program."

"Sweetheart, I didn't bring it up. He did."

"You didn't have to talk about it."

"He tricked me," Elliot said. "I feel like a fool admitting it, but that's the truth. We were going on talking about music, and then right at the end of my time, he sprang it on me. I fell right into it."

Vera went across the room to her own bed and lay down. "That ghastly wall," she said. "I hope it doesn't shine in the dark. Did you really see a cat eat a sea gull?" She tilted her head to look at him. "Then why didn't you do something to stop it?"

"I was inside a building. It was the middle of a geometry class. I like cats more than I like sea gulls." He closed his eyes again and rubbed his fingertips against the wallpaper. The blue of the wall lay like a veil within his eyelids: against it, he saw the ring of white feathers.

Elliot went downstairs soon after, relieved that the worst was over, and that it had been so easy. He wanted nonetheless to get out of his parents' house. The rooms downstairs were too thick with his past, clamorous with old responsibilities. He wandered from the smaller living room (his wedding picture on an end table, he striding—with what assumption of knowledge!—down the church aisle, Vera leggy, elegant, shining with hope, beside him), where he toyed for a moment with the piano, across the hall to the dining room, then up into the large-windowed room that looked out over Lake Michigan. The fireplace was roaring and crackling: logs tumbled together, blazing. The room was terribly hot. Elliot went to the windows and looked out at the dim lake, three hundred yards down the wooded bank and across the expressway. It looked vast and somehow depthless, like an endless plane of indeterminate pale blue, cold to the touch.

Margaret's "office," where she devised the week's menus and figured the household accounts, a small skylit glassy chamber filled with ivy and green creeping plants, was an alcove fixed like an insect to the back of the house on the second floor. In summer sixteen years ago, water-skiing behind the Van Blanks' speedboat, he could look up to his house and see his mother bent at her desk, the steel-rib supports of the shell's exterior gleaming as though they were molten. In that dazzle, the plants had seemed a solidity, a protection against gravity.

Now the tangled profuse greenery against the glass reversed his sense of the exterior: the great dim lake, framed by leaves, was a Japanese painting.

"Are you all unpacked?" Margaret asked, putting down her pen. "Is Vera feeling better?"

"Yes to both questions," he said.

"And your room is not too much of a shock? It's a guestroom now, of course, but it's still most importantly your room."

"I like the change," he said, grinning.

"Comfortable?"

"I'm sure we will be."

"At least you are not shunted off on the west side of town anymore." She had a tucked-in, curiously gratified smile. "Your crotchety old parents will be able to see you."

"That will be nice. I do have to fit in my rehearsals and the concert, however." He liked the way she looked now: strikingly pretty for her age, with her tender powdery face full of confidence for him.

"You'll have no problems with your concert. You're not really worried about it, are you?" Behind her head, the leaves broke the lake into a million ice-blue shards. The sun glittered for a moment on the seams and edges.

"A little," he confessed.

"Vera will be coming down later?"

"Sure." He did not wish to begin discussing the television program, and did not amplify on Vera's condition, though it was clear that Margaret wanted him to. The sunlight along the chips of lake made him stretch restlessly in his chair.

"We all have some little insecurity," said his mother. "When you see your father tonight, be sure to compliment him on his suit. My car is downstairs, if you want to take it somewhere. I had it filled up and washed this morning."

He would not go to Anita's house. She was a white uncertain lucency in his consciousness, a troubling presence. What were his responsibilities? It was a difficult question. Anita had presented a closed face to him—or so it now seemed—when he had last talked to her. That afternoon, and the memory of Andy and Anita pausing at a counter in the frantic pre-Christmas Gimbels Grand, their heads together, a suggestion of great closeness. It was as though she were willing him to think about her. Elliot felt as though he were physically being pushed back into the sensations of four years before: as if, over a great distance, he were being manipulated by her. He knew that she expected him to come to her house, and that when he arrived she would confound him once again.

He turned the car onto the entrance to the lakefront expressway; now he was long past the turnoff to Windmere Court and Leecham Street. He felt a twinge of guilt like a dentist's gentle prodding of a drill into a diseased tooth. His responsibilities clung. A flock of sea gulls dipped like a cloud over his car and settled on the tennis courts in the little park alongside the expressway. When the lights changed, he gunned the engine and fitted smoothly into the line of cars.

Aimlessly he followed the traffic as it swept around the War Memorial. The architect's extruded planes and angles seemed to tilt precariously toward him, slabs and edges brilliantly honed. In the forecourt stood the black glossy monolith carved with lists of names. When the car before his turned sharply left to enter the parking lot, he impulsively followed. He took the car through the gates, parked it, and walked back along a cleanly shoveled path to the pool and the monolith. The weather report on the radio had said that the temperature was twelve degrees, but in his short walk to the terrace, Elliot felt that it could not be so cold. His heels rang on the pavement, his breath ascended in clouds. When he reached the pool, he saw that it had been drained, and that the monolith was upended in a ruck of pulped newspapers, sandwich bags, soda bottles. He scanned the names for one he recognized. Capt. Charles W. Steenborg, between Capt. David Stedman and Lt. Horace F. Steermayer. Dead, they were soldiers for eternity. No Denmarks were named on the giant slab. His ears had begun to ache with the cold. Which of these had beaten the girls Herman Glauber laundered and sent home?

Slapping his hands together, he wandered slowly back along the path toward the parking lot. I know what I'll do, he thought: I'll visit Kai. He felt an overwhelming curiosity, compounded with respect, for the old survivor.

chapter 15

From the War Memorial he drove south, following the tracks of
the old tram line down First Street all the way, past the cream-
colored brick of the huge Mother Beilburg bakery, a series of stolid
red brick apartment buildings that housed secretaries who worked
in south-side offices and aged immigrant couples, Lithuanians, Poles,
and Latvians, then past body shops and gasoline stations, small brick
machine shops, the Curtis Etheridge shoe factory, and by then he
was descending Mitchell Avenue past gray buildings, and there was
a bitter smell of chocolate in the air from the chocolate factory.
Mitchell Avenue continued its descent into the valley. Elliot could
see ahead of him the great turning faces of the Chambers Denmark
clock, a golden ornament above the tops of buildings; then he was
truly in the valley and the buildings closed in about him, concealing
the clock. Here the factories were dense, and the smell of chocolate
was overtaken by something grittier, a smell more urban and metallic. For Elliot, it was this odor, hot and bronzy, which meant *city:*
when he was at Columbia he had breathed it in the IRT stops, and
felt at once at home.

Crammed in the streets between the factories were the tenements—
these of a red brick so deeply stained as to be a dense dark brown—
and small bright eateries, passed-over shops and family groceries,

drugstores and movie theaters, of the Puerto Ricans. Elliot's first impulse was to push down the locks of the car doors, as his father had always done when driving through the fourth ward, and he smiled at this reflex. A brown Santa Claus rang a bell outside Woolworth's. Elliot turned onto MacArthur Avenue at the Pérez-Ricardo Loan Company office, which had plastered on its facing wall an enormous poster for Jefferson Glee. The earnest raccoonlike eyes peered out of the smooth face; one plump hand had removed the alderman's gold spectacles and held them, in a lawyer's pose, a little lower than his chin. RE-FLECT GLEE. Beneath, someone had spray-painted the words BURN WHITEY. The poster was torn at the bottom, revealing an ocher strip of side wall.

He turned left again at the next stoplight, and was now on Ward Street, where fifty years ago Polish newcomers, then the inhabitants of the valley, had built an incongruous street of white frame houses with fifteen-foot lawns and white picket fences. Kai's room was in the third of these houses: they had all been broken into tiny rooms and apartments, and Kai shared his house with the sons and daughters and various cousins and aunts of the Méndez family.

Elliot parked before the house and opened the gate. Even here, on this deceptive quiet street, the odor of factories was in the air, a thin bitter acridity. He rang Kai's bell. The door was immediately opened by a thin black-haired teenage girl in a dark leatherlike coat. She eyed him thoroughly, making no signs of recognition. He could not remember if he had seen the girl before. "Miss Méndez?" he said.

The girl nodded, moving her mouth about her chewing gum. "What you want?" she asked. "We paid the insurance last week."

"I'm not here about the insurance. I came to see Mr. Glauber. Is he in?"

"The old man's always in." She stepped back, allowing him to enter. "I'm just goin' out. You know where his room is?"

"Second floor, on the left," he said. "Okay?"

"Okay," she said. "Go on up." She gave him a rapid, smirking look and sidled through the door.

He went up the dark stairs and knocked on Kai's door. There

was only silence from the room. He knocked again, saying, "Uncle Kai, it's Elliot." When the sounds he had made dropped like stones into the silent room, he slumped with dejection. Another series of knocks had the same result. One more try before I leave, he thought: he may be asleep. He reached his hand toward the doorknob and touched it. The door parted silently from its frame and swung inward. The room was dark. Elliot could make out only the rigid silvery outline of Kai's desk. "Uncle Kai," he whispered, knowing that the old man was not there. A faint odor of age and perspiration drifted to his nostrils.

He stepped within and groped for the light switch. When he had found it and seen his shadow leap instantly to the wall, he turned to look into the room: his heart was accelerating, and he realized that he had thought, at some inner depth, that he might find Kai dead. But Kai was not in the room; the cot, neatly and tautly made up, was empty. Elliot groaned. He had been looking forward more than he knew to a long talk with Kai; at the moment, Kai seemed to possess some answer that would resolve his dilemma. From the ironic mouth, stitched in the upper lip with pain, would come some clear unsentimental phrase. Elliot was tired: the morning's move to his parents' house, a chilly Tessa supervising, had been a drain on his emotions, on his control. He closed the door, went toward the desk, and sat heavily, his topcoat still about him, in the chair. Kai would soon return. A minute later he shed his coat and threw it over the cot. The drapes were closed, as he had always seen them, and the room's atmosphere, hot and unfresh, seemed to settle upon his shoulders, in his hair. He turned to rest his elbows on the desk. The high old typewriter and the square pile of yellow paper were the sole objects on its surface. It looked just as it had when he and Vera had been in this room the week before. Even the stack of yellow paper seemed the same size. There were no signs of occupation or labor, no pencils or erasers, no notepapers, no file cards. It came to him again: he did not believe in Kai's book. Kai probably arranged, noted, wrote a few words each day, knowing that he would never truly finish.

Elliot looked at the metal filing cabinet beside the desk. He could confirm his suspicions with one glance, if the cabinet were unlocked. He glanced up at the top-right-hand corner and saw the key inserted in the holder: the cabinet was unlocked. Should he look? It was unfair to the old man to bare his secret, his self-deceit; but it could make no difference to how he felt about Kai. In fact, looking into the file might clear his suspicions by revealing an actual manuscript. He was rationalizing. This embarrassed him. What he wanted to do was to look into the file. His curiosity was enormous. Why not look? He pulled the chair toward the cabinet, scraping its legs along the floor, and pulled out the drawer labeled MSS.

Leaning over and peering into it, he saw only a flat yellow folder, untitled. He pulled it out and looked at it, then bent back the outer cover of the folder. Within was a much older folder, marked with water spots, small brown stains, the impress of a boot heel. The pencil lines were so faint that at first he could not see them; then, detecting the thin light lines, he squinted and read them. *Notes on Faust.* His heart plummeted. He turned back the covering. Inside the two folders were thirty yellowing pages, each numbered at the top. These too were covered by the faint markings of the pencil, and when he looked closely enough at one of the pages, he saw that the writing was in German.

Elliot tilted back his head and exhaled. Kai had not done any work on his book for twenty-five years. It was all an invention. He dropped the folder back into the drawer and closed it. The bleakness—Kai's bitter winter landscape—seemed utter, completed. There was no comfort to be given or received. Elliot felt horribly depressed. He stood up, pushing back the chair, and moved to the windows. He pulled the drapes apart. A cold gray light streamed into the room. The tiny backyard of the Méndez home, gray snow flecked with black, ended at a white fence a few yards from a solid black wall—the back of a factory. Pipes and fire escapes, an elaborate geometry crested with white. At the back of the little yard stood a Bernadette grotto, leftover from the Poles. Sparrows hopped erratically on the dirty snow. He pulled the drapes together and went back to the chair.

There was one more chance. Perhaps Kai kept his typescript in

one of the other drawers. He opened the CORRESPONDENCE—
GOETHE drawer. This was surprisingly full. He pulled out the thick
top folder: it was filled with typed letters in German, most of them
with university letterheads. Herr Professor Schiff, Herr Professor
Fuerst, Herr Professor Lieberbalt: Heidelberg, Bonn, Freiburg. The
letters were dated from 1951 to 1955. In the next folder, the dates
began in 1949 and ended in 1951. Below this was another fat folder.
He squared the papers and inserted the top two folders back into
the drawer. The dating was decidedly odd: it suggested that Kai had
continued to make scholarly inquiries long after he had abandoned
work on the book itself, and that he had abandoned even this spade-
work fifteen years ago.

Only one drawer was left. The PERSONAL label deterred Elliot
for only a moment. Having gone so far, he thought, I might as well
finish it. "Poor old Kai," he whispered. Yet how could he pity the
old man? In the general muddle, he had come through with at least
an intact surface. The number of consolations one could expect the
world to grant seemed to shrink with each decade. For Kai, perhaps
simply to go on living was labor enough.

He pulled open the lower file and looked into it. No manuscript
was within. At the bottom of the drawer lay an oddly familiar brown
leather box with tooled sides and cover. His memory fumbled, then
caught: his grandmother Denmark, a straight uncompromising
woman with perfect eyesight and black hair when in her seventies,
had owned such a box to hold thread, needles, pins—none of these
had he ever seen her use. Even the raised pattern of the lid felt
familiar to his fingers. The leather box was surprisingly light in his
hand, as if it were empty. He put it on his knees and lifted the lid.

The bottom of the box was covered with old photographs. There
seemed to be about twenty or thirty of these, yellowed and in-curling.
At first they appeared to be all the same picture. He picked up a
handful and turned toward the desk. There, looking more carefully,
he saw the differences. In most of them, a young man was posed
against an emphatic background: Elliot recognized the Paris loca-
tions, the tower, the Trocadéro, the steep steps of the Sacré-Coeur
In other photographs, the young man was in the garden of what

seemed to be an Italian villa, or at the Schoenbrunn, or outside the Pitti Palace or leaning elegantly against an open automobile. In some of the pictures the young man was Kai, young and dark-haired, broad and deep in the chest, his face split with health and content- ment; in others the young man was Harrison Upp, an intense- looking muscular man in lounge suits and Sea Island sweaters. He was only barely recognizable as the boozy acquaintance of Lake Point Drive. One of the photographs showed a spider monkey perched on his shoulders, the country beyond a veiled distance which must have been Tuscany. In several of the photographs, the two young men appeared together, standing loosely beside a river or a *Schloss*, their arms about one another's shoulders: in these pictures, especially those located in the gardens of the villa, the two young men shirtless, there was an almost unbearable sense of overwhelming physical satisfac- tion. The young Kai looked out at him from his unlined face, happy and (he saw) even then doomed by the ten years yet to come. Elliot dropped the photographs back in the box, the box back in the file. He could no longer stay in the room while Kai might return.

The face of the young man Kai had been flamed in his mind as he slammed the door to the stuffy little room and double-jumped the stairs down to the front door and the street. None of the usually unavoidable and gregarious Méndez family appeared, a small favor for which he was grateful. The face was wide open, as open as a sun; it was not mere contentment which had set that expression there, of a blessing given and conferred; it was, blindingly, the face of love. Elliot's bowels were tremulous, scalding. Was that the face Vera had seen six years ago, when he had unlocked the door to Jaeger's kitchen, the face she had questioned night after night for assurance? It was a bitter proof that these moments passed, that loss endures, cruel and natural as winter. He could not go much longer without seeing Anita again. And how had Harrison Upp's face looked, what was its expression? Nerviness, tautness, gloom and with it, something like mastery. The face of an uneasy king. The kind of man who would wear a pistol near his heart. Wingbeats loudly di- vided the air, as of a flight of angels. A monstrous possibility beat in on him, a mad speculation that had the force of Truth. He *must*

talk to Anita, and talk to her alone, without Andy French: her violent face seemed turned against him.

He turned the car up second Street at the traffic lights. Soon the
factories had vanished behind him, and the shops were boarded, their
facades still scarred by fire. The Gimbels marquee hung useless over
chained doors; up to the third floor most of the windows had been
broken into sawteeth or stars. Each breath brought to him the heavy
odor of chocolate.

"We all have to act on faith," his father was saying, his voice a shade
more playful than usual, "though of course we must exercise a fair
degree of scrupulosity in defining its objects. It is a secular world,
despite the efforts of men like my good friend Father Squier. He,
by the way, has taken to allusions to the Diamond Sutra and the
Upanishads in his sermons, and I must say it makes for an improve-
ment. I was getting a little weary of the I-Thou relationship and the
existential moment. Won't you take some more wine, Vera dear? I
can recommend it." He offered the bottle, Robert having vanished
momentarily into the kitchen, and delicately poured two inches into
Vera's glass. "Some examples. Elliot has faith in his music, in music,
in general. Just think of Bach, of Beethoven or Schubert, all of those
elitist sensibilities scratching their way through day after grubby day,
surviving only because of some persistent voice inside repeating *I, I,
I.* Elliot's friend Pittman, scribbling away in his hovel at yet another
unreadable would-be masterpiece: *I, I.*" Margaret made a wry face
at Elliot from across the table. "Elliot has to have faith in orchestras
and musicians. They at least are external to him."

"I like Pittman's novels," said Vera.

"Not quite the universal response, I gather, but more power to
you. My problem may be that I was overexposed to Pittman the
adolescent, a pimple-laden jangly bundle of neuroses, when he and
Elliot were classmates at Walkins, and consequently I cannot be serious about those massive heroes he puts in his books."

"Pittman is," Elliot said, smiling.

"Please," said Margaret.

"Think of Bobby Seale bound and gagged in a courtroom. Perhaps these things don't happen in Paris, but it is these terrible events which comprise the real experience of our moment in history. We owe a responsibility to such events, to our own moments—novels cannot keep up with our responsibilities. From what I understand of Vera's uncle, Kai Glauber, I think that he would understand me." He smiled at his son. "And you are dying to point out, Elliot, that this too is merely another faith."

"Well, *I* don't understand you when you talk this way," said his mother. "I don't think responsibilities are so abstract. And I wish you wouldn't sound so pompous when you explain your ideas."

"He's talking about unselfish awareness," said Vera, breaking in. Her illumination seemed to falter.

"Beautifully put."

"And he's implying that . . . oh, I don't know. That artists are selfish, and that old verities and values are obsolete. Like living for God or for a family, or for a job—"

"I think you are extending what I said too far, my dear. We can still pick and choose among objects for faith. Some things still stand. Teddy Wilson's piano. Scarlatti. Decent manners. A respectable mode of dress."

"I'm mad about your suit, by the way." Vera had remembered: Elliot saw the gratitude flicker over his father's face as his hand went involuntarily in the direction of his lapels.

"What do you have faith in?" asked Vera.

"I have faith in the Monuments Commission. I've made an appointment for tomorrow morning"—this with a quiet look to Elliot—"with the chairman, Walter Lyte. Walter is an old friend of Hilda's. And I have faith in Jefferson Glee. I have an unlimited faith in the probity of I. F. Stone."

"Well, I'm mad about him, too." Vera grinned, amused by these combinations.

"I can't read that man," said his mother. "I know I should, but can't. How *are* your rehearsals going, Elliot?"

"Don't ask," he replied. His father began to speak again. Robert entered from the kitchen with a tray. Presumably, Robert would be given the day off when his father filled the house with Black Panthers.

His thoughts stuck. "Our first loyalty is to our values," his father was saying, Vera looking relieved that he was not directly discussing Nun's Wood, Margaret anxiously glancing at him. He smiled at her, explaining with a look that nothing was wrong. "...because everything else proceeds from values."

The rehearsal that day still hung heavily within him, as did its astonishing aftermath. His uneasiness about Kai, about Anita, had made him unnecessarily abrupt with the musicians, some of whom had drifted in late. Ettenheim was the last to appear. His hostility to Elliot seemed to have grown since the first rehearsal. When they were finally set up to play—Elliot's temper already frayed, and the first orders given, his command, slapping his hand on the podium, that "You all come in on time from now on, you hear? On time!"— Ettenheim lounged through his first section, singing without expression or color. "This isn't *Sprechstimme*, Ettenheim," he said. A cool glance in return: "I'm aware of that. It's a rehearsal." In the transition passages, Ettenheim paced around the stage, throwing off his old duffel coat, peering into the theater where only Himmel sat, the boy grimacing when the first clarinet faltered. The grimace implied that bad conducting, not acoustics, was at fault. One of the tympanists giggled. Then, a bar before his entry, he was back at his music stand, hands on hips, ready to sing. He now had the proper degree of strength in his voice, a perfectly timed vibrato, as slow as the tides, his back-of-the-throat voice thrillingly powerful.

In the cold air,
The spirit
Hardens.

It had been a performance laden with contempt, an extra edge in the voice. When they had gone twice through the song cycle, Elliot called for another, simpler piece, one that had gone well in the first rehearsal. Ettenheim sighed and jumped down from the stage to sit in the first row of seats. He did not go near Himmel, Elliot noticed happily.

He heard in their playing that the cellos had been rehearsing together privately. Himmel must have been coaching them. They were playing together, with the right bite in their attack, and were attending carefully to his signals. Thank you, Nathan. The battle with Ettenheim continued. What would the boy say if he saw the Edwards television program? He would dismiss Elliot as a fraud, as a pretender to modernity.

"You're not Bjoerling yet, Mr. Ettenheim," he had said to the boy, then wandering about the theater, "and I suggest that you sit down and pay attention to what is going on here. This is a rehearsal for everybody." A few smiles from the musicians. The black cellist raised his hand in a fist and gave Elliot a companionable grin: right on, baby. Ettenheim moodily returned to his seat in the first row and began flipping through his music. They started again from number fifteen. From then on, things had gone reasonably well, though he could still sense the tenor's spitefulness, and this rankled like a sore on his lip, a persistent irritation.

"Don't worry about it," Himmel said to him later in the Edwardian Room, "the kid's a personality fuckup. He thinks he's got the world by the balls. And maybe he does. Just apart from his voice, maybe you've got it knocked when you're twenty-two. I can't remember anymore. But next year he goes out into the jungle, and the animals will mess him around a little."

By the time they left Longman's it had grown dark, and wind sliced through the open toplighted spaces of the car park, cutting deeply into him. Elliot was on the fourth level; Himmel had told him that he'd had to wind up to the ninth before finding a space. He trotted across the freezing length of concrete between the elevator and Margaret's car, squeezed in beside a pillar, and unlocked the door, his hand shaking with cold. The seat covers sent a chill radiation upward through his coat, a motion parallel to his anger, his tension. Elliot had a sudden vision of Anita weeping, her face roughened with tears. He punched the heater button, then turned on the radio. "Frosty the Snowman" by Ella Fitzgerald, Nat Cole singing

"The Christmas Song." Himmel's white Cortina slipped past him in the rearview mirror, its headlights on. He waited until the end of "The Christmas Song" and then swung out backward and went slowly down the curving ramp.

On Grand Avenue the stores were still open, and light spilled from the giant windows. Above the street, arches of lights shaped like trees oxidized the night to purple. "Santa Claus Is Coming to Town" gave way to a commercial and he switched off the radio. Himmel, caught in the traffic, was only a block ahead, and Elliot slowed, driving up to Second Street, so that the light would change. The Cortina went over the bridge above the Plechette River and vanished around a curve as he braked, the lights yellow, in a cacophony of horns.

He drove the rest of the way to Leecham Street in a concentrated calm, passing the dark angles and abutments of the War Memorial and then going steadily north past houses picked with red and green lights. Listen, Anita Kellerman. Listen to me. We have been through much together, you and I. I will not allow this to drift away. We are all experts in loss, we all know how to harden ourselves to it. Now it is time for you to tell me. Is Ronnie Mark's father? Yesterday I saw twenty photographs of . . . What? Love's face, and the face of mastery. I do not want us to have to make that terrible choice. Love is the dread of loss, and the shoring up against it of a million acts of charity. All this I will never say.

The lake a dark definitionless volume to his side, a blackness between the bright houses, Lake Point Drive became Windmere Terrace, then the sharp turn on Leecham. On Himmel's white lawn Santa's whip curled frozen over the plastic reindeer. Elliot slewed the car up against a drift across the street from Anita's house and, jamming the keys in his pocket, jumped out. A dim light showed in a ground-floor window. The air tore at his ears, his hands. He ran across the street.

A loud pause from within the house after his ring, and then he heard footsteps coming toward the door. Listen to me. We must talk, my love, my puzzle, my sister.

Andy French opened the door.

Music was faintly audible behind her. "Telepathy," she said, and he recognized *Five Introductions*. He looked past her into the house, but the entry and hall were dark. A mild light emanated from the living room.

"You don't look very happy, Elliot." She smiled questioningly at him. "Why don't you—"

"Is Anita home? She isn't."

"—come in?"

They looked at each other, Andy puzzled. She shivered. "I'll give you a drink. It's too cold to stand out here."

"Yes, give me a drink." He stepped inside, clapping his hands together for warmth. "She's not at home, is she? I wanted to talk about something with her." Hanging his coat in the closet, he looked into the living room: a bottle and glass on the coffee table, newspapers strewn on the floor, one light casting a pool about a chair. His nervous anger lifted uselessly under her gaze, changed key.

"Anita and Mark are out, that's right. They went to Ronnie's for dinner."

He grunted. She took him into the living room.

"So I was playing your beautiful record and reading a book and getting quietly drunk. It was a novel. *Traveling Loose*, by—"

"By William Pittman," he said. "I read it." He saw splayed open on a chair the garish paperback cover of Pittman's book, a young hood in a motorcycle jacket embracing a naked blond.

"I like the descriptions." She seemed embarrassed.

Elliot sat down on the other side of the coffee table. He felt hopelessly like Kai, adrift. "What time will they be back?"

"Anita? I don't really know . . ." Her voice light, puzzled. "Sometime before twelve. Mark enjoys Ronnie, and it's always a struggle to get him to leave. It wouldn't be before eleven."

He looked up at her, and saw for the first time that she was wearing a loose green long gown that gathered softly at the waist and then fell softly to the floor. In this garment Andy resembled a witch, or a Druid. She hovered in his scrutiny for a moment, her hands going from breasts to waist. "I'm sorry," she said. "You wanted to talk to her."

"It's all right." He felt sour, disappointed. The question was still hot within him and he longed to utter. *Is Ronnie Upp Mark's father?* "Really, it's all right. I like your outfit. You are beautiful in it."

"Ronnie gave it to me," she said. "Admire our tree for a second, and I'll be right back with a glass for you." She smiled at him and nodded to the front of the room.

He turned in the chair and looked into the darkest corner of the living room, where the bookshelves met the front wall. In this corner used to hang the photograph of a blooming, full-sailed Anita leading Frank Kellerman across the lawn. Now he saw the dark mass of the tree. Andy, returning at once with a second glass, set it on the table. She moved to the tree and stooped to push in a plug. A glow of red and green, the tree went alight. "We bought it yesterday. Mark loves it so much he gets dizzy watching it."

Andy came back toward him and sat on the floor beside his chair. "That's the way I feel, sort of, listening to *Five Introductions*. I really do think it's beautiful, Elliot."

Not knowing what to say, he said nothing. Then: "I like the ending." The ending came. The next piece began. "Would you mind playing something else?" he said.

Andy stood, using his knee for a support, and carefully took his record off the turntable, put it in its sleeve, and pulled out another from the shelf. A jazz piano record, soft, with giant open chords. Elliot sipped at his drink.

"So you are stuck with me," she said, returning to the floor beside him. Andy looked up sideways, tilting her head, and smiled again. Elliot felt guilty for having ever regarded the girl as an enemy. He could smell whiskey, a biting sweetness in the air. "You don't mind anymore, do you? I've been sitting here for hours, just drinking. I'm so happy you're here, Elliot." She took one of his hands. He remembered how he had felt about her the day they had driven out to the field; he remembered how he had first seen her. She stroked his hand. "That's the extent of my advice," she said. Her hand moved slowly on his.

Shortly afterward they went upstairs to her room. He could later remember the shock of his mouth meeting the roughened skin of her scars, the calculation of her movements, her cries. It was only when she staggered, removing her sandals, that he realized how much she'd had to drink. That, at least, was his explanation. But in the midst of her abandonment, at the last moment, she said, "I don't take anything—don't do it in me," and he poured himself out on her belly. "We'll never do this again," she said softly into his ear. When he looked down at her face, she was coolly smiling, already detached.

He could see no further than the events of the past two days. He had been angry, anxious, approximately lustful, curious, sarcastic, tender, confident, confused: it did not cohere. He had not asked his question. He looked across the table at Vera, still listening to his father with an expression of complete attentiveness.

"I was thinking yesterday about Mr. Von Heilitz," he said. "Tell Vera about the time he invited you to the party. It's a lovely story."

Margaret burst into laughter. "Yes, do tell Vera about Lamont's party, Chase. I'm sure Vera will want to hear it."

"Please tell me," Vera said. "He was the man who had the dogs, wasn't he?"

"Let's not rake that up," said Elliot, seeing his father irritably stroke downward at his necktie. "That's another story." He looked across the table at Margaret, who seemed even more mirthful, recalling the debacle about the dogs.

"No, let's not," said Chase. "Lamont never forgave me for hitting those ridiculous old dogs of his. For a time, he even thought I had done it deliberately, which was very foolish of him. It spoiled what had been quite a satisfactory relationship. In many ways, I quite respected Lamont. *There* was a man who took his values seriously."

"As the story proves," said Elliot.

After checking to see that Vera was still attending, Chase said, "It does, rather." He signaled for Robert to divide the small remainder of the wine between Vera and Elliot, and paused while it was being poured. "The others have heard this story, Vera, so I am telling it just for you. As Elliot indicates, it is significant as well as amusing." He had recovered his humor. "Two things should be remembered about Lamont Von Heilitz's party. The first is that this was in 1944, during the war—a time when everything seemed endangered in this country. We at home had to keep things humming, use our factories for war production, we had to maintain morale. When the news from Europe finally took a positive swing, there were balls the like of which have not been seen since, in my estimation. We saw this as our part—it may have an odd ring in these times, but I still think we did a real service. If we were fighting for anything, it was to preserve the way of life that we did our best to continue during those years. Of course we and the people we knew did much war work as well—running the factory to satisfy the government contracts. My cousin Walter directed the War Production Board for this area. The country was working as a unit, as a team, for perhaps the last time it was possible for it to do so. There were the occasional rogues, such as Roy Zamon, who made a career of an artificial limb—you children wouldn't remember him. But there were heroes as well. Ralph Nieder, a young man of good family and an acquaintance of mine, who won his Silver Star in Germany. He killed himself here in Plechette City when he came back shattered from the war, and his death shattered many of us, I may assure you of that. I damn near *saw* him shoot himself. And there were others. That was twenty-five years ago, and it was a different America, an America that could still believe in heroes and heroism."

"Lamont's party, Chase," said Margaret.

"I am explaining the background to the party, my dear. These days, we would see it all differently. Our priorities have changed. Well, a man in Chicago named Montana Kingsmill threw a party in the winter of 1944 that was one of the wartime's grandest statements."

"It was lavish," said Margaret, enthusiastic. "We were both young, and we appreciated that kind of thing then. Oh, the flowers! And the music! There must have been five hundred people at the Kingsmill party."

"And we knew most of them. Old Jimmy Steenborg was striding around with his cane, a handsome devil of a man in his uniform. That was the last time I saw old Jimmy, but he looked firm and erect as ever—like his son, a real man for the ladies. Bryce, the coffee millionaire, Simpson and Watkins, who invested heavily in MGM and were both squiring actresses, Phil Morgan-Lime, Lotte Ramp, Count Zlydockwyczk, Edgar Burren, the portrait painter, Len Gamble, Hal Fisch . . . I could go on giving you the names for an hour. Shipman Kylody, who knew more about money management than any man in Chicago. Half a dozen famous theater people. Wanda Wylie—her picture *The Millionairess* had just had its premiere. All of these people had glamour, the real substantial glamour that comes from doing things grandly and publicly. Montana had got Benny Goodman's band to play, *and* Guy Pollack. There hasn't been a ball like it since, despite all your Truman Capotes.

"I said you had to keep two things in mind," said Chase. "The other is the character of Lamont Von Heilitz. When we moved into this house in 1940, Lamont was in his late fifties, and he hadn't done a day's work in his life. His father had been a stock millionaire who had invested in the auto industry right at the beginning, and unlike many of the twenties millionaires, he had been a cautious man. The Von Heilitzes had houses in France, Switzerland, and Florida— another killing there, in land. As a young man Lamont had been to school in Geneva, and then went to Princeton. He married young, a girl named Rose Ten Broek from upstate New York—one of those dowdy wealthy girls of the time who never spoke above a whisper. After their marriage, Lamont devoted himself to living well. In this case, that meant living with the greatest possible propriety.

"He and Rose were living in the light of an ideal—an ideal that commanded certain ceremonies of them. Lamont changed his clothes three times a day. They both dressed for dinner every night of their lives. Lamont was the most ceremonious man I've ever met, and probably one of the dullest, and Rose simply retired behind him like a voiceless shadow. I think they lost any sense they might have had of how other people lived. They never read the newspapers, never owned a radio, Rose read only novels by Jane Austen and Rose Macaulay. When Montana Kingsmill had his party, Lamont and Rose were of course invited, and equally as expected, they declined. But some description of the ball must have got back to Lamont, for he—as gently as could be—began to pump me for information about it. This went on for weeks. When I went out for a walk, Lamont would suddenly appear from behind a hedge, asking me who had been invited, how people had dressed, if there had been decorations, what the food had been. Who were the musicians? When he asked me if it were 'done' to invite single women to large parties, I knew that he was planning to emulate Kingsmill. Why, I still have no idea. He and Montana Kingsmill were as unlike as any two men could be. But that was precisely what Lamont had in mind to do, and he began his preparations that April, planning the party for August of 1944. One afternoon he invited me into his house to see his guest list. Rose was standing in the dining room beside this enormous stack of papers. She looked as proud and regal as a newly crowned queen. When she lifted the top page, I saw that it was all one long roll of paper, folded like an accordion—there must have been something like a thousand names on it. I saw right away that the first three people on the list were dead. They were old friends of my father's who had died before the war. He and Rose were so pleased with their work that I could not tell them, and I hadn't the heart to look at the rest of the list. I went home with my head and my heart in my hands, let me tell you.

"He and Rose kept at it all during that spring. It was a beautiful spring too, the news from the front was encouraging, and the weather turned mild very quickly, as if nature were redressing the balance for the terrible winter we'd had. All during that beautiful spring, Lamont was making ready for his party. He hired Guy Pol-lack's band, on my recommendation, I recall. Each week he'd done something new. Planned the menu, hired the same caterers Kings-mill had used, rented roulette wheels. He was happy as a boy.

"Then the disaster struck. In the late summer of that year, we had a particularly vicious measles epidemic. You could see the quar-antine notices all over the city. The Von Heilitzes were as good as in quarantine normally, living as they did, but somehow, in the last week of July, Rose was infected. She'd never had measles as a child. Lamont hung on until the last minute, hiring a nurse full time and caring for his wife as well as he could, and then he came down with something as well. Fatigue, I expect. Nervous shock. I didn't see him for a week. By the time he realized that he'd have to cancel his party, it was too late—the band was committed for the rest of the fall, the caterers had sent him a notice that they were beginning to prepare his order, the flowers had all been paid for. He had paid several thousand dollars in deposits and rentals. Yet all the spirit had gone out of it for him. Rose hadn't moved from her bed in a month. He was exhausted. In the end, two weeks before the date of the party he hired someone to send out regrets to the people who had accepted his invitation. I hate to think how many telephone calls he must have had from sons and daughters and nephews, saying that Father or Uncle had died five years before.

"For days trucks and vans were coming up to his house—we could see them at work in the back gardens, setting up tents and a bandstand. A team of gardeners resodded parts of his lawn. Colored fountains. Spotlights sunk into the lawn. The liquor was unloaded in *cases*, dozens of them. To use a phrase Elliot was fond of as a boy, 'the whole schmear.'

"Then the day came. Debeek's men, the caterers, began arriving about noon, an army of them, with boxes and crates containing the food and the silver and the glassware. Anything that wasn't rationed. The band came in a bus. It was all very peculiar to see, and very funny and very sad at once.

"Our phone rang about six. When I answered, I heard a faint whispery sort of voice—it took me a moment to recognize that it was Lamont. 'I would like to invite you to our little party,' he said to me. 'You may come at your convenience. Dinner will be at nine-thirty, Chase, but it is not necessary that you dress.' I thanked him, and he hung up. So: at eight o'clock I walked across the lawn to his house. The band was playing, waiters were waiting, the house was lighted up like a fun fair, and no one was there but me. I sat at a little white table under a striped tent and was served drinks while I listened to the band. I was sure that, somewhere up in the house, Lamont was watching. I applauded each number Pollack played. They did an entire show while I sat there. 'Honeysuckle Rose,' 'Flyin' Home,' 'American Patrol,' 'One O'Clock Jump,' the drummer danced on a drum, a girl singer named Florence McCall sang 'Green Eyes,' Guy Pollack told jokes between numbers. Nobody looked at me. They were as embarrassed as I, and I felt that they too could sense Lamont watching them from up in the house. At nine-thirty, Raoul, Debeek's headwaiter, escorted me into the dining room. He put me at the central table, before my name on a place card. It was like being the captain of a deserted liner—all that white linen and sparkling glass. 'Will Mr. Von Heilitz be joining me?' I asked, and he said, 'Mr. Von Heilitz will be dining in his room tonight, sir'—as though he oversaw scenes like this every week.

"The wine steward, also one of Debeek's men, greeted me by name and asked my preference in the wines. They were all from Lamont's cellar, and I knew he had a good Puligny-Montrachet and an equally good Margaux, so I asked for them and had a half of each bottle—that was for Lamont's sake. The dinner was superb. When I had finished with my dessert and coffee, I had a small glass of port—Lamont never took brandy after dinner—and walked back across his garden to our house. I waved good-bye up at the house, but didn't see anyone there. One fellow in the band waved good-bye to me. It was the damnedest evening I'd ever had in my whole life."

"And the next week . . ." Margaret prompted.

"The next week Lamont popped out from behind his hedge again as I walked by, trailed along silently for half a block, and then asked me if I enjoyed his party. 'I'm so very happy,' he said. 'I caught glimpses of you from my windows, and I thought that you had quite enjoyed the music.' "

He smiled at Vera.

"I thought it was going to be a funny story," she said.

"Sometimes it is," he said. "But you really cannot deny that it has a great deal to do with values."

chapter **16**

The next day the mail brought a Unicef Christmas card from Joanie Haupt and two letters, each addressed solely to Elliot Denmark.

Dear Vera:
Just a note to thank you for how kind you have been to me. I don't know who else would listen so sympathetically to my wretched problems. The situation seems better now. Lawrence is very contrite—*not* the way I like him best. He gave me a dog named Marcuse. Cute? Let's meet for lunch sometime next week. Love to you and Elliot, and Merry Christmas. Have a happy. Thanks again.

> All love,
> Peace,
> Joanie

Elliot:
Just shamblin' along, footloose/careloose/jobloose. We went to Philadelphia for a week's gig the day after your rehearsal (two days after? I don't remember) and it turned out that the place we were supposed to play in was run by some mafioso who

said he'd smash our instruments if we didn't do four sets a night—us sweating ourselves into greasy little puddles for about thirty bucks—so we quit after two days and went straight on through to New York. Well, livin' the blooz, like the song says. We have a new manager, an ace, who says that he can get us good gigs and a record contract if we hang around here & do a lot of rehearsing. In the meantime, it's cold asses hustling down East Twelfth Street between our "loft" and the local greaseria. Mucho coffee, señor! Sí. Big grins here. I try to keep from getting panhandled by guys who look just like me. A genuinely freakish experience.

Yet, yet, yet—I really do love this city, gritty and bitter and hostile as it is. It's like one long speed experience. (We've been living on hamburgers and Cokes, and that might have something to do with it.) I'm in the middle of reading *The Glass Bead Game*, Hesse's great mindbender, and it's like going from your music to Jimi Hendrix, reading that while hearing the police cars scream by at night. We're rehearsing in what our manager calls a "loft," but in reality is a watery basement in a warehouse. It goes well, old teacher mine. We'll begin working before long, we've got lots of new songs (and a genius new bassist from Memphis) and I'm feeling like I'm finally getting into place, into what I should be doing. We're having a demo heard by Sextant records. I got the money from my parents to buy an echoplex outfit for my guitar, and it really makes fantastic sounds. MAKE MUSIC—that's the only thing.

All this means that I'll miss your concert, for which I here maketh my apologies.

Has anybody seen the wolf lately? I got a big lift out of reading about that big ragged creature patrolling around the suburbs. This may be due to my Hesse binge. What do you think the bastard lives on? I bought a dog the other day, a furry little bundle who eats potato chips and lima beans.

Well, *Dragnet* is on the radio now, four guys just got shot between commercials on the tube, another guy is playing B. B. King on the stereo, I just finished *Traveling Loose* by William

Pittman, a strung-out novel everybody here is reading, so the context is mixed, as always. After all, I'm not William Bendix and this isn't *Beat the Clock* . . . or is it? I saw Roy Rogers selling a disease on TV the other night, just a day after copping an old 45 of "Happy Trails." When I was an *enfant pas terrible* I used to daydream about Dale Evans' boobs. *La vie imite l'art, hein?* (What *is* that verb?)

Until we meet again
Roy Baltz

Dear Elliot,
It was quite a pleasant surprise to get your signature on our statement in the mails this morning, and I write to express my gratitude and appreciation. To reciprocate, I am planning a little surprise for you, one I hope you will like, so do watch for our appearance in the newspaper.

With best wishes,
Dr. Pierce Laubach

"That sounds unpleasantly sinister," said Vera. "When a man like that uses the words 'a little surprise,' I begin to wish I had someone to taste my food for me."

"I don't think it means anything. Maybe he put my name first on the list. He could use my picture for all I care."

"Well, you've certainly burnt your bridges," Vera said. She was referring to his argument with Tessa, and she smiled at him: Elliot knew that there was no rancor left in Vera over the incident. The Glaubers too seemed to have resolved to forget it. Elliot had spoken with Tessa on the telephone yesterday morning before the rehearsal, and she had twice called him "darling." The peace was official.

"When you were a boy, did you daydream about Dale Evans' boobs?" Vera asked, still smiling.

"I was more in the Jane Russell—Faye Emerson era," he said. Andy French, an uneasiness threading up his spine, came clearly into his mind. It had the flavor of defeat. He completely saw for a long

moment her face magnified beneath him, the violent lines like ar-
teries and rough to his lips.

We'll never do this again.

What?

*You heard me. This is it. Sex this casual makes me feel like I'm back
in college.*

I'm sorry that you didn't like it.

I like it enough. She had grinned at him, stretching her arms above
her head. *I loved it, in fact. You're considerate. Thanks for not mentioning the fact that I still am in college.*

You must be the only girl in America who doesn't take the pill.

Did I say I didn't take it? Poor Elliot. When he was buttoning his
shirt, she said, *Lots of us don't take it anymore, Elliot dear. Don't worry.*

"Would you mind if I visited Uncle Kai alone today?" he asked.
"I'd like to go over there sometime after lunch."

"Tomorrow night we go to Anita's party?"

"If you want to."

"I'd love to. You've been hiding her from me, you know."

"I don't think so," he said. "It just worked out that way."

She was silent for a moment, toying with a giant transparent
cigarette lighter on the table. "Be easy with Uncle Kai, Elliot," she
said.

"Who's going to make him be easy on me?"

"And I think you should have a talk with your father, too," she
said quietly.

He only barely heard her. All centers of his guilt seemed to be
converging; since he had seen the photographs, Kai was horribly
linked in his mind with Ronnie Upp. Images of fistfights, raw bleeding flesh, purple bruises, filled his inner vision. He could not enter
Anita's house as long as Andy French was there. Pale light washed
over them, reflected from the ice shattered and heaved up at the
edge of the lake.

His father was playing "Ain't Misbehavin' " on the piano in the
lower living room, and he must have heard their voices, for he called
out, "Aren't you children chilly in there? Why don't you make a
nice crackling fire?" *Da da da bumpbump, da da da bumpbump,* the

piano continued. "By the by, our northern visitor, the *lupus*, was seen again this morning, according to the news commentators. It crossed Jackson Drive in full view of several automobiles, and then streaked away into the fields. It was going generally southeast. Perhaps we should outfit ourselves with weapons."

Driving along the lake expressway toward the valley, Elliot tried to draw things into order. First, the rehearsals showed that the concert would at least not be an utter failure: with one more long run-through on the day of the performance, they could at least make it plausible. It was not enough, but it would be sufficient. Second, the moment with Andy had perhaps been inevitable. He had let the girl grow too large in his imagination. Andy was only a girl—no more than twenty-two or-three. A graduate student. Like many girls her age, she was apparently capable of controlling her emotions. Third, Anita. For an instant, he saw her as some white defenseless thing, trapped, caged, at the mercy of more powerful forces, frightened . . . Well, she had been frightened. Upp had slapped her hard enough to raise a bruise. They must have had a falling-out before she summoned him from his parents' house. Somehow, he would use her party to talk about it with her. He also promised himself that he would have a long talk with Upp. And some words with Andy. Then he felt his panic begin to rise in him again.

Elliot swung the car up the curve around the War Memorial—the lake, catching the sun behind, flashed once in his car mirror—and crossed to the inside lane. Looking sideways to see if traffic were coming, he caught sight of a slender, elegant man in a short brown coat who was walking briskly before the leafless trees along First Street; he was instantly convinced that the man was Ronnie Upp. A flock of pigeons took off from the War Memorial's plaza to his right and wheeled away like the souls of the dead into the dark air. When the traffic light flashed green, Elliot accelerated, recrossing the two lanes in a blare of horns, to get closer to the figure in the brown coat. Just as he drew near, the man stepped jauntily into a side street, and Elliot, braking, saw his slim back join a crowd of people walking toward the festooned entrance to a department store. Elliot lost sight of the man and began to look desperately for a place to park.

He cut savagely into an alley, tires whining, and drove down to the other end past the rust-colored backs of buildings. Just as he slammed the car to a halt, he saw the man, partially hidden by shoppers, cross the alley's entrance. He jumped out. He had no idea of what he would say to Upp. He began to walk quickly down the crowded street. His body seemed to be plummeting. The man came into view, crossing the street, only fifteen feet away. Just then the pigeons banked overhead, their wings loudly beating, and the man turned his head to watch their flight. He had a bony beardless face, round-nosed. It was not Upp. It was only a boy. Elliot's relief was so great that he slumped against a shop window. Trembling, he drew his hands over his face. He realized that he had intended to leap at the man, to flail him with his fists. Shocked, he continued to knead his face.

"I was rather expecting you, Elliot," said Kai, opening his door.

The apartment was just as it had been two days before; the odor Elliot remembered drifted over him again, a snuffy sleepy smell of age. The drapes were closed against the depthless sun. The blocky old typewriter still stood on the desk; Goethe and Celan and Storm marched above it. Elliot looked guiltily for an instant at the filing cabinet he had rifled on his last visit: had Kai noticed anything? Seeing the elegant old man again—his actions on that day seemed utterly unwarranted, an invasion. Nothing he had done seemed the right thing. Kai smiled at him and gestured to one of his chairs.

"You look as though you had better sit, Elliot," he said. "You are shaken." He held his gesture until Elliot removed his coat, laid it across the cot, and sat in the chair. "To give you one more proof of my percipience, I'll tell you that I bought some coffee on my last shopping spree. You would like some coffee?"

"Thank you, yes," Elliot said. "I'd love some." Kai nodded briskly and went toward the curtain. He parted it and disappeared inside. Elliot heard the pounding of water into a percolator. Then the sliding of a tin from a shelf; the gas made its small explosion. Kai reappeared through the curtain.

"Now," he said. "Our only artist is here at last, but he resembles a fugitive from justice. Do you want to tell me what happened? If it is something private, I will withdraw the question."

"I guess I can tell you," said Elliot. "It isn't any earth-shaking thing, really." Where to begin? He could not recount his history with Anita. For a moment he feared he might be sick. "It's all tied in with a man named Ronnie Upp," he said. "I thought I saw him on the way down here, and it was like seeing someone who is supposed to be dead—some old enemy. I wanted to kill him. There are some personal problems of mine tied in here." He shot a horrified look at Kai, who seemed unmoved by the reference to Upp and continued to regard him calmly. "Well, I can't go into that. It's probably unimportant anyway. It has to do with an old attachment of mine. As I say, probably unimportant. But I'm feeling hemmed in by the man. And that thing in the car just now—when I went to follow him—it makes me feel soiled. Filthy. I'm terribly confused about what I'm doing."

"I think you could use your coffee," Kai said, and went again behind the curtain, returning with two cups on a tray, which he set on the table beside Elliot's chair. Elliot sipped from his cup: the coffee was rich and strong, and he drank it gratefully.

"Of course you know about the Nun's Wood business," he said. "I'm involved, really in only a small way, with that, acting against Herman. I blew up at Tessa one night when she nearly accused me of treason, and that could be part of it, I suppose. The scene created some uneasiness between Vera and me. That's only natural, and it's over by now. This Upp is one of the principals in the Nun's Wood matter. Lately, everything seems to be part of some plot, almost, a plot in which I'm just wandering around, trying to build meanings out of dropped cigarette butts and old envelopes. At times I think I'm on top of things, and then something happens, and I'm back again where I started." Elliot realized that he had probably not made much sense. Talking about it made him feel worse. Kai was leaning backward in his tall desk chair, his white hands folded on his lap.

The foxy old face was tilted forward, concentrated on him. "I can't ... I mean, I'm grateful to you for listening to all this gibberish. I thought I had more self-control. I wanted to jump on that man and beat him to hamburger. That's really why I'm upset—it was like finding an enemy inside me, someone vain, savage, deluded ..." Kai did not move. He was watching Elliot very calmly. He is waiting for me to confess about the files, Elliot thought. "A couple of days ago, I wanted to talk about everything with you, to stage some sort of confession scene, I guess. But I don't think I have to do that now."

"No," Kai said. "Confessions are a luxury." He gave his wintry smile. "They are very old-fashioned. The absolution we can get from others is liable to be of little value."

Then we are all self-bound, Elliot thought. Miles of stony distance seemed to separate him from Kai. "I suppose you're right," he said. "But I distrust that kind of statement."

"I do too." Kai smiled. "I distrust the whole apparatus of defensiveness. Forgive me if I overemphasized your use of the word 'confession.' I merely felt that you were not saying everything you wished to say to me. Nor do I mean to imply that we can look no further than ourselves. That you are here, and that I am happy to have you here, should tell you otherwise. I do feel that it is necessary now and then to walk out of the confessional into the street, to see if the sun shines, if the several square miles we inhabit have altered in any significant way."

"They've altered, all right," Elliot said.

"And that is what you cannot talk about."

"Yes."

"That is fine. I do not wish to probe into your private life. And I think you are too young to have any confessions I would find essential." His glance here was ripe with irony. "You and Vera can go on undisturbed, can you not?" Elliot nodded. "Then you are better off not speaking."

It seemed to Elliot that their footing had subtly changed. He sensed some purpose in Kai that he could not decipher, a strategy. He hoped with his whole being that Kai had not noticed that his files had been violated.

"Herman told me the last time we spoke," Kai said, "about the arguments with Tessa, and he mentioned that he thought there was some trouble between you and Vera. This does not annoy you? He is merely solicitous of Vera's welfare. He always has been."

Elliot's panic began to ebb. Kai wished to talk about Vera, so he could not have noticed anything wrong with the files. "No, it doesn't annoy me," he said. "Herman can't believe that Vera is happy living out of the country."

"He never could believe that," said Kai. "You need not concern yourself with that shortcoming of my brother's. And"—he smiled again—"you do not."

"I cannot."

"No, we are not responsible for other people's illusions." Kai crossed his legs, and his hand rose to the curling vein on his temple. "Is the Ronnie Upp you mentioned the young man who shot his father during the fifties? They lived quite close to your parents' house, I recall."

He does know about the files, Elliot thought. He felt sickened, exposed. "Yes, that was the boy, son of Harrison Upp," he said. "Uncle Kai, I have to explain . . ."

"No, I have to explain something to you," Kai broke in. Astonishingly, he took Elliot's hand for a moment, and then let it fall back on his lap. "I want to show you something." He lifted out the leather box and held it on his knees. "When I was in the camp during those years of the war, I thought I had learned a few hard lessons—learned them absolutely. After I learned them, I chose not to forget. Other men, even women, went through what I endured, and sealed it all off, to the extent that it could be sealed off. But to return into the dream of normal life was defensiveness, I thought—no, *knew*. I trusted the work I was doing, because that was an almost impersonal act of consciousness. It also kept me away from anything that might have diminished my sense of what I'd learned. If what I learned was painful, then I had at least to keep my pain alive." He opened the lid of the box, held it up for a moment while he looked within, and then closed it gently.

"All that time, I was half-harboring an illusion, a myth, without being conscious of it. And I only became aware, shamefully aware of it, when I read in the newspapers about the death of Harrison Upp. Listen to me: I ran outside, holding the newspaper, weeping with joy and at the same time for my own dishonesty. Half of what I had thought about myself was shown up for a fraud." He passed the tooled box to Elliot. "It was a terrible moment. It put me back into the camp just as though I had never left it." He looked wryly at Elliot, who held the box, awkwardly, on his knees. "Only then could I finish my book. I began again on it, and spent years doing it, but I finished over a year ago."

"Your book is done?" Elliot gasped. "Where is it?" He turned his head to the files, then back to Kai.

"I detest those metal files," Kai said gently. "Herman gave them to me years ago, when he was purchasing some new equipment for his office in city hall. I made the labels to please him, but I've never used the files for anything important. I've been keeping everything up here." He rose from his chair and went to the closets on the other side of the room. He opened the double doors. On the shelf above his clothes stood a rank of red manuscript boxes. "All of my work is in these boxes. The notes, the drafts, the typescript, everything. I sent a copy off to a university press when it was finally done, and several months later they wrote to say that although it was contrary to their policy to publish works by people not affiliated with universities, they were pleased to accept my book."

"But why didn't you tell anyone?" Elliot heard himself nearly shouting. "Why didn't you tell Tessa and Herman?"

"Because I am old enough to act as I choose," Kai said, looking as handsome as Eliot had ever seen him. "And I chose not to subject myself to the miseries I knew would follow. Would you like to see the letter from the publisher?"

From the shelf where it had been lying next to the manuscript boxes, Kai plucked an unfolded sheet of paper with a letterhead Elliot could read across the room.

"No, Uncle Kai," he said. "That isn't necessary." He swallowed, and watched Kai replace the paper on the shelf. "What will you do when the book is published?"

"I will give them a copy. And that will be my absolution." Kai closed the closet door and went back to his chair before the desk. "Elliot, instead of sitting there in such evident discomfort, why don't you just open that little box? I want to talk about some things with you, and the photographs in the box are where I have to begin."

W hen I found myself out on the lawn of Herman's house,
Kai said, with the *Herald* wadded up in my hand and me sobbing
as I had never before done in my life, I was thrown back almost
physically into the camp at Blini. I could see the rows of barracks,
three long buildings hedged by barbed wire, the railroad line coming
into the camp which was visible from the *Appelplatz* outside the
barracks, the two large buildings to the west of them where we
worked in the laundry or the kitchens or the prisoners' store—all of
this area was called the *Wohnlager*, and it was all surrounded by
wire. Because I could see the railroad line and the *Lazzarett* I knew
I had been ordered out into the *Appelplatz*: and when one found
oneself alone there it meant one thing only. You were to be executed
for some minor infraction—for disobedience, for theft, for something
of that sort. At five every morning we were led out to line up there,
and the guards took a special delight in exempting from the formation any man who was to be shot that day. He stood apart from
the other prisoners and watched, while the rest of us marched away
and thanked God we were not in his place. I could see even the
dusty pebbles of the gravel beside my feet. It was the only hallucination I have ever suffered, but my lack of practice did not save me
from having it complete.

Yet it did not make sense, my being there. Executions were rather rare among the workers in the barracks, and I felt a horrible confusion because I could not remember what I had done. I wished that I had requested a transfer to the *Totenlager*, the upper camp where the ovens and burial tips were located. The workers there never lasted longer than a month or two, and men who were scheduled for execution could win another few weeks of life by pleading to be put up in that section of the camp. I could not imagine why I had been so stupid as to let that last chance slip by me. All of this took place in seconds, I am sure. My hallucination faded as completely as it had come. I sat down on the grass until my terror left me—that odd calculating terror which was so familiar—and until I felt that I was once more in control. I was very badly shaken. A huge globule of perspiration came up under my shirt and soaked me. I spent the next two days in bed, trying to feel my way through what happened, though I had known immediately, sitting on the grass soaked in my own juices, that Harrison Upp, the father of the young man you have mentioned, was at its heart. Harrison Upp, and my relationship with Harrison Upp, and how that relationship ended, though I think it did not really end until that moment. I had gone on being Harrison's prisoner until the day I learned of his death.

I have loved and hated only one man in my life, and in the end the hate drove out the love, killed it so that it was no more than a dry little seed. Yet any strong emotion is a connection to its object. It took Harrison's death to free me of him. Curiously, it is similar to the feeling of having finished the book on Goethe. No purpose is left to me, no fuel—it is the sensation of being beached, run aground; a uselessness. To be fanciful, I could say that it is like being one of my sister-in-law's antiques: an old barrel, a brass bed warmer—those pathetic objects that lately have made me hate entering her home. As I tell Herman, I wish to die, but I do not wish to be reminded of my death by images of it.

The photographs in the box were taken from 1925 to 1933, the years I spent largely with Harrison Upp. Upp traveled a good bit on his own, returning frequently to America, but even toward the end of that time when we had to struggle to remain cordial and fought bitterly nearly one day of every three, he and I must have spent half of every year together. I wrote to Herman that I had "seen through" Harrison sometime in 1930, and that I had left him in Paris and gone to Bonn. That was a very careful lie, a prudent lie—and, as it happened, a prescient lie. By 1932, when I had become well established in Bonn, the situation with Harrison was unbearable. He tyrannized over me, and he was a cruel and capricious man whose tyranny was very inventive. "Seeing through" him, unfortunately, did not stop me from being tied to him. After every separation we were impelled to meet again—as though there were some thread we had to follow through to its end. The photographs show us in the exuberant moments when peace seemed possible, but those had become painfully rare by the thirties. Upp would arrive without warning from a visit to New York and demand that I leave with him for Paris: I'd argue and fight, very truthfully pleading my scholarly work as an excuse, I'd finally give in in despair and then at the last minute he'd leave again without warning. At times I would come home from the university to find him in my room with some girl he had brought there—and he would insist on taking us both out to dinner, torturing us both throughout the evening, and it would end with the girl scornful, sarcastic, upset . . . twice he amused himself by sending me home alone with one of these girls. There were, of course, other young men as well. Harrison gave a party in his Paris apartment in 1930 that was my first collision with his puppetmaster aspect. More than half of the guests were street boys, and Harrison made it clear that they'd have to vie for him. I was sickened by the scene that followed. The next day I tried to talk about it with him, to see why he had done that to me, and he answered, "I thought you might be amused by my little game, my dear Kai." I remonstrated as violently as I dared, and he merely shrugged. For weeks after, he humiliated me in small ways, constantly demeaning me. Yet we always returned to one another, and there would be one of those explosions of good will that cemented us even more firmly together. At some point, I recognized that although I had to come to Europe because of him, I was in effect taking care of him, supporting him physically, buttressing him, and that tied me to him even more firmly.

During one of those summers, Harrison bought a pistol, a beautiful little black Italian weapon, which he wore in a holster from a shop on the rue Passy. He used to lay it very delicately on the table when he was unusually playful or especially unhappy or vicious, always parodying the gestures of a man *in extremis*: at times, it was the performance of a madman, and it terrified me. He would toy with the pistol, aiming it at my head, and then flick it away. "I am going to be married in America," he said to me, "and, little friend, if you object, I will *plink* and *plink* with my little pistol until nothing is left of you." Then he turned up the butt of the gun so I could see that the clip was not in it. I would have been delighted if he had made a happy marriage, and he knew it.

He had a little monkey then, and the animal would run chattering up the drapes when Harrison enacted one of his dramas with his pistol. You can see the monkey in one of the photographs taken at the villa of Bruno Larella, the costume designer—it was a hypertense little beast, and it shat all over the floor when it panicked. One day in Bonn he set the monkey on a table and began toying with his pistol. "Do you see Fritzie, Kai?" he said. "Naughty little Fritzie? I'm sick of him." He pointed the gun at the monkey, and the animal scampered off the table, chattering, to make a run at the window ledge. "Should I kill him?" he asked, and I said, thinking that the clip was out, "You know I hate the beastly little thing. Do what you want." He played with it, pointing the gun and then dropping it, while Fritzie dashed screaming over every surface in the apartment. I couldn't bear the noise the animal was making—its terror. Finally the monkey hid himself behind the drapes. Harrison shot it twice through the draperies. I had really thought the gun was unloaded, as it usually was, and I jumped with the shock. The noise of the firing had seemed so small, almost insignificant. I had thought it would make a terrible explosion. But Fritzie was bunched on the carpet, bleeding, his body suddenly shapeless, like a pulpy rag. Harrison told me to wrap it up in newspapers and put it in the dustbin. He was drunk on that day, of course. I had always detested the little creature, and it was all I could do to touch it, but I opened an old suitcase I hadn't used in years and prodded it in with my foot. Then I took a tramcar and dropped the suitcase in a canal.

I had to use the tram because Harrison had ruined his automobile some months earlier while driving us back to Bonn from Remagen, in the Rhine valley. He insisted on driving on the smaller country roads, and on driving recklessly fast, especially when drunk. He never let anyone else drive his car, a Marmon he had brought back with him from one of the trips to New York. There was a young man with us, a boy really, whom Upp had picked up in our hotel at Remagen. He was a naïf, but a rather charming, witless sort of person. He was twenty, named Karl Frisch, and his mother had just married a horrid little official from Mainz; the mother was only too happy to be rid of him when Harrison proposed bringing him back to Bonn with us. A rather slight boy, blond, with a face like a crushed rose. Frisch had been drinking steadily during the day, and sat in the tiny backseat of the Marmon, singing and bellowing at the other cars and at the farmers driving their hay wagons. I was furious at Harrison for bringing the boy with us, and I was in a rage at the boy for behaving so boorishly—he was anything but charming that afternoon. He insisted we stop at a hotel in another village further up the Rhine for more bottles of hock, and Harrison pretended to be delighted with the notion. He was flattering the boy relentlessly, and I could see that, even drunk, he was enjoying seeing the way Frisch was making a fool of himself. Later, this would all be used as a lever against the boy. I could see Harrison exulting. We stopped at a *Gasthaus* for wine, and then, in a sudden shower, continued. The boy continued to drink, he and Harrison passing the bottle between them. Then just as we were heading toward the roofs of another village, down a slope from where we were, the rain increased heavily, and Frisch began to shout for more wine. He was delighted with himself, delighted with the car, the shower, the village where we would be able to get more wine—as he lurched forward to grab the wheel away from Harrison, I saw his face, and it was terrifyingly happy, bestially happy, the brain guttered out with speed and pleasure and egotism. He fell sprawling over the steering wheel, tumbling into Harrison, and the Marmon went straight for the side of the road, as I remember, Upp in his confusion pushing the accelerator instead of the brake. I saw his mistake, and could do nothing: I was frozen. We overturned, the car flipped onto a rock ledge and crashed down into a ditch. Frisch was killed when he fell half out of the car and was crushed against the ledge. The Marmon dragged him along beneath it when it went down the rocky face. I was thrown clear when we overturned, and fell onto the ledge—when I opened my eyes I saw Frisch being soundlessly mangled by the car, dragged down the slope by its weight. Harrison simply fell out and clung to the ledge.

He explained to the police that the boy was a friend, that he had tried to grab the wheel as a drunken prank—he seemed absolutely sober as he talked to the police. I, the Herr Professor Glauber, would act as witness. He arranged everything. We were held over three days, one of the farmers we had passed testified to Frisch's drunkenness, and afterward we continued on to Bonn by train. Harrison left for Paris several days later and stayed there for a week or two. In the interim, of course, he'd shot the monkey. I think he was in a bad psychological condition—all nerves and guilt and recklessness. Before he left, he mentioned to me, as if it were only a casual passing remark, that he wished *he'd* been the one to die. I knew it was more than that, and that made him even more restless to leave. And he knew that the accident stayed with me, and would stay with me a long time—I think he knew that I had resolved to make a final break from him. He wanted to allow the usual healing that took place whenever we were separated. But I could not look at him without seeing the Frisch boy. It didn't help that my motives were anything but completely moral and that I was disgusted with myself for the tangle of my own emotions.

After his return we fought about my leaving. I had already found another flat nearer to the university, and I planned to move at the end of that month. It was July of 1933. Bonn was bakingly hot, everything was unsettled in Germany, one saw appalling things everywhere. The country was just about to take its final lurch into disease. Yet I was determined to keep on at my work, somewhere in the south, apart from Harrison. We were on a tramcar going into the city when he said that he had finally arranged false papers for me—a necessity if I were to remain unharrassed in the country much longer. "I'll take the papers because I need them," I said, "but I can't live with you any longer. I'm going to hide myself in some farm town to work on my book. You can do what you want, as long as you don't do it near me." Just as I was finishing my piece, which I had been practicing for weeks, waiting for him to return from Paris, an old rouged dandy in a white linen suit, an obvious toupee gummed to his scalp, boarded the tram. His eyes lit on Harrison. His hands fluttered. He spoke with a Berlin accent, in an educated, precise, drawling voice. "My dear Harry, what a delight to see you again!" he crooned, moving across the crowded tram toward us. "Such old friends as we should never have lost touch. . . ." On and on in this fashion. I could tell that Harrison, who'd had several large brandies before leaving the apartment, was flushing with anger. The old man's face had been powdered, and you could see the line on his neck where the healthy-looking makeup ended and his dead-white skin crept down into his collar. "You are looking well, your distinguished friend looks well, and I too am looking well today," said the apparition. "I must take my time . . . arranging . . . in the mornings, but we will all grow old. Yet art may provide where nature fails; we may all look young, with proper care." The old man was half-crazy. It was the pathetic craziness of those who cannot distinguish their reality from their performance, who are swallowed by their fantasy. He invited us to dine with him. "Not at the old place, Harry, I couldn't keep it up anymore, but at my flat on . . ." He named a decrepit street in the area near the city buildings. Harrison told him to shut up, just in that way—his voice was as chilly as a steel blade. He was in a rage, and I could recognize the look he got, his face red and indrawn, when he was on the edge of fury. "Shouldn't speak to me like that," the old man stage-whispered, so loudly that everybody turned to stare at us, "after everything I've done for you. You are a silly little wretch, Harry, a silly terrible little fool." His face was trembling, and he picked up one of his hands to touch Harrison. In a moment Harrison was on his feet, wrenching the old man out of his seat. He dragged him down the aisle to the door, the old man bent in half like an old piece of paper, and pushed him off the tram. I saw the old man go down on the tracks, smearing his suit with black from the cinders. He looked as though he were crying, muttering to himself. I wish I had in that box a photograph of that rouged old creature, crushed bit of human candy that he was; kneeling in the dust he looked like only a filthy bundle of clothes sporting a clown's face. An S.A. man on the tram laughed and clapped Harrison on the back. "You should have let me do him," he said. "All right," Harrison said, coming back to the seat, "I'll send you your damned papers. We'll finish this charade." Then he put his face beside my ear, in such fury and compression of movement that I thought he was going to bite it off. He patted his suit under his shoulder where he carried his pistol and hissed, "I'd like to shoot you, you know. Just shoot you dead, right here. But if you're fool enough to stay in this country, I won't have to." I got off at the next stop. At the end of the month I moved into the new flat. By summer, I had arranged to rent a farmhouse in the country west of Rüdesheim. I used the name on the papers Harrison had given me.

Within a year I knew that I had made a mistake. The farmers were suspicious and snooping, my work had lost its direction, and it became clear to me that Germany was the wrong place to be. But then it was too late to leave. I was arrested in 1934, kept in jail in Berlin for three years, and then removed to Blini. The name on the papers Upp had given me was Traum. Artur Traum. Arthur Dream. I thought that Harrison, who knew many Nazi officers, had betrayed me to them; and I thought that he had decided to do it that afternoon on the tram.

If you can give me more time, I want to tell you the rest of it. I have been silent too long. Try to picture the way rats live on a garbage heap, fighting for spoiled food, lifting their snouts for clean air, all of them carrying disease, living in it, in a strict hierarchy— except that we rats were directed by the officers at Tiergartenstrasse 4 in Berlin, Bouhler, Brock, Blankenburg, Professor Heyde, names none of us knew then.

THREE

The Beginning of the Concert

The evening paper carried on the first page of the local section a brief story headed FALSE SHOT, DOG DIES, concerning a Mr. Georgiou Stampos, of 5580 Pearl Drive, Willowbrook Meadow subdivision, who had shot and killed with a .22 long rifle a German shepherd dog when it approached the fence at the back of his property. "We know the wolf was headed this way by what we read in the papers," Mr. Stampos said, "so we figured we had a right to defend ourselves. For the time being, people should keep their dogs locked up, or more unfortunate tragedies like this are going to happen." A special detachment of men from the sheriff's office, along with a volunteer from the Plechette City zoo, were spending the weekend patrolling the area south of Willowbrook in an effort to capture the wolf. Suburban gun owners were advised to lock up their weapons and telephone the police if they caught sight of anything resembling the animal.

"This business about the wolf is incredible, truly incredible," Chase said. "Incredible and poignant. Don't you see the potential in it? Old Simmons Speigner, the zoo director, is going crazy trying to capture the thing before somebody shoots it. Meanwhile, madmen with guns riddle their picture windows with bullets and shoot all the family dogs in sight. In the interstices between flying bullets and newspaper columns, the animal careers around the city, popping up here and there like the Scarlet Pimpernel. A loose wolf hasn't been seen within two hundred and fifty miles of here for a hundred years, maybe longer. We don't know how to deal with it. It's like science fiction, a time-travel story. In a way, it reminds me of what I was telling you last night about Lamont von Heilitz." His gaiety seemed forced to Elliot, but Margaret overrode it.

"Oh, Chase, now you are being fanciful," she said. She looked around the dining room of the City Club, where they were seated at the "Denmark" table—theirs because Brooks Denmark had graced it—with Dr. Laubach. A black pianist, whose whispy melodic traceries of show tunes were upheld by a bassist and snare drummer, played dance music at the edge of the room's tiny dance floor.

"Elliot," Margaret said, tapping the back of his hand with a finger, "I think I see an old friend of yours across the room. Isn't that Lawrence Wooster there, with that lovely blond girl?"

"I hope not," Elliot said. He looked. "My God, it is. Don't catch his attention, please." He had no desire to trade banalities with Lawrence Wooster, now, as his mother had written him, a junior trust officer at the Guaranty Bank. "Oh," he said, "Lawrence Wooster," remembering, and looked at Vera. She seemed dismayed at the prospect of meeting Joanie Haupt's lover.

"No, please, Mother, he's not a friend of ours."

"It sounds as though you're hiding a deep dark secret," said Margaret, her expression piqued and amused at once. "I certainly don't mind your going out all afternoon without saying a word about where you've been"—Vera, who knew that he had seen Kai, slowly stirred the ice in her vodka martini—"after all, you're a grown man now, but I can't *imagine* what could be amiss with dear little Lawrence Wooster. Not that he was ever really little, but he certainly seemed harmless enough. Why, I can remember on your commencement day from Walkins how all the boys in your class smiled when he went up on the stage to get his diploma. *Cum laude*, too, as you were, Elliot. You were all grinning like Chinese cats! Mrs. Wooster wasn't three rows away from us, and she looked terribly proud."

His father surprised him then: he reached out to his wife and gently patted her wrist. "Let's not bother with Lawrence, if the children don't wish to see him." Even more surprisingly, his mother took the rebuke gracefully. She merely nodded, saying, "Well, it's just that he was at Walkins with Elliot." Chase received the sentence gloomily.

He had been uncharacteristically quiet all during the day, Elliot recalled. Shortly after coming in from some errand, he had gone into the lower living room and played the piano—played it for hours. Elliot had left the house shortly before lunch, and when he returned, frustrated and upset by Kai's long recital, Chase had gone upstairs to work. This was not unusual in itself, but what work could he possibly have on the twenty-third of December? Vera had wanted to hear about his conversation with Kai, but he had been unable to recount that long story. "Yes, he told me some things," Elliot had said to his wife, "but I think it was in confidence." Of course he could not tell her that the book was very nearly published; that much was certainly in confidence. "He said a lot of things about Harrison Upp. He thinks Upp might have betrayed him to the Nazis and had him put in the camp. Kai had false papers with a Jewish name." Vera looked sickened. "What else?" "He said they lived like rats on a garbage heap." Vera said, "I don't think I can hear any more about it. But did talking about it seem to help? I thought . . ." Seeing his helpless look, his shrug, she had nearly cried. "I don't know, I just don't know," he answered. "I guess he had to talk about it, yes."

Elliot thought that Kai would never have told him his story if he had not blurted out his disconnected version of the Ronnie Upp affair, and, perhaps, if he had not been so shaken, arriving at Kai's apartment—or if Kai had not noticed that his files had been disturbed. But, that granted, what followed? Elliot could not help feeling that Kai had been doing more than unburdening himself of a complicated and painful memory; the old man was too reticent for that. He had almost certainly caught some echo of Elliot's affair with Anita; if not the affair, then his distress about his former mistress, and the long story had been intended as a reflection of that confusion. He had offered his own history as parable. Some insight seemed to elude him here, his brain could go no further, and he had given up. Elliot remembered ruefully the clarity he had felt that morning, driving along the edge of the lake. It had been no more than a respite: it was certainly not the grand summing-up he had thought. The false sighting of Upp, Kai's history, these had drowned that momentary optimism in doubt. All afternoon, he had longed to call Anita.

So his father's unexpected retreat into Fats Waller and then into the upper part of the house had not been unwelcome. He could have bantered with Chase only feebly, and that would have evoked irony, superiority, a lurking sadness. Chase was pleased that he had signed Dr. Laubach's statement; it was undoubtedly the reason for the doctor's inclusion in tonight's outing, though dinners at the City Club normally were almost overbearing "family" occasions. The doctor, at least, seemed to have nothing serious in his mind. He had chattered to Elliot about music, flirted with Vera, and was now gaily talking to Margaret about, of all things, the Walkins School, where he and Chase had been classmates.

"It was discipline," he said, "that made Walkins a great school. Chase's grandfather and Brooks knew that if they wanted a first-rate private school in Plechette City, they had to have high standards in every department of school life. That is why they began with an entirely English staff, and I am convinced that it was no mistake."

"No one any longer thinks it was," said Chase.

"Of course not, Chase."

Years ago, Walkins had been known as "the English school," even after no more than two or three English masters remained on the staff. But, Elliot thought, why in the world did Pierce Laubach feel it necessary to utter this belated loyalty pledge? The label had helped, in time, to attract pupils: Brooks's whim had, like nearly everything else in his life, earned its way. Listening to Dr. Laubach go on about the school, Elliot was puzzled by the man's entire manner, which seemed propitiatory and soothing.

"A great school, and a real contribution to the community," he was saying. "It helped change the face of the city in an entirely positive manner. When it turned out artists, they were *real* artists, like your son, not layabouts and beatniks."

"The school was never intended to nurture composers or any other kind of artists," Elliot said. "What it wanted to make was business-men. They might name Pittman and me in their list of distinguished graduates, but that's only to leaven the loaf. Everyone else is a banker, like our friend Wooster across the room, or something equally respectable."

"Well, you can't expect them to honor failures," said Dr. Laubach.

"No, Elliot is right," said his father. "Our goals might have been too narrow from the start. The school turned out four generations of real-estate salesmen and lawyers and manufacturers of roofing and siding. Babbittry, in a way." He reflectively sipped at his drink.

The club's manager, Jacques Mortrent, approached deferentially. In atrocious English, he said that the young lady's lobster would require another fifteen minutes to cook, and asked if they would care to order another drink before it came.

"Oh, *let's*," Margaret said. "We should celebrate. Elliot is going to be on television tonight." Chase gloomily nodded.

"Canadian Cloob for Mrs. Denmark . . ." He took their orders and left them, snapping his fingers at a waiter.

"Excuse me a minute," said Elliot, rising. "I won't be a minute." He walked out of the dining room, skirting the other tables and the polished tiny dance floor.

He rushed down the curving staircase to the ground floor, passing a portrait of Brooks Denmark glaring from a brass frame, and crossed the dark red carpet to the members' lounge. An adolescent in a striped waistcoat inclined toward him, but Elliot shook his head, smiling, and the boy again stiffened into military posture, glancing, as he straightened, at his wristwatch. The members' phones were on a table at the back of the lounge. He pulled the fat floppy book from the table and turned to K. In a moment he had found the name, and he began dialing. The waiter discreetly wandered to the farthest side of the lounge. Elliot heard the telephone ring twice in Anita's house, and looking up, saw himself caught in a huge gilt mirror. He looked distracted, out of place, his hair fluffed at the back of his head to puff out behind his ears. *Useless*, he thought. He began to smooth his hair. He did not know what he would say to Anita. Merely talking seemed of value. But as the trilling continued, he looked into the mirror again and saw himself staring out like a bushy simian in the zoo, and felt helpless, foolish. The telephone continued to ring.

His real place was upstairs in the dining room, with Vera and his father, helping them in their difficult evening. Both were unhappy, Vera with her usual sensitivity, Chase uncharacteristically somber and unironic. He had so far not uttered a word about Nun's Wood. The conversation had revolved, like a great clumsy dancing bear, about the Denmark family. Dr. Laubach had been at pains to describe the essential Denmarkness of Walkins School. It was as though the Nun's Wood battle had already been lost. It was lost, of course, but those two men would not admit it. They saw themselves as leading a squadron of wheelchairs and ball gowns up over the ridge, about to conquer the sharpies and carpetbaggers; holding the line, like pathetic Lamont Von Heilitz, like Hilda Usenbrugge's Preservation Society. The recollection of the scattered old woman brought it back to him: Chase had mentioned an appointment with Walter Lyte, the chairman of the Monuments Commission. He had tried to save Brooks's clock. Elliot had forgotten all about it—forgotten it once again, and it was terribly important to his father. He smacked himself on the forehead with his palm. His father must be feeling wretched. The boy across the room jumped as though Elliot had shot himself. He lifted his eyebrows, took a step forward. "No," said Elliot, "no, thanks, I'm all right. I just remembered something."

When he entered the dining room and threaded back through the tables, Lawrence Wooster and his wife, the wife in Elliot's chair and Lawrence backstraddling another chair pulled away from the next table, were cozily seated with the Denmarks. Vera, he saw, was in agonies. Lawrence leapt up and embraced him.

"Ellie!" Wooster pounded his back, then held him at arm's length. "You old sonofagun, I haven't seen you in years! You look terrific!" He scrutinized Elliot's face like a drill instructor: Elliot saw the amused glance at his hair. Lawrence Wooster, for his part, looked considerably more substantial than he had in prep school or at the Columbia mixer. Now Wooster's semicrewcut had grown out another inch and his waistline ten, his shirt sparkled, his teeth gleamed. His jowls owned a bankerish heaviness. "Sylvie and I were sitting across the room, and I said to her, 'I bet that's Ellie Denmark over there with his wife.' And you know I had to recognize your father and mother, even after all this time. Gee, Sylvie was a little shy about meeting you, she adores your music." Elliot perceived Sylvie's hard glossy vapidity as she gave him a voter's smile, and understood Vera's agony. "And she knew we were friends, so I promised to introduce you. We've been having a nice little powwow with Vera while you were away."

". . . away bleeding the lizard," he expected Wooster to say, but, like his haircut, his manner had changed. He wanted Wooster to leave as quickly as he could suggest it, but said, with a passable facsimile of sincerity, "How nice to see you again, Lawrence. It's a pleasure to meet your wife. Hello, Sylvie."

The girl lifted the corners of her mouth. "An honor to meet *you*." She was pretty in a blond, Breck-shampoo barbecue-clique way, but her voice was mesmerizing. "We are both looking forward to your concert. Lawrence had told me that he was a friend of yours from school, and I was so anxious to meet you." Another alto like Andy, with a grainy New York accent.

"Well, tell me," Wooster said, "Ellie, how do you like being back in the Fatherland? You going to stay over there forever?"

"I don't really know. How long is forever?" He wanted these people to leave. His mother was looking at him with disapproval. "We have a nice home, so we'll probably stay a few years. Vera's got a teaching job, and I can get a lot of work done there."

"You've got to come out and see our new place," said Wooster. "I'll throw a log on, and we'll have a real talk."

"Well, I'm not sure," said Elliot. "I'm a little busy . . ." He shrugged.

"No kidding, I'm really serious. How does the old country look to you? We were over in France ourselves last year—stayed in Sarlat, in the Dordogne valley. You know the place? I had two weeks off, and we just lazed around in the sun. Skipped all that tourist stuff they've got around there. Then we hit the Riviera for a couple of days, and then went back up to Paris. Paris is a really feline city, am I right? Of course, I love Gothic, and Sylvie's crazy about it, so we were right on home ground there. What I say is, you can't beat the food and the churches, but I sure didn't get anyplace with the citizens. You have that trouble?"

"No, we don't," Elliot said. He smiled.

"It helps if you can speak French," said Vera. She was enjoying Elliot's general awfulness.

"Well, anyhow, come on, pal, answer my question," said Wooster. "How does the old country look to you?" He tapped Elliot lightly on the arm. "Are you going to be one of these expatriates?"

"Technically, I suppose I am an expatriate, yes. I live out of the country." Chase looked disturbed, while pretending not to listen. "But I'm not sure what you mean by the word. I don't think of myself that way. I'm just trying to get my work done."

"That's my Ellie, always working." Wooster beamed down at Vera and his wife. "Can you folks make it out to my house next week? Let's nail it down for, say, Wednesday."

Vera looked up questioningly at Elliot. "I'm not . . ."

"I think I'll have to call you back about that, Lawrence. We have a number of important engagements, and I can't remember the dates."

Sylvie stood up. She was taller than either Lawrence or himself. Her face, seen in relation to her body, looked surprisingly petite, insectlike, less hard. "That's a pity, Mr. Denmark." Clearly, she had registered the rebuke to her husband, though Lawrence had not. "I'm afraid I've been sitting in your chair. Lawrence and I were just on our way out, and I don't want to keep you standing."

"Just give me one more minute, will you, sweetie? I haven't seen Ellie in years."

Dr. Laubach, patently bored with Wooster, turned back to his conversation with Chase.

"Have you seen any of the old Walkins crowd? Who have you

been seeing? I mean you and Vera, of course. Catch up on any old friends?" Wooster crossed his arms over his chest, his smile a shade less confident.

Sylvie—really a towering woman, Elliot saw—went to her husband's side. She was clearly uncomfortable. She knows what the bastard is angling for, he thought. "I'll go to the powder room, Lawrence, and wait for you downstairs. Lovely to meet you both, and you, Mr. and Mrs. Denmark. Dr. Laubach." His father and Pierce Laubach stood in the same instant. Sylvie strode from the room, holding her head up. Her posture suggested tension, strain: Elliot remembered the bright glossy face she had turned to him, and felt a tingling of shame that she had seen his contempt for her husband.

"Join me just a second, will you, Ellie?" Wooster nodded to the entrance of the dining room.

When they were standing together in the hall at the top of the curving staircase, Wooster said, his whole being aglow, "I guess you've been talking to Joanie Haupt. So you know the story."

Elliot was wild with impatience, thinking of his father. "No, I don't. It's not my business, Lawrence. Why don't you go downstairs and join your wife? She seems to be in trouble."

Wooster was impervious to even blunt suggestion. He seemed radiant with pleasure. "Sylvie's okay. It's the rag or something. They lose a lot of calcium right around then, did you know that? Calcium loss makes them irritable—it's all in Adelle Davis. Sylvie's a good wife, but a little high-strung, you know what I mean?" Before Elliot could protest that he did not, Wooster continued. "I just don't want you to get the wrong idea about me and Joanie. She's been upset for a couple of weeks, but I want you to know one thing—I take care of her." He beamed at Elliot, then looked down at his shoes. "I know we weren't ever the closest friends in the world, but I've been following your career, Elliot. I bought your record, and I got tickets for your concert. I just want to speak my side of the story, that's all. Joanie and I had a little fight the other day, and she told me she was going to talk to Vera. You could have knocked me over with a feather. I didn't even know she knew you people. I begged her not to—Christ, I even slapped her. So she called me a sadist. That's all there was to it. Otherwise, we've got a terrific relationship, a really *human* relationship. It makes me feel bigger than life, Ellie. No shit, it's the greatest thing I ever did in my life. And listen—she's terrific in the sack. The best sex I ever had in my whole life, really *human* sex." He leaned back and put his hands in his jacket pockets. "Isn't that what it's all about, Ellie? Maybe I can tell you something for a change. Taking care of someone like Joanie, that's what it's all about, that's the body's message. Now don't you know that's right?"

"I know you have to be careful to restrain illusions from messing up facts," Elliot said. "I have to go back inside, Lawrence."

"In a minute. I just told you the facts. Sylvie's a Catholic, I can't get a divorce. Besides that, she is a child emotionally. I kid you not, Sylvie's a great woman in her way, but I'm married to the last Victorian lady. Believe me, I know what I'm talking about. She still believes in stuff you only find in books. Well, we're all sensual creatures, aren't we? It's got to be expressed. An artist like you, I don't know why I'm telling you. What I'm talking about is experience, and you must have seen plenty of it. Did you ever read *The Prophet*?"

"You're an ass, Lawrence," Elliot said. "I'm sorry, but I have to get back to my table."

Wooster straightened his back. "I'm going to forget you said that, Ellie. That's your temperament speaking, not you. Maybe you could use a good Reichian analysis. I might just be a clod of a banker, not some fancy composer, but I think you could do with some real experience in your own country. You might be getting a little out of touch." He brightened again. "*Touch*. Now there, you see—"

"Thanks for the advice, Lawrence." Elliot extended his hand. "I think you'd better join your wife."

"Just one more thing. I think your father is doing a bang-up job on this Nun's Wood business. Ronnie Upp is an egotistical little pain in the ass, and a cold-hearted bastard to boot. I'll tell you what your father has, Ellie. A social conscience. I signed his petition myself, and I was happy to do it."

"That's nice. I'll tell him," said Elliot wearily.

Instead of saying good-bye, Wooster held up the two first fingers of his left hand, and then went down the staircase to the ladies' lounge. It took Elliot a moment to understand what the gesture meant.

"Just because Lawrence Wooster's manners are execrable is no excuse for yours to be the same," said Margaret, neatly parting a section of duck from the bone. "He is a child and his wife is as high-strung as a kitten. I wouldn't be surprised if you terrified them both."

"I think that Wooster probably terrifies his wife himself," answered Elliot, "and I couldn't even make a dent in him, much less scare him. He gave me the peace sign when he left."

Dr. Laubach giggled. "Bankers are becoming very mo-dish," he said to Chase.

"Wooster is a lout and a bore, no matter how modish he is," said Vera. She looked glaringly up at Elliot. "And I'm sure I know what he wanted to brag about to you." She'd had another hysterical telephone call from Joanie Haupt that afternoon.

"I'm sure I don't care what it is," said Margaret. "His wife is much too good for him."

Elliot merely nodded. "Did she know anything about music?" he asked Vera.

"She plays the guitar."

"Modish bankers must have modish wives," said Dr. Laubach. "Lawrence Wooster is one of the signatories of our statement, Chase. He was the only man in his trust department to sign, I believe."

"Well, maybe Walkins did something for him after all." Chase did not appear to be elated by this possibility.

"Folk songs?"

Vera smiled. "John Dowland."

There was silence while they ate.

"Elliot," Chase said after a while, "there is something I must tell you. I'll try to put a good face on it, but it is bad news."

"I know what it is. I realized downstairs that you'd been unhappy all day." Looking over at Vera, he saw that she had noticed it long before. It was, he could see, the reason for her suggestion that morning that he talk to his father.

"Astute of you," said Chase. "Forbear from interruption, and I'll describe the morning's events. Pierce has been kind enough to join us tonight, and I'll have to ask his forbearance as well, for he already knows what I am about to say."

Dr. Laubach seemed to glitter with amusement. "Genre painting," he mystifyingly said. "A Dutch tavern scene, with glandular cases loitering in corners. Or a Goya court scene, with Walter Lyte as crippled king, and Ronnie Upp as *éminence mauve*."

"Oh, I'm sorry," said Vera.

"Pierce can always keep me amused." His father ignored Vera's condolence. "This morning I went early to Walter Lyte's house to speak with him about having the Monuments Commission give their sanction to Brooks's clock tower. Pierce joined me, at my request. Pierce and I were shown into the foyer, were divested by a mollusk of our coats, and left to admire the parquetry. In a moment, another old lobster showed us into a drawing room. He lifted a sheet from a couch and two chairs and mutely bade us sit. At this point, engulfed in the gloom of Victorian breakfronts and maroon carpets, I felt like a figure in a Charles Addams cartoon. The image was miraculously apt. A whirring noise emanated from the hall. Piqued, I went to the doorway and looked up the staircase.

"Shock followed shock. Gliding like Bela Lugosi down the banister and supported in an evil network of straps, a gnome was delivered to us in a chair. The gnome in his basket reached the bottom, fumbled peevishly at a lock, and was dropped gently onto the floor— still in his basket, of course. The basket began once again to purr, and brought him forward. As he motored toward me, I saw a gigantic dry old head, eyes nearly closed and as rimmed with black as though they were rubbed with kohl, two withered, palsied hands, a trunk and body that seemed no more substantial than the thin antlers on the drawing-room walls. All of this midpart was encased in a substance curiously like a winding sheet—or so I thought, until I realized that it was simply a shirt which had twisted about him so thoroughly that I could not see the buttons. He raised a sparrowlike paw to my hand.

"I escorted him back into the drawing room, where he stationed himself before the couch. Pierce and I sat there, in the dark sea of tartans and sheets, under Walter Lyte's Egyptian gaze. With some difficulty we brought our matter to his attention. He squinted up his face so that it appeared to be one huge spot, liverish in hue, and offered the information that a charming Mr. Hop had been to see him months before, and had obtained his signature on a paper. The Monuments Commission had mightily moved, and could not move again."

"A sub-stantially true account," said Dr. Laubach. "Though somewhat embroidered, my old friend."

"Upp had already been to see him?" blurted Elliot. "He took care of it before."

Shockingly, Chase's face dissolved. "He took care of it," he said. "We're finished. There's nothing I can do. That senile old man signed Upp's papers months ago. Upp convinced him that the tower was structurally unsound. He said it's a miracle that it's stood as long as it has." He held his hand over his eyes.

"Come, Chase," Margaret said firmly. "Let's finish our meal, and we'll go home to watch Elliot *do his thing* on television."

"He's a filthy plotter," said Chase, still holding his hand over his eyes. "Forgive me."

"He's been like that all day," said Margaret. "You know the pride Chase has in the family. He's never forgiven Robert Denmark for selling the factory to Ronnie Upp, and the tower was the last straw." She glanced sharply at Elliot. "He wanted to talk to you in private about it this morning, but when you went out without saying a word, he went back to pounding the poor piano."

"I would have stayed, if I had known," said Elliot. "The last thing I wanted to do was desert him."

"I know that, Elliot, but he doesn't. All that talk about Lamont Von Heilitz—don't you see that he thinks he's like that poor silly old man? Chase thinks the whole world is slipping by him. It's the worst thing that can happen to a man, to see himself as outmoded. Or impotent. Or useless. All of this sending out checks to criminals is his way of convincing himself that he is still in touch. That there is still something he can do." She nodded toward the bust of Freud on the bookshelves. "It's why he bought that bust. He wanted to show that he's at least in the right century." It was the first time in years that Elliot had seen his mother so angry. "Do you think that Pierce Laubach would react in the way your father has? That any of his old friends would? Chase is a deeper man than any of them. He's also an optimistic man, as you are, but the past few years have been hard on him. When he came in this morning with Pierce, he was ashen, positively white in the face." She sat straight-backed in one of the new chairs and looked at him sternly.

"What can I do?"

"Talk to him. Let him talk to you."

They heard a car door closing down in the drive, and Elliot went to the window. Dr. Laubach's Lincoln was taking its stately way out toward Lake Point Drive; the taillights flashed once, and the long car drifted like a barge northward.

"Letting people talk to me seems like the only thing I've done since I came here," he said. "When I buy a pack of cigarettes I think I'm going to get a life story with my change."

"I told you why he wanted to talk about Lamont Von Heilitz, Elliot," said Margaret. "Your father thinks he was born thirty years too late."

She stood and joined him at the window. Dr. Laubach's Lincoln was still moving northward, going heavily against the whiteness. He felt her hand smoothing the hair at the back of his head. "He's your father, Elliot," she quietly said. From the upstairs living room, the television set dimly burst into theme music. "Let's go see how you look on television," she said. "He's proud of you for this, you know."

Chase and Vera were seated before the set, where an oval-eyed woman was caressing a soapbox. From the couch, his hands toying with the huge transparent cigarette lighter, Chase gave Elliot an uncomfortable, embarrassed glance from the August sky of his irises. He smoothed down his necktie with one hand. "It just started," he said. "Mr. Edwards has promised us a 'slam-bang show for Christmas' and told three sub-Johnny Carson jokes." He looked critically at the crease in his trousers.

Margaret sat beside Chase on the sofa and took his hand. Elliot leaned on the back of Vera's chair, not knowing if he would be able to watch himself turning into a spouting didactic fool. "Are your parents watching this mess?" he said. Vera turned her head to him, and nodded.

"It's all right," she said.

A zoom shot: Ted Edwards in a chair before a fireplace, leafing through a magazine, then Ted Edwards' face, sleek and gangsterish, filled the screen, as if in amazement. The audience laughed. "I was just getting to the juicy parts." He opened his mouth, winked, closed his mouth. "Well, they won't let me tell you about it," he said. "But it's nothing that doesn't happen in kitchens all over America." More laughter. "Our first guest is a luscious bit of southern honey who graciously gave us a little"—a long pause—"of her time before she starts filming her next picture. One of the greatest actresses of our time: *Lola Walker!*"

To enthusiastic applause, a woman strode onstage. Her hair was achingly red. Halfway to her chair, she did a parody bump-and-grind, kissed Edwards, and mock-demurely sat on the guest's chair. "Ted dear," she wheezed, "I wanted to sit on your lap but the management said it was reserved." Whistles, laughs. "I *told* them there was room enough for both of us."

"Does anybody want a drink?" Elliot asked. Chase shook his head, and Margaret and Vera both said no. "I think I'll make one for myself, then."

A long pan of the audience, which Elliot had scarcely noticed when he was on the stage, walled behind the cameras and the lights: rows of women with open mouths, some waving hands, a poster reading FREMONT HS WOLVERINES, a few stunning girls in the front seats.

"I'm going to make that drink," Elliot said, and pushed off from the back of Vera's chair. A local commercial came on the screen.

Elliot went to the door as Edwards' face reappeared in mid-syllable, saying, "And now, something a little different. Plechette City, currently in the midst of a civic Waterloo, a blockbuster re-zoning issue to decide the fate of many acres of woodland, is also the birthplace of one of our finest modern composers. I've been talking to this man downstairs, and I think you'll find him as charming and entertaining as I have. Let's have a hand for a real force in modern music, Elliot *Den*mark."

He walked before the camera: always a surprise to see yourself this way. Elliot hung just inside the door, watching his image shake hands with Edwards, his gestures a little stiff, then take his chair, jerking up his trousers as his father did. The image-Elliot, big solid face like his grandfather's and hair curling over his ears, tilted his head toward Ted Edwards, crossed his legs. Compared to Edwards, he seemed somehow unprofessional, unfree. "I never heard all that stuff about the city," he said to his parents and Vera. "I was away off to the side, and when he said my name, somebody gave me a push."

"Shhh," said Chase, who was leaning forward, his hand still held by his wife.

"That's what I thought," said Vera. She smiled at him.

"It's why they wanted you on the program," said Chase, his mustache bristling. "Pure and simple."

On the screen, Edwards' razor-slit eyes were narrowing, as if in concentration. Then, Elliot had not noticed the amusement in the man's face, the lifted eyebrows and nods: he looked like a man giving serious attention to a child. Then Elliot's own voice, as the camera stayed on Edwards' face for a moment: "...the breathing of the music." Edwards opened his eyes and took a conspicuous breath. Then a medium shot of the two of them, Elliot talking, moving his hands; but the damage was nearly total. Edwards had managed to communicate seriousness to him while the camera recorded urbane amusement. "Composers need system to characterize space," his voice was saying, "and they need not fall back on the tradition of the centralized hierarchy of triads. All this is Germanic and nineteenth-century, the kind of music we know best." "*Do* we?" said Edwards gaily, and the audience laughed again. Elliot left the room.

He made a drink in the kitchen and sat beneath the rows of shining pots on hooks. He tried to make his mind empty. What else could he do, except what he had done? But the fiasco of the interview

seemed of the same fabric as his humiliation and confusion before
Kai, Ettenheim's insolence, his perpetual turmoil over Anita, the
whole business of the petition. Andy French. From the hall, he could
hear Vera speaking quietly to her parents on the telephone. That
was another mess. He finished his drink and moved into the hall,
passing Vera. She winked at him.

The television set had been switched off. From the end of the hall
he saw a spreading green-tinted light which meant his mother was
in her office. Elliot continued back to the living room. Chase was
standing by the big windows, looking out at the black lake, hugely
visible through his reflection, and turned to him as Elliot entered the
room. His change in mood was immediately apparent. He was beam-
ing, his eyes clear and brilliant. "They'll have to get the ice cutter
out soon," he said. "The whole harbor is icing up. Vera is talking to
her parents? Your father-in-law must be something less than pleased
by all this." He waved a hand in the direction of the blank television
screen. "Herman has no one to blame but himself."

"No, Herman was very good about it," Elliot said.

"Of course. I had forgotten that he drove you down there for the
taping." He was standing very straight before the windows. "Son,
I've been in the dumps all day long, but you've lifted me right out
of them. I can't tell you how proud of you I am. That was a very
brave thing you did just now."

"Just now I went into the kitchen and had a drink."

"Whenever."

"And it wasn't very brave. I was just tricked into it. Edwards was
playing me along and then when I was ready to say anything at all,
he brought up Nun's Wood."

"But the way you did it!" Chase moved his arm emphatically
down and across his chest, fingers balled. It was a gesture of forceful
approval. "You put it so judiciously and yet so firmly. And I didn't
know that Upp owned some land out near Richmond Corners—that
was a very telling point."

"I'm not sure about it," said Elliot. He sat heavily on a chair. His
reflection looked at him: skin the color of egg whites against the
lake's flat blackness. "I mean, I'm sure about the land, but I'm not

sure that it means anything. Or that my talking about it will change anybody's mind."

Chase went softly around the room, patting at his suit-jacket pockets. "Don't you fool yourself, Elliot. You've done us a real service by what you just said. We've been making news in Chicago too, if you're not aware of it. What we are doing in this city is significant, and you gave the reason for it precisely in what you said to Edwards. Upp's plan would be an ecological disaster."

"I know I said that." Elliot saw the dying fox, its small teeth exposed, at the bottom of the brush pile in Nun's Wood.

"Of course you did!" Chase had by now circled the room, moving exultantly, and he sat on the couch across from Elliot. He picked up the transparent lighter and tossed it in one hand. "I want to tell you something. While the women are out of the room is a good time, because I don't want Margaret to hear it."

He leaned forward and gently set the lighter back on the coffee table. "I've been in utter despair for this entire day. It seemed to me that everything I believed in was dying, on its way out, all the traditions of my family. I kept thinking about one of the boys I mentioned to you earlier, Ralph Nieder, who was the brother of George Nieder, a good friend of mine at one time, before he went off to Pittsburgh to buy into a chain-store operation. Ralph killed himself when he came back from Europe, you know. He'd been a hero—there was a picture in the *Herald* of Eisenhower himself pinning a medal on Ralph. Well, I was at the Nieder home when the girl, Ralph's girlfriend, called. She was hysterical. George kept telling her to calm down and explain what happened. Finally, he went sort of white, and shouted into the phone. *What? What?* He raced out of the house, and I followed him. We drove out to Lone Pine Lane, just past the Hunt Club, where the girl lived with her parents. Then there were as many farms out that way as houses, and Ralph's girlfriend lived in one of the new houses set back from the lake. Better frontage than we have, and a lot more of it. It looked pretty peaceful as we drove up, but when we got inside, the girl was screaming. She had blood on her fingers where she had touched him, and she was smearing it on the walls, on her dress—she looked crazy. George and I ran upstairs to her bedroom, and found Ralph's body up there, naked on the girl's bed. *On* it, not in it. He had broken in when she was at school, gone upstairs, taken off his clothes, unstrapped the false leg the army gave him, and shot himself on her bed. It was the worst sight I'd ever seen in my life, and it's stayed with me for the past twenty-five years.

"Now, listen to me. Today I was thinking, Elliot, if that might not be the right way to finish things off after all. I could see Ralph's point. But I was wrong, Elliot, wrong as wrong could be. And that's what you've done for me. Despair is no answer. I feel full of plans again."

Chase's new enthusiasm, couched in such terms, was nearly too much for Elliot. "I don't believe you were thinking of killing yourself," he said.

"Who said I was?" Chase drew himself up again and pursed his mouth. "I said I saw his point. That's all I said. The sight of young Ralph lying there made quite an impression on me, kid. No, no, no"—he was shaking his head vigorously—"suicide is a coward's way out, a low unmanly way of canceling your problems. And poor Ralph Nieder had his leg blown to bits by a German mine, and he couldn't deal with the adjustments back to peacetime. Two powerful motives—besides those, he'd been a boy who never thought beyond the end of his nose. If that is the organ in question. But today, I was thinking about him with more sympathy than I'd had before."

"I see," said Elliot, not wanting a moral lesson he knew would follow.

"Why, certainly you see. You're a Denmark. The way to conquer your problems in this life is to face them out, squarely, to take the worst and not knuckle under to it...." There was more, but it was all familiar to Elliot.

When they were lying together in Elliot's single bed, Vera said, "Don't feel bad about that program, Elliot. Your father needed something like that. I was so *sorry* for him when he started to cry. By the end of the program he was back to himself again."

"So I learned."

"And my parents weren't too bad about it. You know how Daddy is—he said one more oar in the water wouldn't stir it up much more. Mother was a little bitchy, but in kind of a nice way. She says that more people are calling up about the wolf now than about Nun's Wood. They all want the alderman to rush over to their houses with a shotgun."

She put her hand on his chest: a light cool density against his skin. Elliot, sensing some ultimatum, bent his neck so he could see her face. "He said, 'If your husband is such a genius, why can't he buy me a Rolls-Royce for Christmas?' "

"Jesus, I've had an incredible day," Elliot said. In seconds he was asleep, still holding Vera to him.

In the morning he moved sleepily to one side and found that she was still in his bed. She tentatively moved her hand to him, and his mind just clearing from a dream, he entered the soft immensity of their mutual pleasure as if it were the means of restoring his coherence. For minutes at a time, he thought they were back in their house on Villa Beauséjour.

chapter 19

How do you feel about this?" asked Elliot. He was parking his mother's car six houses down from Anita's house, before the only vacant curb space he could find on the block. "It looks like a big messy party." He gestured at the other cars illuminated by the soft nighttime shine of the streetlamps.

"I'm not sure," said Vera. "You're not really talking about the size of the party, are you?" Her face, lightly touched with makeup, which made her seem abstract to him, a harder and more complicated version of Vera, gleamed toward him in the light from the dashboard. A moon, a continent. "You've seen her a couple of times since we've been back, and I haven't seen her at all. You didn't sleep with her, did you?"

It was what she had wanted to ask the previous morning, before he had left for Kai's apartment. The question now seemed to come from the personality suggested by the makeup: yet it was merely another proof of her courage. "No, I didn't," he said. "I didn't even want to."

"Then she's just another woman who lives in Plechette City. A person I used to know. I suppose you're closer to her than I am. That's all."

"It's just a friendship now. I get a kick out of seeing her. And that's all for me." Saying this, having said it, he felt a yearning toward the condition he had just defined, as if the emotions he had felt rumbling and barking within him on the first night he had seen her again—a thinner Anita bearing the traces of a bruise—had been willed, created. Kai's story about Harrison Upp stirred within him, then dissipated like fog before strong sun. He would ask Anita his question. He would talk with Ronnie Upp: Elliot managed to stifle the feelings that arose with the name.

Vera leaned across the seat and kissed his cheek. "It's too cold to sit in the car when we have a nice messy party to go to. Let's go inside where it's warm." She turned her head toward the window, where heaped snow mounted to the top of the lock's thin column. "I'll get out on your side."

He climbed out onto the street. White narrow stripes showed the progress of the plow's razor, traces of snow a glasslike ice interrupted by the duller material of the asphalt, and he said, "Watch out, it's slippery." He held out his hand and helped her from the car. Vera wobbled, lurching toward him, and then steadied herself. They moved slowly on the street between the twin rows of cars. Fifteen yards before Anita's house, Elliot released Vera's arm and ran ahead three long strides that became a swooping glide along the ice. The winter air needled at his face. He staggered, one of his feet slipping sideways, then windmilled his arms. "Elliot!" called Vera. He knew he was going to fall: he fell in that instant. The whiteness broke and dissolved before him into points of light. His back hurt. Elliot opened his eyes and was looking straight up toward the black sky. A single enormous star hung above him.

From the porch, in the cold anticipatory moment before the bell answered, they could see through the windows into the living room: the bright edge of the tree, a shifting mass of people holding drinks. A steady buzz of voices overlay the music swelling from the speakers. For an instant, it seemed to Elliot a summation of all the parties he had ever been to, lively, jumbled, a bright erotic confusion.

Anita, flushed, opened the door. "Elliot and Vera, come on in, dears, I was just wondering where you were. I'm so happy you came!" Elliot followed Vera through the door into the foyer, Anita taking Vera's arm.

They put their coats in Anita's study, across the little hall from the dining room, where the big dark table was covered with chafing dishes and plates of hors d'oeuvres, salads, spreads. A group of men had collected around the impromptu bar at the end of the room. As they walked by, shedding their coats, Elliot saw Rubin and Heldenweit, two of the members of the Melos Quartet, juggling plates and their drinks back across the main hall to the living room, but he said nothing. There was time ahead for all that. In the glimpse he had, the living room seemed as crowded as it had looked from the porch: a moving wall of people. Himmel glanced toward him, raising his glass. His mouth opened.

"Andy and I may have overextended ourselves," said Anita as she closed the door to the study. "You can see what kind of a madhouse we've got here. We just went around inviting people for weeks ahead of time, and unfortunately, I think they've all shown up!" She exhaled, leaning back against the door. "But here we are, together again at last. I'm so happy you're here. Let's just relish the few seconds we've got before all your other admirers sweep you away." Anita blazed out at them, her green eyes moving from Elliot to Vera, then flicking back. "Promise me you'll stay for a long time," she said. "I want to be able to talk to you."

She's overdoing it, he thought, but Vera surprised him by saying, "We'll probably stay until doomsday, Anita. It looks like a lovely party."

"At the moment it looks like Dante's fourth circle to me, I'm afraid. I just don't know what to do with so many people!"

"Let them take care of themselves," said Vera. "How are *you* doing?" In Vera's voice, lower than usual, and in her stance, her head a fraction forward, Elliot could read her impatience. She did not want a reunion scene.

"Dear friends and sweet people," was all Anita said.

"Well . . ." said Vera.

"It's time to feed you to the lions." Then she moved closer to

Elliot. "You were wonderful on Ted Edwards' program. I was so proud of you, Elliot. You make me so happy, you really do."

"How did Ronnie think I was?" Still looking at Anita, he saw Vera, barely disguising her impatience, begin to move toward the door.

"Oh, Ronnie knew all about it. He was there in the audience when you did the taping." She reached sideways, still glowing at him, and took Vera's hand, intercepting her progress. Vera looked skyward. "You'll see him tonight, and he'll tell you about it. Ronnie is very eager to see you, in fact. Now—to the lions."

She opened the door and they went into the living room; immediately they were swept into the party, and Elliot lost sight of Vera.

"This isn't a party, it's a menagerie," said Himmel. He gave Elliot a glass and half-filled it from a bottle in his hand. "La Kellerman and *la jeunesse* invited every other person in sight. Old-fogydom, us Agee-alcohol set, cheek to jowl with the with-its." Himmel splashed liquor into his own glass and then set the bottle on the bar table. "The with-its, Miss French among them, are blowing their minds out in the television room."

"Why are there all these kids?"

"Half the university symphony was invited. It's by way of being your party, Denmark. You're lucky Ettenheim isn't here to do his Tito Gobbi act in the midst of the festivities." Himmel's beefy face slackly indicated glee. "Where's the beautiful Vera?"

"I lost her getting through the dining room." Elliot looked over heads. In a crush by the door, he saw Vera talking to the dean. "She's talking to Jaeger," he said.

"The nincompoop? Watch out, my boy. He's going to try to hire you back, if he can remember your name correctly. Look—" Himmel grasped his arm and spilled some whiskey on his trousers. "Let's us scout around and see if there's any available maidenly beauty. My wife is at home minding Saul. She never quite forgave Anita's not apologizing for the time Mark hit the kid with a hammer. Nor Andy, for that matter. Andy damned near makes her shit in her pants."

"She does look a little wild," Elliot agreed.

"Wild? She glares like a hungry tiger. The only time I tried to talk to Miss French, she damn near scorched my eyebrows. How do you get on with her? I saw your car parked out in front here for a couple of hours when Miss French was home alone."

"I couldn't say," he said, wanting to change the subject.

A tall thin familiar-looking girl in glasses was touching his sleeve. She greeted them both by name.

Himmel's demeanor changed. "How nice to see you, Roberta. Have you been introduced?" The girl shook her head, tucking her lower lip between her teeth. "This is Roberta Potocky, Elliot. One of your cellists. I think she wants to tell you how wonderful you are."

"You're unfair," the girl said to him. "I just wanted to say—" Here she looked at Elliot, who saw that the girl had a fragile, brittle kind of prettiness. She reminded him of Sylvie Wooster.

"Thank you," he said.

"Well, that's all I really had to say."

"I'm happy you said it." The girl still hovered by, clearly hoping for more. "You don't think I'm too much an ogre at rehearsals?"

"I love it when you're like that," she said, and blushed so hotly he thought she would faint. "And I saw you on television yesterday night, and I thought you were wonderful. He *was* wonderful," she said to Himmel, looking for support, "wasn't he?"

"He was a dream."

"I thought I was a buffoon."

"Oh no, you were perfect." The girl smiled up at him, bit her lip again, and fluttering her fingers, said, "I'm looking forward to the concert." Then she backed away into the crowd. Elliot watched the top of her head move toward the living room.

Himmel clapped his right hand about the elbow of his left arm, raising his left hand in a fist. "Perfect!" he bellowed. "Perfect."

Carrying their refilled glasses, they elbowed through to the living room. Near the tree, Anita waved at them before turning back to a furry young man in a denim suit. He could not possibly be Ronnie

Upp. "Bob Cratchit, believe it or not," Himmel breathed in his ear. "That's his real name. He's in the psych department. He and Kellerman have long tender discussions about white rats."

"Have you seen Ronnie Upp?"

"Wouldn't know him if I saw him," said Himmel. "Not unless he drove that Jaguar into the room. I see it parked out in front of here now and then. Cratchit now, he drives a dune buggy."

"Here?"

"No, you pedant. On the beach. He gave a lecture about the psychoaesthetics of dune buggies and tattoos to the Student Union Forum one night—what is he doing in this room, though? He ought to be snuffing out his consciousness upstairs with the kiddies."

"One of the new academics."

"One of the newest."

On the other side of the room, Elliot saw Vera talking to the black cellist from the university symphony. As he watched, she laughed at something the boy said, and held out her palm toward his own. "No *way*," he heard the boy saying, "no *way*." He and Vera both laughed.

"I'm telling you," Himmel said, "you could do worse than Roberta Potocky. A trifle skinny, but she's got a great little tush." He swirled his glass. "I'm dry," he said, and pushed his way back to the bar.

—You're Denmark. You're sweet.

He had maneuvered his way to the front of the room, looking vaguely for Anita, and turned to see an ample girl, her red-blond hair longer than Anita's used to be, bubbling up at him.

—You don't know me yet.

—Sweet sweet sweet.

"I don't like that adjective." He smiled at her starry eyes.

"Where's your head, sweet Denmark? Do you want to turn on with the real people?"

"No," he said. "I hallucinate."

The girl held her cupped hands up to her eyes. "I see you," she said. "I really, really see you."

"What do I look like?" He sought for a ready excuse to separate himself from the bubbly girl.

"A biiig bear." She made her voice gruff. "A coyote. A sad man."

"_____"

Hearing a female voice enact a wordless slide from a perfect D flat to a perfect G, he turned, his ear tingling. Then he met disappointment. It was Rosa Heldenweit, chubby wife of Ernst Heldenweit, violist for the Melos Quartet. He had met her no more than three times before, once over thin sherry at a music-department party in Thatcher Hall (now uprooted and replaced by the concrete-and-glass of Usenbrugge Hall), once at a stuffy gathering at Jaeger's house where she had talked about her son Raymond, accepted on early admission to Harvard and a gangly surly lump he had later encountered at a party, the third of these, at Himmel's house, where Rosa had snubbed him, then an hour later confronted him with the words: "Why don't you ever invite us over? Ernst and I have been wondering." Quoth charmer Raymond: "Forget it, Mom, he's a snob." A worse disappointment was her company, two men standing as if in straitjackets, each expressing by rigidity his disdain for the surroundings. Wattman and Donadio, musicologists and co-authors of *The Poverty of the Modern*, where he had been given a caustic footnote. (Donadio, in the infinitesimal flurry after publication, had written an article for *Gramophone* on "Surveying New Composers" in which Elliot's work was described as "engagingly arid.") Wattman and Donadio looked no happier to see him than he felt seeing them, but Rosa Heldenweit, still pursuing a world of perfect sociability, put a plump hand to his wrist. "Elliot, I thought it was you. Ernst told me he'd heard you were back, but I forgot all about it until I saw you standing there." She smiled, full of baffled goodwill.

"Yes, it's me," he said.

"Denmark," said Donadio. Wattman twitched his shoulders in a gesture intended as a greeting.

"Hello, gentlemen," he said. "Still pursuing the good?"

Wattman showed his teeth. "Always the comedian."

"Ernst would love it if you would come to our house for cocktails," said Rosa. Elliot could imagine the Heldenweit cocktail hour: South African sherry and damp things on crackers, while Heldenweit mumbled complaints about Himmel. He invented an excuse.

"Hold on a sec there, Denmark," said Donadio. "Do you still like that stuff under Stravinsky's name in the *New York Review of Books*?" He was alluding to a dusty series of arguments, conducted with a choked fury on Donadio's part, from his second year of teaching. "Wouldn't you say the old boy has been getting awfully thin lately?" He smiled aggressively. "You subtract all that overrated wit, and how much content have you got?"

"About enough to make three other composers. Or twelve musicologists." Elliot laughed. "What are you working on now?"

"Caustic, aren't we?" said Wattman. "That's a pretty poor defense, I hope you know that."

"We're doing a book on Elgar. *Elgar's Musical Failure.*"

"Maybe just *Elgar's Failure*," mused Wattman.

"I didn't know that he'd had one," said Elliot.

"You're going to have to learn," snarled Wattman, "that you can't joke your way out of serious discussions. I'm convinced that going to Paris was the worst move you could have made. That hothouse-Boulanger atmosphere, that superficial glossy chasing after fame, that worldly-wise atmosphere, that *avant garde* posturing, whatever, that's all bad for your work."

"You're beginning to talk the way you write," said Elliot.

"Hold on a sec there, Denmark, we're trying to make a point," said Donadio.

"Give me a call when you've made it," said Elliot. "Good-bye, Rosa."

He went back through the crowd to the bar and refilled his glass, took two long swallows, and then refilled it again. The whiskey ignited in his throat and burned unpleasantly down his chest. Someone in the living room changed the record. Elliot heard Roberta Flack sinuously gliding through a key change.

Elliot sipped again at his drink and started to walk away from the bar. "Oh, Elliot," he heard Jaeger saying, "what a nice surprise to see you here." The dean separated himself from a group and came toward him. "We've all been following your career very happily. You've done some very impressive things during your sojourn abroad."

Elliot thanked him.

"You've freshened your drink? ... Then perhaps you wouldn't mind stepping into a quieter area to have a talk with me." Jaeger led him out of the dining room into the hall, where they could talk undisturbed. Several feet away, a boy Elliot recognized as the tympanist from the symphony was leaning up against a girl, prisoning her against the wall and talking to her in a fast undertone. When Elliot and Jaeger approached, he looked up and, glaring at Elliot, led the girl up the staircase. "I must say, I haven't been at a party quite this ... exuberant in a number of years," said the dean. "It rather reminds me of my student days."

"It reminds me of my grade-school days," said Elliot.

"Oh, things have changed in the university," Jaeger said, not quite appositely. "Some of the formality that might have bothered you years ago has been eradicated." Jaeger was thinking of the stir that Baltz had created, Elliot saw. "We've tried to follow some of the newer lines of thought, you know, in an effort to adjust to changing realities. For example we now have only three required courses for music majors—or is it two? Something in that line. And the piano requirements for the M.A. exam have been severely moderated. I don't know if you keep up with this sort of thing"—Elliot shook his head—"but I think you will find that we here are very nearly in the vanguard of educational reform. When I go out and talk to various groups, raising funds, you know, and explaining our program, I'm quite surprised to see how radical we've become." He laid two fingers on Elliot's sleeve. "It may be an improper time to broach such a suggestion, Elliot, but I'd like to sound you out on possibly returning to the university. You were quite an asset to us in those days, my boy, and we'd be terribly proud to have you with us again. I'm sure everybody in your department would agree."

Elliot smiled wryly into his drink. "Well, thank you," he said.

"But I'm doing quite well on my own, and teaching does take up a lot of time."

"I think you'd find the salary a recompense for any time lost," said Jaeger. "And of course, as a distinguished composer, you wouldn't be expected to teach more than four hours a week."

"Four hours?" asked Elliot. It was less than the chairman taught.

"If it meets your approval."

"What would the salary be like?"

Jaeger coughed delicately into his hand. "It's as yet an unofficial offer, Elliot, so I can't say anything definite. And you know that we've had budgetary problems for the past two years—cutbacks in federal spending play havoc with our salary systems. But as you'd be coming in with a good deal of substantial work behind you, and would perhaps be able to bring in other distinguished musicians and composers for brief visits, I think I'm free to name an approximate figure of about . . ." He named a figure which made Elliot with difficulty restrain a shout of triumph.

"How much?" he asked, for the pleasure of hearing it again.

Jaeger repeated the figure. He began to frame an elaborate sentence containing the words "pride" and "responsibility," when the boy on the landing above them shouted at the girl with him. "Come *on!*" "*No,*" the girl shouted back, *"I'm not going to,"* and began sobbing. The boy turned to glare at Jaeger and Elliot staring up at him, and then wrenched the girl into what Elliot knew was Anita's bedroom.

"That's quite a figure," he said.

Soon after, fortified by another drink, he went upstairs to the television room. Bob Cratchit and a handful of students were watching *Niagara,* and Elliot smelled the heavy perfumed odor of marijuana. Marilyn Monroe's figure was surprisingly lush, more Gibson Girl than Elliot had remembered. "You fucking zombies can't even see that face," Bob Cratchit was saying. "You were all wetting the bed when they made this movie." In the students' laughter, Elliot saw the bubbly girl he had spoken to downstairs. She said, "It's Mr. Coyote." Andy French, seated in the darkness on the couch, saw him, and left the room to join him. She kissed him in the hallway. "Hello, Mr. Coyote," she said. "Cheryl is right. That's who you are."

Then they were back downstairs, going through the dining room to the bar. "Miss French," said Himmel, bowing. "Be easy with me, Miss French." He was drunk. Bob Cratchit had followed them, and he threw an arm around Himmel's waist. "Let me introduce you two music pushers," he said to Nathan. He was being aggressive, edgy, and he looked at Elliot as though he wanted to fight, his teeth shining from his beard. "Two humanists," he said.

"Nathan, I think you need some fresh air," Andy said, ignoring Cratchit.

"Then walk me around the block," said Himmel. "Up and down and around and around. I'll take you away from this discount Hemingway."

"Your imagery is out of date, friend," said Cratchit.

Someone was touching Elliot very gently on his arm.

"Well, what do you know about Ravel?" asked Himmel. "What do you know about any music, for that matter? I won't be drawn into altercations with these *chazzers*."

Cratchit insinuated his bulky upper body between Himmel and Andy. Elliot saw with surprise that he was shorter than either of them. His furry head waggled; he seemed to be speaking into Himmel's jawline as though it were a microphone. "The trouble with you humanistic types is that you can't follow an argument," he was saying. For all his bristling, it was a weak rejoinder, and Elliot thought that the furry little man would not actually start a fight. "I don't care about that," Himmel said in a lordly way. "You are a gnat." Cratchit began to froth. There was some dialogue Elliot couldn't hear—people had begun to crowd around. A man put his hand on Cratchit's shoulder. "Systems are my lifeblood, Tiny Tim," retorted Himmel. Cratchit balled his fists, bent lower, and sent a left hook to Himmel's chin, sending him sprawling backward. A girl screamed.

The pressure on Elliot's arm subtly increased. A soft Oxford-accented baritone voice said, "Couldn't we go someplace quiet to talk,

Denmark?" and Elliot turned around to see a short, suntanned, smoothly boyish man with a neat cap of hair which concealed his ears, square amber glasses, and he knew that the man was Ronnie Upp.

"We have a lot to talk about," Upp said. "I think you know who I am."

"Yes, I know who you are," said Elliot. Of whom did the grown Ronnie Upp remind him? It was not Ted Edwards, though they shared a sleekness which suggested that both men lived much of their lives before mirrors. Then he recalled an evening at a high-vaulted drafty French theater, and remembered an actor he had seen in a provincial production of *Hamlet*: a miscast elaborate young man, ambitious and uncomfortable in the role of Fortinbras. A tense black-tighted young man, an unlikely victor. But perhaps this was a new model for conquerors. "You're the man behind the scenes," he said.

Upp glittered at him, as if delighted by this description of himself. "Your imagination is not always that theatrical," he said. "Perhaps it's the setting." He moved his eyes, mockingly, toward Himmel. A girl was dabbing at the cellist's mouth with a handkerchief. Elliot saw that Himmel's chin was splashed with blood—he must have bit his lip when Cratchit's blow landed. "If we want to have a reasonable discussion, I think we should go elsewhere."

"Hello, Ronnie," said Andy, her voice cool. She left Himmel's side and came slowly toward them.

"Andy, my dear." Upp looked at Andy like a man keeping a disagreeable secret. Elliot looked around the crowded dining room for Vera or Anita, but saw only Donadio and Rosa Heldenweit, piling their plates with food from the table. The mood of the party downstairs had shifted: though the music was still raucous, the people were quieter, drawn into groups. Himmel had left his chair and was weaving into the kitchen. No more than five or six people had seen the fight. "I want a word with Elliot Denmark, and then I'll join your lovely party." He lifted one hand and placed it atop the other. "Before it dissolves."

"That will be sweet, Ronnie," said Andy. "Anita will be pleased that you are here."

"Let's go into the study," said Upp. He cocked his head toward the other side of the room. "I think we might take our drinks with us."

As they walked into the hall from the dining room, Elliot saw Vera and Anita, close in conversation, moving across the entrance to the living room. They were outlined by the pattern of books behind them. Neither woman looked in his direction.

Upp lifted the coats from a padded leather chair and dropped them on the floor. Elliot took the only other chair in the room, high-backed and hard before Anita's desk. It resisted the contours of his body, and this discomfort increased his unease at finally being in the same room with Ronnie Upp. The shorter man looked at him steadily, his dark eyes shining with amusement behind the big tinted lenses. "You don't look terribly cozy," Upp said, and Elliot remembered more accurately who it was Ronnie recalled to him: not the tense young Fortinbras, but the photographs he had seen of Ronnie's father, with his glittery edgy glamour. His hostility, brushed up like a cat's fur by Bob Cratchit, began to fade. "It's been a long time since we've met, Ronnie," he said.

"So it has. And in the meantime, nearly everything has happened. Everything of importance to either of us." Upp's smile was brilliant, boyish. "But I hope you don't mean to waste time reminiscing."

"Where do you want to start?"

"I think we could begin with Anita, don't you?" The smile continued. "She is important to you, I gather."

"I don't think that's your affair, but I don't see why I shouldn't admit it. She is important to me. She's a friend. I feel involved in Anita's problems, and I want to give her any help I can."

"And your notion of help is to talk about how much you love her. Then she tells you she loves you, and you both feel better." Ronnie's smile tightened. "Or you try to alarm her with horror stories about killing animals in Nun's Wood. Anita and I have few secrets from one another. We met in Cambridge—our Cambridge, not theirs—

when Frank Kellerman was doing a year's research. I owned the house they rented. And we became friends there. Three people from Plechette City—we were very close. After Frank's death I took up much of the payment for Mark's treatment. That may be a surprise to you."

It was.

"That's because you don't understand money," said Upp. "Your entire attitude toward the Nun's Wood business says that. Elliot . . . that foolish performance on Ted Edwards' program!" Upp looked at him gently, chidingly. "Do you really believe in that sentimental soap opera about ecology your father has been deluding himself into believing? I can't really imagine that you do. I'll confess that I was distressed to see you rambling on like dear old Hilda Usenbrugge. She's scarcely a reputable model, do you think?"

"I wasn't aware that I had taken Hilda Usenbrugge for a model," said Elliot.

"Yes, I think awareness *is* the problem." Upp smiled as if he had some secret knowledge.

Elliot could not define Upp's attitude. His tone, a school-masterly unctuousness, mixed confusingly with the slightly menacing glee of his manner. Two weeks ago Andy had told him that Upp thought of himself as superior to other people, and perhaps it was this condescension which was the key to his attitude. Yet condescension was usually a fool's refuge, and Upp did not appear to be a fool. Nor did he appear merely condescending. He seemed to be deliberately setting out to create unease.

"What distressed you? That I talked about your other property out there?"

Upp put his hands in his jacket pockets and sank deep into the padded chair, his face showing a mixture of surprise and incredulity. "That? No, that scarcely seemed significant. And it is not really significant, is it? Tell me, if your father were not fighting us on the Wood question, would you have bothered bringing it up? And with such vehemence?"

"I would have been happy to ignore the question altogether. But my motives don't change the action."

"I'm not going to let you take refuge in evasions, Elliot. But your honesty on the point is refreshing. So I will be similarly honest with you. It wasn't at all your talking about the other property or even your misguided references to me that I found upsetting. I thought it was a pity that you're wasting your energies on a foredoomed issue."

"Is that all?"

"It's also a pity that you waste them on hostility to me. I could do a great deal of good for you."

Upp was still slouching deep in the chair, his eyes shining at Elliot. Elliot sipped slowly from his drink. He felt Upp's tension like a wind; but that was not all he could feel. Upp's manner was that of a man concealing a trump card. That, and the tension he could feel in the man, began to make Elliot nervous again. It was like talking to a betrayed husband.

When Elliot did not speak, Upp went on. "Your father-in-law and I had a long talk about you the evening I dined there. I suggested to Herman—out of Mrs. Glauber's hearing, by the way—that I thought it might be possible to arrange a place for you on Ted's program. Ted Edwards is an old friend of mine, and I thought he could put you on his schedule. There are a number of other favors I could put in your way, if you were to go back to your main concern, which is making delightful music."

"Herman didn't..." Elliot stopped. He thought that Upp had shown his trump card. "The favor rather backfired. Herman seemed unruffled, however."

"He's a sweet man," said Upp. "Herman Glauber is unencumbered by ancient grudges."

"Well, so am I," said Elliot. "But I think this conversation is getting tedious. I don't think you need to buy up Nun's Wood, but you're not interested in what I think about that. You could be a hero and buy the place as a park. Probably I'm boring you. Why don't you say what you want to say to me?"

When Upp stood and walked toward him, Elliot expected to be threatened. Upp's handsome boy's face maintained its affability only with effort. He stood no more than a few feet away from Elliot, his hands still in his pockets. "I think I've said most of it. Let me ask you a question. How much money do you make in a year? Don't bother to answer. Combining your income with your wife's, fifteen thousand? Twenty? Most of that would be her salary. About enough to pay for the mortgage on your romantic home and buy score paper." The smile deepened, became more malicious. "You're an industrious ant, Elliot. You don't even live in the real world. You made a tiny substitution for it and convinced yourself you're comfortable there. Let me tell you something about money. I'm an expert on money—I respect its energy. Money is a metaphor, it has its own will. People like you make the mistake of thinking that money is a term for leisure or ease, when it is really another term for electricity, for war—for a hurricane of will. Where there is money, engines turn, darkness scatters, because there's a tiger on the loose, and you've goddamned got to keep it fed. Because it's the biggest tool in the game, Elliot, the one hand you can play that makes everyone else put down his cards. It's too bad you were raised as a rich boy, so you could never see it."

"Weren't you raised as a richer one?"

Upp leaned against Anita's desk, crossing his arms over his chest. "Let me tell you how I was raised. I'll condense it into an anecdote, so it won't bore you." He leaned backward on the desk, letting his heels rise inches off the carpet. Elliot noticed that he was wearing high brown suede boots. A dandy, he thought, like my father. Upp squinted toward the light. "At the time of the anecdote, I am eight, and we are in Lausanne. My father is having our house there redecorated, and men are in and out all day long. My mother is usually in bed, resting. Sometimes there are parties, where lots of young men play with me. Since it is summer I'm not at the *école*, and I can stay up late at night. One night my nurse, Martine, brings in a sheep dog during one of my father's parties. It's my dog. A surprise for me. The young men fuss over it, put ribbons in its lovely shaggy fur, make it drink champagne from bowls. My nice doggy. I went to bed—fell asleep on the couch, actually—very late, full of dreamies about my doggie."

He looked down at Elliot from his perch on the desk and folded his feet under himself crosswise. "Take a little sip of your drink, because here comes the heartbreaking finale. I woke up on the couch headachy and ill. The dog was whining and shuffling around the floor, where people had spilled food. The room was a mess, not just the usual mess from the decorators, but a sort of last-days-of-Pompeii mess. Broken glasses, spilled drinks, cigarettes. I saw the dog sniff around a wine bottle standing on the carpet, nose it over, and then lap up what spilled out. It was whimpering and yowling, crying, making a terrific racket. My father came fumbling out of a bedroom and down the stairs, still tying his bathrobe about himself, and I could tell by the way he was walking that he had a hangover. He was in an evil mood, and I tried to run away, but he grabbed me and pulled me out into the backyard. Then he went back in and pulled out the dog, which was still whimpering. 'Which would you rather have,' he said, 'this dog or a thousand francs?' I started to cry. 'I asked you a question,' he said. When I didn't answer, he went back inside, and then came back with his pistol. 'Choose,' he said. 'You shoot that wretched animal, and I'll give you a thousand francs. You can do whatever you want with the money.' He held it out to me. He ordered me to hold it while I made up my mind." Ronnie looked teasingly down at Elliot. "I was fascinated with the pistol, of course. All kids are. He'd never let me touch it before. Well, the dog looked sick. It was sort of baying around the garden. So I tried to shoot it without looking at it. I fired and missed. The dog ran toward the fence, but it couldn't run very well. I aimed and pulled the trigger and missed again, and then my father took the pistol and shot the dog in the head. He was a wonderful marksman. Later he gave me fifty francs in cash and put the rest in my bank account. Bye-bye doggie. But when I was holding the pistol, my arm numb from the first shot, I remember thinking that if I shot my poor old hung-over bastard of a daddy, I'd have it all." He smiled at Elliot. Perched on the desk with his feet tucked under his legs, he spread his hands, palms up, so that the light gathered on their smooth pink skin.

Upp raised one hand, leaned over, and touched Elliot lightly on the forehead.

* * *

"If you are asking me what I think you are asking me, I think the answer is yes. I've always thought so." Anita sat across the kitchen table from him and looked at him levelly, her short mannish hair catching and glowing with the light. Nathan Himmel was slumped where they had put him, in a chair near the oven. "It was the act of a terrorized young boy, and he has been paying for that act all his life. And there's another thing. I don't know how much you know about Ronnie's father—"

"Too much," said Elliot.

"Then you know that he probably deserved what he got. He was undoubtedly an ill man, but illness is not an excuse for what that man did, for the cruelty, falseness, and deception of his entire life." The green eyes, now seeming almost depthless, looked at him squarely. "I think he was lucky to live as long as he did. And probably he wanted to die. He was killing himself with liquor, and his wife, in what must have been an intolerable situation, was doing the same. When if finally happened, I don't think that Ronnie himself knew that he was doing it purposely. I am sure he thought, with the largest part of his mind, that he was doing what his father would have done, shooting at a burglar."

Elliot sat quiet for a moment. "I don't know why I'm talking to you about Ronnie, since you are determined to defend him."

"I'm defending him only because I know him much better than you do," she replied. "Dear one, for years I've been putting Ronnie together. Don't be foolish about Ronnie Upp."

"I'm trying not to be." After a moment, he said, "As I'm trying not to be foolish about you. What kind of thing do we have? What sort of connection is it between us?"

"Maybe that is up to you," said Anita. "But remember that for a year while we lived in the same city, you retreated into your marriage. What sort of connection did we have then?"

"A frustrated one."

"Because it was all we could have. You chose to have it that way."

"But it doesn't stop there," he said. "Sometimes I think I'm simply obsessed with you. I carry you around in my head. I probably think of you once every ten minutes. There's an area in me that simply belongs to you." Kai, and Kai's story, stood as a rebuke to sentimentality. "It might be that all we've got is friendship. Yet even if that's so, it is an exceptionally resonant friendship."

"One reason I love you is that you always say the right thing," said Anita, once more baffling him. "Dear Elliot, I love you. I depend on you."

"Well, you confound me." He rubbed his face with his hands. "You puzzle me. It's not a bad state—maybe just a sort of emotional polyphony. It's not always at the same strength, but it's always latent. At least I think it is."

Ronnie Upp's voice, rapid and gratingly English, came from the living room, followed by a burst of laughter. When the two of them had returned to the party, Upp had been immediately surrounded by Jaeger, Wattman and Donadio. Vera had been talking to Andy French, and both had looked questioningly in his direction when he and Anita had left the room together. Bob Cratchit and several of the students had left, but many others were dancing, in the small crowded space of the living room, to an old Beatles record. "All I wish is that you'd be more open with me."

He returned her steady gaze until Anita made a pouting gesture with her mouth and looked down at the table. "I've always been open with you, Elliot."

"Then why did Ronnie begin his spooky little tale by asking me about you?"

She did not reply. Her face down-tilted, she showed him only the broad plane of her forehead beneath the sideswept short blond hair.

He asked his question. "Is Ronnie Mark's father?"

She lifted a radiant, assertive face. "I don't know. He could be. Ronnie thinks he is."

Himmel, who had begun to snore, stirred in his chair. He lifted his head. *"La belle Denmark,"* he said. "What time?"

Elliot looked at his watch. "One-thirty," he said. Himmel nodded exaggeratedly, then leaned back to rest his head against the sink. "Hemingway," he muttered.

"I could never have told you," Anita said. "But I'm glad you thought enough about it to ask. I knew Ronnie for a long time before we met. He had the virtue of not being an academic. And I wanted an affair, and I had one. Oh, Elliot . . ." She glowed at him. "I really am happy that you guessed. Ronnie is no threat to us."

"His power doesn't go that far, you mean." He put his hand to his forehead, which had begun to throb. His back still hurt from the fall on the street. "Does Andy know about all this?"

"I've never told her. Andy works for me." That was Anita's gift: to imply that all other relationships were secondary, insubstantial. "And you know how she feels about Ronnie. I think she's a little jealous of him."

"Well, I'm not sure that I'm not jealous of him."

"You dear fool," she said. "I told you I felt like a nun."

Her statement filled him with an extraordinary relief. Anita's having a child by the odd, tormented Ronnie Upp could not shake his feeling for her. Now that she had freely admitted the truth of Mark's parentage, it lost the charged significance it had held for him. If the matter was of supreme importance to anyone, it would be Frank Kellerman, and he had slipped into history when his car had stalled on a freeway. Elliot thought that he could understand Upp now: he must have felt insecure in his relationship with Anita, on unsteady ground. Hence his bribes, his peculiar manner. He feared that Elliot would once more begin an affair with Anita, and injure his relationship with Mark. Yet at this moment he felt a grateful distance between himself and Anita—she was irretrievably apart from him. In all of this, there was a large, lifting, and complex relief.

Yes, Elliot thought, my real life is in Paris with Vera. Kai had been implying just this sense of detachment—it was the meaning of his story. He felt suffused with warmth. As he looked across the table at Anita, he felt an irresistible sexual stirring. He remembered the taut planes and soft hollows of her body, and wished to touch them again.

Anita was still talking about Andy. "She has been monopolizing me lately. Andy and I see one another for most of every day, you know. We work in the same department, and then she takes care of Mark when she's not with me. I'm afraid that the Kellermans have

been absorbing most of her emotional life. I really have been unfair
to Andy. Mark and I are a refuge for her, a sweet safe little den.
We are very close, but Andy has become sort of overprotective lately.
I think it will be good for all of us when she finally leaves."

"And what about Mark?"

"Mark will be taken care of, one way or another."

"That's how you got *this*," he said, holding one hand up to his
cheek. Anita nodded, her face defiant, almost warlike beneath the
shining helmet of her hair.

"I was going to give Nathan some coffee," she said. The percolator
on the stove was making a staccato popping sound. She walked
around the table to stand beside him. "Why don't you come over
here tomorrow?"

"If you want me to." His body seemed forcefully impelled to her.

"Does your back hurt, darling? You've been rubbing it all night."

"I fell down in the street." He took his hands away from the small
of his back and let them dangle, unsure of what to do with them.
"It doesn't really hurt."

She began to stroke his back, slipping her hand underneath his
jacket, with short intense caresses. Her hand was very warm.

"Oh, Elliot, have you seen the news? On television?"

"No," he said, "I've just been talking to Anita." But Andy knew
that. She seemed gloomy and distracted. She had spoken to him as
he walked past the sofa, carrying a drink, and when he looked down
at her, she seemed small and defenseless, the tribal face showing an
almost pathetic eagerness to talk to him. Elliot sat beside her. The
couch was warm, as if someone had just left the place he now occupied. "What was the news?"

He could see Ronnie near the tree, talking to Anita and Roberta
Potocky. Several yards away from them, and watching Ronnie Upp
with great fascination, Wattman and Donadio were devouring the
last of the food. When Wattman glowered at him, Elliot felt unrea-
sonably elated.

"They showed your tower," Andy said. "That clock tower. The
announcer said that new plans for it were approved, and then he

showed an architect's drawing. It's going to be taller than the old one, but not so . . . grandiose. Did your father know that it was that final?"

"He just found out. He was upset at first, but he cheered up when he saw me on television."

"Because of what you said about Ronnie?"

He nodded.

"He's going to dedicate the new tower to Brooks Denmark, did you know that? With a plaque."

There were two reasons for her bitterness, and he chose the less complicated. "You are very unhappy with Ronnie, aren't you?"

"I'm unhappy, if that's the word, about his treatment of Anita. I'd like to see her free of him."

"I think she is free of him, in any important way," he said. When she merely looked at him, he said, "Why didn't you say anything about this when we went for that ride?"

"I didn't know how much I could trust you. How much you could be trusted."

"And now?"

"Now I know you can't be." Laughing, she patted his hand like a child's. "It's good that you can't, in that way. I wish the same could be said for Ronnie. Sometimes I think people should be a little more faithless. They'd be less screwed up." She smiled, still a little cool.

"I don't think I've seen enough of you," he said. It seemed to him that Andy had just echoed his thoughts.

But she looked at him as though she detested him. "Then why don't you come over tomorrow sometime? One or the other of us is sure to be in." Andy continued to hold her eyes on his. "Ronnie was just telling me you'd be around," she said. "I suppose he told you about trying to shoot that dog. It's what he tells people at parties."

"Well, I talked with your two women," said Vera. They were near the bookshelves, apart from the rest of the party. "And I had a short talk with Jaeger. Did he make you his offer?"

"He did, and it was a lovely offer."

"Are you going to take it?" Vera looked at him questioningly, her eyes full of danger.

"I don't think so. It was flattering, but I don't think I could live in Plechette City anymore. It's too complicated."

"Even with all your admirers?"

"I don't want admirers," he said. "There's something poisonous in it."

"She's pathetic," said Vera. She did not have to specify the "she." "There's something wrong with her. I feel sorry for her, and that's quite a reversal. It's like she's crippled somehow—or that she always was, but that she was too full of energy for anyone to see it. Or maybe she had you and whoever else she had to hide it. It was like talking to Joanie Haupt."

He could not meet the bitterness in her voice. "What about Andy? My other admirer?"

A light, amused look passed between them. Elliot was intensely curious about his wife's reaction to Andy French.

"Andy will do," Vera said. "Andy is straight. I like her. I think she should get out from under Anita's thumb."

In a little while there were only three or four people left in the room, and the Denmarks were not among them.

chapter **20**

Elliot sat, holding a cup of coffee and the morning's *Herald*, in the dining room of his parents' house. Disturbed by his dreams, slightly hung-over, he had risen and dressed long before anyone else was up, and then gone down to the kitchen to put the pot on the stove. Now, fifteen minutes later, it was still only six-thirty and black outside. He'd had only four hours of sleep. Even Robert would not be up for another hour.

He had been pleasantly surprised to find the newspaper in the mail slot, entirely unsurprised by the contents of the front page. The headlines speculated about Vietnam and Cambodia. The President was to make a speech next week—when Elliot would be back, he thought with relief, in Paris. On the front page was a photograph of a captured Vietcong hung by his heels, surrounded by grinning South Vietnamese boy soldiers. He read the caption, skimmed the articles, and looked at a story on the bottom of the page. Simmons Speigner, the zoo director, had not found the wolf, which was thought to be wounded. One of the sheriff's party had apparently hit it with a long-range shot over the weekend. Speigner was quoted as saying that it might have found a secluded spot and died in the fields around the southern subdivisions bordering the airport.

The dining room was cold and oppressively dark. Elliot felt

penned within it. He folded the paper under his arm, and took the cup and saucer across the hall, going up the short flight of steps to the upper living room. In the big-windowed room over the lake, he set the newspaper and coffee cup on a low table and pulled open the drapes.

The big room seemed immediately colder. Looking east across the black lake, visible as a denser darkness than the sky, he saw only a faint hazy ribbon of light on the horizon. The single lamp he had switched on glowed orange in the window, and Elliot could see the tall fluffy-haired outline of his body wrapped in a robe. Down at the edge of the lake, a few giant jagged blocks of ice shone a pale gray. His dream made it all ominous.

Kai's disturbing story was behind it, he knew—it weighed on him still. He had been walking through a grassy field, like those around the small farmhouse in Beynac he and Vera had rented one summer. The sky was black, shot with broad lurid threads of pink. Andy French had been walking up a hill about fifty yards before him; Elliot followed her, knowing that she was leading him to something appalling—he was impelled to go toward it. He smelled some sweet terrible odor. After walking a little of the way, he tried to run, but each step was made with great effort. After struggling uphill for some minutes, he saw what looked like one of the little prehistoric stone huts which had dotted the fields in Périgord. Andy looked at him coldly as he approached her. The scars on her face stood out as though they were about to come to life. He saw that there were bodies on the ground around the hut. He moved toward it, and saw that it was not a hut, but a pile of something shaped like one of the little stone constructions. It was burning. Small flames curled out at its edges like a hundred tongues. The odor grew worse. He bent to his knees in front of the burning pile, holding a hand before his face to shield it from the heat. In the tangle of arms and legs which made up the pile, he saw a corner of material, and pulled at it. One of the bodies came away. He pulled it out onto the grass and scattered ashes off its face. In the lurid glowing darkness he could not distinguish its features. It was a woman. Then he saw that it was Anita. He had come suddenly awake, his heart pounding and his mouth cottony, with an almost painful erection.

He had been dreaming of Anita for several nights in sequence. None of these dreams had been obviously erotic. Often he saw her alone in a room, her hair as long as it had been years before, spreading out in wild tangles over the white shoulders of her nightdress as she went around the room trying the doors and windows. Her face, even when she began to weep, retained an extraordinary calm, as if she knew she were a figure in a dream. In another dream a pigeon flew wildly back and forth in a skylighted chamber, battering itself against the windows at the top. He could not bear to think of the bird killing or maiming itself and he tried to catch it, but the pigeon was far out of his reach, skittering from window to window. There had been an odd specific terror in that dream, but last night's was the most harrowing. He had tried to fall asleep again, but the sense of threat and fear was so immediate that he could not. The blue wall on the far side of the room had seemed to be moving imperceptibly toward him through the darkness.

Anita still weighed heavily on his mind. But things seemed at last stabilized between them. His dreams to the contrary—and what were they but testimony to his sense of her importance to him?—Anita Kellerman had her own life in which she solved her own problems. His homecoming had shaken her weak connection with Ronnie Upp. This was teasingly satisfying to his ego. Beneath the sleekness and smoothness, Upp was an uncertain juvenile who resented Elliot's relationship with Anita. It was possible that he had undertaken the Nun's Wood business and the destruction of the clock tower to wound the Denmark family. No, that could not be true: his father had become interested only after Upp had made an offer to purchase the land. Now, however, Upp was no doubt delighted by the prospect of blocking the Denmarks.

Yet that was more his father's problem than his. In the cold gray darkness of the morning, Elliot felt that his own problems might be moving toward a clarification, a resolution. Anita had always possessed a significance for him that was nearly mythical; he had seen her as though she were a giant figure in an epical drama of liberation, and now he could approach her more practically, with a realistic love which honored their situation. Anita herself found no unfairness in the stringent conditions imposed upon them. He would have to see her again; if time could be found, today. His love for Anita, with all the distancing necessary in it, entailed like all love a responsibility: otherwise everything was loss and disorder, was wild chaos.

He folded the first section in half and took up the second section of the paper, the local news. Alderman Jefferson Glee had given a speech at a black church citing the Nun's Wood affair as a white ploy to divert attention from the issue of civil rights. Was that good news or bad? Vandals had set fire to a fourth-ward junior high school. It was only six blocks from the school where Vera had taught, and Elliot felt a tic of relief that she was no longer working there.

Then his knee jumped as he saw his own name in one of the heads on the inside of the first page. COMPOSER DENMARK SPEAKS ON NUN'S WOOD. The story recounted his appearance on the television program, and laid great emphasis on his remarks about Ronnie Upp. "Ecological disaster," "reckless building," "the arrogance of wealth": he had actually spoken this drivel. The writer implied that he had spoken violently, decisively, as if he had used the Edwards program as a platform. Chase Denmark would be delighted by the story. Rona Bender would show the piece to her husband. All of this threw Elliot back into the dejection his dream had aroused in him, the sense that important matters were beyond his control. It must be the lack of sleep, he thought, but the idea only brought Anita's party back to him. In retrospect, it was a depressing evening. He saw Ronnie Upp's smooth face before him, talking about shooting a dog. He drank his coffee and reread the article, then pitched the newspaper to another chair and stared for a minute at the grim expanse of the lake. The room had become intolerable.

Upstairs, Vera still lay asleep in her bed, the pillow a little smudged with makeup. Elliot looked at her closely and then took off his robe and began to dress. He fumbled in a drawer for his old blue jeans and found them by touch. Then a clean shirt from the laundry, which he tucked into his jeans while sliding his feet into loafers. As an afterthought he pulled on a sweater. He closed the door and went softly downstairs. On his way out he took from the closet near the front door an old sheepskin jacket he had worn at Columbia as an undergraduate; worn and dirty, it suited his mood, and it was the warmest thing he owned.

It's too cold to walk far, he immediately thought, and decided to go only as far as the traffic lights at the eastern end of Jackson Drive, where it intersected Lake Point Drive. The *Herald* article was not enough to justify freezing oneself, though he could only guess at Tessa's reaction to it, and the discomfort she might cause. The evening he would have to pass at the Glauber house became gigantic in his mind, and he began to go south along Lake Point Drive, from time to time slipping on patches of ice, brooding about it. His nose and ears stung with the cold, but Elliot, far into his thoughts, scarcely noticed. He put his hands up over the collar of the jacket and held it close to his ears. When he reached the traffic lights, he absently glanced eastward, where the band of light above the lake had fractionally broadened. The streetlamps, still burning, canceled any sense that it was yet day. He continued walking. He remembered going to work this way years ago, driving in the winter darkness along the drive toward his morning classes. Now he could not recall what days he'd taught. His teaching life seemed impossibly long ago, the person he had been then lost. Everything was different and everybody had changed. He was a foreigner here. As if to confirm that he was alien, a cruising police car, the only automobile on the road, slowed as it went past, and the two uniformed men in it turned their heads to stare at him. Should he wave at them? They were clearly suspicious of him. Nobody walked down Lake Point Drive at seven in the morning.

Elliot remembered that he had no identification with him; it came to him that he did not even have a house key. The police car was now traveling so slowly that it was keeping exactly abreast of him. He was walking past the huge houses of Lake Point Drive, the great gray Gothic buildings. He could probably name the owners of three out of four of these houses—would that convince the police? One of them was talking into a radio. Elliot was suddenly aware of his ears and nose, now almost numb. One of the houses he was passing was almost certainly the home of Walter Lyte. Elliot shoved his hands deep in the pockets of the jacket and put his head down and continued walking.

The policeman on Elliot's side of the car negligently turned his head, and the car gradually picked up speed and pulled away from him. Humping his shoulders, Elliot continued on in the direction the car had gone. Now he was half a mile past the lights at Jackson Drive; the next traffic lights would be at the turnoff of the lake expressway. Far ahead he saw them glimmering red through the darkness, a little hazed by the oncoming of the sun. He had gone much farther than he had expected to, lost in his brooding about the article and the party. But that the police had not stopped him had left him somehow buoyant, and he walked another block in a dislocated peace and lightness, almost relishing the cold. He began to walk consciously toward Anita Kellerman's home. It was much too early to find anyone awake or dressed, and he had no idea of what he would do when he got there. As Baltz had said, the activity was enough—he relished this walking, dressed in old clothes, to a woman's house. It was as though he had been translated out of his daily life into another existence, free of consequences—he felt fifteen years younger. He had a brief vision of himself and Anita talking about the newspaper article, both of them laughing: he was now so close to Windmere Terrace that turning off the drive toward Anita's home was irresistible. In any case, he had to stay away from his parents' house for at least an hour, so that Robert could let him in without waking the whole house.

Ten minutes later, when he was turning into Leecham, he recognized that the vision of Anita laughing with him in her old vibrant way over the reporter's misreading of his performance on Edwards' show was an impossibility. Ronnie Upp had interposed himself between them; he could no longer predict what might make Anita laugh. For a moment he felt as threatened as he had by the police car, a dark heavy helplessness. If everything—the country, his city, his parents—had changed, then Anita had changed most of all. Yet the optimism of his mood carried him into the reflection that the change in Anita was after all not an essential change—people could not alter so drastically. What he was feeling was much like the old rich emotional confusion she had caused in him, the product of what he had thought of as her masque. Now once more within it, he thought he understood its mechanism. Certainly none of *that* had changed: Anita was still Anita, and he was bound to her.

Her house seemed, like its inhabitants, unawakened. Looking at the quiet brick and wood of its face, he felt a wave of tenderness washing through him. The dislocations of being up so early in the morning! Elliot felt whole and entire, standing across the street from Anita's house. He forgot the newspaper article entirely. The house was much like its neighbors, all of them two-story modest structures with big Midwestern porches. Even in winter the brick's muted reddish-brown, interleaved with creamy mortar, seemed warm. His depression now seemed insubstantial—a vapor from the dream. The house expressed peace, comfort, mystery: Elliot was swept back into thinking of how many times, in what wildness or exuberance of feeling, he had entered it. Ronnie Upp was not Harrison Upp any more than Elliot was his own father, any more than Mark was Ronnie. One had to take short views, be grateful for temporary satisfactions. Herman's words, and Kai's, seemed to move in his bloodstream. He thought of Anita lying asleep in her familiar bed, her knees tucked up and her skin shining.

The sky had perceptibly lightened to a pinkish gray, a true city color, and the air smelled alive and clean. Whether he had meant it or not, Kai had said this, Elliot thought: he had cried not from hate but from love. Badly or ignorantly chosen, love remained, the best of all small satisfactions and stays against chaos. He remembered Anita's slipping her warm hand down the length of his back. Kai's story had been about the giving of love, and the sufficiency of the gift: any strong emotion is a gift of spirit to its object. After the death of Harrison Upp, Kai had been bereft of the person who had evoked the strongest response from him; and so was overtaken by a dim gritty tide of loss. Elliot felt charged with a rich emotional surge of meaning, everything understood; he felt American once more. He began to speculate on Kai's similarities to his father, and then saw with regret how far Kai had been diminished in his imagination. The world spun, a gaudy controlled toy, between Anita and himself.

He was freezing, freezing and awash in feeling. He could not merely stand on the street and watch Anita's house. In one of the upstairs windows, a light suddenly appeared. Someone was up. The streetlamps switched off with a surprisingly loud click. The day had begun. He crossed the street and went up the stairs to Anita's house, moving as if he were sleepwalking.

Before he touched the door he knew it would open. When he put his hand to the knob, it swung noiselessly in. He stepped quickly through. None of his actions seemed to entail consequences. He stepped across the narrow porch and gently pulled down at the old-fashioned handle of the next door, and moved into the hallway. The house was suffused with pinkish-gray light. The pale colors of the walls, the dark colors of the woodwork, were as if new to him, softened by the spreading light. He went forward in the hall and saw the ruined mess on the dining-room table, the cloth blotched and stained, plates and serving dishes strewn this way and that. A large silver spoon was stuck to the tablecloth with a congealed yellow mass that had been fondue. Three or four plates had been carelessly stacked at the end of the table, particles of food littered about them.

No attempt at all had been made to clean the living room. When Elliot went across the hall and stepped through the arch, his foot toppled a glass and released a gold spreading stain on the carpet. The smell of whiskey lifted to his nostrils like a ghost. There was a humming. From across the room he saw that the turntable was still revolving, the needle clicking uselessly within the blank end grooves. Elliot walked over the strewn floor and switched off the machine. Like the street lamps, it made an abnormally loud clicking noise which hovered for a second in the air. The carpet was a mess, a bedlam. Overturned ashtrays, glasses, record sleeves, a necktie. Some white plates dotted the floor, two of them still half-piled with food. The whole house seemed to smell of ashes. In the odd light it all looked strangely beautiful, every object picked and defined by the beams easing in through the windows. Elliot went across the room to the source of the light, his old sheepskin jacket weirdly altered by it in color, and put his hand to one of the panes. The palm was black, his fingers nearly transparent. Our lovely temporary bodies. Then he pushed up at the frame and forced open the window. Cold air streamed over him.

When he turned away from the window and went around a chair back toward the center of the room, his foot crunched down on a pile of slippery black fragments. A record, he thought, stepping aside and looking down. It had been broken into quarters, then snapped piece by piece until it was in a dozen sections. He saw a fragment of the label. Printed on it was a dog cocking a floppy ear to the bell of an old gramophone. Red paper: RCA Red Seal. He idly separated the fragments with his foot. One piece bore the entire word MODERN. "Oh no," he whispered, and bent down. On another piece he saw:

MAINST

I Fiv

II Mom

RCA Sym

Pierre B

Marcas Regi

STEREO DYNAGROO

It was his record. Some of the grooves had been pounded into gray powder, and all were thickly fingerprinted.

Elliot jumped back to his feet and moved quickly to the shelf of records. The sleeve was lying flat across the tops of the other two records, and it was empty. In disbelief he went back to the small black heap beside the chair and looked down at it. Someone had deliberately broken up his record. The pieces lay in a jagged heap just now touched by the light. He could still see the word MODERN. The room's atmosphere had changed. The pinkish light seemed wrong, somehow sinister, threatening, as did the disorder on the carpet. He had to see Anita. His body did not fit the room. Stepping over the fragments of the record, he drove his ankle into a hard edge of the chair; a plate slipped away beneath his foot. He heard it crack. He felt sluggish, too large for the house.

For a second he hesitated at the bottom of the dark stairwell. A black line of shadow diagonally bisected the stairs: below, whiteness tinged with unearthly pink; above, dark gray of a lintel's shadow. Why had Upp destroyed his record? He could see the dapper little man effortlessly snapping the record, then grinding it with his boots—what for? He might have hurt Anita again. Elliot went quickly up into the darkness of the stairs.

On the next floor nothing suggested that anyone was yet awake. The hall was still night-dark, and Elliot kicked a small table with his shoe before his eyes adjusted. His ankle flamed again. A pot wobbled back and forth on the table's surface, rattling, and Elliot gripped it with his hands. Then he walked slowly down the hall to Anita's door. The doorknob was temperatureless to his fingers: the heat of a stone. He could hear no noise from within. He gently turned the knob and swung the door in.

Four identical eyes looked into his, two neat boyish heads lifted from pillows. They looked like brother and sister, or like sister and sister: when the man threw back the sheet, their bodies seemed for a second of clarity duplicate creatures, each pink, nearly hairless, molded . . .

The illusion broke when Anita scuttled back under the sheet in a frantic knifing movement and Ronnie came naked toward him across the small sunlit floor. "Go downstairs," he said, his voice powerful. "Now. I'll be with you in a second." In the next room Mark began to scream.

It was catastrophe. He collided with Andy in the hall, nearly knocking her down. She uttered something that sounded like "Poor Elliot," and then pulled her nightgown about her and rushed through the third door, from where came the high-pitched screams, as eerie and urgent, mechanical, as those of a rabbit in a gin.

The terrible screaming stopped when he reached the bottom of the stairs, cut off as if a pillow had been placed over the boy's face. The echo of the screams seemed a part of the walls, the high hysterical tone carried in the wash of pinkish light. Elliot cast back and forth in the living room, stepping on cigarette butts, feeling seared. His eyes burned. Had he known that Upp was in Anita's bedroom? Had he then invited this wretched confrontation? No, no.

"What are you doing to me?" he said when Upp, gathered into a blue silk robe and carrying the amber eyeglasses, padded into the room. He was as neat as a cat. "Where the hell is your goddamned car?"

"I'm freezing," said Upp. He ran his hand through his hair and gave a few dexterous fingerings which made it fall perfectly into place. He looked around, his mouth down-drawn, at the chaos, and slid the glasses over his eyes. The bows disappeared into thick hair at his temples. "The window," he said, and went across the room to close it. Elliot hoped he would struggle with the frame, but it came down effortlessly, as if on oil. "My car is where I left it, I suppose. There was such a crowd here last night that I had to park it blocks away, and then I had a beastly walk to get here. You throw off the heaters in these old houses, you know, if you let cold air get to the thermostats."

He shoved his hands into the pockets of the robe and stood watching Elliot. Beneath the hem of the robe his legs smoothly protruded, straight and hairless. He had small pretty feet. "You look terrible. I take it you've walked over—you're still carrying the cold with you. Why don't you sit down for a minute, warm up, and let me run you home?"

After a minute when Elliot sat in silence, staring at him, Upp said, "I like you. Let me take you home after you've calmed down. Neither of us wants the obligatory scene, so I can't think why we should suffer through it."

"I think you're despicable," said Elliot.

"No you don't. You're just upset." Ronnie stood gazing at him, his eyes soft behind the big lenses. "Isn't this room appalling? The worst thing about parties is cleaning up afterward. In fact, I only came last night because Anita very much wanted me to. I thought I should have the opportunity to talk to you longer, but as luck would have it I was captured by those two dreary musicologists."

"Wattman and Donadio."

There was a rushed rustling noise on the stairs, and Elliot looked up wildly, hoping to see Anita.

"Wretched polecats," said Upp. "Do people like that actually teach? They might be brothers."

Elliot was still numbly watching the door.

The complex noise continued, and Ronnie too turned his head, an annoyed expression on his face. Andy entered, half-carrying Mark, who was rubbing his face on the sleeve of his pajamas. When the boy looked up, he at first gaped at Elliot, his eyes wide and mouth in an astonished O. He began to scream.

"Stop that," said Ronnie. "Let him go, Andy."

The boy sagged, then went taut, his face terrifically red. His screams caught in his throat.

"Come over here, Markie," said Upp. He held out his hands, and the boy raced toward him, scattering a litter of ashes and cigarette butts from an upended ashtray. The soles of his feet were gray when Upp lifted him. "Nothing's wrong, Markie Markie. This is Mr. Denmark. He's a friend of your mother's, and Mother and Andy like him very much."

Andy glared at Elliot, challenging him to speak. "Is that all?" she asked, her eyes on Elliot.

"Yes, dear," said Ronnie. "Go upstairs and help Anita get dressed. Elliot's given us all a bit of a *turn* this morning."

Andy wheeled out of the room. When Mark stopped his sobbing, Ronnie took him back upstairs. In a little while he came down dressed, his suit and shoes different from those he had worn at the party. He drove Elliot home.

Elliot was back walking up the driveway at eight-fifteen, just in time for Robert to see him through the little window in the kitchen and to let him in the back door. "Cold for a walk, Elliot," was all Robert said. Elliot went upstairs and showered.

That evening at the Glauber home, Elliot saw that Tessa took his chastened manner as an apology for his remarks in the *Herald* article. "I suppose I'm the only one who thinks of Ronnie," she said. "He struck me as a very sensitive man." Vera, knowing that her mother intended this as the last word on a Delicate Subject, took her aside.

These were their presents: perfume, an antique brass bowl, a striped shirt, a nightgown, a copy of *Lives of the Composers* ("I told the clerk, give me something for someone interested in music. You can exchange it if you already have it," Tessa said), a John Updike novel, a game called Diplomacy. Elliot feigned suspense, surprise, gratitude, all the appropriate responses.

This is what Kai was telling him, he thought, *this*: you are your fate. He could not escape himself. His insights all seemed fledged, insubstantial, drained by the weak and corrupt creature he was. When he thought of Anita, he saw only the white pigeon of his dreams, battering against the windows. There was no emotion in it. Trumping him, Ronnie Upp had finished that.

chapter **21**

Roy Baltz's question as to what the Plechette City *lupus* found to eat was drastically answered during the late evening of December 24, when the wolf attacked and severely injured a child, an eight-year-old girl, who had been making her way across a field near the airport. She had been playing with a friend and was coming home to dinner when the animal, starved and unseen, had come circling out of a ragged, dying stand of elms. The Christmas-morning edition of the *Herald* contained a picture of the field, rumpled and spotted as a bedsheet after lovemaking, interviews with the girl's parents, a photograph of the girl, thin and spectacled in her class picture, and an Olympian roar from the zoo director. A small army of sheriff's men was spending Christmas threading the southern subdivision and airport fields.

"It's finished," Chase said, "it's dead already, blown away. Before this happened, I was fond of the beast. It must be a glorious animal. If it had come down from wherever it came from in the summer, this would never have happened. One of Speigner's men would have shot it with a tranquilizer, and by now it would either be in the zoo or back where it belongs. A pity. Either way, a pity."

" 'Pity' is hardly an adequate word," suggested Elliot. "The girl will probably die."

"What else? 'Tragedy'? We don't have tragedies anymore. Our beliefs aren't large enough. Look at Vera's uncle downstairs. If anyone among us is qualified to use the word, it is he, certainly as much as the parents of that poor girl, but how does he spend his time? Writing a book about a dead poet. The man could be a witness, but instead he's elected to be a failed scholar. Though Kai Glauber does appear to be a charming man. He and Pierce Laubach would like one another, don't you think?"

Elliot did not answer, and both men looked for a time through the glass where Chase had parted the leaves and vines in Margaret's dark office. A single large bright star vibrated in the sky.

It was perhaps twenty minutes before dinner; Chase had left the upper living room, where the Denmarks and the Glaubers had been sitting uneasily over drinks, and when he had not returned, Elliot had gone upstairs to look for him. Chase had been muted all day, except for brief flashes of gaiety when, before the arrival of the Glaubers, they had exchanged gifts. Vera was delighted with the book of Italian paintings and he with the volume of Berg's letters to his wife she had given him. Then, Chase had been impish, dealing out the presents with barbed little jokes. With the Glaubers' arrival he had changed. When Elliot found him in Margaret's office, he was sitting beside his wife's desk, chin held in hand, looking out at the sky's first star, the room darker than the night.

"Earlier, only a few generations ago, everybody knew the stars," Chase said. "Earlier still, they were figures. Myths. The only constellation I can now distinguish is the Big Dipper. My father once pointed out Orion to me, and it looked like a great white-handed giant, but now I wouldn't know Orion if I held a chart of it in my hands. We don't read the Greek plays not only because they are not close to our experience, but because they are scarcely comprehensible. Margaret and I saw a performance of the *Oresteia* in Athens years ago, and it might as well have been a ballet—lovely movements, nothing more. It was like a trip to a costume museum." He fell silent.

"Are you going to come back downstairs?"

"And stop sulking up here. I take your meaning, Elliot. But I

don't want you to think I'm merely sulking. Perhaps I'm just catching my breath—charging my batteries. Tessa Glauber is a bit of a
burden. She's been lowering her eyes at me all evening, when she
was not sitting there frozen-faced, and I was finally so uncomfortable
I thought I'd come up here for a bit. This is one part of the house
where there is always a feeling of purpose and accomplishment. How
is your mother doing downstairs?"

"Perfectly."

Margaret had immediately made Herman and Kai feel easy in her
home, guiding them by instinct into conversations where each could
freely talk; an easier task with Herman than Kai, but she had kept
it flowing by tying it to Elliot and Vera, and Kai could always talk
about Elliot's music. He had been gentler with Elliot's work than
was his habit. Only Tessa had resisted Margaret's efforts. She had a
self-possessed, icy edge to her, smiling only with her mouth. Yet
even Tessa had loosened after seeing that Herman was not going to
be insulted. Elliot saw also that part of her stiffness was a fear that
Kai would embarrass her. He explained this to his father.

"Then the woman's a fool," said Chase. "Kai is even more old-
fashioned than I am." He pulled open a desk drawer after switching
on a lamp. "I really came up to find these old photographs of you
and some of the places we've been." He took an old album from the
drawer. "Looking at dull pictures is a marvelous way of calming the
nerves. Let's go downstairs, son."

Somehow, the evening passed. After dinner—Tessa uncertain of
how to deal with the problem of Robert, and solving it with an
elaborate steely politeness—Chase led them all back to the smaller
living room. After preparing them all with drinks, he began to play
the piano. For Elliot, the success of this ploy was astonishing. Tessa
was as pleased as a child by his father's rattly bouncy jazz, and after
he had played "Ain't Misbehavin'" and "Rosetta," she began to call
for other songs. "A Fine Romance," "The Lady Is a Tramp." "Oh,
Chase," she said, her whole being expressing pleasure, "this is such
a treat. I can see where Elliot gets his musical talent. Do you remember 'This Year's Kisses'?"

"One of the finest," said Chase. "Just you wait to hear how we old masters play it."

Where Tessa led they all followed. Herman, his face gleaming with amiability, a brandy glass prisoned in his fist, sat down on the bench and began to sing. Later, after Chase had left the piano, he led him aside and the two men had a long quiet discussion on the couch. At Tessa's request, Margaret took the other woman back to the upper living room. "I love your views," said Tessa. "Have you ever thought of changing to colonial?" Elliot and Vera went to Kai. When the two men went up to join their wives, Elliot could hear his father's light dry voice beginning to tell the story about Lamont Von Heilitz's party.

"Your father has worked a miracle," the old man said. "He's won Tessa completely."

"Uncle Kai," said Vera, "I think you're the miracle. Imagine what she would have been like if you weren't here."

"That's only partially the truth. Tessa has been afraid all evening that I might use the wrong fork or commit some other dreadful social solecism. Yet"—he smiled at them—"her real fear is not that I might be awkward, but that she might. At some level, she's proud of me."

"Oh, I know," said Vera. "Dear Kai."

"Just the usual mixture of feelings," he said, still smiling. "Tessa is too powerful for her own good. She has too much force to function as smoothly as she'd like."

"Well, she's honest," said Vera.

"She and your husband."

"No, Elliot is like you," said Vera. "You both have secret lives. Mother would like to, but she's not subtle enough." The rebuke in her words was modified by her kindness, and Elliot saw that she was talking entirely to Kai, not to him.

"If I have any secrets, they are all out-of-date by now," Kai said. "But even that no longer seems significant to me." He seemed relaxed, a little tired, paler than usual. "What we keep secret," he said, "isn't really half as important as what we tell."

Vera took his hand.

Kai was right, Elliot knew. He had been half-consciously waiting
for Anita Kellerman to telephone, but he thought none of that would
ever happen again.

The Glaubers left soon after. Margaret stood waving in the door,
but Chase went outside with Elliot and Vera as the others went to
Herman's car.

"Thank you again for coming," said Chase. "When all of this is
over, this upset, I do hope that we can see more of each other."

Tessa nodded and said, "We owe you a dinner now."

"We'll be sure to collect." Chase had not even winced.

"Too bad it's such a long haul out to Richmond Corners," Herman
rumbled. "And I don't suppose you think much of the sights along
the way. We should try to meet for dinner at a restaurant somewhere
in between."

"A marvelous idea, Herman. Let's try to do that. When all of this
is over. And thank you again for your offer. We'll arrange a meeting
about it after the kids leave."

"You got your meeting," said Herman. "I always said there should
be no hard feelings from this business. I was annoyed as hell at the
start, but . . ." His voice dropped, and he shrugged his shoulders. "I
suppose you were too. We just have to see how things go at the
hearing."

They were all shivering with the cold, and the night hung massively above them. Tessa went around to the passenger's side of the
car and let herself in. The lights were off in Lamont Von Heilitz's
old house and in the lower floors of the two houses visible across
the street. Chinks of yellow shone through blinds in the bedroom
windows. When Elliot turned back to look at his parents' house, he
saw his mother standing inside the first-floor windows, still waving.
Vera went up to hug her father, and Chase moved toward Kai, who
had been standing a little apart.

"You're probably the only man among us who can answer my
question," he said. Kai bent his head, smiling. "When I went upstairs
to find the photograph album, I saw a large single star or planet

right through the glass in the back of the house—my wife's office. It was the only star in the sky. Is that the North Star?"

"No, that was more likely to be Venus," said Kai. "The evening star. It is always more conspicuous than any other, and it is the first to appear."

"I thought you'd know," said Chase. His whole body expressed satisfaction. Both of them—and Elliot, his chest constricting, imitating—lifted their faces to look. The December wind blew about them.

"Come on, you people, get back inside," said Herman. "It's too cold to stand around out here stargazing." "Especially this close to the lake," came Tessa's muffled voice. Herman opened the car door, bent the seat back for Kai, and then got in himself. "Merry Christmas," he called to them. They were already on their way back up the drive to the house. "Merry Christmas."

"Merry Christmas."

"Merry Christmas."

"Merry Christmas."

When the doorbell rang the next morning, Elliot was working at the piano, trying to rough out the new piece he had begun several days before, a setting for the Theodore Roethke poem *The Waking*. It had to be kept to the simplest essentials, just piano and voice, with a six-verse structure which would modulate by intricate repetitions from the quiet dreamlike beginning to something more somber: an unfolding from the villanelle's rhymes to a swelling baritone-register conclusion. He had heard it from the first as for a baritone, with a patterned series of lifts and surprises in the music. When completed, the song could stand as a synthesis, an epilogue, to *Words for the Wind*, another voice entering to dominate. But the simplicity had to evolve from a tough density of tone which would advance the tenor's insistence in the earlier work. He had done three of the verses, then stuck at the fourth.

This morning it was going better. Normally he did not work at a piano, but spun it out in his head, testing the alternatives with his inner ear; the change was temporarily exhilarating. When the bell rang, he ignored it, thinking that Robert would answer. Then he realized that Robert had the day off. Vera was still upstairs. His parents had gone to visit Pierce Laubach and his sister: a "brunch," Dr. Laubach had said, the quotation marks audible in his voice indicating his disdain for his sister's vocabulary.

The bell rang again. He looked at his watch: ten to eleven. He was pleasantly surprised that he had been working so long, nearly two and half hours. He decided to save Vera the trouble of coming downstairs. Just as he was crossing the room Vera called from upstairs.

"Oh, Elliot, what a bother. Do you want me to answer it?"

"I'll get it," he said, and went to the door.

At first he did not recognize the good-looking hippie-ish girl outside. Then she said shyly, "Elliot," and he saw that it was Joanie Haupt. In five years she had grown up. Even red-faced, as now— from the cold? from crying? she was pouched beneath the eyes— Joanie was remarkably prettier than she had been. Perhaps it was merely that she no longer looked innocent. Her hair was much longer, and her face had a strained, sleepless quality that made her look in some way doomed. Momentarily, Elliot felt a shade more sympathy for Lawrence Wooster. He asked her to come in.

"I don't want to disturb you," she said, "but I had a terrible day yesterday. I had a really black Christmas. I thought I'd come to see Vera. I was in the car for half an hour, debating whether or not to ring the bell. I saw your parents leave. I didn't want to come. I'm sorry." She looked down at her feet. "I don't even know you very well."

"Don't be silly," he said. He took her coat. "Vera's upstairs somewhere. She'll probably be glad to have someone to talk to. I've been working down here all morning, and she's just been keeping out of my way."

"Oh, you're *working*," Joanie wailed. "I'm interrupting you. Baby, be still."

"Excuse me?"

"I had to bring him with me because he hates being alone in the house, and then it was so cold in the car." From one of the deep pockets of her coat she lifted a small liver-colored dog. The dog squirmed in her hands. "This is Marcuse," she said, holding the squirming little dog out so he could see it. She appeared to be a little less mournful. "Larry bought him for me. He's fully grown, and he only weighs four pounds. Isn't he *tiny*?"

Elliot agreed that Marcuse was tiny. He glanced back toward the room with the piano.

"Marcuse keeps me company. Maybe what I really needed all the time was a dog, not a man. Larry keeps *hounding* me, and I can't keep hanging up the telephone when I hear his voice." She looked at him again, the dog struggling in the crook of her elbow, and he saw that she was on the point of tears. "Should I go?"

"No of course not, come on in," he said, looking around for Vera. He was holding Marcuse when Vera came into the hall.

"Vera, I had to come," said Joanie. "I'm sorry."

"There's nothing to apologize for," said Vera. "Come on upstairs. We'll keep out of Elliot's way, and then the old ogre will be able to work." Elliot gave the wriggling dog back to Joanie, and Vera led her firmly upstairs. She cast Elliot an apologetic look before disappearing.

Elliot washed his hands and splashed water on his face and returned to the piano. Marcuse began to bark, off in the direction of his bedroom: a yappy two-syllable popping. He played the song setting through from the beginning. An idea formed. The barking stopped, resumed, stopped again. He could very faintly hear Joanie Haupt's soft full bruised voice.

Twenty minutes later—two lines of music which were a dissonant variation on the second verse—he heard a car coming into the driveway. The door punkily closed: since it did not continue into the garage, it was not his parents' car. He stood up from the piano and went to the window. Anita Kellerman, her hair ruffling in the wind, was striding up the walk.

He went to the door and opened it just as she was about to ring the bell. Her eyes swam luminously toward him.

"I had to see you," she said. "When you didn't call, I decided to come over. Do you mind?"

"No, come in. I was working, but . . . come on in."

"I'm so happy you were working," she said. "You're so much better than the rest of us. What's that noise? It sounds like someone is breaking bottles."

"It's a dog. A friend of Vera's just came over and she brought her dog."

"You look spiky today." Anita's face was questioning, uncertain. She fidgeted in the hallway, and he drew her in and removed her coat.

"No, come in," he said. He felt tired. They went into the living room. Anita went toward the couch, and watched him moving around the room.

"I wish that hadn't happened, that morning," she said. "You won't understand it, and it's going to change everything. Oh, damn. I wanted to say something else, and just looking at you I can see that everything I wanted to say was wrong."

He sat on a chair. He looked at the piano. "You don't have to explain anything. I shouldn't have just come in that way, of course. I was in an odd mood—a disconnected sort of mood. The night before, I hadn't had much sleep; then I saw a piece about me in the *Herald*, an absurd story. I had to get out of the house, and I started walking, and I wound up at your house. So I came in."

"As easily as that."

"Yes."

Neither of them spoke for a second.

"You think I've been lying to you," she said.

She had never seemed more distant to him—sitting there before him, she seemed packed with history, with her past that was her life.

"I suppose you're right. For a while, I thought you might be sleeping with Andy."

She laughed gloriously, holding her fingers over her mouth. "Dear Elliot. What should I say? What Hollywood people say, I guess. We're just good friends."

He felt a great self-loathing: his remark, utterly factitious, had been intended to wound her. Then he recognized that, at various points in the past two weeks, he had indeed wondered about the relationship between Andy and Anita. He had never quite allowed this fear to become conscious.

"Andy says that people should be selectively unfaithful. She said something like that to me at your party. I guess she was trying to help me along to enlightenment."

"Oh, I can't bear you when you're being so heavy and ironic." Anita was very confident. "I wish you hadn't come barging into my bedroom, but since you did, I don't want it to damage what we have together." She looked at him questioningly. "Don't be so distant from me, Elliot. I can't bear it."

"All right. I won't be distant." He looked at her: her short hair shining, the forceful face turned squarely to him. "None of this makes any sense," he said. "I don't have any claims on you. But I guess I took you too literally when you said you felt like a nun."

"I meant you to take it literally. I do feel like a nun."

He caught a faint whiff of her meaning: a purpose cold and direct as a bullet.

"Elliot..." She looked as though she wanted to take his hand, and he slumped deeper into the chair. "Elliot darling, I've always rejoiced in your marriage. *Rejoiced* in it. And I've always loved Vera—I told her that once."

From upstairs, over Marcuse's *yap yap*, Joanie Haupt's voice was faintly audible.

"I don't know much about you and Upp," he said. "I don't want to know much about it. But I don't like your 'rejoicing' in my marriage. That makes me feel invaded. It's intrusive and presumptuous. You don't know Vera at all. You just made a little model of the perfect wife, someone discreet, sympathetic, not too bright to be threatening, and you pinned Vera's name on it. That's not Vera—that's not any real person at all."

"And you don't know Ronnie. Nor Mark." There was a flicker of appeal in her eyes, but the tone of their conversation had irrevocably darkened, and the appeal became depthless as he waited for her to continue. "Ronnie loves Mark, and he always has. You're a childless man. Mark is unreal to you. You couldn't begin to know how to deal with him. With all Ronnie's problems, he is terribly supportive for Mark. I'm beginning to think that we might be able to keep Mark at home, if Ronnie can spend more time with him. This year has been a wasteland for all three of us, but I think Mark might be coming out of his terrors. Ronnie may be right. I'll at least give him the chance to try. You wouldn't do as much."

"I think I would," he said. Yet perhaps Anita was right. He could not imagine himself as Mark's father; he might repeat the pattern he had set with Baltz.

Then her anger softened. "Ronnie was afraid of you, Elliot. He didn't know what might happen when you came back. He's still uncertain. That was the reason he struck me, a month ago. I'd just heard that you were coming home, and I couldn't help looking pleased. I think Ronnie has always been afraid you might come back."

The history of this sentence slowly beat in on Elliot. Upp had known Anita long before he had first returned to Plechette City.

"Nothing has changed," she said. Marcuse, upstairs, barked. "And after all, dear one, it's you who live in Paris. Not me."

He stood up smartly, moved around the couch to the piano and struck a series of chords. He tried one of the runs from the Scarlatti sonata in E flat major, but misfingered it badly. He played it again, willing it to be right. The second time, it was technically correct, but sounded wooden to him, lifeless.

"That was beautiful," said Anita.

He sat on the bench and looked over the top of the piano at her.

"Play for me what you're working on," she said. "I'd love to hear it. What is it?"

"A song setting. Another Roethke poem—the villanelle called *The Waking*. I'm not satisfied with it so far, though."

"I'd love to hear it," she said. "I always love your music. Will you play it for me?"

He nodded. He was in a savage mood. He played through the first four verses—the morning's idea came back to him as he struck the last two lines of the fourth verse—and then, without a break, thinking of the shattered record on her carpet, he played "Ain't Misbehavin' " out of tempo, in no key.

"Elliot, that's the loveliest thing you've done yet," she said. "It's just beautiful."

"I like the ending," he said.

When he took her to the door, she put her arms about his neck and said, "I know everything will be the same. Tell me you love me."

"I love you," he said. "What difference does it make?"

She misunderstood him gloriously.

Ten minutes later, seated back at the piano, he again heard wheels crunching against the snow at the side of the drive, followed by the closing of a car door. Andy, he thought; he did not desire Andy French's sympathy. Elliot walked around to the windows and, looking out, saw a red Porsche parked outside. Whose? Another intruder. The doorbell rang.

When he opened the door, furiously impatient, Lawrence Wooster, coatless and in a blue pinstripe suit, strode in, his pink face flushed and embarrassed. "Ellie baby!" His hand was damp. "I'm on my lunch hour, Ellie, and I tried to get in touch with Joanie. When I didn't get her at her place, I had a quick bite at the club and thought I'd take a swing around this way. I spotted her car outside your place here. Is she . . . ?" He paused. His breath suggested that the quick bite had included more than a little gin.

Elliot nodded. "She's upstairs with Vera. Do you want to go up?"

Wooster surprised him by blushing. "Gee, I don't know, Ellie. Maybe I ought to let her talk it out, do you think?" He was standing nervously in the hall, rising and falling on the balls of his feet. "It's awkward of me to show up here, I know, but I've been trying to get ahold of Joanie for a couple of days now, and she won't cooperate. Jesus, Ellie, I'm going out of my mind. Do you suppose I could just stay down here with you for a little while?" He tweaked the hair at the nape of his neck.

Wooster looked as though he might explode, and Elliot wished to cushion him. "Sure, come in and sit down," he said. "I'm trying to get some work done, so I won't be able to talk, but if you just want to wait a few minutes . . ."

"Yeah, I'll take a pew," Wooster said, badly imitating what must have been his habitual manner.

Elliot returned to the piano. Before he had played the ridiculous ending to Anita, he'd had a minute needling of what to do with the fifth verse, and he began to toy with it, bar by bar, trying to ignore his visitor.

Wooster left the chair and wandered about the room. He picked up Elliot's wedding picture, sighed, and put it back on the table. "Sorry," he whispered. "Can't seem to stay still." He went back to the couch. "Say, could I make myself a drink?"

"In a cabinet in the kitchen. To the left of the oven." Elliot kept his head down, and his hands on the keys. Wooster said, "Gee, thanks," and moved heavily across the room and into the hall. Elliot heard him discover Robert's swinging door which led back and forth between the kitchen and the dining room. A sound of cabinets being opened and closed. Marcuse barked, but Wooster seemed not to hear. Then the clatter of an ice tray rapped against the sink.

Wooster reappeared in the living room, pink-faced, a short glass with a bobbing olive in his hand; he looked too young for his suit. "What's it like, working at home?"

"That depends." Elliot looked speculatively at Wooster, who was now back at pacing the room. "Sometimes it's a little difficult."

"Jesus, I envy you. No office to go to, no regular hours, no boss. That's the way everybody should live. But you know? I think most people in the U.S. aren't ready for that kind of life. They're whipped into line by their jobs so . . ."—he groped for a word—". . . much . . . that they wouldn't know what to do without them. Take anybody you can name at the bank. Take the trust department. If those guys tried the *vie bohème* like you, they'd go to pieces." He sat on the edge of his chair. "Take me. I make one step out of the pattern, and they call me on the carpet."

Elliot looked up. "Joanie?"

"Hell, no." Wooster glanced at the ceiling, then brought his round blue eyes back to Elliot. "I mean that damned thing I signed for your father. Walt Clement, the head of the trust department, called me into his office yesterday and gave me a long powwow about steering clear of public issues—said my future could be at stake. I think someone in the estate department squealed to him. Ronnie Upp's a big investor with us, you know. Clement sees him three times a year. When I said I was trying to use my social conscience—I had your father in mind there, Elliot—he damn near took my ear off."

Wooster gulped at his drink. "Indirectly, sure. Indirectly, Joanie's probably been affecting my work. A load like this is a tough thing for a man to carry. Then I spent a couple of months in analysis, and my whole head was turned around. Elliot, I saw things. I saw things you never dreamt of in my philosophy. Joanie's been a great help to me—the sex alone has changed my life. All my values changed. I was never a deep thinker, but now I'm into things that make me take a whole new look around. Some examples." He spread his hands as if he were opening a portfolio. "I used to be a straight-down-the-line party Republican. Straight ticket, all the way. Back our boys in Vietnam. Had a flag decal on the station wagon—the old Stars and Stripes. Then after I met Joanie, I started to blow a little grass with her friends. I started to think it couldn't be *that* bad. Hell, she was doing it, and *I* was doing it. I got in touch with Dr. Loomis, my therapist. Gave the wagon to Sylvie and bought myself the Porsche. Grew my hair a little. Ellie"—his eyes grew charged with sincerity—"I read books. I subscribe to *Rolling Stone*. I began to see what it was all about. Sure, I stayed within the system, but I figured that was the way to change the system. Picture hundreds of guys like me, thousands of us, working in banks, lawyers' offices, brokerages... Elliot, you wouldn't believe the talks I've had. I used to think of Joanie as my teacher. I learned things about love I never learned in eight years of marriage with Sylvie. Oriental things—Indian things. Joanie went the same way I did, you know, but she started earlier, when she went to college at Madison." He gloomily stared into his drink.

Elliot closed the lid of the piano. "You think Upp tried to get you fired?"

Wooster came back from his reverie. "Something like that. He swings a lot of weight down at the bank. Clement told me that if my work didn't pick up, and if there was one more incident like this, I'd be in the market for another job. He said I'd better make my image fit in a little closer with the bank's. Then I come home, and Sylvie is playing her damned guitar or talking to some priest or giving me some shit out of the nineteenth century. I give her a good home, a car, a social life, every credit card under the sun, but she's not satisfied. She wants to stand in the way of my development. She tries to hold me down. She hates my friends. And now, things are going to hell with Joanie. I didn't think she'd ever want to get away from me, but it looks like I have to chase her all over town just to talk to her." He looked pleadingly at Elliot.

The dog's barking carried faintly down the stairs. "Jesus, that's Marcuse," Wooster said. "I gave her that dog for Christmas, and now I think she loves the dog more than she loves me. I even named it for her. I better go up." Wooster had suddenly come close to tears.

"No, sit still," Elliot said. "I'll go up instead." Wooster regarded him lovingly with his round eyes. Elliot left the piano and went into the hall. He could now hear more loudly the dog's insistent *yap yap yap* and Vera's voice calmly, lowly talking. He went up the stairs.

Joanie, her head propped against the wall, jumped when he entered the room. She was leaning weakly back in a chair; her face looked powdered, dead white. The clean lines of her mouth and jaw touched some internal point in Elliot. "You scared me," she said.

Vera stood up: he saw that she had had enough of Joanie.

"Has he left yet?" she asked.

"No, he wouldn't leave," said Joanie. "I can't get rid of him. He buzzes around me like a fly. When he can't get me at home, he calls me at work. He's absolutely, utterly like glue. I feel so *harassed*." She carefully smoothed her forehead with one hand. "You people are so good to me," she said. "Larry was so sweet when we started—I used to think of him as being so straight and dependable. He was so innocent. Everything he did, he acted like it was the first time anybody had ever done it. 'I'll take care of you,' he said to me, 'just let me take care of you.' But now I feel like I somehow created him. He never stops talking about how much I mean to him. He sort of went all mystical. He's not very bright. He confessed to me one day that he cheated his way all through high school. In college, he bought term papers from his fraternity—they had files. I was so excited by what I could do for him! But damn him, he won't stop talking about it."

Vera, standing near, put her hand on Joanie's shoulder. "What do you want to do about it now?"

"I just . . . just . . . just don't know." She faced Elliot, using her eyes. "If I go down now, he might hit me. There's a whole side of him that's in a terrible darkness, and you never know how the darkness will express itself. Marcuse, get down from there."

The dog was rooting in a stack of score sheets beside Elliot's bed. Hearing his name, he lifted his head and looked worriedly around at Joanie. "Get off," she said sharply. He sprang from the pile of papers to the bed and began to roll on it.

"I had to get away," she continued. "But getting away is killing me. Sometimes I feel like I'm in this terrible sort of physical slavery to him. I love him. When he's all strong and quiet and just touching me, he's the most wonderful man. But then he starts to talk about it! He jumps up and reads something out of a book. I don't *want* him to be like that. I don't *want* him to talk the way my friends talk. When I hear him on the phone, he's all gruff and serious to begin with, the way he should be, and then he ends up all whiny and pleading. Oh, I hate that."

The dog was still rolling on Elliot's bed, rotating the small stick of his tail; the bedcovers puckered and bunched about him. The score sheets lay in a rumpled heap.

"Lawrence Wooster isn't going to hit you," said Vera. "I think you should go down. We'll come with you." She moved toward the door and took Joanie's hand. Over her shoulder, she threw Elliot a look of wild impatience. "Come on, Joanie."

Together, they took her to the staircase. Halfway down, Joanie began to weep. "Marcuse," she sobbed, and raced back up to the bedroom. Cradling the wriggling dog in her arms, she reappeared and started again down the stairs.

Wooster met them at the bottom of the stairs. "Joanie . . ." he said, unable to continue.

"Don't be so *pathetic*," she snapped at him, and clasping the dog in her arms, sailed past, snatching her coat from the rack in the hall before running out. They could hear Marcuse squealing as if injured.

Wooster goggled at Elliot and Vera and then blushed furiously. "Excuse me," he whispered, already moving toward the door. He dashed outside, and they heard Joanie's car starting up and going off down the street. "Ellie, thanks for the drink and your company," he called to them from the doorstep, then slammed the door behind him. In a moment the Porsche roared, and Elliot heard its wheels whining for a second on the road.

"He's nineteen years old," he said to Vera, still astonished.

She said, "So is Joanie." She put her arms about his waist. "Elliot, let's get away from these people."

chapter 22

E lliot moved from landscape to landscape, turning the pages of the book he had given Vera, virgins succeeding nymphs on the big colored plates, Ucello's snaked line of soldiers overwhelming a smooth Botticelli girl, half-asleep in a thick wood. A long-haired man, his muscles lovingly delineated, slept near. It was Mars. Beside Elliot lay a bookmarked *Bech* and a proof copy of Pittman's latest novel, sent with a note from Alicante. *Inge's packing to leave, as sick of me as I knew she would be, as sick of me as I am of her. She uses tiny leather bags no larger than her ass. Go, go—it makes me feel like Papa Lowry, hung upside down in an amusement park, watching everything he owns fall out of his pockets to the roof of the car. Inge-less, I'm dedicating this to you. Take it and run.* The note was taped to the green backside of the flap, two pages away from his name. *For Elliot Denmark.*

Some of the paintings recalled the photographs he had seen in Kai's room. The pale green misted landscape of the Domenichino frescoes—lush Daphne extruding leaves from her fingers to evade rapacious Apollo—and the lyrical long plane, softly brown, of Pollaiuolo. He deliberately flipped the page, and the plate fluttered. Here was a perverse, delicious Piero di Cosimo, half the canvas filled with dogs—aimless patient creatures. Had Kai walked along that lake?

His past was as formalized as the paintings, concentrated to a pattern Elliot had read. He looked in the index, then opened the book again at the Botticelli *Venus and Mars*, two languid figures in a wood. At the right, his head thrown back, Mars was about to be blown to life by a fat goat-satyr puffing into a shell, a horn: an instrument. Elliot looked closely at the first satyr, and knew he had been right. Its impish chubby face was that of the cherub in the Glaubers' garden.

And the Bellini portrait of the doge, an image which had haunted him for weeks, that stern amused old face was Kai's. Indeed, had he not known it from the first? Kai the survivor—the face rebuked him.

Anita said, "The entire subject is something we shouldn't talk about. It'll ruin what we have together, and I wish you'd be more reasonable about probing and prying into what's only an old story. I love you. I need to love you. If I also need to love Ronnie, and you'll remember that I told you that on the first night I saw you after you returned, you've always had Vera. I'm selfish about my needs, but all needs are selfish anyhow. When I came to your house the day after Christmas I thought we had settled all this. Elliot, I'm heartbroken to see you still upset. Count on me, Elliot. Depend on me. Trust me."

"I trust you to *be* you."

"So you really don't think that I've been honest."

"No, but I don't think that I have either."

"Oh, but you are," she said. "You're honest, and you're fair, and you're not a fool."

Elliot signaled to the waiter for another drink, and turned to look at the turning faces of the clock. By summer it would be a heap of shattered brick. Further south loomed the two golden domes of a Polish church, and, to their right, the bare winter beach, visible between buildings, of a south-side yacht club. "For a behaviorist, you're being awfully mystical," he said. Then he knew it was a mistake. She liked his talking that way.

"You might be right," she said, smiling. "What I mean is that if you hadn't come back here, I would have shown up on your doorstep in Paris one afternoon, just to keep you in my orbit. I can never lose you, Elliot."

There were chords enough, he saw, but they were the wrong ones.

"Ronnie was never really paranoid. He was just frightened. He remembered what happened when you came back here from Columbia years ago. We'd had a rift, a falling-out. I hadn't seen him for weeks when I first met you. And I kept him away all during our first year together. But then when it was over, and I met Ronnie in Sweden, I knew that everything would hold. That we were all tied together."

Where he had looked for a clear hard vein of purpose—in Anita—he had found the deepest nonsense. Seated across the polished table from her in the dark circular room, their glasses half-empty, he wanted most to throw a switch to cause some hard bright illumination over all of them, a light impossibly clear—other people were always as hidden as not, always objectifying one another into emblems and excuses. He wanted to abstract himself, to complete the wounded retreat of his emotions.

Yet he could not be so arbitrary. It was the impulse to go back into his work, into the house on Villa Beauséjour rich with old Poltovnin's possessions. Perhaps he was more like Tessa Glauber than he imagined.

"You've just gone away," said Anita. "Come back."

On New Year's Eve the Denmarks went to a party at Nathan Himmel's home, and Anita, who had spent much of the first half of the evening speaking quietly with Vera, found Elliot in Himmel's study, where he had been letting Roberta Potocky, the student cellist, assure him of his artistic magnitude. Under the barrage of her compliments, Elliot had grown increasingly uncomfortable. He saw that she was pleading with him—she wanted to impress him with her seriousness. She was just finishing her work at the university, and she was looking for a symphony position: he knew that she was clumsily preparing to ask for a recommendation. When Anita entered the room and gave one glance at Roberta the girl scampered through the door as though she had been seared. Elliot felt annoyed, relieved, pursued.

"How did you make her leave like that? It was very impressive."

Primed with assurance, Anita glided magnificently toward him, eyes and face alight. He thought she would embrace him, and he unconsciously stiffened, but she stopped a foot away. In her elegant simple clothing, a rich modulated ocher which brought out the depth of her eyes and the starkness of her face, Anita was the most breathtaking woman at the party; Elliot thought it possible that Roberta Potocky had been literally shamed from the room. She gave him a deep humorous glance. "I only have you for a few more days," she said. His old illusion: she looked like the woman by whom all others must be judged.

From the living room Elliot could hear a faint buzz of voices, and over them, Glenn Gould playing the fourth Bach partita. Strong steely music. "Why isn't Upp here?"

"He wanted us to have some time together. He knew I'd rebel if I couldn't see you alone some more before you left."

"And Andy?"

"She's at home with Mark." Anita gave her answer almost shruggingly: as though everything were finally understood between them. "Vera is still uncertain of me, but we basically like one another. I can't tell you how much I want Vera to like me. All of us are friends now." Her glance meant that "friends," between them, was code.

It was nearly nightmarish, her misreading of his mood. She was convinced that he would be in love with her for life.

She came toward him, and he, countering, drew her toward the door. When he glanced at her face, he saw that rejoining the party was precisely what she wished to do. It suited her masque: if he were surly, it would suit her masque; if he kissed her—the taking for granted of her implications—she would be distant. Ronnie Upp and Vera were now part of her internal ordering. It was easier to leave the study. The partita's brisk gigue, its last movement, accelerated, slowed, accelerated through the low voices.

"Now that you've finished the song, what are you going to work on?" They were just entering the living room. Vera, on the far side of a crowd of faces, was talking to Himmel, who held one meaty hand on her shoulder. Anita would always assume that he was "going to work" on a new piece.

"I've had something in mind," he said. "Something for an unaccompanied chorus, with big blocks of sound. Almost medieval in feeling."

"What is it?"

"More poems," he said. "I'm thinking of calling it *Four Hymns to Marriage*."

She showed puzzlement only for a second. "It's perfect," she said. "You couldn't do anything else."

At midnight, when everyone blew out razzing raucous blasts on noisemakers, Wattman and Donadio sulking beside the bar, Himmel set on the turntable a violent cheerful piece by Shostakovich, and in the blare of sound, faces bending to kiss all about him, Elliot looked for Vera but found himself being turned by a firm female hand on his shoulder and then beneath his lips those, a little sticky from champagne, of Rosa Heldenweit.

"Please come over to our house, Elliot," she breathed to him. She stumbled, and he was forced to catch and hold her with the length of his body. "Please do come. I'm so sorry."

Italian Renaissance Painting lay beside the chunky pop-art cigarette lighter on the coffee table, a folded newspaper and three glasses the only other objects on the table's smooth expanse. It was the late evening of New Year's Day; far out in the lake, Elliot could see the red lights of a harbor ice cutter inching southward. It had been at work all during the day, casting back and forth and moving toward open water.

"So you have seen the *Herald*," said Dr. Laubach, nodding toward the paper. "My little surprise for Elliot. Hilda thought of inserting it in the January first issue instead of the January second. A marvelous in-stance of feminine connection to yearly rhythms, the woman's sense of symbolism. I am forever observing this in my sister.

"A new year, a new beginning. We have this impulse when we make resolutions for the new year. We know we can't change our skins, but at least it *feels* as though we might. Perhaps the community as a whole might alter its priorities. Especially when advised by so luminous a character as yourself, Elliot." Dr. Laubach gave his thin saurian smile.

A week ago, the newspaper statement would have infuriated Elliot; today he was calmer. His picture looked somberly up toward the ceiling, the same photograph to be used on posters and programs for the concert. Its distracted, rather shifty appearance did not well suit the italicized comments beneath it, which had been taken from his interview with Ted Edwards.

"It's a good thought, Pierce, and good of you to have given Elliot such prominence in the ad, but I'm afraid we are on the losing side of this battle. On Christmas Day I talked to Herman Glauber, and he intimated to me that he has five certain votes on the commission. Jeff Glee is our only chance, and he's a slender reed." Chase tugged at his cuffs. "Of course, we've had a decent exercise in participatory democracy, and that may be of value in itself. At least Upp did not clear us off the board in one move, as he did in the clock-tower business."

"Hold on to the faith," said Dr. Laubach. "Hold on to the faith, baby," He grinned wickedly at Elliot. "Did I say it correctly?"

"Ask Lawrence Wooster," said Elliot.

Dr. Laubach looked from Chase to Elliot, then back to Chase. "I take it that you do not entirely approve of my redesigning of our statement."

"Oh heavens, Pierce," said his father. "I think it's lovely."

"It's fine by me," said Elliot. "I wish there were a photograph that made me look less like a butcher with his thumb on the scale."

"You look the image of your grandfather," said Dr. Laubach, "and a good deal like old Brooks with long hair. We put in the quotations at the last minute—another of Hilda's inspired notions. They improve the layout, don't you think?" He held up the paper and turned it toward Elliot.

"The layout is fine."

"Fine," echoed his father.

Dr. Laubach put the paper aside and took the huge book onto his lap. He opened it near the middle. Then he took his eyes from the

Uccello which Elliot could see upside down, glare from the lamp obscuring half the plate so the warriors marched into a dissolving whiteness, and said, "We are all working together on a serious issue. Don't be defeated now."

"I'm proud of the *fight*," said Chase, "but I don't think I care anymore who wins it."

Far out beyond the crisp outline of his head the red light of the armored harbor boat swung inward for the last time.

"It seems from the evening news that the wounded girl will live," said Dr. Laubach. "She will have a few scars, but plastic surgery can fix anything these days, I gather. Ah!" He propped the book up with his hands. "Florence!" It was meant as a general accolade to the arts, and as the ice cutter's red light inched toward the frame of the window, Elliot ironically bent his head.

Y
ou have only a few days left among us. Andy will miss you,"
said Ronnie Upp, grinning pleasantly at Elliot from behind the giant
ornate mahogany relic that had once been Brooks Denmark's desk.
Everything else about the office had been changed from the times
when Chase had taken Elliot as a boy up to the suites on the top
floor of the factory. Where an old richly colored Turkish carpet
("Make a wish and you'll be able to fly on it," his grandfather had
said. "If it is the right wish.") dully glowed from desk to door, there
was now a single dark patterned green sheet like a country-club lawn
after a summer shower; the walls had been repainted from their old
sober colorless color to a light snapping blue, interrupted at regular
intervals by large abstractions—black whisked over white—signed
with a famous name. Brooks's delicate monoprints of Paris, preserved
by the Chambers family and the various Denmark cousins who had
used this office, were gone. Wood and aluminum in strong linear
patterns: if the old office had implied labor, moral seriousness, an
idiosyncratic Francophilia, it now suggested coolness, distance, vistas.
Only the desk and the great windows to the east remained. Immediately beyond them the side of the clock tower gigantically revolved.
Seen so closely once again, it reminded Elliot of a still from a Harold

Lloyd film—a little man hanging from a huge clock hand. "We will all miss you, naturally. But particularly Andy, I think."

"Because she will lose an ally."

The two men looked at one another with self-conscious irony. Upp had welcomed Elliot into his office with no coolness—the magnanimity of a man who had won every hand. Elliot, sitting across from him in this cool transparent office, felt vestigially shabby, displaced. Upp was dressed in the manner of a wealthy young English viscount with a fondness for Tommy Nutter and Savile Row. Even his secretary—a beautifully elegant young man—had regarded Elliot with a limp superiority. Yet Upp had seemed unsurprised to see him, had even appeared to be expecting him, this morning after the disastrous public hearing.

"Let's not be nasty," said Upp. "I'd never hold that absurd newspaper thing against you. In fact, I'm sure that wasn't your doing at all. You're not that kind of man. I am certain that your father's cohorts thought of using those quotations from the Edwards taping. It was typical misplanning. That kind of thing does more harm than good in Plechette City. And you are not really a Savonarola type, are you?"

"It seems not," said Elliot. "That was never one of my problems." He looked at the edge of the clock.

"You've just proved my point, Elliot. One of the things I've learned from Anita is that there are two reactions to stress, fight or flight. That's the jargon of her trade, but it is accurate. You choose flight. That's fine! If things had worked out differently, I think we could have been friends. Perhaps we still can."

"I didn't come here to be your friend," said Elliot. "I just wanted to get another look at you."

"Curiosity?" Upp's smile was now nearly intolerably superior. "You once caused me a year of misery—I wouldn't be human if I weren't interested in the man who was capable of that. You must know that Anita picked you blindly. Willfully. You were an accident, Elliot. No more than that. You know, our friend Anita is incapable of living without a man. Before me, there was one of her husband's colleagues, before that a graduate student. I fear that Bob Cratchit may be the latest of these footnotes. Don't be shocked. After all, you know Anita's temperament. She must have told you about the astrologer who told her she was lascivious. Anita's proud of that."

"So you're contemptuous of her." Elliot felt sickened.

"No, I'm hardly that," Upp answered. "I know her too well. Anita fulfills a necessary function for me. When I need a hostess she is a good one—she is an impressive woman. I really cannot do without her. For years we've had a good firm relationship. It's tricky at times, but what relationship isn't? I tolerate her foibles, she tolerates mine. Elliot, you should be grateful you can see the true situation at last. I was almost grateful when you walked in on us that morning. I thought, now we can all begin to build from here. Don't look so downhearted. We both want you to think of us as friends. I'd like to look you up when she and I come to Europe next summer. I know a clinic in Geneva that can do wonders for Mark."

Upp stood and went around the desk. He touched Elliot lightly on the shoulder and then motioned toward the door. "You have your last rehearsal to fit in today, if I remember correctly. It's a pity we can't have lunch together, but some other time. And, Elliot"—going back around the desk, he slid the glasses back over his eyes—"remember this. We all got what we wanted." He smiled. "Perhaps you should call on your father before your rehearsal."

Elliot had one more question. "Why did you shatter my record?"

The other man surprised him by grinning. "Oh, did you see that? I'm terribly sorry. But I am not your culprit. Mark broke it, I fear. And I'm sure he picked it utterly at random. It was on top of the other records. The boy used a hammer. Much better that he attack objects than people or animals, don't you think?" Upp waved him out of the office.

Elliot parked in the lot behind the Moore Building on upper Grand Avenue, pushed down all the locks, and walked swiftly, turning up his coat collar, toward the back entrance. His feet were damp from the gray slush. Against the building someone had set a beer bottle, and it had frozen during the night, so that now it was like the still frame of an explosion; brown shattered glass buried in thick brown ice. He kicked it over with his foot, and the misshapen thing snapped in two. He had gone to Upp's office in a tigerish mood, but had failed—the man had evaded him as neatly as a fish slipping around the edges of a net. In his muted eggshell of an office, he was impenetrable. Anita was his. The hearing, despite Rona Bender's feverish verbal assaults, had gone smoothly beneath its frantic surface. The wood too was Upp's. And now, thirty minutes before the last rehearsal, he was following Upp's advice and going to see his father.

Still, for all Anita's mysticism—it was how he thought of her faith in the permanency of love—he felt that she was stronger than Upp. Upp's smoothness, his blandness, his air of bullying superior graciousness, these fitted him less well than did his foppish clothing. For all his calculated air, Upp broadcast a sense of pain. Anita would not see this. Entering the elevator in the immense brown lobby of the Moore Building, Elliot remembered what he had said to Upp. "I didn't come here to be your friend," he repeated with satisfaction. A man with a swollen jaw—the lower floors of the Moore Building were a phalanx of dentists—visibly started, and Elliot realized that he had spoken aloud. He looked down to his ruined shoes, to the filthy winter floor of the elevator, then shifted his gaze to the panel above the door. *Next stops 4 6 7 12.* When the elevator stopped, *4* vanished and the other man moved very quickly out into the hall. Elliot watched while all the numbers before *12* went black.

Jefferson Glee had been his father's last hope on the commission. There were twelve aldermen seated on the platform above the audience in the hearing room, and Herman Glauber had told Chase that nearly half would vote for the proposed rezoning, no matter what comment came from the audience. With one exception, the others were uncommitted. Archie Holton, Chase's alderman, and perhaps two or three others would vote against. "You never know what Glee's going to do," Herman had told Chase. "He got elected by making speeches about the white devil, and he never stopped making them, even while he was doing deals right and left with the white men. And whatever way he goes, the other two black aldermen will follow. The trouble is, Glee's slippery. He can't look like he's playing up to the whites or he'll lose face in his ward. But if he goes with me, maybe he'll think that I'll support him on programs for his ward. And maybe I would. Glee and I have never got along very well, to tell you the truth. If he goes your way and votes no, you could tie it, and we'd have to schedule another hearing."

Chase had been silent throughout the speeches. To his son, he looked gray and already defeated. When the new sound system in the hearing rooms sputtered and squealed, he held his hands over his ears. Dr. Laubach, in contrast, rushed around the chamber like a ferret before the start of the hearing, speaking to each uncommitted alderman, seating Rona Bender and her friends in a bloc at the front of the room before the platform. When Elliot came in with his parents, he saw Dr. Laubach leading Jefferson Glee toward a quiet corner. Glee's face was stony and aloof. He was older, more grizzled than his posters indicated, and his eyes were a lionish yellow around the irises. When Glee mounted the platform and sat behind his microphone, Dr. Laubach scurried around to Chase. "I think we may have him," he said. "Glee is too can-ny to say it now, but in the end I think he'll go with us. One thing the minorities hate is middle-class suburbanites, and he'd have no interest in putting companies out there to lower their tax base." Chase merely grunted.

Rona Bender, scanning the room, saw Elliot in the back of the chamber. She signaled to him with a commanding wave, and when he went up to the front of the room, she stood to meet him like a man. Rona's manner had altered from their first meeting. She seemed still hypertense, aggressive, but beamed at him with an overwhelming good will. When she began to speak, he saw that he had become a hero. "You really told 'em," she said. "Boy, did you ever tell 'em. And now we're going to squash them flat. I've got a whole list of arguments right here"—she lifted her purse—"in case I forget any. I really have to hand it to you. Boy, you really laid it on the line. When I first saw you I wasn't sure about you, but I take it all back. I agree with everything you said. You're your father's son, Mr. Denmark. I should have seen what you were doing that day out at our place. You were getting that Ronnie Upp's number. I should have seen it then. I don't see him here, do you?"

Elliot said that he did not think Upp was in the chamber.

"Because he's afraid to show his face. Oh, we've all got his number now, Mr. Denmark. He knows what's going to happen to him to-night." Rona's voice was rising, and her face was a little flushed. People in the near rows stared at the chunky little woman. He was reminded uncomfortably of the mad woman in the department store. "I'm a great admirer of straight talk, Mr. Denmark, and you talk straight, and all of us are going to talk straight tonight. You can tell that to your father." She had clamped onto his wrist. An angry-looking man in a turtleneck was coming toward them, his eyes fixed on Elliot; behind him, others followed. Elliot removed his wrist from her grasp. "I'd better get back to my seat," he said. He nodded at the rest of the people who were gathering around him, and then glanced up at the alderman's table. Jefferson Glee was looking down impassively, his gold spectacles twinkling in his hand. To Elliot, the crowd of people in the chamber seemed brilliant and tense, volatile; whenever the loudspeakers hummed or sputtered, the noise level rose.

The council meeting began calmly, then disintegrated into disor-der. Rona Bender began to heckle other speakers in the audience. The microphones and amplifiers wailed like electric guitars. The head of the planning commission, an old alderman named Max Fest-linger, gradually ceased banging his gavel and let the arguments rage. He supported his chin on his fist and pointed into the crowd to select the speakers. At the epicenter, Rona Bender put on her glasses and fished in her purse. She stood and shouted down a man in the middle of the room who was rambling about taxes. Clippings fluttered in her hand. "I've got some advice for you, mister," she called. "And for you too, Mr. Festlinger." Elliot never heard what the advice was, because her next sentence was drowned in a storm of booing from the right of the chamber. Jefferson Glee and the other two black aldermen swiveled their heads from side to side, expressionlessly, like observers of a tennis match. None of them had spoken. Then Elliot heard, with a shrinking feeling of horror, his own name. Rona Bender began to read from her clippings.

In the end, three hours later, when Rona's voice had become un-bearably shrill, a hoarse Max Festlinger silenced the audience and called for a vote. Herman Glauber calmly recorded an Aye. The four aldermen to his right did the same. Archie Holton showed the first Nay. Then one more, then another. Then the sixth Aye. When the next man showed a Nay, Rona and her section of the audience applauded, cheered. Chase, too, dryly clapped his hands.

"Mr. Glee," called Max Festlinger. Elliot heard his father stop breathing.

"Abstention," said Glee, very calmly and clearly.

Dr. Laubach, on the other side of Chase, patted his fingertips together. "The son of a bitch," he whispered.

The final vote was six to four in favor of the proposal to rezone the land. "Mr. Festlinger, you've murdered our children," screamed Rona Bender. Boos, shouts, applause.

Elliot and his father, along with a silent Pierce Laubach, left the council chambers soon after. Out in the corridors of the vast building, Elliot noticed that all of city hall smelled of floor wax and tobacco smoke. Walking through the lobby, trailing his father and Dr. Laubach, Elliot paused to look at the murals of Jimmy Steenborg icily regarding Père Plechette and his ring of muscular braves. Someone had recently retouched them, and they shone gaudily in the harsh light. Then they were outside, going down the rank of marble steps to the plaza, and hunching their shoulders against the black cold.

"Democracy is overrated," said Dr. Laubach before he left them to go slowly up the plaza in the bitter wind toward his car.

Elliot waved to his father's secretary and opened the door to his office. "Welcome, son," said Chase. He was seated gray-faced behind his desk. "It's good of you to come." He went to one of the leather chairs, motioning Elliot to another. When Elliot sat, he noticed on the far wall of the office, near the windows and facing the aerial view of the city covering one wall, the prints of Paris which had once belonged to Brooks Denmark. So that was where they had gone; it was odd he had never noticed them here before. But for the prints and the two opulent chairs, Chase's office was as bare and neat as Kai's room.

"Pierce is very bitter," said Chase, crossing his legs. "He was even more involved than I in the effort to stop the rezoning. Hilda and he were in it from the first. They were the real soldiers. I think I was just a sort of hanger-on. I gave them a few ideas. Looking back, I'm not sure I ever thought we'd really stop them. The world's changed too fast for me. Years ago, I suppose we would not have even considered trying to do anything about Nun's Wood. We would have let that side of town go on about its own business."

"I wish you weren't so damned discouraged," said Elliot. "Maybe it's better to be bitter."

"I'm too realistic for that," his father snapped. "We were amateurs fighting the professionals. Nothing could have won it for us. Upp knew from the beginning that if he got Herman Glauber on his side, he'd eventually get a majority vote from the planning commission. The hearing was just a sideshow. Herman told me as much on Christmas Day. A less worthy man would have gloated, but Herman didn't permit himself that satisfaction. He was admirably level with me. Fifty Rona Benders screaming at the tops of their lungs wouldn't have changed the final vote, except to alienate more of the commission. From the beginning Upp had all the cards. *Finis*."

He looked glumly out of the window. "I keep wondering what my own father would have done. I think he would have invited Jeff Glee and his whole family to dinner, and sent a case of Scotch around afterward. Don't look disgusted with me, Elliot. I should have seen from the beginning that Glee was the key to our winning or losing. Pierce thought all along that he'd go with us. If we hadn't been so stupidly optimistic, we would have sent round petitions, forced a referendum."

"You could still do that."

"No, we've lost our moment," said Chase. "Pierce, Hilda, the Wiltshire Drive people, I, all of us are antiques now. Dusty things in a lumber room. We'd be split up for kindling if we kept it up any longer. Ronnie Upp is the new man now—he's stolen all the best Denmark methods."

Though he recognized the truth in what was said, Elliot laughed aloud, amused by his father's self-consciously despairing language;

Chase shot a single bright glance at him. "Laugh at me, you decadent lounger," he said. "I used to wonder if you'd ever understand me."

"No, I don't think so," said Elliot, still smiling.

"The Denmarks have always been contradictory types," said his father. "Your grandfather would have bought up that acreage himself and sold it off for a fortune, and then agonized about it, wondering if he'd done the right thing. Old Brooks would have done the same, but made a speech about contributing to the progress of Plechette City. At least young Upp spares us that. You are smarter than the lot of us. You make your own world. I wish I could say the same."

Elliot went on looking out the window, where a parade of flat roofs heaped with snow led off to the bright blue glowing tear of the Gas Company's flame. The sky shone white.

"Have we given you and Vera a good Christmas?" came his father's voice.

"Of course," he said.

"I've been thinking about Harrison Upp lately. Your mother and I used to see him now and then, you know, in the days when you were just a boy. Your asking about him on the telephone the other day started me off, and since we've been locking horns with his son, I've found myself recalling him, little things he did."

Elliot was now facing his father, and something in his glance made Chase smile. "Silly, isn't it? The man's been dead how long? More than fifteen years. Nearly twenty years. It doesn't seem that long ago to me. The fifties are quite present to me—it was a good decade, better than it is represented these days. Certainly better than the sixties. Less surreal. I've read all the books, all the new books, and I know that we're not supposed to think this way. In some ways though, I think the books are wrong. In the fifties a certain surface calm prevailed, but currents were always present under the surface. It was probably the last of the America we used to know, but all the mutations and variants were cropping up. Didn't that fellow Ginsberg begin writing in the fifties? All that gloomy talk about the Bomb. At the time, none of us could read phenomena of that sort. What I've been thinking lately is that Harrison Upp was a sort of harbinger, in his own way. Then, we used to think of him as simply 'wild,' you know, and some people went further than that. He was not a universal favorite.

"I rather liked him," said Chase, "because like Lamont Von Heil-itz, though a Lamont turned one hundred and eighty degrees about, he had his own sort of code. I think perhaps he was a moralist, and I think I should have paid more attention to him."

"What do you mean, a moralist?" said Elliot.

"Well, I now think that Harrison Upp possessed the kind of sophistication that never allows itself to be violated. He invariably knew what he thought and what he wanted—he was like a chess master. He seemed so immensely vital as a man. Do you remember his taking his family on safari in Africa? That was pure Harrison Upp—he nearly got himself killed, trying to get a lion. When I went past his house at night, out for a walk, I'd see cars all up and down the block, jazz music would be pounding out the windows, there'd be throngs of people who claimed to despise him, but who couldn't stay away. And he loved shooting, hunting—it was the way he loved drinking. Harrison had built up his father's fortune the way his son has built up his own. He sold all the property he owned on Second Street when land there was at the height of its value. I'm sure that he saw then what would happen there—Jeff Glee was a sort of protégé of Harrison's. Upp sold off his properties to men who were convicted that there'd be a larger market down there eventually; the expansion principle, I suppose. Upp knew better. In fact, he *always* knew better in business matters. He saw what industries would begin to make money, and he saw it a few steps ahead of anyone else. Many people hated him for that, when they couldn't afford to despise him.

"I don't want you to think he was a Gatsby," said Chase. "Harrison was too self-possessed and too violent. All those guns! But he did have, I gather, a past as disguised as Gatsby's. He'd traveled everywhere, met everyone. Vera's uncle has something of this air about him—of more experience than most of us have seen, as though most of what is significant about the man is hidden. Maybe what I felt was that the most important part of his life was in the past: that his future could never be as substantial. For all Upp's bearishness, I always felt that he was calculating his actions, keeping himself concealed in some essential way. He was like a survivor of the twenties, with his drinking and his safaris and his parties; but it was his attitude of mockery about it all that made it compelling. It was like he didn't give a damn about it, or about his fabulous success, and like he thought that was funny too."

"He does sound interesting," Elliot admitted.

"I rather think old Brooks Denmark and Harrison Upp would have liked each other. If I were your age now, I might like Ronnie Upp. Twenty years ago I was too narrow-minded."

"I thought you said you did like the father."

"I said, I think, that I rather liked him. It was a highly qualified affection," said Chase, smiling to himself. "Unlike most of the people we knew, unlike Margaret and myself, I don't think Upp liked the fifties at all. He was too conspicuous. It was no secret that he liked boys as well as girls—in those days, it was a thing you hid, it put you pretty much beyond the pale. Harrison flaunted his differences, but, again, I now think that he did it from a kind of ironic sense. That was what made him so glamorous. He never seemed exactly happy, even at his wildest. What does cruelty come from? Some kind of desperation? That may be merely a liberal's answer. Whatever it was, it could be unsettling. He mistreated his wife very badly; he humiliated her at parties. Margaret still cannot mention him without showing her loathing. But many women found him devastating. You'd be shocked if I listed all the respectable women from this area who chased after Harrison Upp. And who caught him."

"Is that what you meant when you said *nihil nisi bonum?* Queerness? Promiscuity?" A flight of heavy gray pigeons dropped diagonally past Chase's window; they settled on one of the ledges below, pecking and cooing. In their midst, plumper than the others, was a beautiful soft brown bird, its coloring so subtly varied that it appeared to have been laid on with a paintbrush.

"No, not really," said his father. "It was a feeling I had. Nothing I should talk about."

"Well, for God's sake don't clam up now," Elliot said. He was torn between leaving for his rehearsal, scheduled to begin in fifteen minutes, and hearing whatever last insight into the dead Harrison Upp his father could give him. The pigeons were wheeling away again and dropping down farther toward the street. The beautiful little brown bird among them was lost to his sight, somewhere far down among the buildings.

"I suppose it doesn't make any difference what I think," said Chase. "And although I appreciated Upp's skill at managing people and events, I was always a little intimidated by him. I thought buying that pistol was an outright mistake, especially since he didn't keep it locked up with his other guns. He wasn't in any sense a careless man, and that troubled me, leaving the pistol lying around. Carrying it in a holster. His reputation at that point was as low as it ever got—the men who'd bought into Second Street were beginning to feel the first slump in their business, and people were talking about Upp and a young man, a brainless kid from Chicago who had just tried to kill himself. The last time I went to one of his parties, he drunkenly told me that he'd given his son permission to use his pistol to defend the house anytime he was out. 'He's a weak little shit,' he told me when I tried to argue that it was irresponsible to give a child license to handle any weapon. 'It's one chance in a hundred,' he said. Upp looked terrible, his skin seemed to be on the point of falling off his face, he was drunk, and I didn't understand what he was talking about. And I was afraid to press him—he was still capable of violence. A couple of weeks earlier, he'd been beaten up in a fight in a very sordid bar on Booker Place. So you see my point. When he was killed, it crossed my mind that he'd almost planned for his son to shoot him. I think he'd been taunting his son for months. His motives? I don't know, couldn't begin to guess, apart from what I've just told you. I think it no longer mattered to him if he lived or not."

"My God," uttered Elliot. "If that's true, how can you say he was moral?"

"Maybe you don't understand your own country as well as you might," said Chase. "You'd better go off to your rehearsal."

"But you're saying that he was mad. Crazy."

"Yes, I suppose. Crazy." He smiled thinly, and stood. "But he always got what he asked for, and in the end, I imagine that he got the last thing he had been asking for. And his family got the fortune in insurance, not that they needed it, which a suicide would have taken from them. Hadn't you better rush? I'll see you at dinner. Robert is going to outdo himself in cooking some sort of tribute to your concert, so be sure to demonstrate your appreciation." Before he went back to his desk, he added, "It was just an idea I had at the time. I could easily be wrong. But that I could think it at all shows you something of what kind of man he was." He went back behind his desk, and Elliot left the office, rode down in the dark elevator, cut through the lobby, and walked out into the cold white air.

Of all the results plotted separately and jointly by Herman Glauber and Chase Denmark, one had unequivocally occurred: standing in a passageway far behind the stage in the Usenbrugge Auditorium, Elliot could hear, unmistakably, the sounds of a large crowd assembling. For nearly half an hour, people had been streaming into the auditorium where, during the past two weeks, he had seen only Vera and Nathan Himmel seated—two small white faces in a sea of rich red and gold. Now it was a beehive of voices, a perpetual buzzing and humming. His stomach momentarily fluttered. Was the music on the podium? Elliot's knees seemed fluid, watery. Of course it was there. He had spoken to the boy twice. Most of the musicians were raggedly gathered in the gray-block cavern behind the stage, some still carrying their coats. (The architect had apparently forgotten that culture did not hibernate during winter, and on the far wall of the cavern hung a single short rack of curved hooks. A huddle of coats lay beneath, crumpled, trod upon, arms folded or outflung.) The musicians too seemed nervous, but brilliantly nervous, as though they were hosting an important party. The last rehearsal had been the best to date, with no faltering in the sections, no hesitations or gingerliness; some of the pieces had sounded really right for the first time. When they had given the entire program a final run-through, he had been deeply pleased by their playing. Now if they could only conquer their jitters—and he, his—to duplicate that last performance.

In their suits and long dresses they looked different than they had during the course of the rehearsals. He had, unthinkingly, been expecting tuxedos or tailcoats—his own had been meticulously pressed by Robert that afternoon—to be worn by the males; now he was grateful they were not so formal. Some did not even wear suits, but came in the same sweaters and jeans they had worn to rehearsals. Ettenheim was seated on the concrete floor with his back against the hard wall, his eyes closed. The others bounced on the balls of their feet, laughed at some comment from the stringy-haired exuberant boy who played first trumpet, or talked loudly with their friends. Another group of musicians clustered around the edge of the aperture which allowed them to see the audience. Their arms rested loosely across their backs and shoulders—like Kai and Harrison Upp, both squinting shirtless in the sun and the camera on the terrace of a villa. While one part of his mind snagged on the memory of the photographs, another section recorded that he had never been made so aware that they were students.

"May I?" He was at the edge of the cluster around the aperture. Roberta Potocky was sarcastically describing her mother's dress, and the giggling ceased when he spoke. *Why*, he thought, *this is more an event for them than it is for me*. They broke apart as if he had shouted. "Oh, it's wonderful, Mr. Denmark," said Roberta Potocky, turning her nervous, glancing face toward his. "We're nearly filled! I've never played to so many people before. Just look at them all! I even saw my mother, and she never goes to concerts—she's in the tenth row, wearing her schoolteacher dress—a purple dress. The only thing she ever went to before was my Master's recital. Which she didn't even like!"

"Will she like this?"

"Oh, I don't know," giggled Roberta. "She'll probably like the singing."

"Well, I like the singing," said Eliott. The students glanced at one another, as if he had uttered a significant admission. "As of four hours ago, I like the playing too," he added. Pep talk, paternalism.

He bent to the aperture and looked out at the audience. The vast middle portion of the orchestra section was nearly filled, and more people were still stepping down the side aisles.

The complimentary tickets must have been all from the same roll. His parents were seated in the third row, on the right side, next to Herman and Tessa Glauber. Herman looked flushed, hot, delighted; Tessa fumbled in her bag beside him, and took out a comb and ran it through her hair. Chase leaned across his wife and made some comment to Herman which caused his bullish face to split with good humor. Vera, beside her mother, smiled too, and reached over to touch her father's hand.

Then he saw a moving flash of yellow hair coming down the far aisle and knew before he saw the face that it was Anita Kellerman. He had not thought that she would come; that, he saw, was foolish. Slim, preoccupied, she was marching down the aisle unguided by an usher; Andy came behind, carrying the tickets. She was comparing the row numbers with those on the flimsy paper tickets, and kept turning her head from side to side as they came forward, her lips pursed, her forehead drawn up. Men stared at her face. Anita moved like a distracted queen straight for the correct row. Her certainty released a bubble within him: he could not maintain his hostility. They were, after all, friends. As he watched, Anita paused at a row a little back from the Denmarks and Glaubers; Andy, checking the tickets, nodded sharply. They went in toward the middle of the hall and took two vacant seats beside a placid heap of a woman in purple.

"I see your mother," he said to Roberta, who hovered beside him.

"You saw that awful dress? It's what she wears to *functions*. It makes her look so ghastly, like someone at a funeral. Let me look." She bent her head close to his. "Oh, dear Mother," she whispered. "Now she's got those two exotic creatures beside her, I suppose she'll be nervous and not hear a thing. Wait. Isn't the blond one Mrs. Kellerman?" Her face, half an inch away, registered dismay. "I'm sorry, I didn't . . ." She turned half-hysterically back to the opening. "I mean I think Mrs. Kellerman is beautiful. When I was an undergraduate, boys took her classes just to look at her for an hour. She's a good friend of yours and Mr. Himmel's, I know . . ."

"It's all right," he said to her profile. "You didn't say anything."

"My goodness! Look at that! That couple up in the boxes. If music is the food of love, they'd better leave right now." She giggled again, and trying to point, dropped her music on the floor. Elliot leaned over to put his head where hers had been, and looked up at the row of boxes. Most were empty. You could see only half the stage from there, and with the hall's acoustics, you'd be lucky to hear even that. He saw a tangle of hands, two heads together in a kiss. The man browsed along the woman's lips, her cheek. Since they were seated, only their heads were visible above the plush railing, giving them a Punch-and-Judy look. The man—it was Lawrence Wooster—broke apart from the woman and traced a finger down the side of her jaw. Joanie Haupt caught his finger and slipped it in her mouth. Elliot turned away from the aperture, full of chagrin and amusement. Roberta Potocky was still stooping above the concrete, assembling the loose pages of her music.

"I saw you on television," said Ettenheim. He had stationed himself two feet away, and looked as though he might break into a run. "You were okay. I thought what you said made a lot of sense."

"About Nun's Wood?" Elliot was incredulous.

"No, what you said about music. I'd like to hear some of your newer work sometime. I mean, I was really persuaded by what you were saying. I've been thinking along those lines for about a year, and when you were talking to Ted Edwards, you made a lot of things fall into place for me."

Roberta, now kneeling on the floor, looked up at Ettenheim with amazement. The boy jammed his fists into the pockets of his jacket and glared at Elliot. "I mean, it's just the way I felt. I was just wondering what kind of thing could be done with a vocalist in the sort of music you were talking about. We don't talk about really new music very much here, and I kind of feel like I've been stumbling along in the dark. Is there anyone I could write to?"

"You could write to me," said Elliot. He fumbled in his pocket, but found no pen, no paper. Ettenheim handed him a shabby notebook with a ball-point clipped to the springs, and he put down on a blank page his name and address.

Then everything happened. Roberta finally finished assembling her pages and fluttered across the cavern to where the musicians were lining up to go onstage; Ettenheim shoved the notebook in his pocket with a perfunctory thanks and took his own place in the formation. At a signal, they swept onstage. Elliot watched them take their chairs, bathed in light and applause. When they had finished flipping the pages before them and the applause had nearly ceased, the ritual of tuning completed, he started to walk out of the wings toward the podium, head back, using long determined strides—the conductor's march; but before he had even properly begun, Nathan Himmel appeared from nowhere and embraced him. "You can't lose," Himmel whispered, and released him. Elliot grinned at his friend, turned his back toward the lighted stage, and walked out in his normal manner, as if he were going down the block to buy flowers. The moment he stepped out into the light, he was drowned in renewed applause. None of the faces he dimly saw looked familiar.

One last glimpse of Elliot Denmark: he is seated by the window in the backseat of his father's immense black automobile, so crowded by his mother, whose knees project upward in a clean elegant nylon line, her feet placed on the floor's central hump, by Tessa, who is all elbows-in and hurtled together, and by Uncle Kai, of whom only the outline of a gray sweater and a gray tweedy angle of legs are visible, that he is jammed up against the rear door, his side dug by the armrest. The front seat is less crowded. Chase and Herman Glauber sit, with enough room to turn and gesture, on either side of Vera.

"Are you sure you have your tickets?" Tessa leans forward abruptly, forcing Margaret to list to the left, and transfixes Elliot with her long eyes. While Elliot assures her that he has them in his pocket—the long holders rest there beside a letter from Baltz (a demo made, a girlfriend, another dog, two weeks in Max's Kansas City)—he sees his father tighten with impatience. It is the third time Tessa has asked about the tickets.

Herman rumbled with laughter. "You don't want to have to say: I wish the grand piano were here."

"Oh, I know that one," Margaret sang out. "They are at the Harvard-Yale game, and you can't get a seat for love or money because it's the crucial game of the season."

"A shortcut," says Chase, turning the car at the War Memorial building to follow First Street down into the valley.

"You don't use the expressway?"

"I'm sure this way is faster. The expressway takes you so far east that you lose all the time you gain while you're going south."

"Just check to see if you've got the tickets, Elliot. To put my mind at ease."

"He *has* them, Mother, Jesus Christ."

"I always use the expressway myself. You can really belt along until you get to the Pulaski Avenue turnoff."

"And the wife says, why do you wish the grand piano were here?"

"Oh, I did forget something," said Elliot.

"I knew it."

"No, he has them, Mother. I saw him put them in his pocket."

"It was the proof copy of Pittman's novel. I just remembered that I left it up on one of the beds."

"If your mother finds it first, she'll burn it."

"I hate to put you to the trouble, but could you mail it to us?"

"Is that the book Vera was telling us about? It sounds wretched."

"Then he says, because that's where I left the *tickets*."

They were sailing down the long hill to the valley past a billboard for Jefferson Glee; everyone in the automobile but Kai looked at it as they accelerated past.

"You don't have to break the record, Chase, we're in plenty of time."

"Better safe than sorry."

"It's been wonderful to have you here, dears."

"Maybe we can come back next summer."

"Your mother and I will probably come over if you don't. I haven't seen Paris since I was twenty."

"Oh, have you been to Europe? I envy you."

"Don't encourage them, Tessa, they'll never come back."

The gold top of the Chambers Denmark clock revolved above the buildings, showed its gleaming faces, then was lost among the rising gray and red brick of factories.

"You kids today have all the breaks."

"Now *you're* encouraging them."

"I wish you could stay longer."

"How is your book coming, Kai?"

"It's a secret."

Soon they were out of the city. The houses scattered apart as if a bomb had dispersed them, little frame buildings made to look like dwarf ranch houses. Fields hemmed them in with barbed wire.

"A lot could be done with this ward. Already, a few companies are making noises about relocating out here, to take advantage of the land price."

His father and Herman began to talk about the planning commission, the new proposals for extension of the expressway. Elliot looked out of the window to the sparkling fields. "Now they think it was a dog that attacked that girl," said Margaret. "Did any of you see that in the morning paper? One of the neighbors had a savage dog that he kept to guard his home. It's such a ghastly thing. The dog ran away on the morning the girl was injured. The man was afraid to tell anyone, but his wife made him go to the police." He and Tessa, crowded shoulder to shoulder, tried to remember what breed of dog it had been. Doberman? German shepherd? Off to his right, dashing across the field, Elliot saw a swift dark shape. It was loping, not running; in mid-stride, it rolled over on its back like a puppy and squirmed deliriously in the snow, nosing, writhing. When it got to its feet again, now dusted with white, it ran, keeping pace with the car for a few moments, then fell back. The animal looked like no dog he had ever seen. No one else in the car had noticed it. Herman pointed his finger upward at the windshield; a giant silvery jet was planing away eastward, seeming to move very slowly and trailing plumed white ribbons. After a second they were hit by its sound.

EPILOGUE

5 Verbena Blvd.
Boulder, Colorado
29 November 1970

Elliot Denmark
6 Villa Beauséjour
Paris XVI
France

Dear Elliot,
I don't really know why I'm writing to you, unless it's because
I see both of us as Anita's victims. At times last December, I
could almost see your brain working, see all the wheels and
judgments and decisions whirling around, trying to grasp how
she and I related, how you fit in. I wanted to protect you—to
keep you from seeing what you were eventually made to see.
Maybe it would have been kinder, on the day in the field, to
have explained everything; but I couldn't, I could not be certain
that it would not be a kindness for the sake of cruelty, and you
were too open, too vulnerable for that. I wasted too much time
being jealous of Anita, jealous about you, about Ronnie, about
Mark—she seemed to have engineered everything, to have
made everything possible for herself—and in the end I

simply became superfluous. She wouldn't understand this, with her gift for optimism. (Perhaps I should say, with her gift for power—but that may be residual malice. In the end, I was fired, although she tried to disguise that reality. I didn't know how you could fire someone from friendship.) I always felt very ordinary beside Anita, like something small and cosseted, and this is miles away from my normal conception of myself.

I'm finding this a very difficult letter to write. As you will have perceived, it's taken me months to get organized enough to even try. And maybe I'm still confused, metaphorically out in the cold, away from the circle of Anita's affection, friends, lovers—maybe, I mean, she was our victim and not we hers. But if that's true, neither of us will ever be certain. That gift of hers for optimism and illusion-making might be our blessing as well as hers. I suspect that we both still love her. (Oh, a little voice says, didn't you know? I had the classic little-girl/gym-instructress crush.)

Life here in Colorado (observe, she said, the rapid change of scene and subject) is pleasant, unhurried, purposeful; the university near to mountains and clean air. In the summer it smells of mountain flowers and streams. I have a half-time job in a good clinic, the people I work with are to a man Western and gregarious and friendly. A gang of them climbs mountains on weekends. Nobody ever wears a necktie. My boss is the exception, and he wears one of those string ties you see on country-and-western singers. *Autre temps, autre* neckwear. I expect none of this interests you, though I think you'd like the sheer peculiarity of the landscape. It's jumpy and lyrical, unexpected, like your new record. *Marriage Hymns*, indeed.

I'm going to mail this now before I change my mind, and then to the library to add another fifty or sixty notecards to my vast mound of them. Please don't feel that I expect an answer.

All in love,

Andy

P.S. I'm almost glad the sixties are over. It's like: *Now* I can start growing up. Which I guess you have to leave home, or whatever you replaced it with, to do.